Praise for the Sharpe & Donovan Novels

CARLA NEGGERS

LIAR'S KEY

mira

mira

ISBN-13: 978-0-7783-3024-0

Liar's Key

Recycling programs
for this product may
not exist in your area.

For questions and comments about the quality of this book, please contact us at
CustomerService@Harlequin.com.

www.Harlequin.com

Printed in U.S.A.

For my mother,
again and always with thanks and love

LIAR'S
KEY

1

Gordy Wheelock washed the dried blood off his face and checked the damage in the mirror. Not too bad. The blood was from a swollen scrape behind his left ear, at his hairline. It wouldn't be visible if he combed his hair right and wore a collared shirt and sport coat.

For the life of him, he couldn't remember what had happened.

He stared at his reflection. Gray stubble, bags under his eyes, flab under his chin, hair completely gray, what was left of it, anyway. He was still in the slacks he'd worn on yesterday's flight from London.

Damn. He looked like an old, out-of-shape has-been.

He hated that.

He picked up his bloody shirt off the bathroom floor. His left knee ached. It felt swollen. He didn't remember any problems with it when he'd checked into the Boston waterfront hotel around seven last night. He'd had a drink and gone out to get some air and have a cigarette, never mind that he'd quit smoking decades ago.

That much he remembered clearly. After that...

He grimaced and limped into the bedroom, where he'd awakened on the floor, in a major stupor, fifteen minutes ago. He tossed his shirt on the untouched bed, then walked over to the windows and pulled open the drapes. Had he shut them after he'd fallen—or hadn't he fallen? Had he been clocked? *Damn.* He didn't remember, but he figured he must have shut the drapes himself. The hotel wasn't bad but it didn't have a turn-down service.

Cold water and now the morning sunlight didn't help him separate memory and nightmare, but blood, pain and a palpable sense of fear and foreboding suggested that what was stirring in his aching head was more reality than the dregs of a bad dream.

He made coffee in the Keurig machine and dug a Kit Kat out of the minibar.

"Shirt. I need a clean shirt."

He saw his overnight bag by the door. He remembered dropping it off in the room before heading down to the bar off the lobby.

He tore open the candy. Coffee and chocolate would help him wake up, come to—both.

They did, and he didn't like it.

This is your only warning. Back off.

A ragged low voice, maybe male, maybe female. Who knew these days?

A gun in the ribs.

Felt like a gun, anyway. Gordy didn't know for a fact what it had been.

A pro? Not sure about that, either, but whoever it

had been had managed to deliver the warning and stay out of Gordy's line of vision. Probably would have taken less skill just to beat him over the head.

Gordy was disgusted with himself. He was rusty. Back in the day, he'd have had his attacker's ass in the harbor.

He rubbed his lower back and discovered a bruise where he'd been jabbed. Given his fuzzy head and general aches and pains, he hadn't noticed until now.

His head throbbed. He hadn't been shot, grazed by a bullet, anything like that.

"I fell."

He heard the disdain in his voice. His attacker had come at him from behind at the top of the stone steps near the hotel, stuck a gun, club or whatever in his ribs, grunted the warning and given him a good shove. It'd been dark. Gordy had stumbled and hit his head and banged his knee on the steps.

Never had a chance to light his cigarette.

It was all coming back to him.

He drank his coffee and ate his candy bar, forcing himself to stay loose, relaxed. He'd done that last night with his attacker, too. He hadn't wanted to fight, risk serious injury, call attention to himself, have to explain to the police—all of which his assailant had clearly known and counted on.

Gordy figured if he was supposed to have come out of this thing dead, he'd be dead.

The warning meant he wasn't grasping at straws. He was on to something.

He tossed the cup and candy wrapper into the trash. He'd have to tough out the pain from his bruises. He got a collared shirt out of his bag. He'd opted against a suit and tie, but he did have a navy sport coat. He wouldn't be dressed as if he were off to play golf, at least.

He hadn't planned to change his slacks despite having slept in them, but he noticed blood on his right hip, visible and obvious against the light gray flannel. He must have touched the blood on his face and then his pants. He dug out fresh trousers. He saw he had a scrape on his right hand, probably from breaking his fall, but it didn't bother him.

Getting dressed hurt. Walking would hurt, too. Hell, *thinking* hurt. The attack hadn't been a coincidence. He'd asked for it, sticking his nose where it didn't belong. But who all knew he was in Boston?

Once he was dressed, he checked his reflection in the mirror above the small desk in the corner. Better. He looked as if he'd had a bad night, but he didn't see any visible sign of blood or bruises.

He took the elevator three floors down to the lobby. After a moment's deliberation, he checked out and left his bag with the bellman, a different one from last night.

He went outside, the sunlight making his head hurt worse. It was a warm spring morning, at least by Boston standards. He walked past the wharf where the New England Aquarium was located, a crowd assembled at the entrance. Parents, toddlers, students and teachers on spring field trips. A few retirees. Not many. Gordy figured he sort of blended in and people could think he was meeting his grandkids, but he'd chosen his hotel for its proximity to his ten o'clock meeting with the FBI. A little late to cover his tracks, anyway. Whoever had attacked him had obviously known where to find him. Followed him from the airport, then waited for him to come out for a smoke? What if he hadn't? Maybe his attacker had nailed the wrong guy. But Gordy didn't think so.

He dug out the pack of cigarettes he'd bought after arriving at Logan, tapped one out and lit it with the disposable lighter he'd bought at the same time. If he hadn't been sneaking a cigarette, would he have been blindsided last night?

Moot point now.

He took two puffs and tossed the cigarette onto the sidewalk. He ground it out under his foot, scooped up the butt and pitched it into a trash can. Never mind someone assaulting him. If the local cops saw him litter, they'd be all over him.

Gordy chuckled to himself, feeling better. Now that he was awake and the caffeine and chocolate were taking effect, the warning and his tumble last night had fired up his adrenaline. He was tuned in, confident he was back in the game. Almost a year playing golf and hanging out with his wife and the kids and grandkids in North Carolina hadn't softened him up too much. He wouldn't be caught off guard another time.

A chilly gust blew off the harbor. A stab of pain seemed to go through his eyeball, but he shook it off. Hell, he might even survive May in Boston. He thought he'd never get used to living in North Carolina again, but here he was, shivering.

He glanced at his watch. He'd have to hoof it not to be late for his meeting with the FBI, specifically Special Agent Emma Sharpe.

The hell with that.

He'd take his time. He was an FBI legend. Emma could wait.

2

At first Emma didn't recognize the man standing in her office doorway. Gordy Wheelock? Had to be. People didn't just walk into her small FBI building on the Boston waterfront, and she was expecting him. He'd called her last night to set up their meeting. "Ten o'clock sharp, Emma. Funny, huh? Sharp, Emma. Emma Sharpe. Ha."

That was Gordy, always with the lame humor.

He rubbed the back of his neck, looking pained. "I know. I look like Yank's drunken uncle these days. Sorry. I should have warned you."

Yank—Matt Yankowski—was the senior agent in charge of HIT, the specialized FBI team of which Emma was a handpicked member. She doubted he had a drunken uncle.

Yank and Gordy weren't friends.

"No problem," Emma said. "Come in, please. It's good to see you."

He stepped into her small office. She did her best to hide her shock at seeing him. Gordon Wheelock was an FBI legend who'd taken the investigation of art crimes to a new level during his thirty-year career, but he didn't look like a legend this morning. He had dark circles and puffy bags under his eyes, and he'd put on weight—at least fifteen pounds. His hair was sparse and totally gray now, not the salt-and-pepper of just a year ago when she'd flown back to DC to attend his retirement party. He wore a collared ice-blue shirt without a tie, a navy sport jacket, tan trousers and scuffed leather walking shoes. The clothes were wrinkled, as if he'd pulled them out of a suitcase or a laundry basket.

Before joining HIT and moving to Boston last March, Emma had worked with Gordy in Washington for several months. Like her, his area of expertise was art crimes. He understood as a law enforcement professional the intersection of major art crimes with other major crimes—embezzlement, extortion, kidnapping, money laundering, drug smuggling, illegal weapons trafficking, murder and even terrorism. He didn't have a background in art but considered that a strength. She had a degree in art history, and she was a Sharpe—her grandfather was a world-renowned private art detective. Matt Yankowski had urged her to join the FBI and then had chosen her for HIT specifically because of her expertise, but Gordy had warned her not to get distracted by her knowledge and interests. *We don't investigate protocols, controversies and cool stuff going on in the art world, Agent Sharpe. We investigate potential and actual federal crimes.*

Word was he'd been ready to retire, but Emma had never asked him for his reasons.

He nodded to the papers, index cards and Post-it

notes she'd arranged on the inexpensive sofa against the wall opposite her desk. "Anything interesting?"

"No, unfortunately. I'm sorting through the contents of some physical files."

"Anything interesting, you wouldn't let me near it."

She forced a smile. She noticed a nick on his jaw where he must have cut himself shaving. He'd always been so crisp and professional when she'd worked with him.

He gave her a frank once-over. She was dressed professionally in slim-cut dark pants and a cream-colored shirt, with a lightweight leather jacket hanging on a peg behind the door. She had good walking shoes, no visible sign of wear. Her hair, fair and shoulder-length, was neatly pulled back. "You look good, Emma. Kick-ass and pretty as a picture." He grinned. "You're blushing. It's okay. I can say whatever I want now that I'm retired."

"One of the perks, I guess. Did you just get into town?"

"Last night. I flew in from London. I used to fly all the time, all over the country—all over the world. Jet lag never bothered me. These days a pop fly from London to Boston knocks me on my ass."

"What were you doing in London?"

"Whim."

It was obviously an incomplete answer, but he didn't seem to care. She decided not to push him. "Did your wife go with you?"

He shook his head. "Joan's home in North Carolina with the gang. Our youngest is having another baby. We have four grandkids now. Two boys, two girls. This next one will tip the scales back to the girls. Joan's excited. Loves babies."

"That's great, Gordy. Congratulations." Emma paused, a hand on the back of her desk chair. "If this is a personal visit, why don't we wait and have lunch?"

"It's not a personal visit, but I'm not going to keep you."

"Would you like to sit down?"

"Nah. I'll stand. Sciatica acted up on the flight." He walked over to her one window. The main offices, including hers, were on the second floor of a former warehouse, one of many rescued buildings of Boston's waterfront past. "Alley view. I bet Yank has a harbor view."

He did, but Emma made no comment.

"Security's tight here but it's not a fortress," Gordy added. "The world's changed since I broke into my first sweat at the academy."

"You had an amazing career, Gordy." Emma sat on her desk chair, swiveling to face him. "What brings you to Boston?"

"I'm on my way to Maine for the open house at the new Sharpe Fine Art Recovery offices on Saturday. I'm invited. That wasn't your doing?"

"No, it wasn't. I'm not part of the business. You know that."

Founded sixty years ago by her grandfather, Sharpe Fine Art Recovery was relaunching itself under the leadership of her older brother, Lucas. Although still relatively small, the business had grown since Wendell Sharpe had set up his first office in his home in Heron's Cove on the southern Maine coast. He'd been a young museum security guard, following his interests, hoping for the best. Now he was semiretired, living in Dublin since his wife's untimely death fifteen years ago. Emma knew Lucas had never expected to take the helm so young, or on his own, but he'd taken to the work—or at least he was good at it, dedicated, tireless.

Gordy glanced back at her, a touch of the no-nonsense Agent Wheelock she'd known in his incisive look. "Any regrets about joining the FBI instead of the family business?"

"No. Gordy…"

"A touch of impatience. I like that. I don't intimidate you anymore."

She didn't respond. He'd never intimidated her, but she'd always respected him. In his mind, the two often went together, and either or both could be used as leverage to get what he wanted. Answers, cooperation, his way.

She tilted back in her chair. "Let's do this. You talk. I listen. Okay?"

He moved away from the window but didn't sit. "Sure thing. I stopped in at a high-class tea party in London on Sunday. Champagne, chocolate, scones, loose-leaf tea. It was at Claridge's. Damn fine hotel. I didn't stay there—too pricey for my wallet. The party was in celebration of the opening of a show at the Victoria and Albert Museum featuring art and artifacts from the late antiquity period." He paused. "How'd I do? Pretty good, huh?"

Emma didn't buy his act. "As always."

"I've picked up a few tidbits. Late antiquity bridges the classical era and the Middle Ages, around the time the proverbial shit hit the fan with the Roman Empire, at least in the west. It lasted from the fourth century to the end of the sixth century. That's AD, or CE, as we say these days. But you know all this."

"It's a fascinating era."

"I guess so. The party was relatively small, maybe forty people."

"How did you know about it?"

"I still have contacts in London," he said. "Getting the invitation to the Sharpe open house stirred me up, I guess. I'd hoped to go out on a high note and I went out on a dead end. That's the way I looked at it. Anyway, I'm at this London tea party, and no sooner did I help myself to fancy tea than lo and behold, who do I see? Want to guess, Emma?"

"You go ahead, Gordy."

He grinned at her. "I hope that's my training you're putting to use. I ran into an MI5 agent I know, a guy as knowledgeable as anyone in law enforcement and intelligence on the illegal antiquities trade and its connections to terrorism and terrorist funding."

Emma sat straight. Gordy had her interest now. "Did you speak with this agent?" she asked.

"Sort of. He marched over to me and told me to drink my tea and then pack my bags and head home. I told him I only had one bag. He laughed."

"Most people appreciate your sense of humor."

"Yeah, right. More like he humored the old fart who doesn't know enough to stay home and play golf. He wouldn't tell me why he was sniffing around at a fancy London party—denied that's what he was doing." Gordy settled back on his heels and narrowed his gaze on Emma. "I thought you might know what his interest was."

"Why would I know?"

"Because your pal Oliver York was there, too."

And there it is. Emma remained very still. "Keep going."

"English mythologist. A wealthy loner with a tragic past. He witnessed his parents' murder at their London apartment when he was eight years old. The killers kidnapped him, but he escaped. They're still at large thirty years later." Gordy's voice wasn't without compassion. "Awful business."

"Yes."

"How long have you known York?" Gordy asked.

"Not long. Gordy—"

He held up a hand. "It's okay. I don't know anything that wasn't in the papers. He got mixed up in an investigation into a private security firm this winter. You almost got killed. You already knew him by then, though, didn't you?"

"Sort of. Keep talking."

Gordy paused, studying her.

"Is Oliver York working with MI5, Emma?"

"Why do you ask?"

"Instinct. The MI5 guy is a real bastard. If he's got York by the short hairs for some reason…well, it's no wonder York is doing MI5's bidding. But what could British intelligence have on a lonely mythologist?"

Tons, Emma thought, but she didn't respond to Gordy's question. Given his experience as a federal agent, he would know she couldn't. It wasn't that she didn't want to. For a decade, he had chased a serial thief who'd broken into museums, businesses and private homes in a dozen different cities in Europe and the US, making off with a fortune in artwork. Wendell Sharpe, Emma's grandfather, had also hunted for the thief, who had especially enjoyed taunting the world-renowned art detective. Last fall, while on an unrelated case, Emma had helped identify the thief as eccentric English mythologist Oliver York. Oliver had never admitted his guilt, and he would never face arrest and prosecution for any of his brazen heists—in part because of lack of evidence, but mainly because he'd agreed to help the United Kingdom's Security Service, popularly known as MI5.

"I guess I wouldn't answer that question, either," Gordy said. "Oliver York's London apartment—the same one where he witnessed his parents' murder—is a short distance from Claridge's. He also owns a farm in the Cotswolds. Again, though, I'm telling you something you already know, since he's your pal."

"Oliver isn't my pal."

"Is he one of your grandfather's eccentric pals?"

"You'd have to ask him. Did you speak with Oliver at the party on Sunday?"

"No, I didn't. He saw me and took off in the opposite direction. Coincidence, maybe."

Emma doubted it. "What else, Gordy? I can't get worked up about MI5 and an English mythologist showing up at a high-end London party."

"Your parents were there."

Now this was news, Emma thought, containing any reaction. She could see he was gauging her response as the experienced agent he was. As a member of HIT, short for High-Impact Target, she worked on investigations focusing on elusive criminals with virtually unlimited resources. But she had only a little over four years on the job. Gordy, retired just a year, had decades.

"I haven't talked with them in a few days," she said.

"We said a quick hello while the MI5 agent was looking daggers at me. They're living in London now, I understand. It's temporary?"

"A year. That's what they say, at least. The idea was that a dramatic change of scenery would help my father with his chronic pain."

Gordy winced. "Terrible. A simple fall on the ice and his life is changed forever. Your brother had to pick up the reins of the family business sooner than he expected. I hear old Wendell is retiring, but I'll believe it when I see it."

Emma got to her feet. "Gordy, if you're here because you want me to give you information, you're wasting your time. I appreciate any information you want to give me, but it's a one-way street."

"Yeah. I get it." He picked up an index card that had fallen onto the floor and set it back on the sofa. "You heard Alessandro Pearson died about two weeks ago? Funeral was a week ago Tuesday. He had a heart attack and fell down the stairs near his apartment. Heart attack is what killed him, though. He was eighty-eight. He had a good run."

Emma nodded. "Yes, I heard."

"Old Wendell was at the funeral. I didn't realize they were friends."

"He consulted with Alessandro a few times."

"Archaeologist specializing in ancient mosaics. I thought your grandfather steered clear of antiquities."

"He does these days. Look, it seems you should be talking to him instead of me."

"Relax. I'm just curious. I'm at a party celebrating an antiquities show with MI5, this Oliver York character, your parents and a few other people, and everyone's buzzing about Alessandro Pearson's death."

"He was a respected expert in antiquities."

"Know anything about ancient mosaics stolen recently in London, Emma?"

It was a calculated blurt. Despite his disheveled appearance and obvious fatigue and aches and pains, Gordy had clearly come to this meeting prepared. He watched her closely.

"No," she said. "What do you know?"

"Not much. I overheard rumors at the tea party. Word is several sixth-century Byzantine Christian mosaics, possibly illegally obtained, were stolen a few weeks ago from an unnamed London collector. I'm no expert on mosaics but I did some quick research. Mosaic art flourished from the time of the ancient Greeks through the fall of the eastern Roman Empire—what we commonly refer to as the Byzantine Empire—in the fifteenth century. Sort of fell out of favor during the Renaissance." He steadied his gaze on Emma. "Interesting, isn't it? A mosaic expert dies and these rumors surface."

"Are you suggesting the FBI should get involved?"

"No." Gordy rolled his left shoulder, as if to work out a muscle spasm. He breathed, shuddering. "I kinked up on the plane yesterday."

"Are you sure you won't sit down?"

"Yeah. I'm sure. You don't know anything about these stolen ancient mosaics?"

Emma saw no reason not to be straight with him. "I haven't heard a peep." She sat down again. She wished she'd had him meet her in the conference room instead of her office. He would be taking in everything, from the way she'd unloaded the files onto the sofa to the tidiness of her desk and her choice of artwork—or lack thereof. "Where are you off to now?"

"No firm plans yet. It's only Thursday. I don't have to be in Maine until Saturday. Are you going to be at the open house?"

"I'll stop in, yes."

"When do you head up there?"

"Later today." She didn't elaborate on her plans. "You have my cell phone number. Let me know if you need anything while you're in Maine."

He leaned toward her, his gray eyes serious, his skin more ashen with the light from her desk lamp hitting his face. "Emma, do we have an active investigation involving stolen ancient mosaics? *We* meaning the Bureau."

"You know I can't answer that."

A bit of color returned to his face. "Figured I'd try. What about your fiancé? Is he going to be at the open house?"

Gordy's question took Emma by surprise, but she knew it shouldn't have. He would have checked with his contacts for her latest news, and her engagement definitely fit under that heading. "We'll see. Do you know him?"

"Of him. Colin Donovan. A rough-and-tough type. Good for you, Emma. Engaged to be married, wedding in a few weeks, member in good standing of an elite FBI unit. Quite a change from your days with the Sisters of the Joyful Heart, isn't it?"

She noted the edge to his voice but made no comment.

"The paths started and abandoned in life," he said.

"Why didn't you tell me you'd been a nun before you joined the FBI?"

"It wasn't a secret. It was just something I didn't talk about."

"And you never reported directly to me," he added, almost knocking over folders stacked on the arm of the sofa. "I only found out a few months ago. I had to hear it through the vine. You think Wendell would have said something. We were in touch when you were in the convent."

"I doubt it was relevant."

"I guess. You've never riled easily. Those years as a postulant and novice must have helped. It's true Yank recruited you out of the convent?"

"Yes. I never professed my final vows."

"Whatever that means. The Sisters of the Joyful Heart. I like that." There wasn't a hint of sarcasm in his tone. "They specialize in art education, preservation and conservation and have a beautiful convent on the Maine coast. Life could be worse." He eyed her, as if he were trying to picture her as a nun. "Sister Emma." He wrinkled up his face. "That's a hard one to wrap my head around. Except Emma wasn't your name as a nun, was it? Didn't you have to take another name?"

"I was known as Brigid then."

"Good Irish Catholic name."

Emma inhaled deeply. "Anything else?"

He grinned. "I like the impatience. I'd have threatened to throw me out the window by now. Do the good sisters work on restoring ancient mosaics?"

"I don't know. They primarily work on pieces that can be safely transported to the convent."

"They don't fly out to archaeological digs?"

"Not that I'm aware of."

"Fair enough. Is Oliver York coming to the open house?"

Another blurt designed to throw her off her stride. "As I said, I'm not involved with the open house, up to and including the guest list."

"But you'd know."

She got to her feet. She wanted to maneuver Gordy out of the small confines of her office. He was fishing. He wasn't even trying hard to hide it. She nodded toward the door. "Agent Yankowski's office is straight ahead if you want to stop in on your way out."

"That's okay. Yank knows I'm here. He can poke his head out of his office if he wants to see me. He's got work to do, and we didn't part on the best terms. We never saw eye-to-eye on his idea for this team. I'm not convinced I was wrong but results speak for themselves. Water over the dam now. I'm retired. A dinosaur." There was no self-pity in his tone. "I should get moving. I might go see the penguins at the aquarium, or I might skip the penguins and drive up to Maine in time to take old Wendell out for a pint."

"I'm sure he'd like that," Emma said, her tone neutral.

Gordy started past her but stopped abruptly. "I hoped you'd level with me, Emma."

"That's a two-way street, Gordy."

"I always believed there were no secrets between us. I should have known better. You're a Sharpe, after all."

"Sorry the fishing expedition didn't work out for you."

He laughed. "I had that coming. You're tougher than you used to be. Maybe you had a little of Sister Brigid left in you when you worked with me. Or is the smart remark your fiancé's influence?" He winked at her. "I bet you complicate his life."

"I'll see you on Saturday," Emma said.

"Another careful answer." Gordy pointed a finger at her. "That's good, Emma. Be careful, because your grandfather will burn you if you aren't. Mark my words."

"Can you find your own way out?"

"Not a problem."

"Take care, Gordy. You know how to reach me should you need to."

"And you know how to reach me."

She gave a curt nod. "Yes, I do."

"Good to see you, Special Agent Sharpe."

After Gordy left, Emma texted Oliver York and her parents, asking them to get in touch, and then she went into Matt Yankowski's office. His windows overlooked Boston Harbor, glistening in the morning sun. Yank had her sit on a chair facing his desk and he didn't interrupt her report on her brief, odd meeting with the retired agent.

When she finished, Yank grimaced. In his midforties, he was a good-looking, straight-arrow, buttoned-down agent out of central casting—except nothing about him was that simple. It was a lesson Emma had learned early in the four-plus years she'd known him. "Do you have anything on these stolen mosaics?" he asked.

She shook her head. "No."

Yank's eyes narrowed. "But?"

"It's entirely possible Alessandro Pearson's death

triggered the rumor mill. Something to do with his estate, maybe. Wild imaginations. I don't know."

"Could York and MI5 be creating the rumors to stir the pot?"

"Anything is possible."

"Right now I wish your brother and grandfather hadn't put Gordon Wheelock on their guest list. Do you know which one of them had that bright idea, when and why?"

"I don't."

"But you're going to ask," Yank said.

"I'm heading up to Maine after I'm done here."

He heaved a sigh. "Did you know about this London party?"

"No."

"But your parents were there as well as Oliver York. I was afraid his name would come up when I heard Gordy Wheelock had an appointment with you. Does York know Gordy investigated the thefts?"

"Undoubtedly."

"What about Gordy—does he know Oliver's the serial art thief he and your grandfather chased for years?"

"I don't think so, but that's only a guess. Gordy's certainly suspicious of my relationship with Oliver."

"He'll figure it out, then."

"I would bet on that."

"Was Oliver at this party because Gordy was, or was it the other way around and Gordy was there because of Oliver?"

"I've already texted Oliver asking him to get in touch with me."

"You said please, since he's a British citizen protected by MI5?"

Emma shrugged, ignoring Yank's sarcasm. "Whatever it takes."

Yank looked pained. "I was hoping we were done with him for a while."

"Same here."

"Yeah. I ran into Gordy before he left. He invited me outside for a cigarette. Sarcastic SOB. He knows I don't smoke. I said no. He never approved of HIT. He wrote a letter to the director articulating his disapproval. No love lost between us, but there's no question he was one of the best." Yank pushed back his chair and rose. "When I'm done with this job, I'm going quietly. I'll go for long runs on the Esplanade, take up tai chi and help Lucy run her knitting shop."

Emma got to her feet. Lucy was Yank's wife, a psychologist who'd been reluctant to move from their home in northern Virginia. She'd finally agreed to move north and was adapting to Boston life, moving into a Back Bay apartment and opening a knitting shop. She and Yank had no children, and he was convinced she would go back to psychology. Colin was, too, but Emma wasn't. Lucy Yankowski was getting into yarns, needles, knitting patterns and classes.

"Oliver's an expert in tai chi," Emma said finally, with a slight smile.

Yank scowled as he came around his desk. "Do we have a bored retired agent on our hands who's trying to connect dots that don't connect because he wants to feel relevant, or is Gordy Wheelock on to something?"

"I can't say for certain."

"I'm not asking for certainty. I'm asking for your gut take on what he's up to."

Emma tended to be analytical and objective, gathering bits and pieces of information and evidence and letting them point her in the right direction. Gut takes were Colin's strength, given his training, experience and natural instincts, and an asset in his work as an undercover agent.

"Gordy was deliberate and reasonably well prepared," she said. "But he wasn't in great shape, whether it was jet lag or what, I don't know. I didn't work with him during his last few months on the job. I'll look into what he left unfinished."

Yank nodded. "Good. Gordy could have made up the rumors to get in here and try to pump you for information. Him, MI5, Oliver York and your family. Not my favorite combination." He heaved another sigh. "I don't need more Sharpe trouble, Emma. I really don't."

"Understood."

She headed out of his office, shutting the door behind her. To get to her own office, she had to pass through an open-layout area of tables and cubicles where HIT team members could meet or work on their own. Sam Padgett, the newest member, had set up at a U-shaped table with his wireless keyboard, laptop, separate monitor, a stack of printed spreadsheets and notebooks and several Sharpies. He was a dark, ultrafit, good-looking Texan, full of contradictions and foiled stereotypes, an expert marksman, a whiz at numbers and a total wimp when it came to New England winters. He'd arrived in Boston last fall and Emma swore no one had ever been so happy to see the green grass of spring.

He looked up at her. "Bad?"

"Not great. A retired agent was just here. Gordon Wheelock. Did you see him?"

"Nope. I was in my office gathering up my gear so I could spread out here."

"And he didn't see you?"

Padgett shook his head. He had on a dark suit, a crisp white shirt and loosened red tie, but he always managed to look casual. "Why, you want me to tail him?"

"Maybe," Emma said, then explained the situation. "Think you can find out where he stayed last night? Knowing Gordy, it will be convenient and relatively inexpensive."

"I never use *inexpensive* and *Boston* in the same sentence. Convenient to here?"

"He mentioned penguins. Try near the aquarium. I'm concerned he's working his own agenda and could infringe on something he shouldn't."

"A freelancing retiree. Just what we need. I'll go see the penguins. You off to Maine?"

"I'm on my way out now. I'm supposed to have lunch tomorrow with my future mother-in-law."

"Lobster rolls and wild blueberry pie?"

"Very possibly. They're not quintessential Maine foods for no reason."

"No doubt. I've met your future mother-in-law. Nothing fazes her. You can tell."

Emma smiled, some of her tension easing after her visits with Gordy and Yank. "Four sons would do that," she said.

"Especially when all of them are Donovans. We'll stay in touch about Agent Wheelock."

She returned to her office and collected the contents of the files spread out on her sofa, stuffing them into their appropriate folders, then stacking the folders on her desk. She grabbed her jacket off the back of her door. *Was* Gordy invited to the open house on Saturday—or had he lied about the invitation as a maneuver to get her to talk?

One of a thousand questions coming at her.

No wonder Yank had hidden in his office during Gordy's visit.

3

About forty children around ten years old were congregated at the entrance of the New England Aquarium, laughing and elbowing each other as their teachers counted heads, when Emma arrived. She'd decided to take a quick look on her walk back to her apartment. She wasn't surprised not to see Gordy lined up at the ticket booth. A stiff breeze was blowing off the harbor but it didn't freeze her to the bone the way it would have even a month ago. Spring had taken hold of New England, and that meant her wedding was getting closer and closer.

If only Colin were close, too…

She pushed the thought aside and walked the short distance to the nearest hotel, a four-star chain hotel on a small wharf jutting out into the water. It was probably more expensive than Gordy would have liked, but it was an easy walk to HIT and not a bad cab drive from the airport, assuming he hadn't lied and he'd come in from London yesterday.

Emma didn't quite know why she was thinking the way she was—not simply that Gordy Wheelock hadn't told her the whole story about why he was in her office, but that he might have deliberately lied to her—but there it was.

She approached a cheerful bellman, explained who she was and showed him her FBI credentials. "I'm looking for a friend of mine," she said, then described Gordy. The bellman pointed her to a colleague, an older man flagging a cab for a young couple. Emma waited until he finished.

He remembered Gordy. "Sure, sure. You missed him by a few minutes. I just put him in a cab."

Emma stepped back from the curb, away from an arriving cab. "Has he checked out?"

"Yes, ma'am, he had his bag with him."

"Do you know where he was headed?"

"I don't, sorry."

"Was he alone?"

The bellman nodded. "He was, yes. I never saw him with anyone. I worked late last night and I got in early today. I didn't see him leave the hotel, but I saw him come back—he was on foot. Alone. Only weird thing…" He hesitated. "I probably shouldn't say anything."

"Go ahead, please," Emma said. "He's not in any trouble."

"Well, he tripped last night. That's what he said—I didn't see it happen myself. He was bleeding…here." He pointed to a spot behind his left ear. "We keep hand towels by the door for runners. I gave him one. He wasn't real coherent but he thanked me. He said he tripped and went flying on the steps by the aquarium when he went out for a smoke."

"Did you believe him?"

"Yes, ma'am. Of course. Why would you lie about something like that? At first I thought he'd been mugged, but he's a big guy—not the target you'd pick, you know? Then he said he tripped and that made sense to me. I probably shouldn't have mentioned it. I asked him if he needed an ambulance, but he said no, he'd be fine. He looked okay just now."

"Anything else you can think of?"

"There was one other thing. A cab driver gave us an envelope to deliver to him."

"To Mr. Wheelock?"

The bellman nodded. "The driver said he left his passenger window open while he was chatting with another driver, and when he got back in, the envelope was on the front seat. He didn't see who left it. He said there was a label on it but it blew off."

"What did the label say?" Emma asked.

"Just the guy's name and that he was a hotel guest. He'd checked his bag with the front desk. I found it and put the envelope in an outside pocket."

"Did you look inside the envelope?"

"No, ma'am, I did not," the bellman said, obviously offended.

Emma thanked him and headed back to the street. She called Sam Padgett and filled him in. "No wonder Gordy looked as if he was in pain," she said.

"I'll talk to housekeeping and see what they can tell me about the state of his room. Good work, Agent Sharpe. Are you going to call Wheelock and ask him what the bloody head and this envelope are all about?"

"Doing that next."

"He didn't mention falling either because it's embarrassing, tripping while out for a smoke, or he was attacked and doesn't want you to know."

"Or it didn't occur to him to mention it."

"It occurred to him," Sam said with his usual certainty.

"What's your take on the envelope?"

"Was he expecting it or was it a surprise? Something from a source? A threat? Red Sox tickets? Lots of possibilities. We'll stay in touch."

After they disconnected, Emma called Gordy on his cell phone. When he didn't answer, she left a voice mail. "It's Emma Sharpe. Call me."

She continued along the harbor to the tiny waterfront apartment she'd rented upon her arrival in Boston last March to join Yank's team. Happy to be back in New England, working on challenging investigations on a small team led by a senior agent who'd always been her champion, she'd settled into her new apartment and new routines. Not for a second had she envisioned—or even dreamed—that by fall, she would be in love with a deep-cover agent with roots in a small fishing village a few miles from her own southern Maine hometown.

Now she and Colin were getting ready for their wedding.

She smiled, thinking of him. His dark hair, his smile, his blue-gray eyes that reminded her of the ocean.

"I miss you," she whispered, as if he could hear her.

After several months back and forth to Washington, he'd finally disappeared in mid-March on his latest undercover mission. Despite her own role with the FBI, Emma didn't know what his mission was or where it had taken him. She only knew it was intense, dangerous and exhausting. He'd come home for a few days in late April and then left again. Since then, not a word—not so much as a text message, email or cryptic voice mail.

Matt Yankowski knew where Colin was. Yank had been Colin's contact agent on his first deep-cover mission four years ago. Last October, he'd gone out on a limb to get Colin, at least nominally, into HIT and had put up with his relationship with one of his team members. Emma would never ask him to give her hints as to Colin's whereabouts. She respected their professional relationship, but she also respected Colin's silence and his trust in her to handle the situation.

Never in a million years did I think he'd put a ring on your finger, at least not this soon.

That was Yank in November. He'd never been one to mince words. Emma smiled, remembering that rainy Dublin night when Colin had dropped onto one knee in a crowded pub and proposed to her.

Wherever he was, she knew he was safe. She felt it.

As she unlocked her apartment door, she noticed a new sailboat had arrived at the marina that shared the small wharf with her building, another renovated warehouse. There would be more boats with the warming weather.

She went inside and was helping herself to a yogurt out of the fridge when a text message came in. Video chat in ten minutes?

Oliver York. Emma texted him back. Five.

"You look uptight, Emma," Oliver York said in his genuine upper-class English accent. "Or do you continue to insist I call you Special Agent Sharpe?"

"Agent Sharpe will do."

"Mmm. That sort of call, is it?"

"It's always that sort of call, Oliver."

She'd placed her laptop on her coffee table and was seated on the sofa in her small living room. Just as well they were talking here instead of her FBI office. Nothing about her relationship with the wealthy Englishman, sheep farmer, mythologist and serial art thief was regular. He was in his late thirties, with curly tawny hair and lively, light green eyes. His features were deceptively boyish, betraying none of the psychological trauma and physical pain he had suffered as a child.

"I see." He narrowed his gaze on her. "For someone usually so cool and analytical, this uptight look of yours worries me. You and Colin haven't canceled the wedding, have you?"

"It's Agent Donovan and no, we haven't."

"Have you relented and decided to invite me after all? Is that why you texted me?"

"I'm not inviting you to my wedding."

"Is Agent Donovan inviting me, then?"

"No."

"A pity, but I'll send a gift, regardless." He sat back, putting a bit of distance between him and his screen. "You're home early. I recognize the moody seascape on the wall behind you. It's the work of our fair Irish artist friend, Aoife O'Byrne."

"It's a signed print. I can't afford her original art."

"Who can these days? But a signed print is worth something. It's only four o'clock here. That means it's just eleven in the morning in Boston. Did you get fired?"

"Not yet. It could happen anytime with you in my life."

"I see you tried and failed to smile while making that comment. What can I do for you, then, Agent Sharpe? Does the FBI need my help given my expertise in mythology?"

Emma barely heard him. She was looking past him, taking in his surroundings. She recognized the bright, contemporary furnishings and the view from the partially open window behind him of the Irish Sea. "Oliver..." She gritted her teeth. "Oliver, you're in Declan's Cross. You're in a seaside room at the O'Byrne House Hotel."

"I am, indeed. I'm taking in a delightful breeze off the sea as we speak. Spring on the south Irish coast is quite lovely. I believe I'm in the room where you and Colin stayed on your last visit this winter."

"It's not the same room."

"As if you'd tell me if it were."

"Why are you in Declan's Cross?"

"I couldn't resist Kitty O'Byrne's scones."

Kitty was Aoife's older sister and the proprietress of the boutique hotel, which a decade ago had been a rambling old seaside house owned by their uncle. Ten years ago, the house had been broken into by a clever, brazen art thief, still officially unidentified and at large, although the stolen works had mysteriously reappeared last fall.

Oliver did have nerve.

"I'm leaving once we've finished our chat," he said. "Kitty kindly allowed me a late checkout without extra charge. So, my dear, if you're tempted to sic the Irish guards on me, there's no need."

He was referring to the Gardaí, the Irish police. Kitty's love interest happened to be a Dublin-based garda detective who owned a farm in Declan's Cross.

Sean Murphy would love an excuse to interrogate Oliver York.

"I'm not going to sic the guards on you," Emma said. "But if you're hatching a plan to resteal the art you returned to the O'Byrnes, you can forget it. You'll be arrested. MI5 won't be able to save you."

Oliver waved a hand. "You and your fantasies about me, Emma—Agent Sharpe. I flew into Dublin from London yesterday thinking I'd have a pint with your grandfather, but I discovered he's already in Maine. I consoled myself with a quick visit to quaint, pretty Declan's Cross."

"Why did you want to see my grandfather?"

"Wendell and I always have things to talk about."

"He was in London last week before he flew here on Saturday. Did you see him?"

"I shared a dram of an interesting new Scotch with him. Now, what can I do for you, Agent Sharpe?" Oliver made a show of glancing furtively around him, then leaned close to the screen. "Keep in mind MI5 is likely listening to us."

Emma wouldn't be surprised if they were. "You were at a party at Claridge's on Sunday. Tell me about it."

"Tell you what?"

"For starters, why were you there?"

"Why wouldn't I be? Don't sound so surprised. I live in the neighborhood and Claridge's is one of my favorite hangouts."

It wasn't a direct answer to her question but Emma let it go. "Who else was there?"

"Your parents." His brow furrowed. "Did the good Faye and Timothy Sharpe see or hear something of interest to the FBI, or to you personally?"

"I haven't spoken to them. This is a voluntary interview on your part, Oliver, but I'd like to ask the questions if you don't mind."

"Of course. By all means." He sat back farther, clearly relaxed. "Ask away."

"A retired FBI agent was there. I believe you know him. Gordon Wheelock."

"Do I?"

"He investigated your US thefts. San Francisco, Dallas. He's responsible for putting away a number of art thieves and was sorry he retired before he could put you away."

"*My* thefts? *Me?* The still unidentified thief, you mean." Oliver gave an obviously faked yawn. "I want to take a walk before I return to London this evening. Aoife O'Byrne is in Declan's Cross painting sunrises, did you know? They aren't a cliché subject in her hands, although I am partial to her short-lived phase painting porpoises."

Emma refused to be distracted. "Agent Wheelock stopped in my office this morning and told me he saw you at Claridge's."

"Did he? Hmm. He must have been the disheveled American who gave me the dirty look. We didn't speak but someone mentioned he was an American agent of some sort."

"Who mentioned him?"

Oliver made a face. "Take a guess."

"Your MI5 handler?"

He pressed a finger to his lips. "Shh."

"Was he at the party?"

"Obviously you already have the answer, but I'm not going to confirm or deny his presence. It was an uneventful, perfectly civil English tea. No guns, no blood, no arrests. I wish you'd been there, Emma— although given your life these days, I suspect the afternoon would have taken a different turn and ended up in the papers."

She ignored his remark. "Any particular interest in late antiquity or the Victoria and Albert Museum?"

"Of course. Both. I'm a mythologist and I'm devoted to the museum. You've been, haven't you?"

"A number of times. Did you see anyone with Agent Wheelock?"

"As a matter of fact, yes. He arrived alone but he met up with Claudia Deverell. I believe you know her? She's an American who used to work at one of the big auction houses. She specializes in Mediterranean antiquities. She lives in London."

"I know who she is," Emma said.

"That's what I thought. She and her family are no strangers to the Sharpes. Wasn't her mother once a Sharpe client? Victoria Norwood Deverell. She died last year. Cancer. Very sad. The Norwoods were great collectors of antiquities, with a special passion for mosaics. They've owned a house in Heron's Cove for generations." Oliver sat forward, as if he were in the same room with Emma instead of on the other side of the Atlantic. "Is Agent Wheelock meddling in FBI business, Emma?"

She kept her expression neutral. "Did you hear any

interesting rumors while you were at the party on Sunday?"

"Ah. You mean the rumor about stolen Byzantine mosaics. Did that get your retired FBI agent worked up? I know nothing."

"How, when and where did you hear the rumors yourself?"

"I was eating a delightful mini scone with clotted cream and strawberry jam when I overheard two elderly gentlemen say they'd heard someone had nicked a couple of ancient mosaics from a London collector. I got jam on my shirt cuff and went to the men's room. I don't know the gents and heard nothing further before I left."

"Since then?"

"Not a peep."

He could be lying, or he could be telling the truth. Emma couldn't tell. "Did you speak with Claudia Deverell yourself?"

"Your parents introduced us but I didn't linger. Didn't Claudia once date your brother? But that's none of my business, and I must be going. By the way, the sheepskins I sent you and Colin this winter are wonderful in warm weather, too. You'll see."

"Oliver—wait."

But he was gone.

Emma shut her laptop. No point trying to get him back. He wouldn't answer. She rolled to her feet and went into the bedroom. She'd rented the apartment when she'd first moved to Boston, months before she'd met Colin. It was small for the two of them but they'd decided to keep it, given its convenient location and Boston's sky-high rents. They had his house in Maine for more space. Not that they'd needed space lately, given his absences.

She dug her overnight bag out of the closet and set it on the double bed. Thinking about living arrangements was a welcome respite from thinking about Gordy Wheelock and whatever he was up to, and how it involved Oliver York, Claudia Deverell and the Sharpes.

The Sharpes.

Emma unzipped her suitcase. She was a Sharpe, too. She didn't need to remind herself.

Her parents hadn't responded yet to her text. Her father still worked for Sharpe Fine Art Recovery from London in a low-stress research and analysis position. Her mother had left her job as an art teacher. They made a point of socializing on occasion, sometimes because it was good for business but mostly because it was good for them for its own sake. A new procedure in December had provided her father with some relief from his chronic back pain, but Emma didn't know when, or if, her parents would return to Maine, even for her wedding.

She threw a few things into her suitcase. She had some clothes at Colin's house—yoga pants, sweatshirts, hiking shoes, kayaking gear—but she'd need something to wear to lunch with his mother as well as to the open house. Now she had to add checking up on Gordy Wheelock to her list for the long weekend.

Would Claudia Deverell be there? Emma hadn't seen Claudia or any of the Deverells in at least six years. She'd been a novice then. Blonde, attractive and a few years older, Claudia had joined Emma on the tidal river in Heron's Cove. *I can't believe you're a nun, Emma. You were always so worldly and well-*

dressed, and you seemed to enjoy life. But I shouldn't call you Emma, should I? It must be Sister Something.

Sister Brigid. I'm a novice. Are you in town long?

I'm here with my mother for the weekend. It's Fourth of July, or didn't you know?

Emma, wearing her modified habit, her hair pulled back with a wide white headband, had picked up two river-polished stones, handed one to Claudia and then tossed hers into the rising tide. She'd learned not to be defensive about people's notions about a religious life. She invited Claudia to tour the convent, located on a small peninsula near Heron's Cove.

Claudia had tossed her stone into the river. *My maternal great-grandfather was good friends with the man who built the original estate that's now your convent. They were adventurers. They did several trips together in the early twentieth century and brought home all sorts of treasures from the lands of the former Roman Empire. Loot, we might call it now. Eye of the beholder, I suppose.* She'd dusted bits of mud off her hands and smiled. *Good to see you, Emma.*

Claudia never came to the convent for a tour, and Emma left the Sisters of the Joyful Heart a short time later for her new life with the FBI—and now her life included Colin.

She wondered if Claudia had been the one who'd told Gordy about her past.

Emma slung her overnight bag over one shoulder and headed out. Her next logical step was a chat with her brother and her grandfather about Gordy, Alessandro Pearson, Claudia Deverell and the rumors about stolen mosaics. Fortunately, for the first time in years, Wendell Sharpe, founder of Sharpe Fine Art Recovery and one of the foremost private art detectives in the world, was less than two hours away in southern Maine, and Emma wouldn't have to fly all the way to Dublin to see him.

4

Mary Bracken paused on the narrow lane that wound along the cliffs above the village of Declan's Cross. She was winded from walking too fast up the hill, but the lane had leveled off. She was on the headland where Sean Murphy, a garda detective, had his farm. As she caught her breath, she watched a trio of chubby lambs chase each other in the pasture on the other side of a barbed-wire fence. Nearby, two ewes nibbled on the lush green. Mary could hear the bleating of the lambs above the crash of waves on the rocks far below her. She didn't know if the tide was coming in or going out, just that it was somewhere between low and high.

She knew whiskey, not tides, she thought with a smile.

She resumed her walk on the quiet lane, a short distance from historic Ardmore, the ancient land of Saint Declan. She loved this part of Ireland, but it wasn't home. Home was Killarney to the west, a favorite with tourists given its natural beauty, national park and fascinating history. Bracken Distillers, where she worked, was located in the hills not far from the busy village. A good location.

I should be there now.

Mary sighed, frustrated with her obsessing. She'd made her decision. She even had her boarding pass for her flight tomorrow. No point questioning her motives for setting off to America now. She'd fly from Dublin to Boston and then drive on to Maine and a visit with her brother, Finian.

Her priest brother.

One of the ewes spotted her and bleated loudly, as if she knew Mary needed a good talking-to.

She shoved her hands into her jacket pockets and continued on her way. Where would she be now if Finian and Declan, twin brothers and the eldest of the five Bracken siblings, had decided to make a go of the Bracken farm instead of launching their own whiskey business?

She passed another ewe, a lamb at her teats.

Mary smiled. "*That's* where I'd be. I'd have little ones at my teats by now."

As it was, she had a full-time job at Bracken Distillers, running tours and the whiskey school. She loved her work. She and Declan got on well.

They missed Finian.

Mary felt a lump in her throat. "Ah, Fin."

Where would *he* be if he'd made a go of the farm?

He'd be off on a tractor, fixing fences and tending sheep instead of across the Atlantic working as a parish priest in a small Maine fishing village. Fixing himself, tending his church flock—living far away from the reminders of his loss. His wife, his daughters. Gone too soon.

He was a worry, Father Finian Bracken was.

Mary, the youngest Bracken, usually wasn't prone to worry or obsessing, but Finian's choice to enter the priesthood felt all wrong to her and had from the start. Now seven years had passed and he hadn't yet returned to Bracken Distillers and his senses. She feared he never would.

Old Paddy Murphy waved to her from his tractor, across a rolling pasture on the other side of the lane as it curved along the cliffs. She waved back, and Paddy continued his work, which no doubt involved mud, muck and manure. Mary could smell the salt water and welcomed the fresh, clean breeze, no hint of rain in the clear air. As the lane wound closer to the cliffs, she saw the tide indeed was ebbing, and she wished her worries could ebb with it. Yet she knew even if they could, they'd be back, as sure as the tide would rise again.

The lane turned to dirt, narrowing further as she approached the tip of the headland, where a medieval church lay in ruin along an ancient stone wall covered with moss and tangles of greenery. Mary recognized holly, rushes and a small oak, but she couldn't name the spring wildflowers, delicate-looking with their pink and blue blossoms amid the vines and moss. Like tides, she didn't know much about wildflowers. They seemed to hold their own against rock, wind and sea, and were an integral part of the rugged, beautiful scenery.

Three ornately carved Celtic Christian stone crosses stood on a green hilltop above her, as if they were sentries protecting the headland. She noticed a movement, and then recognized Oliver York as he emerged from behind the center cross. "Don't come up here," he called to her. "It's muddy as bloody hell."

Mary stayed put as he trotted down the hillside toward her. She zipped her Irish Mackintosh and felt the stiffening breeze whip through her long, dark Bracken hair.

She thought the mysterious Brit on his way to her might be one of Finian's new friends, too. He disappeared into the church ruin, its partial walls of lichen-covered stone behind the trees and vines on the overgrown wall. Mary didn't know what to make of him. They'd met briefly in February, here in Declan's Cross. Finian had been there, home in Ireland for a short visit.

Oliver squeezed between the oak and a holly and jumped onto the lane, missing a puddle by inches. He was, indeed, splattered with mud, from his Wellingtons to his well-worn waxed-cotton jacket. His tawny hair was tousled and his cheeks were red, no doubt from the windier conditions up by the crosses.

"Mary Bracken," he said cheerfully. "Father Bracken's youngest sister. Hello, Mary. I don't know if you remember me. Oliver York."

"I do remember you. How are you, Oliver? It's a beautiful afternoon for a walk."

"I suppose it is. I'm not much on rambling, I'm afraid." He glanced out at the sea, a deep turquoise in the late-day light. "This is a good spot to nourish the soul, if one goes for that sort of thing."

"Do you?"

"Sometimes. Here, especially. I can't explain."

He shifted his gaze back to her, scrutinizing her with a frankness she didn't find unsettling, perhaps because of his overall good cheer and easygoing manner. She was dressed casually, in leggings, a simple top under her jacket and waterproof walking shoes.

"I didn't expect to walk this far," she said. "Did you just arrive in Declan's Cross?"

"Last night. I stayed at the charming O'Byrne House Hotel. I enjoyed Bracken whiskey in the lounge before turning in and then a full Irish breakfast this morning while I looked out at the Irish Sea. I checked out before I started up here."

"Did I interrupt your contemplation of ancient Irish Celtic myths and legends?"

"Hardly. I was contemplating getting on with my drive to Cork in time for my flight back to London." He tilted his head to one side, his green eyes narrowing on her. "And you, Mary? What are you contemplating on your ramble among the sheep, sea and ruins?"

"I was just enjoying the scenery." It wasn't the entire truth, of course, but she wasn't baring her soul to this man. "I leave for Dublin soon. I have an early flight to Boston tomorrow."

Oliver's eyebrows went up. "Is that right?"

Yet…he didn't seem surprised. Mary couldn't put her finger on why she thought that. She heard a bird twittering in the rushes and suddenly wished she wasn't leaving for Dublin and America but could stay on here for a few days.

"Will you be visiting your brother in Maine?"

She nodded. "I want to see him before his year there is up. I'm staying with him at the rectory. He can't take much time off, but I'll be able to amuse myself."

"I've no doubt. Is this a sudden trip?"

"The priest he's replacing is finishing his Irish sabbatical in a few weeks. If I don't visit now, I'll never have this chance again."

"You hope, if it means he'll be back in Ireland," Oliver said.

"Maybe so."

"Did you drive here from Killarney? Declan's Cross is a bit out of the way if you're on your way to Dublin Airport."

"I know, but I couldn't resist. Have you been in touch with Finian lately?"

"Not in a while, but he and I are great friends. You must say hello to him for me."

"I will," Mary said.

"Did he warn you about me?"

She smiled. "*Everyone's* warned me about you."

"Ah." Oliver's lively eyes sparked with humor. "Let me guess. I'm an eccentric, solitary Englishman steeped in the language of myth, legend and folklore."

"Also that you're a teller of tall tales and, like Fin, friends with dangerous types—such as the two FBI agents who were at the gathering here in February."

"Egad." Oliver shuddered. "Agents Emma Sharpe and Colin Donovan would throw me in irons if I referred to them as friends. That's only the slightest exaggeration, mind you." He kicked a clump of mud off the toe of his boot. "Does your work with Bracken Distillers put you in contact with many dangerous types?"

"Not me personally, no, but we had a brush with smugglers last spring, just as Fin was moving to America. The smugglers used an abandoned section of the old distillery for their illicit activities. They were caught with help from Fin. I missed most of the excitement, or whatever you want to call it."

"Sean Murphy was injured in the fracas."

For reasons to which Mary wasn't privy, Sean didn't approve of Oliver York. She didn't know if his reasons were personal or professional, as an elite garda detective.

She angled a look at the Englishman. "You seem to know a lot about us."

"I suspect Detective Garda Murphy and the FBI know far more about me than I do them. Shall we walk back to the village together, or do you want to ramble some more? I wasn't joking about the mud up on the hill."

"I'll walk back to Declan's Cross with you."

The lane was the only route on the headland to the village. Oliver didn't seem at all out of breath as he walked with her, the breeze picking up as they emerged from the protection of the wall and ruins. Mary found it curious if not suspicious that he'd shown up in Declan's Cross as she was leaving for Maine to see her brother. She didn't know if Emma Sharpe and Colin Donovan would be there, but she expected they would be.

Oliver slowed as they came to the Murphy farmhouse. Paddy, Sean's uncle, had returned from the fields and was cleaning off the tractor in front of the barn. Sean owned the farm, but Paddy mostly worked it.

"I love listening to the lambs," Oliver said. "Can you hear them?"

Mary smiled without looking at him. "I can."

"I have a farm in England. I inherited it from my grandparents."

"It's in the Cotswolds, isn't it? I've been there—to

the Cotswolds, I mean. Obviously I haven't been to your farm. I did one of those inn-to-inn walking tours."

"More rambling," Oliver said with a wry smile. "You went on your own?"

"Yes. It was after the deaths of my sister-in-law and nieces in a sailing accident. I was on summer break before my final year at university in Cork. I needed…" Mary broke off, searching for the right words. "I suppose you could say my solitary walk in the English countryside was good for the soul. Are you here in Ireland alone?"

The wind caught the ends of his tawny hair. "I am, yes."

"Is your visit because of mythology or because of the dangerous types you know?"

"Perhaps both."

He spoke lightly, but Mary detected an edgy undertone, as if her question had struck a nerve. She wondered if his response might be the truth. "When did you arrive in Ireland?" she asked.

"Yesterday. I flew into Dublin."

"And you're leaving tonight. That's a brief visit."

"I'd hoped to see Wendell Sharpe but discovered he'd already left for America. Do you know him?"

"Not personally, no."

"He's gone home to Maine for the first time in years. He's attending the open house for the new Sharpe Fine Art Recovery offices."

"Wonderful," Mary said. "Fin and I will be there. Did you know the Sharpes investigated an art theft at the O'Byrne house about ten years ago?"

"I've heard," Oliver said.

"It wasn't a hotel then. Kitty's uncle owned it. It

was a drafty old place, I understand. The thief made off with several valuable artworks, including two landscapes by Jack Butler Yeats that are worth a fortune now."

"He was the younger brother of William Butler Yeats. A talented family."

"Most of the stolen works mysteriously reappeared last fall." Mary could hear the drama in her voice, but she didn't care. It was a captivating tale. "Only a landscape painting of the crosses and ruin out on the headland is still missing. It's unsigned and probably of little value. Some people think it's an early work by Aoife O'Byrne, but she hasn't claimed it. She says she became an artist in part because of the theft."

"I'm a great fan of her work." Oliver looked out at the sea, past a narrow strip of pasture between the lane and the cliffs. "I own one of her porpoise paintings."

Mary hadn't known that but hid her surprise. "Aoife was at the gathering in February, too. You two, you aren't..."

"We're friends. At least I think of her as a friend. I'm a simple mythologist, Mary."

"I doubt there's much about you that's simple." She nodded back toward the church ruin. "Do you have a particular interest in the three crosses on the hilltop?"

"I'm not working on a scholarly paper, if that's what you mean. The church that's in ruin is named after Saint Declan. This is Saint Declan country. He's one of the great patron saints of Ireland." Oliver smiled, the hint of awkwardness a moment ago vanishing. "Fin's twin brother is named Declan."

"It's a traditional Irish name," Mary said. "I'm not religious. I certainly don't believe Saint Declan was led to this part of Ireland by a bell atop a boulder float-ing on the Irish Sea."

"Not literally, perhaps—"

"Rocks sink."

"But think of rocks flung about in a fierce storm. Perhaps they could appear to float. In any case, I see the power of Saint Declan's story not in its literal truth but in its human truth."

"Now you sound like Finian."

"Also the name of an Irish saint," Oliver said with a wink. "There's no chance of you entering a convent, is there?"

Mary laughed. "None at all. I'd have said there was no chance of Finian entering the priesthood, but obvi-ously he did."

"He's a very good priest."

"He was a good whiskey man, too. And a good fa-ther and husband."

"You don't approve of his vocation?"

"It's not for me to approve or disapprove."

"But you don't approve."

She sighed. "Let's go back to discussing art. It's much safer, don't you think?"

"That all depends," Oliver said.

"Oh, right—helps not to be a thief or the victim of a thief."

He said nothing. The lane descended steeply into the village with its brightly painted homes and shops. Mary found herself wishing again she were staying here through the weekend, enjoying the spa at the O'Byrne House Hotel, indulging in scones, whiskey and full Irish breakfasts. She could wander to Ardmore with its sand beach, stunning cliff walk and impressive medieval round tower. Saint Declan was said to have been buried there. She was almost sorry she was leaving for Dublin and a long flight to Boston in the morning. She didn't *need* to go to Maine.

Except she did. Deep inside her, she knew she did.

"The Sharpes came up in a conversation last week," she said as she and Oliver turned off the lane at a bookshop, its front painted a vivid shade of red. "An American woman on a tour at the distillery mentioned them. We chatted for a few minutes after the tour. She said she was fascinated by Killarney's history, but she herself knows more about ancient Greece and Rome. She said she inherited a passion for antiquities from her mother, who was once a Sharpe client. Small world, isn't it?"

"Antiquities and whiskey. A good combination, I would think."

Mary felt heat rush to her face, but she glanced at Oliver and realized he wasn't making fun of her. "I tend to chat with visitors between tours, lectures and tastings."

"You're gregarious by nature."

"I know much more about whiskey than I do antiquities. This woman was aware I have a brother in Maine who's friends with the Sharpes. It seemed odd at first, but then she explained that she chose our distillery to visit because of the connection."

"Do you recall her name?" Oliver asked.

"Claudia Deverell. I made a point of remembering. She visited the distillery on Friday, but I don't know how long she was in Ireland. She said she lives in London most of the time. Do you know her, by chance?"

"We met at a party on Sunday, as a matter of fact.

Small world. I can't say I've run into her before then. Have you told anyone else about her visit?"

Mary paused, noting a few pedestrians out in the village enjoying the fine spring day. The hotel was a short distance up the street. She suddenly couldn't wait to be there. She felt unsettled, as if she might have said too much to this charming, eccentric Englishman. She *had* been warned about him, after all.

"I haven't said a word to anyone," she said finally. "I don't know why I mentioned her to you. Because she lives in London and knows the Sharpes, I suppose."

"The Sharpes are an intriguing lot."

Mary forced herself to take in her surroundings—a passing car, the scent of roses from a trellis on a small house painted a rich yellow. Best to change the subject, she decided. "Finian's promised to take me sightseeing in Maine," she said cheerfully.

Oliver eyed her a split second longer than was comfortable. "That sounds splendid."

Mary smiled, relieved he didn't press her further about Claudia Deverell. "I don't think I've ever heard anyone use *splendid* in a sentence."

"My grandfather used to say *splendid*. I suppose I was channeling him."

"I'm not making fun of you. It's sweet, using a word your grandfather used."

"He was a good man."

"Did he like the Irish?"

Oliver winked. "Who doesn't like the Irish?"

"What did Oliver York want with you?"

Mary bristled at Sean Murphy's tone. She sat next to him at the bar at the O'Byrne House Hotel, nursing a glass of sparkling water and lemon as he gave her a dark look. He was drinking coffee. She had assumed he was in Dublin, but he'd explained he'd come down to Declan's Cross to visit Kitty and see about his farm. Mary appreciated Sean's rekindled relationship with Kitty O'Byrne, who'd left them alone at the bar.

Mary wondered if Oliver York had anything to do with Sean's arrival in Declan's Cross. She liked Sean, although she didn't know him as well as Finian did. The two had become friends in the terrible months after the deaths of Finian's family. In a way, Sean had saved her brother's life, or at least he'd helped.

Nonetheless, Mary didn't like his tone. "Are you asking as a friend or a detective?"

"I'm both, Mary."

His tone had softened slightly. The spring breeze floated into the quiet lounge through open doors and windows, and she could hear the wash of the tide across the back garden of the boutique hotel. It was located in the heart of the quaint, tiny village. "Oliver didn't want anything with me. I ran into him out past your farm. We walked back here together, and he got in his car and is on his way to Cork for his flight to London." Mary paused, but Sean made no comment. She hadn't touched her sparkling water yet and took a small sip, setting her glass down before she continued. "What's your quarrel with Oliver?"

"Trouble has a way of following him. Let's leave it at that."

Mary eyed Sean. He was a fine-looking man with his dark, thick hair and piercing blue eyes. He had an amiable manner, but she knew better than to allow that to lull her into thinking he was more sheep farmer and friend than alert detective.

"What did you and Oliver discuss?" Sean asked finally, lifting his coffee cup.

Mary shrugged. "Not much. The weather and a few other things."

"What other things?"

She felt more like a recalcitrant toddler than a manager of tours and lectures at a successful whiskey distillery, but Sean had crawled under her skin—and he knew it. In fact, she saw now he'd been quite deliberate about it. She supposed she'd fallen into his trap, letting herself get twisted into knots. "I'm not used to being interrogated," she said.

"I'm not interrogating you, Mary."

"You are, but we won't argue about it. Oliver and I chatted about Saint Declan, whiskey and Finian, since they're friends."

Sean grimaced. "I wouldn't call them friends."

"It was a normal conversation, Sean, which, I might add, this is not." She hesitated, debating how far to go, but she'd never been one to keep her thoughts to herself. "I've had a feeling Oliver had something to do with the art stolen from here ten years ago. Is he a source— a consultant with the Garda, or Interpol, perhaps? He can't be the thief, can he?"

Sean drank some of his coffee and set the cup carefully in the saucer.

Mary waited, studying him. She felt her pulse quicken. "*Can* he? Sean!"

"Forget Oliver York." Sean pushed his cup and saucer away from him on the polished wood bar. "Are you driving to Dublin alone?"

"I am. Oliver offered to switch his flight and drive me if I was too tired or wanted to have a drink before I left Declan's Cross."

Sean's expression darkened. "Mary Bracken, you can't—Fin would have my head if I let you—"

"You don't have a say in what I do, Detective Garda Murphy."

"Provided it's legal," he said.

"Well, of course. In any case, I said no to Oliver's offer, and, as I've already told you, he's gone, on his way to Cork, which, I needn't remind you, is a good distance from Dublin. I'm leaving in a few minutes and driving myself. I debated taking the train, but Aoife offered to let me leave my car at her studio in Dublin. She's here in Declan's Cross painting for a few weeks."

Sean sighed. "You enjoyed riling me up, didn't you?"

Mary grinned at him but didn't let down her guard. "Very much."

"Have you told me everything you and Oliver discussed?"

She relented and told him about the American woman and Oliver's reaction. Sean's jaw tightened visibly as she spoke. "Do you know her?" Mary asked when she finished. "This Claudia Deverell?"

Sean's jaw seemed to tighten more. "No." He studied her a moment. "I wish you'd reconsider this trip to Maine, Mary."

"I promise I'll stick close to Fin the entire time."

Sean turned and stared out the window next to him. It looked out on a strip of lush, green grass with a bench and stone urns dripping with bright spring flowers. Once again, Mary couldn't name the variety of flowers. Begonias, she thought. She had an apartment with a garden in Killarney but she'd killed everything she'd tried to plant. It wasn't a question of aptitude, Declan and her sisters would tell her. It was a question of regular maintenance.

Finally, Sean shifted back to her. "Trouble has a way of finding our Father Finian Bracken these days, too."

Mary breathed in the scent of grass and salt water floating into the lounge from the doors and windows. "It's a good thing it's a fine spring day or I might have to figure out how to poison you, Sean Murphy. I'd get away with it, too, because you'd be gone and you're the best detective the garda has."

"And no one would suspect pretty, blue-eyed Mary Bracken. Well, I suppose the flattery cancels the threat, and I don't have to arrest you." He rolled off the stool onto his feet. "You'd be wise to steer clear of Oliver York, Mary. Let's hope he stays in London."

"You really are going to phone Finian, aren't you?"

"The minute I get home."

"Home to Dublin or to your farm here?"

Sean glanced past her to the doorway where Kitty had disappeared. "Home is wherever Kitty is."

"Such a romantic," Mary said, feeling a pang of loneliness. She had loads of friends and acquaintances, but she'd never fallen in love the way Kitty O'Byrne and Sean Murphy had with each other—never mind they'd needed years and years to figure out they were soul mates. Mary hoped her true love, should he ever materialize, didn't take *that* long to get sorted and there were fewer twists and turns.

But if it was twists and turns she wanted to avoid

in her life, why was she on her way to visit her brother in Maine?

"Find yourself an Irish lad," Sean said, as if reading her mind. "One who likes a strong, stubborn woman, because that's what you are, Mary Bracken." He handed her a card. "Ring me anytime, day or night, if you run into trouble in America."

"I will, Sean. Thank you, but I won't run into any trouble."

He looked unconvinced as he left in search of Kitty.

Mary filled her water bottle, grabbed an apple from a bowl and headed out through the front door for her car. She'd be in Dublin in less than three hours. She considered stopping at the cottage Aoife had rented for her painting retreat. Maybe Aoife could explain Oliver York, the Sharpes, the FBI agents and one Father Finian Bracken, but Mary had detected tension between Aoife and Finian at the winter gathering here in Declan's Cross.

Perhaps best to get on to Dublin and rest ahead of her flight to Boston in the morning.

5

Killarney
County Kerry, Ireland

Colin Donovan was admiring a giant rhododendron with a profusion of white blossoms and thinking of his fiancée, who would appreciate the rhodie more than he did, when Sean Murphy called and ruined his afternoon. Maybe his evening. Maybe his entire Irish excursion. All it took was the mention of Oliver York.

"I'm getting an instant headache," Colin said.

"I live to give the FBI headaches," Sean said, his natural humor intact. "Where are you?"

"Killarney."

"Meet me at the Bracken distillery in two hours."

The Irish detective clicked off. Colin slid his phone back in his jacket. He'd alerted Sean to his presence in Ireland as a professional courtesy, but he wasn't there on FBI business. He was there to plan his honeymoon. He'd put it off for weeks—months—while he focused on his latest deep-cover mission. He'd been to four countries, coordinating with other federal agencies and local authorities as he chased down an arsenal of shoulder-fired missiles and other goodies that had ended up in the wrong hands. He'd posed as a rogue buyer. The weapons were secured. The bad guys were on the run or under arrest in the USA, and he was in Ireland, looking at rhododendrons.

He walked across the soft grass of an expansive lawn to a walkway and got out his phone again. The early sunshine had given way to gray clouds but no rain yet. He'd didn't mind. He'd been in hot places. The cool, damp Irish weather was perfect.

He hit the number for Matt Yankowski.

Yank answered on the first ring. "I thought you were taking a couple of days to decompress."

"That was the plan. I'm walking past flowers right now. I think they're lavender. I don't know, though. They're purple."

Silence. "What?" Yank asked finally.

"I'm at Muckross House. It's a part of Killarney National Park. Mansion, gardens, views of one of the famous lakes of Killarney. Didn't you visit here when you were in Ireland last fall?"

"No."

"Just proving I was decompressing."

"Was," Yank noted.

"Sean Murphy is on his way."

Yank sighed. "Because Oliver York is in Ireland."

"Emma?"

"They talked earlier."

Colin stood by a bench among the flower beds along the attractive walkway. "What do I need to know before Sean gets here?"

Yank filled him in on Gordon Wheelock's visit that

morning with a certain Special Agent Emma Sharpe. "Do you know Wheelock?" Yank asked as he finished.

"By reputation. Legend."

"A retired agent attending a London party a few days before the Sharpe open house isn't cause for alarm in and of itself. I don't like throwing in Oliver York, MI5 and rumors about stolen ancient artifacts, but no point in getting riled up until we know more. Gordy Wheelock and I never got along, but I respected him. I don't want to see him hurt himself."

"I hear you," Colin said.

"Emma's following up with him. In the meantime, if I were Detective Garda Murphy, and you and Oliver York showed up in my country at the same time, I'd want to talk to you, too. We have no reason to suspect York wasn't on the level when he told Emma he was in Ireland to see her grandfather and stopped in Declan's Cross on a whim."

"All innocence," Colin said, skeptical.

Yank grunted. "There's nothing innocent about Oliver York. When he was eight, yes. Now? No."

"If he's gone back to London and I decide I need to talk to him after I meet with Sean?"

"Go. I hate to pull you away from the lavender, though."

"Maybe it's mint. Mint's purple, isn't it? The rhododendrons are impressive. They're not the invasive kind. Emma explained the difference when we were here last fall."

"Well, don't explain it to me. Stay in touch."

Yank disconnected, and Colin continued on the walk to the cafeteria in a newer building next to the sprawling Victorian mansion. He hadn't done the mansion tour but he'd read the tour guide. All that stuck was that it had sixty-five rooms and the gardens had been expanded ahead of a visit from Queen Victoria in 1861.

He'd rather be thinking about Queen Victoria's long-ago visit to Ireland than Oliver York and whatever he was up to now.

Especially if it involved the Sharpes.

Colin went into the modern cafeteria, got rhubarb crumble and a coffee and sat at a small table by the floor-to-ceiling windows overlooking the gardens. It wasn't crowded. He wished he had Emma with him. She knew her flowers from her time as Sister Brigid. He hadn't been in touch with her in weeks, out of necessity. He'd promised he would be home in time for their wedding. Beyond that...she knew little about where he'd been, what he'd done.

Yank had told him she was on her way to Maine for the Sharpe open house.

A fine drizzle started and the afternoon turned grayer as Colin drank his coffee and ate his crumble. He wondered what he'd be doing now if he'd decided on a Scottish honeymoon instead of an Irish one. His throat tightened, and he could feel his fatigue clawing at him, his frustration that his forty-eight-hour break in Ireland had gone to hell.

He got up abruptly and went back out into the gardens, and he kept going until he reached a narrow path into the woods. The drizzle let up, and he stood on a rock outcropping above the gray, quiet lake. He breathed in the mist and let the silence envelop him. He saw himself here in a few weeks with his bride at his side, and he knew he was in the right place. And that it would happen—their wedding, their life together.

Two hours later, Colin wasn't settling into a cozy Irish pub for the evening, as he'd anticipated when he'd gotten up that morning, but was standing in the cluttered office at Bracken Distillers, where Mary Bracken, the youngest of the five Bracken siblings, organized her distillery tours. Sean Murphy was pacing in front of a glass partition that looked out on the main floor. He'd just arrived and wanted to stay on his feet after his mad dash, as he called it, from Declan's Cross to the east.

Declan Bracken, a good-looking Irishman in his late thirties, co-founder with his twin brother, Finian, of the distillery, sat on a tall wooden stool next to a worktable. He was silent and grim-faced. Understandable, perhaps, with an American FBI agent and a Dublin-based garda detective on the premises.

Sean reported on his stop in Declan's Cross and his conversation with Mary ahead of her drive to Dublin and her morning flight to Boston. Colin wasn't surprised anymore by anything Oliver York did, but Sean's mention of Claudia Deverell got his attention. According to Yank, she'd been at the London party on Sunday.

Declan confirmed what Mary had told Sean in Declan's Cross. "Mary told me about Claudia Deverell's visit last week. I didn't meet her myself. She told Mary the connection between Fin and you lot helped her decide on Bracken Distillers for her whiskey tour."

You lot. Not much Colin could say to that. He'd let the two Irishmen interpret the silence. So far, Colin thought he was doing a good job of looking both competent and uninformed given the encounter between Irish Mary Bracken and English Oliver York in a small Irish village—by itself, not a matter for the US Federal Bureau of Investigation.

"If you'll excuse us," Sean said, addressing Declan.

Declan hesitated, glancing at Colin and then again at Sean before giving a curt nod. "I'll be just outside," he said as he retreated, shutting the solid wood door behind him.

Colin took a seat on the stool Declan had vacated and eyed Sean. "You know I'm here to plan my Irish honeymoon, right? For real. No games."

"When exactly did you arrive?"

"Late Tuesday. I spent yesterday catching up on sleep at Fin's cottage in the Kerry hills."

Sean had an ambivalent look about him, as if he already regretted this meeting. "You're not in Ireland because of Oliver York, then?"

Colin winced. "No, I'm not. Honeymoon, Sean. Oliver wasn't on my mind at all. Trust me."

"I've made your headache worse," Sean said with a quick smile. "I got one, too, when Kitty texted me that Oliver was in Declan's Cross. He'd already left by the time I could get there."

Colin listened closely as Sean provided a few more details about Mary Bracken's encounter with the mysterious English mythologist up by the church ruin and old crosses above the tiny, picturesque village. Sean knew as well as Colin did that Oliver was an accomplished, unrepentant art thief who'd begun his larcenous career on the south Irish coast, but Sean also knew, as did Colin, there was nothing he, the FBI or Scotland Yard could do about it.

Or would do, maybe, given Oliver's unique skills and contacts.

"I was due a visit to Declan's Cross," Sean said. "I only wanted a casual word with Oliver. I have no actionable reason to limit his movements in Ireland or to detain him. Then Mary told me about meeting him, and about this Deverell woman."

"You don't think Claudia Deverell's distillery tour and Oliver's visit to Declan's Cross are a coincidence?"

Sean didn't hesitate. "No."

Colin noted the bottles of Bracken Distillers whiskey lined up on a shelf, including the award-winning fifteen-year-old single malt that Finian Bracken had casked himself, before tragedy had changed his destiny. One rainy night after his arrival in southern Maine a year ago, he'd told Colin that drinking the rare peated expression and its nonpeated counterpart was like reaching into the past and touching the man he'd once been.

It wasn't difficult for Colin to picture his friend here as a young man, working night and day, shoulder to shoulder with his twin brother, to convert the abandoned seventeenth-century distillery just outside Killarney into a modern enterprise. Tilters at windmills, Finian said he and Declan had called themselves.

"Do you know this Deverell woman?" Sean asked, bringing Colin back to the late spring evening and the business at hand.

He shook his head. "I don't."

"Her relationship with the Sharpes?"

Colin debated for a fraction of a second. "Her family on her mother's side has a house up the street in Heron's Cove. I don't know any details."

Sean pounced. "But you do know more," he said.

Colin saw no need to respond. He and Sean had met in Declan's Cross last fall, over a murder that had involved both the Sharpes and the Donovans, at least on the periphery. While in the tiny Irish village, Colin had learned about a serial art thief who'd first struck the O'Byrne house ten years earlier and had been taunting the FBI and the Sharpes ever since.

Sean resumed pacing in the small, rustic office. He finally stopped at a large wall calendar of the month of May, almost every day filled with penciled notes in what Colin assumed was Mary Bracken's handwriting. "York's untouchable," Sean said, turning from the ragged calendar. "It's impossible now to arrest him for the thefts in Declan's Cross." The Irish detective sucked in a breath. "I don't need to tell you what he's doing these days."

Working with MI5. No, Sean didn't need to spell it out. "Did York come to Ireland alone?" Colin asked.

"Apparently, yes," Sean said. "I'm checking. Are you certain you're in Ireland only because of your honeymoon?"

"I'm being straight with you, Sean. That's it. That's why I'm here. Fin offered me use of his cottage and that's where I've been until this afternoon."

"I know the place," Sean said.

Colin remembered that the detective's friendship with Finian Bracken went back to the deaths almost eight years ago of Finian's wife and two young daughters. Finian had been working here at the distillery, expecting to join his family on a sailing holiday. Before he could, a rogue wave capsized their boat. Sally Bracken and little Kathleen and Mary had all drowned.

"You didn't sound surprised I was in Ireland. Did Fin warn you I was coming, or do you have my name flagged so you're notified when I enter the country?"

Sean shrugged. "I spoke with Fin earlier."

Colin didn't blame his fellow law enforcement officer for the incomplete answer.

"Fin wasn't concerned about Mary's trip to Maine until I mentioned Oliver York," Sean added. "But he knows her. She's stubborn. She won't change her plans."

"Stubbornness is a Bracken trait," Colin said with a sigh. "Fin knows I'm here arranging my honeymoon but I haven't mentioned it to anyone else. I'm keeping it a secret, especially from Emma. It's a surprise. I want for us to visit Ireland as if we're a pair of regular tourists."

"You don't want your friends pestering you on your honeymoon," Sean said, with the first hint of real amusement since he'd greeted Colin in the distillery parking lot.

Colin grinned. "That, too."

"Well, your secret is safe with me. Where did you fly in from?"

"Rome."

"Via Hell, I expect. I'm glad you're safe, Colin."

"Thanks." He didn't elaborate on his whereabouts prior to Rome, and he knew Sean wouldn't ask, as a professional, whatever his suspicions. "I planned to stay in Ireland through Saturday and head back on Sunday."

"The Sharpe open house is on Saturday." Sean

cocked an eyebrow. "Or is that why you're here instead of in Maine?"

"It's a Sharpe thing. I don't need to be there." Colin didn't know that Emma needed to be there, either. "I imagine Fin's invited."

"He's bringing Mary. She's looking forward to it."

Colin could hear his friend's ambivalence. Happy for Mary to visit her brother and have a harmless adventure or two. Uncertain about her leaving Ireland and her safe world at Bracken Distillers. "I wasn't sure Wendell Sharpe would ever return to Maine," Colin said, deliberately lightening his tone. "But he's there. He wanted to be at the open house."

"That's something, then." Sean stared out at the quiet main floor. "You're reconsidering your plans, aren't you, Special Agent Donovan?"

Colin stood up from the stool. Yesterday's sleep had helped with some of the raw edges of his fatigue, but not enough. "I'm thinking about jumping on a flight to London and going to see Oliver."

The detective turned to him with a smile that didn't reach his eyes. "I was hoping you'd say that."

"I'll bet you were," Colin said. "You know, Oliver has a standing offer for me to stay in the guest suite at his London apartment."

Sean groaned. "Dear heaven. You aren't considering—"

"Not a chance. Just thought you'd appreciate a taste of how hard my job is."

"A sense of humor helps. Oliver York's a character, I'll say that. Quite the charming rogue, and a past I wouldn't wish on anyone." Sean glanced at his watch and stood abruptly. "Come. If we hurry, I can put you on a flight to London out of Kerry airport tonight."

"On what, a carrier pigeon?"

"It's a small airport but it offers several nonstop flights a day to London." Sean moved toward the door. "You have your bag?"

"In my car, which is a rental, by the way."

"I'll take care of it. We want you on that flight."

"The thing about living on an island," Colin said, tugging open the door, "you have to fly or take a boat to get most anywhere."

"Fortunately, everything I need is here," Sean said.

They went out into the main room of the bustling distillery. It was medium-sized, not one of the huge, well-known Irish distilleries but not one of the small start-ups, either. The Bracken brothers had gotten their start before the explosion in independent distilleries and had established a brand known for excellence.

Declan Bracken was waiting for them, and Sean explained that Colin was off to London, a last-minute change of plans. Declan looked as if he had a dozen questions, but he simply nodded and wished Colin a safe flight and a quick return to Ireland. Colin thanked him but noticed Sean was almost to the front entrance.

"When will you be planning *your* honeymoon?" Colin asked as he caught up with the detective.

A quick smile. "As soon as I can talk Kitty into marrying me."

"Have you proposed to her yet?"

"I'm getting there. She's not sure she believes in marriage anymore. That's what she says."

"There's never been a woman who's played hard-to-get like Kitty O'Byrne, has there?"

Sean grunted. "She's not playing."

But the pair couldn't hide from themselves or anyone else how deeply in love they were. Colin wondered if people had the same thought about Emma and him, but he put that out of his mind as he grabbed his duffel bag and tossed it in the back of Sean's car. Two minutes later, they were on their way to Farranfore, the small village between Tralee and Shannon where the Kerry County airport was located. A fine mist had collected on the windshield and the early evening light shone on the twisting road back through Killarney.

"Mary Bracken doesn't live in the world you and I do, Special Agent Donovan," Sean said, driving one-handed.

"I know, Sean. Fin knows, too."

"She's had a devil of a time since Sally and the girls died and Fin turned to the priesthood. Now he's left Ireland altogether and she's afraid he won't be back."

"Father Callaghan is due to return to Rock Point from his sabbatical in a few weeks," Colin said.

Sean glanced at him, looking troubled. "Is he?"

"Do you have information to the contrary?"

"No, but Fin dodges the question when I ask him what he plans to do when he returns to Ireland. But that's a problem for another day. I wouldn't describe Mary as naive, but she thinks the best of people. I don't like that Oliver York intercepted her in Declan's Cross. It feels planned to me."

"He plans his heists. I don't know if he plans much else." Colin watched out his window as the car sped through rolling fields. "I'll talk to him. I appreciate the heads-up."

"I'm sorry I took you away from your honeymoon planning."

"The honeymoon isn't what matters."

"True enough."

Sean pulled into the parking lot of the small airport. The mist was now a soft rain. "Good thing I'm not a nervous flier," Colin muttered. "Have you ever flown out of here?"

"Oh, yes. Of course."

"On what?"

The Irishman grinned. "You don't want to know."

"Funny, Sean."

"No worries. You'll be on a real plane."

Colin grabbed his duffel bag out of the back of the car and headed into the terminal. Sure enough, a reasonable-sized plane was on the tarmac. He'd purchased a ticket on the twenty-minute drive from the distillery. The rain wouldn't cause any delays. He'd be at Oliver York's London apartment within a couple of hours.

With a few minutes to spare, Colin stood by the windows in the small terminal and watched the rain. His undercover assignment had turned out to be more complex and dangerous than anyone had expected. He'd been looking forward to taking a couple of days to relax, dust off the stink and plan his honeymoon before he headed home. He disliked not being in touch with his fair-haired fiancée. That Emma understood he had a job to do didn't make it easier, but it did make it bearable.

She had a job to do, too. He'd had a taste of her work last summer, a couple of months before they'd met, when information from an unnamed art crimes

specialist had helped him locate and arrest a major illegal arms dealer who happened to be in Los Angeles
to indulge his passion for Picasso.

Colin dug out his phone and texted Yank. London
it is. Then he stared at his screen for a split second
and texted Emma. I just had a visit from Sean Murphy.

Her response came within seconds. You're in Ireland?

Kerry Airport. Didn't know there was one.

We drove past it. Easy to miss. Coming, going, staying?

On my way to London to see our English friend.

Colin tried to picture her reaction, where she was—
her. He could almost see her warm, deep green eyes.
Her answer finally came on his screen. Does that explain your visit from Sean?

Yes. Talk to Yank.

Will do. On my way to Maine. I'm having lunch tomorrow with your mother.

Good luck. You'll need it. I learned my best interrogation techniques from her.

Ha. Safe travels. Love you.

You, too, babe.

Colin started to slide his phone back into his jacket pocket but saw he had a response from Yank: Your garda friend has a call in to me.

That was quick. He's good but you'll be okay.

Colin could almost see Yank's roll of the eyes but his flight was being called. He got out his boarding pass. Bad enough Oliver York was on the radar again, but if a retired FBI agent was stirring up trouble and if that trouble involved MI5, Colin wouldn't be surprised if a few agents met him at Heathrow. Then it would be a long night of explaining—but explaining what?

He gritted his teeth. He would find out what he could in London and go from there.

It was a short hop to London. He'd get his head sorted out before he arrived. He wanted to know the truth about why Oliver had been in Declan's Cross and what he knew about Claudia Deverell and her tour of Bracken Distillers, and about Gordy Wheelock—and what, if anything, they had to do with a dead archaeologist and stolen ancient mosaics. And if there was any connection to the Sharpe Fine Art Recovery open house on Saturday in Heron's Cove, Maine.

"And with Emma," Colin said under his breath as he headed through the rain to the waiting plane.

6

Gordy's head was on fire when he mounted the steps to a narrow brick building on busy, upscale Newbury Street in Boston's Back Bay neighborhood. He'd taken a cab from his hotel and had lunch at a hip burger joint then wandered in the Public Garden to try to clear his head, but he still felt terrible. His overnight bag might as well have been a hundred-pound weight.

He hadn't looked in the envelope. It was still tucked in the outer pocket of his suitcase, where the bellman had told him he'd put it. If it contained what Gordy thought it contained, he didn't want to open it, at least not until this next visit was behind him.

Part of him wanted to skip it and go home. A high-end consignment shop was located on the ground floor of the nineteenth-century former town house, down more steps and through a glass door. He could buy a present for his wife. Make amends for being so weird lately.

But he continued up the steps to the main floor.

He pushed open an unlocked glass door and entered a vestibule with stairs straight ahead and another glass door to his left, leading to a small gallery that specialized in Greek and Roman antiquities and contemporary mosaic art. This door *was* locked. Gordy looked for a buzzer and didn't see one. He rapped his knuckles on the glass.

Claudia Deverell looked up from a fussy, ornate desk and swore. He couldn't hear her, but he could read her lips. Not that happy to see him, obviously. Big surprise.

He pointed to the latch. "Open up, okay?"

He had no idea if she could hear him, but she rose and glided to the door, pulling it open. "I should have guessed you'd find your way here. There's no getting rid of you, is there?"

"Hello to you, too, Claudia."

She sighed, opening the door wider. "You might as well come in. The gallery is open to the public by appointment only."

"Makes sense. No one's going to walk in on a whim and buy an ancient Greek coin or a cracked Roman urn."

"The contemporary mosaic art is also a draw. How did you find me?"

"You mentioned you were staying a couple of days with the friends who own this place before you drove up to Maine."

"Oh. Right."

Gordy expected Claudia to go on, but she didn't. He stepped past her into the gallery. It had an upscale, artsy, museum feel to it, with its polished wood floors, industrial-feel shelves and careful lighting. The items for sale, both old and new, were widely spaced, each with a handwritten card, presumably to imply personal service, describing it in detail.

Sure enough, a cracked pottery urn was the first item he noticed. It stood by itself on a shelf next to the desk. It was Greek, though, not Roman. "Fourth century BCE," he said. "That's a hell of a long time ago."

"Yes, it is," Claudia said, managing to make her voice sound like a roll of the eyes. She shut the door and returned to the desk, but she didn't sit down. "You shouldn't be here, Gordy."

"I'm on my way to Maine myself for the Sharpe open house on Saturday."

"You don't really think anyone will miss you if you don't attend, do you?"

He shrugged. "I don't think anyone will notice if I do attend. I like Maine. I went to Acadia National Park once with Joan and the kids. I remember popovers at Jordan Pond, the sunset on Cadillac Mountain and the kids bitching and moaning about not having a TV at our cabin. I haven't seen much of southern Maine. I hear it has some decent sand beaches." He paused, aware that his chitchat sounded stiff and rehearsed even to him. "Your place in Heron's Cove still the same?"

Claudia sank into the chair at the desk and crossed her arms on her chest. Her cool blue eyes deepened and turned hot. "Unchanged since you graced us with your presence," she said with obvious sarcasm.

"Us? It was just you and me, sweetheart."

"Don't remind me."

More than a year had passed between Gordy's last encounter with her in Maine and the party at Claridge's

on Sunday, but slim, blond, wealthy Claudia Norwood
Deverell was as attractive as ever—and as much out
of his league. Intelligent and well-connected, she operated with ease in the high-end art world—first at an
auction house, now on her own. He'd been a nuts-and-
bolts federal agent who'd ended up working art crimes
after breaking an infamous Chicago museum heist of
art worth hundreds of millions.

"When did you get in from London?" he asked her.

"Monday. I wanted to adjust to the time change before I head to Maine. We're getting the house ready
to go on the market. It's an emotional time. My great-
grandfather built it and it's been in the family ever
since, but my father never liked Maine as much as my
mother did. Now that she's gone…" Claudia didn't finish. "The house needs a considerable amount of work.
We rented it out most summers and that's taken a toll,
but it's in a prime location. A buyer might want to tear
it down and build something new on the lot."

"Is that your way of saying you're not going to invite me for a martini on the front porch?"

"Oh, Gordy." She inhaled through her nose, obviously trying to maintain her self-control. "I wish you
hadn't come to London. I wish you weren't here now
and on your way to Maine. It's going to look as if
you're following me."

"You're the one who called me, Claudia."

"That was a huge mistake. I didn't mean for you to
jump on your white horse. I wanted to know if you'd
be in Maine this weekend for the open house. I thought
the Sharpes might invite you." She hesitated. "I wanted
to steel myself."

"Right."

"I don't appreciate your tone. I'm being straight with you."

"No, you're not."

She bit down on her lower lip, which brought back memories he knew would do him no good. Or her. As much as he didn't trust her, he didn't wish her ill, even if she looked as if she wanted to throw something at him—might have done it, too, if it didn't risk breaking a two-thousand-year-old artifact.

"Why don't you believe me?" she asked finally.

Gordy didn't answer. She seemed to know he wouldn't. When Claudia had called him in North Carolina a week ago, asking about the open house and whether he'd heard about Alessandro Pearson's death, Gordy had been inclined to skip it. *I guess I just needed to hear your voice, Gordy. You've never lied to me. You'd tell me if I needed to worry.*

Maybe she hadn't lied, but she'd certainly flung the BS.

He examined a wall mosaic on display, its bright colors and modern geometric design a contrast to the muted colors and obvious age of the ancient objects sharing space in the gallery. Seeing Claudia again, being alone with her, wasn't helping his stomach. It was still off, but he was confident he wouldn't vomit. That'd be the crowning glory to the past twenty-four hours—puking his guts out on ancient artifacts in front of Claudia Deverell.

He turned to her, noticing she had a few fine lines at the corners of her eyes. What was she now? Had she hit forty? When they'd first met almost three years ago, she'd told him she never planned to marry and didn't want kids. *I'm not the maternal type.* But that'd made her even more intriguing. Joan was all about kids, family, making a home. She was the best, but for a while…

Gordy nodded at the displays. "I was expecting statues of naked women."

Now a roll of the eyes for real. "You would. I'm looking after the gallery for a few hours. It specializes in common ancient items of high interest and low controversy. It's not easy to find anything from the ancient world these days that isn't without some level of controversy, especially if it originated in what's now a conflict region."

"Conflict region? I like that."

A hint of irritation in her pretty eyes. "It's just a phrase, Gordy."

He moved to another set of open shelves. "Are any of the items from your mother's collection?"

"Some."

He smiled. "Your idea of heaven, sitting here surrounded by all this ancient stuff."

"I suppose it is." She glanced past him to a display of worn coins at his shoulder. "It's amazing to think an Athenian held those coins in his hand thousands of years ago."

Gordy couldn't deny it. "Sure is."

"My great-grandfather, Horace Norwood, started collecting antiquities on his travels, before modern protocols for the excavation and removal of artifacts from archaeological sites and source countries were in place. My grandfather and mother added to the collection over the years. It was a different world then. As scrupulous as they were, they might do things differently now."

"The antiquities trade has been complicated and

controversial for hundreds of years," Gordy said. "It's easy to get into trouble even if you know what you're doing."

Claudia flushed. "I'll ignore that. As you know, my mother had a particular affinity for mosaics and supported on-site training in mosaic conservation and preservation techniques. I've carried on her work, but I don't know how long I'll keep it up. And I've stopped acquiring any new pieces."

Gordy appreciated Claudia's passion for her family collection of ancient art and artifacts but had never shared it. "I'd rather have a new set of golf clubs," he said with a wink. "How much of the Norwood collection do you figure is fake, looted or otherwise illegitimate?"

"Still the cynic, I see," she said, some of her initial tension visibly easing. "Every ancient piece here in the gallery has been fully vetted. It's authentic, with a clear provenance, and not only legal but ethical to put on the market. A portion of any proceeds from the sale of pieces from my family's collection will go to conservation and preservation efforts. I can't imagine a more fitting tribute to my mother. She always saw herself as a steward rather than a true owner of some extraordinary works of the ancient past."

Gordy studied Claudia, letting her get a little uncomfortable with the silence before he spoke again. "Was Alessandro Pearson helping you sort out your family's collection before he died?"

Claudia jumped slightly, as if startled by his question. "Not really. I was still getting things organized. My mother had already arranged to sell the Norwood pieces on display here. Alessandro was quite elderly but his death was still a complete shock. I heard his heart gave out." She narrowed her eyes, frowning. "Is this why you're all cloak-and-dagger, Gordy? Because an elderly English academic who was an expert on antiquities died suddenly?"

Gordy grinned, trying to look confident, at ease. "I'll cop to being jet-lagged, not cloak-and-dagger. Never did go in for that sort of thing." He nodded to the gallery displays. "Did Alessandro help your mother figure out what was worth selling?"

"He was more interested in her preservation work since mosaics were his particular area of expertise."

"He and Wendell Sharpe were friends."

"As much as the Sharpes are friends with anyone," Claudia said half under her breath. She waved a hand, blushing. "I'm so sorry. That was uncalled for. There's nothing suspicious about Alessandro's death, is there? It's sad, of course, but he was an old man who had a heart attack and fell."

Gordy wondered what she'd have been saying about him if he'd died last night. An out-of-shape old FBI agent who'd tripped and gone flying? An unfortunate accident that could have been prevented if he hadn't gained fifteen pounds?

Who would know he'd been warned to back off and then shoved?

"Wendell was at Alessandro's funeral," Gordy said.

"I know. I was there, too. Timothy and Faye didn't attend. It was good to see them on Sunday at Claridge's. My mother was fond of the Sharpes."

"Including Lucas?"

"Yes, including Lucas, and you can go to hell, Gordy."

"Sorry. I know he's a sore subject." He didn't even try to sound sincere. "How long are you staying in Maine?"

"A few weeks. I haven't booked a return flight to London yet." Claudia stood and came around to the front of the desk, the light catching her eyes, less hot now, more suspicious. "I'm prepared to see Lucas again. Wendell and Timothy and Faye were civil to me in London. I don't know if they're aware of the falling-out Lucas and I had."

"It was over a year ago. Maybe no one cares anymore."

"Would that were true."

"It wasn't my fault, Claudia."

She gave a fake laugh. "You know, Special Agent Wheelock, if you hadn't interfered with my life, I could be Mrs. Lucas Sharpe now."

"I don't know who should thank me more, you or Lucas."

"Bastard," Claudia said, almost smiling. "Lucas knew I was distracted and under a lot of pressure with my mother's failing health and then her death—and I couldn't tell him the truth about you and me, how it was nothing, never meant to be anything for either of us. Oh, Gordy. What we did wasn't just wrong on your end, as an FBI agent, it was wrong on mine, too. I betrayed a man I cared about."

"Don't be so hard on yourself. You were close to your mother and had a hard time with her illness and death. You're only human." Gordy stepped closer to her, realizing he felt nothing anymore—no urge to touch her, kiss her, make love to her. He attempted a smile. "I was still quite the stud when you fell for me."

Not so much as a crack of a smile from Claudia. "I didn't fall for you."

He gave up on trying to make her feel better about the past. Not his call how she felt, how she rationalized their behavior, whether she forgave herself...forgave him. None of that was why he was here. He'd consulted with her in an effort to better understand the antiquities trade, both legitimate and illegal, but also because he was convinced she could lead him to some serious bad guys. He was still convinced his professional instincts had been on target, but his personal instincts—his personal integrity—had led him astray, and Claudia, too.

"Nothing is ever simple and straightforward with you, Gordy," she said, calmer now, her tone almost reflective. "It was stupid of me to call you. It was like lighting dry kindling. You were waiting for something to get you back in FBI mode. How long did it take you to book a flight to London?"

He grinned. "Two seconds."

"See? *Stupid* of me to call. I tried to tell myself I was just an old friend from your FBI days, but I got you all fired up. You couldn't resist. You had to check to see if I was getting myself in trouble."

Gordy stood over her. "Are you?"

"No." Spots of bright color appeared high in her translucent cheeks. "I haven't had any trouble since you retired. That's cause and effect, don't you think?"

The sarcasm and heat were back, but Gordy didn't respond. He checked out three pottery bowls, each on its own shelf, as if they were too valuable, too precious, to brush against anything else. He was surprised by their reasonable price. They weren't much more ex-

pensive than what he'd pay for new ones at Pottery
Barn or Crate & Barrel. He'd done well in art crimes
in part because he could look at art and antiquities
with a certain level of objectivity, without the subjec-
tive passions of a Claudia Deverell.

He leaned close to the handwritten description of
one of the bowls but didn't read it. "Have you run into
Scotland Yard, MI5, MI6 or any other real cloak-and-
dagger types?"

He turned back to her in time to see her furrow her
brow and cross her arms on her chest. She was studying him as if she just got it that he wasn't flailing—he
wasn't here simply to harass her or rekindle their relationship. Finally she sighed, dropping her arms to her
sides. "What on earth are you talking about, Gordy?"
she asked. "What's going on?"

"Is this place bugged?"

"What?" She seemed ready to bolt but got herself
under control. "Don't tell me you've become paranoid.
No, this place is not bugged. No, I haven't had anything
to do with the FBI, the Sharpes or British law enforcement or intelligence agencies. I'm busy with my work,
my family and my friends. Good friends," she added
pointedly, clearly excluding him.

"Who else did you talk to at the party on Sunday?"

"You mean after I ditched you? All sorts. Do you
have anyone in particular in mind?"

Gordy decided not to mention Oliver York. "No
one in particular."

"You did ruin the party for me, if you must know,
but I blame myself more than I do you."

"I've never been good at small talk. I guess I got
used to being the skunk at the picnic when I was an ac-

tive agent." He remembered touching the smooth skin of her cheek, her soft hair. Regrets, he thought. Oh, yes, he had them. "Everything's okay with you these days, Claudia? No problems, no enemies, no threats?"

"I learned the hard way always to be on the lookout for bastards and scoundrels. Even a perceived wrong move in my world and the FBI swoops in with threats to get you to do their bidding, and your life is never the same." She held up a slender hand, the nails cut short and polished in a pale, neutral pink. "I don't want to dredge up the past. I've never done anything illegal and you know it."

"I'm not here to dredge up the past, either."

A touch of exasperation reached her eyes. "Then why are you here?"

Gordy could feel the cut behind his ear, the bruise above his hip. What did Claudia know about the attack and warning last night? But he stopped himself before he could go too far down the rabbit hole of speculation. He needed to be deliberate, contained. "I'm just killing time before I head to Maine."

"Okay. I'll accept that. I was surprised when I received an invitation to the Sharpe open house. My father and brother were invited, too. I suspect it was Wendell's doing. He has a come-one-come-all mentality. Lucas must have wanted to kill him when he found out."

"Will you attend?"

She shook her head. "I wouldn't put Lucas in that position. My father and brother will make an appearance, since there's no ill will there."

"They're going to be in Heron's Cove, then?"

"They're arriving today. They might be there already."

Gordy stepped back from her, overcome by a sudden attack of pure lust. So much for thinking he had things under control. One look from her, and he swore he'd carry her into the back room and make love to her on the spot. But it'd probably kill him, considering the rotten shape he was in, and it'd get him nowhere. And he had Joan, his life with her and the kids.

"Have you ever told anyone about us?" he asked, hearing how ragged he sounded.

Claudia scowled. "Give it up, Gordy. There was never an *us*. There was sex. But no, Special Agent Wheelock, I've never told anyone. I've been discreet for my sake but also for yours, and for the sake of your family. No one would believe you never told me any secrets about your work, but didn't. I was the one who told you secrets."

"Not any that I could use. If you're in over your head, tell me now, Claudia. I can help."

"You've never helped me. You only used me. I lost Lucas because of you."

"You lost Lucas because of your own actions. I didn't help."

"I repeat, Gordy. I've done nothing illegal. I never have. I don't care if you believe me."

"You've heard the term *blood antiquities*. That's when the money that allows an ancient artifact to go on display in an elite Boston gallery such as this one turns up in the hands of violent sons of bitches who will use it to plot attacks in airports and cafés, to buy weapons and pay bomb-makers and—"

"Stop, Gordy. Just stop. My family's collection is

established. It has nothing to do with your so-called blood antiquities."

"You're playing in a dangerous sandbox." He heard the intensity in his voice. "Walk away. Let me help you."

Claudia tossed her head back and gave him a condescending look. "I stay away from people who could hurt me—including you. I'm sorry I called you. I truly am." She squared her shoulders, going patrician on him. "Is there anything else?"

Gordy glanced around the gallery. "I never got the fascination with owning antiquities. Take mosaics, for instance. They were some rich guy's floor."

"Not always. You know that. And floor mosaics are often beautiful works of art depicting flora and fauna, mythological and allegorical tales, biblical stories—they provide fascinating insight into the lives of people from ancient Greece through the Middle Ages."

"None of yours are missing?"

She looked genuinely confused. "My what—mosaics? What do you mean by missing?"

He shrugged. "Stolen."

"Not that I'm aware of, no, but the collection is fairly scattered. Some pieces are on loan to various museums, others are in storage—there's a room full of uncataloged items at the house in Maine. I have to go through them." She waved a hand, clearly exasperated. "Never mind. You look tired, Gordy. Jet lag can be a bitch. They say it's worse as you get older."

"Thanks for that," he said with a grin.

"We've never minced words with each other." She smiled, relaxing visibly as she returned to her chair behind the desk. "I have a conference call in five minutes. I'm staying with the friends who own the gallery. Their apartment is a short walk from here. Why don't I meet you there in an hour? I'll give you the keys."

"Your friends wouldn't mind?"

"They're out of town. You need a nap. They'd understand." Claudia rummaged in her expensive tote bag on the desk and lifted out a set of keys. "I see you have your suitcase with you."

"I checked out of my hotel. Haven't figured out what's next. Are you going to offer me a bed tonight?"

"It's a one-bedroom apartment." She handed him the keys. "You can have the sofa for a nap and for tonight if you need a place to stay."

"Not like the old days, huh, Claudia?"

She ignored him and jotted down the address on a notepad, tore off the sheet and handed it to him. "See you later."

Gordy ate another handful of ibuprofen as he walked up Newbury Street, which was crowded with shoppers and diners on the beautiful May afternoon. He figured Claudia planned to blow him off but he needed a place to crash for a couple of hours. He was dead on his feet. He didn't have any water to go with the ibuprofen, but he didn't mind. He'd practically drowned himself sucking down two bottles of water after he'd gone back to his hotel to collect his suitcase. He was well hydrated. He had no interest in shopping and he was still full from lunch, which had been a bad idea, anyway, given his physical state. Hip or not, his burger had turned his stomach on top of the Kit Kat, coffee, water and being back in an FBI office. Matt Yankowski had his own little kingdom on the Boston waterfront.

He needed to catch some serious bad guys or the new director would shut him down in a heartbeat.

But Gordy wasn't a part of all that any longer.

He turned down a side street, his stomach lurching, his head throbbing. He needed to give the ibuprofen a minute to start working. He wanted a cigarette. He'd quit smoking at forty and hadn't looked back, but he'd been tempted a couple of times since retiring. First time had been after his mother-in-law's funeral last summer. His wife had cried her heart out, and his brother-in-law had been a horse's ass, picking fights with everyone. Gordy had gone out for a pack of cigarettes. Emotions. He'd never been good at them. At least he wanted a cigarette now because he'd had his ass kicked.

He should be skipping the Sharpe open house and leaving Claudia to her own devices. At most, he could have shared his concerns with Emma over the phone. Claudia obviously had been taken aback when he'd turned up in London. She'd all but shut her door in his face. He'd checked into a hotel. He should have forgotten her and invited Joan to join him for a few days instead. They could have toured palaces and gardens, shopped at Harrods and dined at interesting restaurants. Been a normal couple in early retirement.

He walked down a residential stretch of Beacon Street, parallel to the Charles River. It was mostly apartments and condos but with a sprinkling of single-family mansions. He hadn't spent much time in Boston. It was an attractive city, good for walking and packed with history.

The friends' apartment was only another half a block. Thankfully. He needed to take a leak, puke and regroup, preferably in that order—although he hoped to skip puking.

The walk to the apartment didn't kill him, but he figured the hike up the two flights of stairs with his suitcase would. Only when he reached the landing, huffing and puffing, and got the key in the door did he notice the elevator tucked in the far corner of the hall.

He was rusty. No question.

By Boston standards, the apartment was a palace, located on the top floor of a former single-family mansion. The front windows were bowed, looking out on a shade tree with spring leaves fluttering in the sunlight. For what Claudia's friends likely paid, Gordy figured he could have a second home at the beach. Maybe two second homes plus tuition for the grandkids. He couldn't imagine how anyone could afford a condo much less a home in posh Back Bay.

The living room had high ceilings, original dark woodwork, a formal brick fireplace and traditional furnishings, including a bust of some Greek god that he assumed was a copy. He left his suitcase by the coffee table and located a half bath down the hall and made urgent use of the facilities. He checked his reflection as he washed his hands. Not great but not awful.

The urge to puke passed.

When he returned to the living room, he noticed shelves crammed with books and framed photographs of ancient sites and yellowed maps of long-gone empires. Gordy doubted Claudia's friends had a clue she had been a reluctant informant for the FBI.

For *him.*

He sank onto the leather sofa in the living room and took a few minutes to indulge his pain, self-disgust and self-hate. Then he sat up, leaned forward and dug out the envelope from the front pocket of his suitcase. He still didn't want to open it, but he knew he couldn't let fear and denial get the better of him. He'd already held back too much with Emma Sharpe.

With a heavy, resigned sigh, he ripped the top off the envelope and dumped the contents onto the coffee table.

Three four-by-six photographs landed faceup.

No note, no phone number to call, no commentary of any kind, but he wasn't surprised. Words weren't necessary. He got the message. *Back off or these go public.*

Same message as from his attacker last night, except this time the threat wasn't limited to him.

Gordy blinked, his eyelids heavy with fatigue and pain. His head ached as he stared at the photographs. One mistake in his career—one mistake in his marriage—and someone had proof of his screwup and was using it as leverage. Had his visit to London and Claudia prompted the threats? Running into the MI5 agent and this Oliver York character? His call to Emma?

Questions were easy. Answers, not so much.

The woman's features weren't clear, but she was unquestionably not his wife. The long legs, the shape of her hips, the glimpse of her breast…

No, not middle-aged Joan Wheelock.

Pain shot through Gordy's eyes. He half hoped it was the start of a stroke, but if he died, there'd be a death investigation. The Boston police would find the photos. They'd call the FBI. Emma Sharpe would find out. Yank, that sanctimonious bastard.

"Save the stroke for after you figure out this mess," Gordy muttered.

One memorable, mind-blowing, short-lived affair, never to be repeated—except in his mind. He loved his wife, but not a week had gone by since he'd ended things and retired that he didn't remember the long, insane, perfect nights he'd had sex with beautiful, brilliant, slightly shady Claudia Deverell, breaking every personal and professional rule that had guided his life for decades.

Gordy had been harassed and threatened from time to time in his career, but never like this—never over something stupid and embarrassing. He'd had *grandkids* a year ago. What the hell had he been thinking?

And he loved his wife. They'd been going through a rough patch last year, both of them figuring out retirement, where to live, what to do. He had a feeling she'd stepped out on him—but he'd never asked. Didn't want to know.

Joan wouldn't want to know about this. They didn't need a private truth-telling session and certainly didn't need to be dragged into a public one. She liked being married to an FBI legend with a spotless record.

The only positive about the photos on the table in front of him was he looked pretty good. If whoever had delivered them went public, Gordy figured at least he could console himself that he'd been a hell of a stud right up until his retirement a year ago.

He grabbed the photos and returned them to the envelope. He gave himself a minute to calm his breathing, let his head and stomach settle down, and then leaned forward again and shoved the envelope back into the outer pocket of his suitcase.

He emptied the last of his ibuprofen bottle into his palm, downed the three pills and decided a nap was in order. He needed rest, a chance to clear his head.

You're not as young as you used to be, Gordy. You injure more easily and heal more slowly.

His doctor, not two weeks ago.

Gordy hated his doctor. Hell, right now he hated everybody.

He kicked off his shoes and stretched out on the couch.

Sleep, then it was time to start thinking again like an FBI agent.

7

Claudia retrieved her suitcase out of the back room, locked up the gallery and descended the front steps to the busy sidewalk. Thirty minutes after Gordy's departure, she still had to force herself to breathe normally. It annoyed her. Hyperventilating wouldn't solve anything. She had to remember he was as committed as she was to keeping their affair secret.

She crossed busy Newbury Street. Breathing in the spring afternoon air helped. Being among people. She entered an upscale coffee shop and ordered an espresso, the normalcy of her surroundings helping her at least to begin to relax.

She sat at a small table in front of the window and inhaled the pungent scent of the coffee. She took a sip, trying to identify the different flavors, as if it were a fine wine or whiskey. She swore she tasted citrus, chocolate, perhaps a touch of black pepper. She welcomed the round, velvety feel of the espresso as she savored every drop.

Slowly, she felt a restored sense of calm and purpose. *I'll be fine.*

She trusted herself to make the drive to southern Maine without devolving into a fit of uncontrolled breathing and passing out at the wheel. She'd hoped to have the Heron's Cove house to herself through the weekend, but her father and brother had visited her in London last week and announced they would be there for the Sharpe open house. Her father had returned to Philadelphia for a few days and then flown up to Maine this morning. Adrian, her older half brother, had arrived about the same time from Atlanta.

An impromptu Deverell family reunion.

Claudia knew she needed to stay cool and get this trip to Heron's Cove behind her. Staying a week or two in Maine seemed more ambitious now that she was on this side of the Atlantic than it had when she'd planned this trip in London. She hadn't stepped foot in the small Maine village since her mad, brief affair with a senior FBI agent.

Liaison. That was a better word for her encounters with Gordy, she decided. An affair implied love. She hadn't loved him and he hadn't loved her. They'd shared a certain illicit passion, sparked by the hold he had over her and fueled by impulsiveness, risk and fear.

She remembered making love in the sunroom to the sounds of ocean waves, seagulls and the occasional lobster boat.

No, definitely not *love*, Claudia thought.

He'd been the one to end it. *This was stupid and wrong. See you, Claudia.*

A month later, she'd heard he'd retired and was moving with his wife to their small hometown on the North Carolina beach where they'd fallen in love as teenagers. Claudia hadn't seen or heard from Gordy until she'd called him last week after Alessandro's funeral and asked him about the Sharpe open house. She'd *had* to know if he would be in Maine, if he was up to his old tricks. Then he'd turned up in London, and now Boston.

She wouldn't let him ruin her life again.

He didn't have to want to ruin her life—she believed he hadn't wanted to a year ago—but that didn't mean he couldn't do a proper job of it.

"Poor Alessandro," she whispered.

He'd called her the morning before his death and asked her to meet him for tea that afternoon. They'd agreed on a tearoom near his apartment in Kensington. She hadn't seen him in several months and had been shocked at how old and frail he'd looked. He'd been worried and preoccupied about illegal trafficking in antiquities from his former work sites—and convinced, as always, that Victoria Norwood Deverell's only child was as kind, altruistic and scrupulous as she had been.

Claudia was well aware that her retired-FBI-agent ex-lover would have wanted to know about her tea with Alessandro, no matter the cause of his death. She'd learned the hard way that Gordy always wanted to know everything. He would use the most innocent omission as leverage to get what he wanted.

She finished her espresso and wheeled her suitcase out of the coffee shop and up the street toward her rental car, parked at a meter. Gordy would figure out she wasn't coming back tonight. Maybe he'd take the hint and go home. Whatever he chose to do, she was going to pick up Isabel Greene at South Station and head straight to Maine.

Her ambivalence evaporated now that she was almost on her way. She couldn't wait to be back on the rocky coast and in the rambling house she had so loved as a child. She hadn't been back in years, but her mother had wanted to see Heron's Cove before her death. Claudia had flown in from London, met her mother in Philadelphia and had taken her to Maine for one last visit. After her death, Claudia had launched her disastrous affair with an FBI agent and had her falling-out with Lucas Sharpe, sullying Heron's Cove for her. But it was time to go back and put the past to rest.

She couldn't wait to explore the handful of ancient works her mother had stored at the Maine house, although she doubted she'd discover any hidden treasures. As she'd explained to Gordy, most works of any real value were on loan to museums or in professional storage near the Deverell home in Philadelphia. Value, though, wasn't always a question of profit and money, especially with ancient art and artifacts. Regardless, steeped in antiquities from infancy, her mother had possessed an unerring eye and a keen passion for the art and artifacts of the ancient Mediterranean past. Whenever Claudia touched an antiquity her mother had touched, she could picture beautiful, sweet-tempered Victoria Norwood Deverell.

Would her mother forgive her for her reckless behavior?

Would she understand the choices her only child had made—was making even now?

Fighting an urge to hyperventilate again, Claudia placed her suitcase in the trunk of her small rental. *You're fine*, she told herself.

She almost climbed into the passenger seat but remembered she wasn't in England and went around to the driver's side of the car. For the past decade, she'd spent most of her time in sprawling London and had come to hate driving. She didn't own a car, preferring to walk and take taxis and public transportation. Occasionally she'd rent a car for an excursion, but despite seldom getting behind the wheel herself, she had grown accustomed to seeing cars driving on the left. It no longer looked strange and disconcerting to her. She'd had no trouble driving on the left when she'd rented a car in Ireland last week.

She shut her eyes, grasping the steering wheel with both hands.

You're doing the right thing.

The Sharpe invitation, Alessandro, her mad call to Gordy, Ireland, the sudden party at Claridge's, the long, lonely flight to Boston, coping with her obsessions… Next it would be Heron's Cove, the memories… Lucas.

Yes, you are doing the right thing.

You are, you are, you are.

Claudia opened her eyes, sniffling, and started the car. Time to get on with it.

She couldn't wait to breathe in the fresh ocean air.

As she navigated the heavy traffic, she could see her mother standing on the front porch of her Maine house shortly before her death, looking silently out at the sparkling Atlantic. The sun had washed out her already pale skin and brought out the premature deep lines in her face. There'd been no denying the cancer eating away at her. She'd turned to Claudia. *I want you to remember, Claudia, that never have I met a finer man than Wendell Sharpe.*

Her mother's words had taken Claudia by surprise. *Even Dad?*

Your father's a fine man, too. A different kind of fine than Wendell. When you're in financial trouble, you go to Dad. When you're in real trouble...you go to Wendell.

She'd ended the conversation there, with no further explanation.

Maine would be filled with memories, Claudia knew, but she was up to them. More than that, she was ready for them.

"You're doing the right thing," she whispered. "You are."

She eased the car into the Newbury Street traffic, feeling less awkward driving on the right than she had when she'd rented the car at the airport on Monday, wondering when she'd see Gordy again—the Sharpe open house, or Boston? She'd misplayed every contact she'd ever had with him, from the very first time she'd met him in London a few weeks after her mother's death.

Claudia Deverell? Special Agent Gordon Wheelock. I need you to do something for me.

She shook her head. She'd called him last week out of strength, not weakness.

She wouldn't let him manipulate and intimidate her into doing his bidding this time.

"No, Gordy. Not this time."

Claudia drove straight to South Station, where her friend Isabel Greene was already out front, an elegant tapestry weekender bag slung over one shoulder. She and Claudia were driving to Maine together. They'd taken the train to Heathrow together on Monday. Claudia had flown to Boston, Isabel to New York. Isabel had mentioned she planned to take the train to Boston and Claudia had offered to pick her up. A talented mosaic artist, Isabel was entertaining and capable of dispelling any dark mood. They'd have a fun drive to southern Maine.

Isabel waved, as if Claudia might not see her, and jumped off the curb, pulled open the door and tossed her bag onto the backseat. She climbed in front, flipping back her long, curly golden blond hair and emitting a cathartic groan. "What a day," she said. "I'm so glad you're here. The Acela is fast but I'm ready for a break from traveling. I can't *wait* to be in Maine."

"We shouldn't run into traffic," Claudia said. "We'll be there in no time."

Isabel pulled on her seat belt and snapped it in place. She looked put-together despite an almost four-hour train ride, charging through a crowded station with her bag and waiting on the curb for Claudia to arrive. Isabel lived half the year in New York. The other half, she traveled and exchanged apartments with a friend in London. She'd started out working at a New York museum but now supported herself with her mosaic art, which included both portable pieces and installations. She'd spent February completing a mosaic floor in a conservatory in Malibu. The owners had requested a vineyard scene. Claudia had seen photographs of the stunning results. Like her mother had been, she was in awe of the combination of Isabel's imagination and technique.

"How was the train?" Claudia asked.

"Only way to get in and out of New York. I haven't been in New York in May in ages. Central Park is gorgeous. I saw ducklings, of all things. I've been on the go since I arrived from London. I can't wait to kick back for a few days."

"Excellent."

Accustomed to a frenetic pace, Isabel had promised she was looking forward to Maine and wouldn't get bored. Handsome Adrian Deverell, Claudia's older half brother, might have something to do with it, but Isabel denied any romantic interest in him. Claudia didn't want to think about that right now. Sometimes she wondered if Adrian and Isabel had more in common with each other than Claudia did with either of them, despite her brother's indifference toward antiquities. But it wouldn't take much for her to start feeling threatened and sorry for herself. She almost would have preferred if her father and Isabel hit it off but couldn't explain why.

Claudia maneuvered back into the heavy traffic and started toward the interstate north. She didn't need a map or GPS. She knew the way.

Isabel pushed back a few stray curls, catching her breath. "How are you, Claudia?"

After Gordy had left the gallery, even before her restorative espresso, Claudia had decided not to tell Isabel about his visit, for a thousand reasons. "Great, thanks," she said, smiling. "Happy to be home in the US."

"Have you put the party in London on Sunday behind you?"

"Behind me? It was fun. I had a great time."

"Does your father know? Adrian?"

Claudia looked over at her. "About what?"

"Not what. Who. You know who I'm talking about. Agent Wheelock. I saw you two at the party on Sunday.

It confirmed what I've suspected for a while. There is—or there was—something besides consulting on antiquities between you and that married FBI agent."

"You have a fertile imagination, Isabel."

"This isn't my imagination. One way or the other he's the reason you and Lucas broke up and you quit the auction house and went out on your own, isn't he?"

"My mother died. That's why I did what I did. Lucas and I…" She shook her head. "Never mind. We saw each other a few times on his trips to London, but that's about it. And I quit the auction house to focus on my family's antiquities collection."

"At least you could afford to." Isabel frowned, her brown eyes narrowed on Claudia as she navigated Boston's insane traffic. "I remember Agent Wheelock coming round in London last year. I've had my suspicions he played fast and loose with the rules where you were concerned."

"Isabel, please…"

"All right. Whatever was between you two is none of my business. I don't know the guy myself, just that he specialized in art crimes and had you give him a tutorial in the antiquities trade. Antiquities used to be fun, but now—never mind the controversies about the ethics of ownership and stewardship, they can be downright scary with the fraud, looting and pillaging going on in some very dangerous places."

"I know what you mean," Claudia said, hearing the sadness in her own voice.

"We don't need to talk about that now. I'm not sorry you and Lucas didn't make a go of it, you know. The Sharpes aren't your friends. I have nothing against them, but they keep themselves separate from people like us."

"Like us? You make it sound as if we're criminals."

"I don't mean to. Not at all. I mean those of us who are artists, collectors, experts." Isabel waved a hand. "But let's just enjoy the drive."

"I agree. Tell me about New York. What did you do there?"

Isabel took the hint as Claudia threaded her way through heavy traffic. Once they were on the interstate, heading north to Maine, though, Isabel shifted in her seat. "Agent Wheelock isn't a problem for you, is he, Claudia?"

"Isabel—"

"I was only half-serious about you two earlier. Does he know your mother stored some of her collection in Heron's Cove?"

"Yes, but I don't care one way or the other. I have nothing to hide."

"Of course not. I didn't mean to imply otherwise. Anyway, I'm glad you won't be in Maine on your own."

"Me, too, but not because of him. I haven't been to Maine in a long time."

"Not since Victoria…" Isabel's voice trailed off, and she sniffled, staring out the side window. "I'm going to cry when we get there."

Claudia felt tears rising in her eyes. "We can cry together."

8

Southern Maine coast

The gray-shingled Sharpe house in picturesque Heron's Cove didn't look much different from the outside than it had before renovations. Fresh paint, new pots on either side of the door filled with green plants. Emma remembered her grandmother's weathered pots with their plethora of flowers, a reflection of her the-more-the-merrier gardening philosophy. It had been her philosophy about company, too. Emma felt a pang of grief as she headed up the short walkway. Was it possible her grandmother had been gone for more than fifteen years?

The front door was unlocked. Emma rang the bell and went in. She imagined her grandfather setting up his fledgling art-recovery business in the front room sixty years ago. So much had changed since then. Sometimes—too often, maybe—the work forced Lucas to put aside his personal wants and needs, but if he resented his younger sister's decisions about her own life, he'd never said.

Emma went down the hall toward the kitchen. Although she'd witnessed the transformation of the small Victorian into state-of-the-art offices since last fall, the changes still could take her breath away. The space was open, bright and well-equipped for taking Sharpe Fine Art Recovery into its next decades. The hall was decorated with framed photographs of the rocky Maine coast, but Emma noticed a black-and-white photograph of her grandfather at his first desk, an old oak rolltop that unsentimental Lucas had stored in the attic. He'd have gotten rid of it altogether if Emma had let him.

She smiled, remembering their many "discussions" over renovations. Her only stake in the house was emotional, but her brother hadn't shut her out of decisions, even if technically he could have.

The few staff had gone home for the day, and she found Lucas making tea in the kitchen. He was dressed casually, in a dark polo shirt and khakis. Emma was struck by how much her brother and grandfather resembled each other with their rangy builds, green eyes and tawny coloring. She was fairer, slender but not tall, but she did have the Sharpe green eyes.

"This isn't a casual visit," Lucas said, plugging in the electric kettle. "I can tell by your expression."

"Where's Granddad?"

"Out for a walk. He's been gone about an hour. I'm not ready to call the marine patrol."

Emma pulled out a chair at the table. Like everything else in the kitchen, it was new, an oak-top with a base painted a sea-turquoise. Out the windows there were views of the tidal river behind the house. "How's he taking to being back in Maine?"

Lucas shrugged. "Seems fine. Same as ever."

"Not that you'd notice if he dipped into melancholy

or nostalgia on his first visit home to Maine in years. You two are so much alike—cut-to-the-chase, focused on the work and rarely if ever introspective."

"Emma, I didn't expect such compliments from you."

She laughed. "You deserve each and every one."

Since he was now in his eighties, last year Wendell Sharpe had decided to retire and shut down his Dublin office. He was working on the odd project from his home in Dublin, still occasionally talking about returning to Heron's Cove to live. Although the two floors and attic of his former home had been given up to office space, renovations had included a small apartment—really, a guest suite with kitchen privileges—should he return to Maine, whether for a visit or to stay. It'd taken all but a crowbar to pry him loose from Dublin, his birthplace, onto a flight to Boston last week.

Emma sat at the table. "I'd like to talk to you about the open house."

Lucas pulled one of their grandmother's old china teapots off a shelf. "Granddad warned me having an open house would cause problems. Mum and Dad were for it. You've graciously kept your opinions to yourself. It's too late now." He set the teapot on the counter. "Please don't tell me that we have a wanted felon on the guest list."

"I haven't seen the guest list, so I wouldn't know."

"Ha."

She watched him prepare tea. The kitchen had a clean, bright feel with its white cabinets and butcher-block countertops, a contrast to the old kitchen with its worn counters and scarred cupboards.

Lucas set a plate of digestives in the middle of the

table. "One of Granddad's favorites," he said, returning to the counter.

"Mine, too," Emma said.

He grinned. "Figures."

As similar as he and their grandfather were, Emma recognized that Lucas was more businesslike, less prone to operating on gut instinct and not keeping proper files. When he retired, he wouldn't need to spend days doing a brain dump with his successor, as their grandfather had done with him in Dublin last fall. Anything needed to carry on the business would be in the Sharpe Fine Art Recovery files, backed up, sorted and official.

Matt Yankowski often told Emma he'd like to do a Vulcan mind meld with Wendell Sharpe. Not a bad idea, she thought. She'd like to do one with Gordy Wheelock right now. He hadn't returned her call and text, but Sam Padgett was pushing forward to learn more about what had happened at Gordy's hotel last night. Emma wouldn't want to try to get anything past Sam. If Gordy had indeed tripped over his own feet, so be it. But Sam was on it.

"I talked to Mum and Dad on my way up here," Emma said as Lucas placed the teapot and mismatched cups and saucers on the table. "They were at a tea party in London on Sunday celebrating the opening of an antiquities show at the Victoria and Albert Museum."

"They told you they ran into Oliver York, Gordon Wheelock and Claudia Deverell," Lucas said, sitting across from her.

Emma nodded, not surprised he already knew. "Still no love lost between you and Claudia?"

"Still." His tone suggested the reasons were none of

his younger sister's business. "Her father and brother arrived in town a little while ago. I suspect that's where Granddad is. He ran into them in London last week and made sure they'd be here on Saturday."

"I understand Granddad was in London last week for Alessandro Pearson's funeral," Emma said.

"That's right. He visited Mum and Dad at the same time. You met Alessandro, didn't you?"

"I did but only once. I tagged along when he and Granddad had whiskey together after Alessandro gave a guest lecture at Trinity College. That was when I worked with Granddad in Dublin."

"Before the FBI, then," Lucas said, his tone matter-of-fact.

"They talked about whiskey and the weather. Not a word about antiquities."

"It can be hard not to talk business sometimes, can't it?" Lucas reached across the table and poured Emma's tea, then poured his own. "I met Alessandro in London last year—it was a few weeks after you'd moved to Boston. April, I think. Nice old fellow. He'd obviously lost a step or two but he was sharp as a tack. Sorry he's gone. Anyway, what does this party on Sunday have to do with the FBI?"

"Possibly nothing. Are you okay with the Deverells being here on Saturday?"

"Henry and Adrian have said they'll stop in. We haven't heard from Claudia."

"Interesting that she was at the party on Sunday, too," Emma said.

"Makes sense given her background in antiquities. I find Oliver York's presence more intriguing." Lucas settled back with his tea, studying his only sister. "Is Oliver the reason for this visit?"

"Granddad invited him to the open house back in February."

"That was a spur-of-the-moment thing. Oliver hasn't said whether or not he'll be here on Saturday. If he is, he is."

Pragmatic Lucas, Emma thought.

"We invited a long list of people," he added. "We never expected everyone to show up. Maine in May is great but it's not high season. No one will have trouble finding a place to stay but it won't be the best beach and boating weather." He reached for a digestive. "What's up with Special Agent Wheelock? We invited him, of course, but I didn't expect him to respond, never mind say he'd be here."

"When did that happen?"

"Last week by email. He and Oliver York are your friends, Emma, not mine."

They weren't friends, but she didn't raise an objection. She gazed out the window in the back door. More pleasure boats were in the water at the marina next door. Finally, she shifted her attention back to her brother. "What do you know about rumors about stolen mosaics?"

Lucas broke his digestive in half and dipped it into his tea. "Mum and Dad mentioned the rumors when I talked to them earlier," he said finally. "Granddad did, too."

"When did he mention the rumors?"

"I don't remember. A few days ago."

"Before or after the Claridge's party?" Emma asked.

"Before. He stressed they're only rumors. We don't know anything for a fact."

We. Emma helped herself to a digestive. "Do you have any information on the mosaics in question?"

"Early Byzantine Christian. No description." Lucas's voice was crisp, businesslike. "I took the rumors with a grain of salt, Emma."

Emma ate her digestive without dipping it into her tea, a habit she had refused to pick up from her grandfather or her older brother. Suddenly all she wanted was to sit on the back porch, look out at the boats and have tea and digestives. She'd meant to be on her mini break by now, but Gordy's arrival in her office that morning had changed everything.

"Can you let me know if you hear anything else about these mosaics—even it's just more rumors?"

"Of course," Lucas said. "Is Gordy Wheelock in on these rumors? Wasn't he working an antiquities case when he retired?"

Emma finished her cookie and lifted her teacup. It was decorated with morning glories and had been one of her grandmother's favorites.

Lucas leaned back. "All right, Emma. I can translate your silence. You can't discuss Gordy Wheelock and an ongoing investigation, except on your terms. Mum says he's put on weight but otherwise seems fine. Does he know Oliver York is your serial art thief? Gordy chased him almost as long as Granddad did."

"Lucas…"

Her brother grinned. "I had to try."

Emma drank the rest of her tea. She thought of Colin's texts from Ireland and pictured him at Bracken Distillers with Sean Murphy. It was a good image, two strong men conferring about a cheeky English art thief with a tortured past.

Could Wendell Sharpe know something about Gordy and Oliver that wasn't in the Sharpe or FBI files, that he hadn't told her, Lucas, or anyone else?

"I miss the carpenters," Lucas said, reaching for another digestive with an obvious lack of enthusiasm. "They always brought doughnuts. A digestive is not a doughnut."

"I love digestives."

"Does Colin know this about you?"

"He does, and now he's become a fan, too. Well, *fan* might be too strong."

"Where is he?" Lucas asked mildly.

Emma grabbed another cookie and bit into it, welcoming the familiar bland flavor. When she'd worked with her grandfather in Dublin, between her time at the convent and joining the FBI, they'd enjoyed many tea-and-digestive breaks together on his terrace.

Lucas poured himself more tea. "Sorry if Colin's whereabouts is an awkward subject for you," he said, setting the pot back on the table.

"Colin's been in and out of Washington so much lately, it's hard even for me to keep track of him."

"I see," Lucas said, his tone enough to convey he could read into her safe answer.

Emma directed the subject back to the matter at hand. "Did Granddad see Oliver when he was in London for Alessandro's funeral?"

"I don't know. I didn't ask. Oliver isn't our problem these days." Lucas smiled, if faintly. "He sent you sheepskins, not Granddad or me."

She groaned. "Don't remind me."

"Beware English thieves bearing gifts," Lucas said with a laugh. "I bet they're top-quality sheepskins, though."

"Oliver says they're from sheep on his farm in the Cotswolds." Emma kept her tone neutral. "I think he was telling the truth this time."

"Have you seen him since he had you and Colin out to his farm in February—with the FBI's approval, or so I assume?"

"It was with approval and no, I haven't seen him since then. We didn't stay with him at the farm."

Instead, Emma thought, she and Colin had stayed at an inn in a nearby Cotswold village. They'd taken a short break after a particularly nasty case that had involved Oliver, at least on the periphery. It had also included an attempt on her life. Although nothing was said, she suspected Colin had been taking a few days to rest and be with her before going undercover again.

"Thanks for tea, Lucas," she said, getting to her feet. "Let me know if Gordy or Oliver gets in touch, okay?"

"Will do." Her brother rose, grabbing the teapot and taking it to the counter. "Mum and Dad said they still plan to make it home for your wedding."

"That would be nice," Emma said.

"Granddad says he wants to stay here through the wedding. It's only a few weeks away."

"I'd love for him to be there, but if he's homesick for Dublin—"

"Dublin's not going anywhere." Lucas turned to her, some of his earlier intensity easing. "I can keep him busy with work here. He's not as young as he thinks he is, but he's not just any man in his eighties, either."

No doubt about that, Emma thought. She knew—

and she suspected Lucas did, too—that Dublin was home for Wendell Sharpe now, and that aside from brain dumps, walkabouts in the Irish hills and giving up his office, he'd never fully retire.

Lucas walked out with her onto the back porch. "The new offices are working out well," he said. "We have more space than we need. That was the idea. Room to grow."

"I'm sure it helps to be out of temporary quarters. You're happy? You like the work?"

"It's been all-consuming this past year, especially with the folks in London, but we'll return to a more normal schedule soon. I'll have a life again."

"A social life beyond art auctions and gallery openings, you mean. You're on the job then, but an attractive woman could wander in and sweep you off your feet. Are you getting someone to take over the office in Dublin?"

"I don't know yet. I don't want to step on Granddad's toes."

"He understands you're the boss now."

"I wouldn't go that far," Lucas said with a laugh. "At least he keeps me informed about what he's up to—as far as I know, anyway."

Emma looked out at the wide, tidal river and past a narrow channel to the Atlantic, its turquoise waters glistening in the afternoon light. It was low tide, the air filled with the smells of the ocean and a hint of lilacs. Heron's Cove was coming to life again after the dark, cold winter months—shops and restaurants were reopening and summer houses were being aired out and spruced up for the season.

"Are you taking tomorrow off?" Lucas asked.

"I'm having a long-delayed lunch tomorrow with my future mother-in-law."

"Ah."

"That's all you have to say?"

"You're the one marrying a Rock Point Donovan."

Emma grinned, some of her own tension easing as she said goodbye to her brother and headed down the porch steps and around to the front of the house. Lucas clearly had his suspicions about the reasons behind her visit, but he had a good sense of their different professional roles. If nothing else, he knew pushing her wouldn't get him anywhere, and her brother wasn't one to waste time.

Instead of getting right back into her car, Emma walked up the street toward the Deverell house, the mouth of the tidal river giving way to a much-photographed section of the rockbound Maine coastline. She checked her phone, but still nothing from Gordy. She concentrated on the feel of the fresh breeze off the ocean and listened to the wash of waves on the rocks, the distant cry of seagulls and the putter of a lobster boat past a small cove, but she couldn't relax.

Across the curving road were large summer homes, most built around the turn of the twentieth century. The cedar-shingled Norwood-Deverell house occupied a prime elevated lot with stunning views of the Atlantic from its porches, bay windows and dormers. Emma didn't remember when the family had stopped summering in Maine. She couldn't have been more than ten. They'd come for a week at most, if at all, and rent out the house to friends and extended family. Victoria Norwood Deverell, who'd died of cancer last year, had been Henry Deverell's second wife, a quiet woman dedicated to her volunteer work and her family's impressive collection of Mediterranean antiquities. Only in her late teens had Emma discovered the Norwoods had been one of her grandfather's early clients and their Maine home had been maintained by his Irish-immigrant parents—her great-grandparents.

Life's twists and turns, she thought as she paused across the road from the classic 1910 house. It had been spruced up since last summer, with new white paint on the trim and shutters, fresh blue-and-white covers on the porch furniture and a good pruning of the shrubs. A gnarly spruce was the sole tree in the yard. As exposed to the Atlantic as the property was, shade trees were under constant threat from harsh winds and salt spray, but they also tended to spread their branches and block views.

There were two cars in the driveway, but Emma didn't see anyone on the porch or in the yard. With a pang, she realized that Victoria Deverell wouldn't be there. The house that had been a part of her family for over a century wasn't in the best shape but it would sell quickly and soon be owned by someone else.

"Emma!"

Even as she heard her name called she spotted her grandfather loping down the sidewalk toward her, moving with the energy of a man twenty years younger. She laughed, waving back. "Hey, Granddad."

They cut the distance between them in less than a minute. "I didn't expect to see you today," he said, kissing her on the cheek. "What a pleasant surprise."

He'd arrived last Saturday and she'd met him at the airport and put him in a hired car to take him to Maine.

He'd been tired from the long trip across the Atlantic, but he looked great now. She noted his lined, wind-reddened cheeks, lively green eyes and thin, near-white hair. He wore a lightweight jacket, ancient khakis and boat shoes he might have left in a closet on his last visit to Maine, except, of course, Lucas had cleared out all the closets before the renovations.

"How was your walk?" Emma asked.

"Invigorating. The air's different here than in Dublin. For a bit there I almost thought I was fourteen again, off to help my father repair shutters and mow lawns."

She nodded at the house across the street. "Did you stop and see the Deverells?"

"Henry was out on the porch. We had a nice chat. The last time I was here, Victoria…" His smile faded. "As I told Henry, it's hard to believe she's gone. I know what it's like to lose a wife too young. Cancer. It's the bloody devil, isn't it?"

Emma tucked an arm around him. "Come on, Granddad, I'll walk with you back to the house."

"Good. You obviously have something on your mind."

"That transparent, am I?"

"Only when you choose to be."

A seagull swooped low in front of them and perched on a boulder at the water's edge. Emma hugged her grandfather, feeling his bony frame and wondering what she'd ever do without him. Even in Dublin, he was a fixture in her life, a presence she didn't want to imagine not having. Calls, video chats, emails and even text messages were a constant, and they saw each other regularly.

They walked together back toward the river and the village center, the breeze dying down as they approached the inn and the Sharpe house, less exposed to the Atlantic. "You can tell me what's on your mind," her grandfather said finally. "We don't have to do hale and hearty. You can cut to why you're here."

"I'd have stopped to see you even if I didn't have something I need to talk to you about."

"Of course. Goes without saying. What's up, Emma?"

She told him about her visit from Gordy Wheelock, leaving out only what she'd learned about his mishap at his hotel last night. They arrived at the house as she finished. "Anything you can tell me, Granddad?"

He shook his head. "I've heard the rumors about the mosaics. I haven't tried to pin them down. I've been here, trying to get your brother to stop looking at me as if he thinks I'm about to keel over. Don't worry. I told Lucas to quit hovering. Not speaking out of turn."

"As if it'd stop you if you were."

"You've gotten cheekier since you started wearing a badge, or whatever you call it. Or is it the influence of that fiancé of yours?"

"It's knowing you," she said lightly.

"I love having my grandkids blame their smart mouths on me." He squinted across the street at a seasonal restaurant known for its lobster rolls and grilled scallops. "It can't have been easy for Gordy Wheelock to give up the work. For decades, you get up every morning knowing who you are, what you're expected to do that day. Maybe you like the accolades that come with the job, but it's the routines, the boundaries and the sense of accomplishment you miss when the work's not there any longer."

"Are we just talking about Gordy, Granddad?"

"Yeah, who else?" He turned, looking back in the direction they'd come. "I remember walking here with you when you were a tot. You loved to scramble on the rocks. No fear, but you always watched where you were going."

"Sometimes it doesn't help," Emma said. "The rocks can surprise you."

He nodded thoughtfully. "They turn out to be slippery or loose when they don't look it, or a seagull swoops at you, thinking your cookie is meant for him."

She smiled. "I've lost a round or two to seagulls. How do you like being back in Maine?"

"I've been wallowing in the past since I got here. Ireland seems like another life."

"Speaking of Ireland, Oliver York is there, or he was earlier today. He says he stopped in Dublin to see you and discovered you were gone. True or false, do you know?"

"Well, I *am* here."

"I meant is Oliver lying about his reasons for being in Ireland."

"I know what you meant, kid. I saw him last week when I was in London to see your folks before I flew back here. I don't remember if I told him my plans—he damn well doesn't need to know—but I could have."

"So, no help there," Emma said.

"Where is he now? He's not camped out at my house, is he?"

"He was in Declan's Cross."

Her grandfather nodded thoughtfully. "I think he

likes to go to the ruins there periodically as a kind of therapy."

Maybe so, Emma thought, but she doubted that was the only reason for Oliver's presence in the tiny south coastal village, or in Ireland at all. "I didn't realize you attended Alessandro Pearson's funeral last week."

"Mmm. Sorry to lose him, but he didn't suffer."

"Had you been in touch with him recently?"

"We were going to have a drink together when I was in London, before heading here. His idea, but I was happy to do it. I think he figured I'd die on the plane or never come back. That tone of voice, you know? Maybe you don't, since you're so young. Maybe it had nothing to do with me and he just sensed that his own end was near."

"Then a few days later, we hear rumors about stolen mosaics," Emma said.

"I suppose Alessandro could have wanted to talk to me about the rumors, but I don't have any evidence to support that theory. Do you?"

She shook her head without comment.

"Would you tell me if you did?" her grandfather asked, his green eyes narrowing on her.

She smiled. "Maybe."

"Well, there's no indication Alessandro's death was suspicious. It was his heart, not the fall, that killed him. I suppose he might have survived the heart attack if he'd been at home, but it's a moot point now. It's easy to get carried away with speculation, but we know better, don't we, Emma?"

"We do, indeed."

When she'd worked with her grandfather, they'd frequently hashed out ideas over a pint at his favorite pub.

She missed that camaraderie. She'd learned so much from him during those months, getting his insights on preventing, assessing and investigating private issues with fine art and antiquities. At the same time, the complexities of the relationships in the Sharpe Fine Art Recovery world had often frustrated her; not because she wasn't good at unraveling them, but because she wanted more straightforward relationships in her own life—one of the many reasons she'd been attracted to Colin, she supposed. As straightforward as they were themselves, Lucas and her grandfather navigated the gray areas of the complex world in which they operated with integrity, ease and an appropriate distance she respected.

She nodded to her car, parked on the street. "I should go," she said.

"Lucas and I have a client dinner tonight. I could ask him if you could join us."

Emma knew her grandfather and her brother were scrupulous about who they accepted as clients, but they were just as scrupulous about preserving their privacy. An FBI agent at the table could put an uncomfortable damper on dinner conversation. "That's okay, but thanks. It's in town?"

"At a nice restaurant in the village. I remember when it was a dive." He gave a mock shudder. "I sometimes wonder if I remember too much, but it's better than getting senile."

"You've always had a steel trap for a mind. Have a great time tonight, Granddad."

A gust of wind seemed to catch him by surprise, but he hunched his shoulders and grinned. "I love this place. I miss it sometimes in Dublin. Your grandmother loved it here, too. She'd have told me I was crazy for leaving."

"Granddad…"

He waved a hand. "Don't worry, I'm not going to start crying. There'll never be another woman like your grandmother. She was the best."

"Even Claudia Deverell?" Lucas asked, coming out the front door. "And what about that mosaic-artist friend of hers, Isabel Greene?"

"I should throw a rock at you," his grandfather said. "They're both too young for me, anyway."

Lucas grinned. "Doesn't Henry Deverell have an older sister?"

"Yes, and I've met her. Enough said. Never mind me. I'm a million years old and I had the love of my life. I'm a lucky man. What about you, Lucas?"

"I have cats," he said.

The banter between them eased Emma's concern about her grandfather's uncharacteristic bout of melancholy. Lucas knew what to say to him. She'd likely dig him deeper into his dark mood with probing questions, her desire for insights and connections—to visualize his memories of Heron's Cove and his life here, before her grandmother's death, her father's fall on the ice.

Lucas turned to her. "I sent the guest list for the open house to your personal email. It's not like it's classified information. Check it out to your heart's content, Special Agent Sharpe. We've noted those who responded in the affirmative, but people who didn't respond can show up, too. We're loose. We'll have name badges printed but we can do badges by hand for walk-ins. No big deal. It's not like a state dinner at the White House."

"Will you have security?"

"We're not the ones who own expensive art, Emma."

"That means no," she said with a slight smile. "Thanks, Lucas. I appreciate this."

"Better than you having to subpoena me." He winked. "Joking."

"You two," their grandfather muttered.

Emma stayed focused on her brother. "Are you aware Finian Bracken's sister, Mary, will be there?"

Lucas nodded. "She emailed my assistant, who mentioned it to me."

"When?"

"Last Saturday."

After Claudia Deverell had done her tour of Bracken Distillers. But Emma said nothing. With the wind turning chilly, she kissed her grandfather on the cheek, wished him and Lucas a fun dinner and got in her car. As she snapped on her seat belt and watched her grandfather go up the front steps, she swore she noticed a hitch in his gait. Emotion, maybe, more than infirmity—or just the aftereffects of his walk. He'd been hoofing it when she'd first spotted him.

When the door shut, she checked her phone—she had a text from Sam Padgett asking her to call him. "Bellman had it right," he informed her. "Housekeeping found a bloody towel in Wheelock's room. His bed was still made up this morning. They figure he either slept on the floor or didn't sleep at all. How'd he look when you saw him?"

"Not great. He said his sciatica was acting up. I didn't notice any injury."

"Maybe it's nothing. He'd had a long day. Tripping on the pavement while he was out for a smoke wouldn't be unusual, but I don't know if it explains not hitting the sack. I mean, the guy does sleep in a bed, right?"

"Maybe BPD has something."

"I have a call in to them. Nothing more on the envelope yet. I located the cab driver who picked Wheelock up at the hotel after he left you. Dropped him off on Newbury Street. Happens to be a gallery there that specializes in antiquities and contemporary mosaics."

"I know the place," Emma said.

"Figures." There was no sarcasm in Sam's tone. "I paid them a visit. Talked to a young woman in the shop downstairs who described Wheelock and said he had been there with Claudia Deverell. Stayed about twenty minutes. She left a short time later. According to its catalog, the gallery has a few pieces on sale from the Norwood antiquity collection. The contemporary mosaics on sale are by Isabel Greene, a Norwood-Deverell family friend—this from a guy at the gallery, not the catalog. Have you ever been to this place?"

"When I first arrived in Boston. I was curious. Anything else?"

"That's it."

"Thanks, Sam."

"No problem. I'll keep digging."

He hung up, and Emma texted Gordy: Call me.

The sun was low in the sky when Emma arrived in Rock Point, a few miles up the coast from Heron's Cove. Working boats floated in the still water of the horseshoe-shaped harbor of the struggling fishing village where Colin had grown up and most of his family still lived. She felt some of her tension easing as she turned onto one of the cluster of residential streets above the harbor. Before he had met her, he'd bought a small Craftsman-style house above the harbor. It was his refuge, and now it was hers, too.

She went through the back door into the kitchen and switched on the overhead light.

The silence accentuated Colin's absence.

She glanced at her watch. Almost six. Eleven at night in London. Colin would have arrived there by now.

She hadn't opened any windows, but swore she could hear the ocean, even though the house was on a residential street up from the harbor. Three of the four Donovan brothers were out of town. Mike, the eldest, was working a temporary assignment providing private security for a group of volunteer doctors in Africa; Colin, the second born, was presumably in London to talk to Oliver York; and Kevin, the youngest, a Maine marine patrol officer, was doing special training at Quantico. Andy, the third-born brother, a lobsterman, was in town, but Emma would be more likely to run into him at 5:00 a.m. than in the evening.

She opened the refrigerator and smiled when she saw the six-pack of beer on the bottom shelf. In the months since she'd been coming here, she'd added a few items, but mostly nonperishables: flour, baking powder, cornstarch, vanilla, cocoa.

She liked to bake, but not tonight.

Tonight was a night for fish chowder with friends.

She set her bag in the bedroom, then headed out the back door into the cool fog and quiet of Rock Point.

9

Martin Hambly looked as if he was having second thoughts about opening the front door to the spacious, expensive Mayfair London apartment owned by his longtime employer, Oliver York. "Special Agent Donovan," Hambly said with a sharp intake of breath. "Mr. York didn't mention he was expecting you."

"He's not. Mind if I come in?"

Hambly hesitated. "It's rather late."

"Yes, it is."

In his fifties, Hambly had begun his career working for Oliver's grandparents at their farm, now Oliver's farm, in the Cotswolds, two hours west of London. When the elder Yorks had died, Hambly had stayed on the payroll. He hadn't been at the London apartment thirty years ago when Oliver's parents were murdered in front of their eight-year-old son. The killers kidnapped young Oliver, ultimately dumping him in a remote Scottish ruin. The boy had escaped into the rain and mist of the Highlands, where, about to collapse from hunger and hypothermia, he'd come upon a priest out for a stroll.

With Oliver's help, the killers were identified as two contractors who'd done odd jobs for his parents, but the pair had disappeared and had yet to face arrest and prosecution for their crimes. Colin wouldn't be surprised if they were dead. It was the sort of unsolved case that ate at law enforcement officers.

Hambly reluctantly permitted Colin to set his suitcase in the entry and then led him from the elegant entry down a wide hall. Colin had the feeling Hambly had done his best by Oliver for the past thirty years, including, no doubt, suggesting his employer have nothing to do with FBI agents.

He motioned for Colin to enter the library and remained by the wood-panel door.

"Greetings, Agent Donovan," Oliver said, seated in a high-backed chair with a bottle of expensive Scotch and a glass on the small round table next to him. "You must be on Maine time given the late hour. Of course, you're a tough FBI agent. Time means nothing to you, does it?"

Colin didn't smile. "Thanks for seeing me, Oliver."

"I'm reading about ancient mosaics," he said, holding up the thick book he had on his lap. "Greeks loved the form but the Romans really took off with it. Mosaic art became popular throughout the Roman Empire. The golden mosaics in Ravenna in northeast Italy are among the most well-known. Have you been to Ravenna, Colin?"

"No."

"I imagine your fiancée has. I have. Ravenna was

the capital of the entire Roman Empire in the early fifth century. After the fall of Rome, it continued as the seat of the eastern Roman Empire—what became known as the Byzantine Empire—until the eighth century. Its early Christian monuments are a designated World Heritage Site. The Ravenna mosaics are incredible—they're intricate works of art that combine western Roman and Byzantine traditions. They depict Biblical narratives, an emperor or two—I was blown away by the golden mosaics in particular."

Oliver could go off on tangents, but Colin guessed this wasn't a tangent. "They're made of real gold?"

"Not exactly. A thin film of gold was fused to the tesserae—the small pieces that make up an individual mosaic. The gold creates an otherworldly glow that's quite mesmerizing. Of course, most mosaics don't involve gold." Oliver nodded to the book. "The mosaic on the cover isn't from Ravenna. It's from an ancient Greek burial vault. It illustrates the story of Persephone's kidnapping by Hades. Do you know your Greek gods and goddesses, Agent Donovan?"

"Some of them. I was more into the goddesses than the gods."

Oliver sighed, shaking his head. "Truly a wonder Emma ended up with you."

"I can't argue with that," Colin said.

"Hades, of course, was the god of the underworld. He kidnapped Persephone and dragged her to the underworld with him. An appropriate story for a tomb, don't you think?"

"Yep. Sure."

"I'm ignoring your disinterested tone," Oliver said, rubbing a fingertip over the book's slightly worn cover.

"This was on a top shelf of the bookcase over in the corner, behind the chess set. Who knew?"

"You should go through all these books one day. You might find a twenty-dollar bill."

"I'd buy you a pint if I did," Oliver said with a small smile. "The author of the book died recently. Alessandro Pearson."

"I knew this was leading somewhere." Colin crossed the thick carpet and pointed to a chair on the other side of Oliver's small table. "Mind if I sit down?"

"Of course not. My apologies. I should have invited you to sit. You caught me absorbed in the world of ancient mosaics. Something to drink? Tea? Something stronger?"

"No, thanks."

Oliver settled his gaze on his guest, as if really seeing him for the first time. "How are you, Special Agent Donovan?"

"Just fine."

"You don't sound fine. You sound abrupt and tense. Are you on your way home? Will you be in Maine in time for the open house at the new offices of Sharpe Fine Art Recovery?"

"I'm not here to discuss my schedule." Colin realized he did sound abrupt and tense and decided to tone it down. "You just got in from Cork. Are you planning to stay in London for a while?"

"Spring in London is a delight. You and Emma should consider a few days in London for your honeymoon. I can see you two holding hands, wandering through St. James's Park on a beautiful June afternoon."

"Does that mean you have no plans to go anywhere?"

"Nowhere tonight. We'll see what tomorrow brings, shall we?" Oliver threw one leg over the other, everything about him languid and relaxed except his eyes, unwavering as he watched Colin. "Did Detective Garda Murphy ring you, and you happened to be in London?"

Colin shook his head. "It doesn't matter."

"I suppose not, but I'd hate for you to interrupt your plans on my account. It's hard to believe a few hours ago I was walking among atmospheric ruins above the Irish Sea." Oliver motioned toward Hambly, who was still hovering in the doorway. "Agent Donovan and I will be fine, Martin. Thank you."

"Can I bring you anything to eat?" Hambly asked Colin.

"Since you don't have Rock Point's finest haddock chowder, no, thank you. I'm good."

A slight smile from Hambly as he withdrew.

Colin shifted back to Oliver. "All you need are a pipe and smoking jacket."

Oliver laughed. "They're with the tweeds in the closet." He gestured to the bottle on the small table next to him. "Shall I pour you a drink after all? I just opened this intriguing Scotch from the Isle of Lewis in the Outer Hebrides. The Spirit of Lewis, it's called. It's from the Abhainn Dearg distillery. That's Scottish Gaelic. It translates as 'red river.'"

Colin repeated the name, pronounced *aveen-jarek,* and noticed the bottle's distinctive red label.

"It's a young spirit matured a short time in a sherry cask," Oliver added. "Everything at Abhainn Dearg is done by hand. Distillation, bottling, labels, shipping."

"Is it any good?"

"It's quite robust for a new spirit, but it's brash—more like the less refined spirit of old. I'd love to get Father Bracken's opinion. Emma would hate it, but you might like it."

"I'll pass for now, thanks. Talk to me, Oliver. I'd like to hear about the party at Claridge's on Sunday."

"What a perfect event it was. You know Claridge's is my favorite hangout. It's a great example of the art deco period, which is one of my favorites."

"Did you crash this party?"

He sniffed, feigning insult. "I never crash parties."

"Then you were invited," Colin said.

"After a manner. Your future in-laws were there."

"They have nothing to do with this visit."

"Have you spoken with your fiancée, the fair Emma Sharpe? We had a nice video chat earlier today. I was at Kitty O'Byrne's hotel in Declan's Cross. It's as chic and charming as ever. I lingered into the afternoon. I've only been back in London a short time."

Colin was tempted by the Abhainn Dearg. Just a sip, enough to remind him of the few quiet days last June when he'd first met Finian Bracken and they'd become friends over a bottle of Bracken 15. By September, he'd met Emma. By November, Oliver York. Nothing about his life was ever simple with the Sharpes, or with Oliver York.

"The FBI has no authority in the United Kingdom," Oliver added.

"You're stating the obvious."

"Maybe. Of course, I have no authority anywhere. I am a simple Englishman enjoying a single-malt Scotch. Have you ever been to Scotland, Agent Donovan?"

"No."

"Queen Victoria's 1854 visit to the southern Highlands north of Edinburgh helped launch the small village of Pitlochry as a tourist destination. Much the same happened a few years later with her 1861 visit to Killarney, Ireland. Have you visited Killarney National Park?"

Colin kept his gaze on Oliver. The guy was a lateral thinker. Slippery. "You know I have."

"I don't know as much about you as you think. Have you been there with Emma?"

"To Killarney?"

"You don't need to be deliberately dense with me, Special Agent Donovan."

"Unintentionally dense is okay?"

"I doubt you're ever unintentionally dense." Oliver reached for the open bottle of Abhainn Dearg and splashed some of the single malt into a second glass on the table. "I insist you at least try it."

Colin accepted the glass and took a sip, both out of curiosity and because he knew Oliver wouldn't give up until he got his way. "Whoa. Yeah, it's different."

"It has notes of honey and citrus but there's a power to it. I was surprised it has a nice sweet finish."

"You and Finian can talk. I'm getting better at all the notes and noses and finishes, but for the most part I just know if I like it or don't like it."

"And?"

"It's good."

Oliver seemed pleased. "But you're not here to talk Scotch, are you, Colin."

"No, I'm not."

Oliver narrowed his eyes, again with a hint of the intensity and intelligence that had made him impos-

sible to catch as an art thief. "You know I am sched-
uled to fly to Boston tomorrow."

After a moment's hesitation, Colin nodded. "Yes, I
know." He reminded himself that he was, technically,
Oliver's guest. "This is your apartment, Oliver, but
don't play games with me, not if you want to board
that flight."

"Ah. There we have it. The veiled threat."

Colin shrugged. "I didn't think it was that veiled."

"You're every bit as snarly a bastard as my MI5
handler. I only made my reservation this afternoon,
but I should have assumed you knew I'm off to your
beautiful part of our planet. Am I on some FBI watch
list or does MI5 keep you informed of my travels?"

"Could be both."

"I'm not officially barred from entering the US, but
you want to know when I do."

"Close enough." Colin took another sip of the
Scotch. He agreed with Oliver that Emma would probably hate it. "Are you attending the Sharpe open house?"

"I am, indeed."

"Inviting you was Wendell's first sign of senility."

"Hardly, and you know it. Well, I'm glad we can
avoid any awkwardness and nonsense about my return to Boston, and to Maine, of course. Regardless
of the open house, what's a trip to Boston without a
stop in Maine?"

Colin didn't respond.

"I assume you're also aware that Mary Bracken
is flying to Boston tomorrow. She'll be visiting her
brother Finian, our priest friend serving the Roman
Catholic parish in your dreary little hometown. Do

you suppose our Father Bracken regards his year in Rock Point as a sort of penance?"

"Penance for what?"

"Not being with his family when they died. Not being able to help them, or to share their fate. He was working and he got left behind."

Colin studied the Englishman, noting the seriousness in his light green eyes, but also the unexpected warmth and empathy. Another side to the brazen thief, maybe. Like the Scotch he was serving, it was easy to note the brashness first, before noticing the layers and subtleties to his personality.

Oliver cleared his throat, as if he recognized he'd gone too far. "Father Bracken is performing your wedding service. When I spoke to Emma this afternoon, she told me I'm still not invited."

"That's correct."

"A pity. I'm a great wedding guest. Ah, well. May I ask what you are doing in London?"

Colin cupped his Scotch glass in his palm, uncertain what Oliver's game was. As well as an accomplished thief, Oliver York was an expert in *shorin-ryu* karate and tai chi, a brilliant, largely self-taught mythologist, a successful sheep farmer and a wealthy Englishman who operated with ease in exclusive circles from Hollywood to London. He could take on various personas—in fact, he had worked as a mythology consultant in Hollywood under an assumed name. He'd escaped detection and arrest for a decade in part because of his ability to read people and situations. His experience as a young boy with fear, violence and profound loss, his solitary ways and his expertise in martial arts and myth, legends and folklore had all combined to make the complex, intriguing man sitting in front of Colin.

But Colin didn't buy Oliver's bored-aristocrat act any more than his other acts.

Bottom line, the guy was a thief.

"I flew in from Ireland tonight," Colin said. "I was there on personal business."

"There, you see? You can give straightforward answers when you care to." Oliver sat back again, looking more at ease. "I assume Sean Murphy told you I was in Declan's Cross and ran into Mary, since he arrived as I was making my exit. Good timing, that. He contacted you, didn't he?"

"Irrelevant."

"To you, maybe. I suspect you're familiar with a few of my friends in MI5 and MI6 and they could have told you I was in Ireland. They weren't pleased when they found out. I got a proper tongue-lashing when I returned to London earlier this evening. They're a rough lot."

Colin tried not to smile. He knew Oliver's handlers, and they *were* a rough lot. One in particular, who had, in fact, checked in with him as well after he'd landed in London. *Sharpes, Deverells, Oliver York and ancient Byzantine mosaics. What do you know?*

No mention of Alessandro Pearson, the dead archaeologist. Colin had put off the MI5 agent, at least for the time being. "Are you alone, Oliver?"

"Intensely. Always."

"I mean here now in London. No guests?"

"Except for Martin, no guests."

"And Ireland—were you alone there?"

"On my own. I didn't have a travel companion.

Martin was at the farm and arrived in London about an hour before I did. I did see Kitty O'Byrne, Mary Bracken and old Paddy Murphy in Declan's Cross. Paddy offered to buy me a pint, if you can believe it. I explained to my MI5 handler if he'd tried to follow me or bug a headstone in the Irish ruins, Detective Garda Murphy would have found out, and you and Emma would have found out. *I'd* have found out, and you'd all never see me again. I'd disappear into the wind."

"That'd be a feat," Colin said. "Slipping into the run-down O'Byrne house and making off with a few artworks is different from cutting out on the UK intelligence services."

"And the FBI."

"That assumes we give a damn, doesn't it? If you put a toe out of line, your MI5 handler will see to it you're arrested and prosecuted for breaking into a London home and helping yourself to two prized oil landscapes."

Oliver grunted. "Least of my worries with him."

No doubt. Colin set the Scotch glass on the table. "What's your game, Oliver?"

"No games."

He recorked the Scotch and set the bottle on the table. Colin waited, if not patiently. He hadn't seen Oliver since winter. He had nothing to do with the English thief from day to day, although he was aware Oliver was working with MI5. It made sense, given Oliver's particular expertise with art crimes. Emma was in a position, both as an agent and as a Sharpe, to know more about what Oliver York was up to these days.

"One day you, Emma and I will have to have a proper tour of Bracken Distillers," Oliver said. "We can have a wander in Killarney at the same time. The national park is a treasure trove of adventures. One can imagine leprechauns hiding in the ancient oak forest, or hearing the wail of a banshee in a remote glen. Have you ever been out to Innisfallen Island in Lough Leane?"

Colin gritted his teeth. "No, Oliver."

"Early medieval monks had a monastery there and wrote down pre-Christian Irish tales. Of course they added their own spin to them, but they still are of enormous value. You can get a boat ride out there from Ross Castle, another fascinating place."

"Let's save the history of leprechauns, banshees and Irish monks for another time."

Oliver sighed, his gaze leveling on Colin. "We're never going to be friends, are we, Agent Donovan?"

"Probably not."

"If I do succeed in talking Emma into inviting me to your wedding, you won't have me barred at the convent gate?"

"Whatever makes her happy."

Oliver smiled. "I knew you'd say that." He raised a hand. "Not to worry. I'm in no way suggesting I can read you or know you well. I understand you FBI agents like to be inscrutable."

Colin recognized that he'd walked in here tired and surly, without sufficient information or clarity. His purpose was unfocused, a mix of personal and professional—and likely to get him in a mess if he didn't get a handle on himself and what was going on.

"Tell me about Claudia Deverell," he said.

Oliver sprang to his feet. "I wondered if Mary would tell anyone else about her. I assume Detective Garda

Murphy got it out of her. I'm afraid I'm not going to be of much help. I don't know Claudia. I'm learning about her. Her family on her mother's side has a history with Heron's Cove and the Sharpes. They helped Wendell establish his name. That by itself is curious, but Claudia also has a history with Gordon Wheelock." Oliver turned to Colin, who was still seated. "Are you familiar with our venerable retired art-crimes investigator, Agent Donovan?"

Colin gave a curt nod. "Of course." He looked for any sign Oliver was manipulating, fishing or giving him plain old BS, but saw none. Which, he knew, meant little. "What history?" he asked.

"Agent Wheelock consulted Claudia here in London before he retired last year. He was working on a case involving fraudulent antiquities. That's about all I know."

"You left yourself wiggle room with that answer."

"Did I? I wouldn't know. I don't pay attention to such nuances because I have nothing to hide. I don't know Agent Wheelock personally. Emma worked with him for a short time."

"He came close to catching you."

"Catching me… I have no idea what you mean."

Another act Colin didn't buy. "Was Agent Wheelock in London last week because of Claudia Deverell?"

"I wouldn't know. I saw them together at the tea at Claridge's on Sunday."

"Why was MI5 there?"

Oliver walked over to the tall windows that overlooked St. James's Park. "I don't ask questions."

"You just do as you're told," Colin said, not bothering to hide his skepticism.

"That is correct. The Tower of London looms large in my imagination."

"Right. I can get in touch with your handler, you know."

Oliver glanced back at Colin with another sigh. "Or no flight to Boston and no party at Heron's Cove on Saturday? Is this what you call playing hardball, Agent Donovan?"

"Not even close."

"Ha. Touché, my friend."

Colin ignored him.

"All right, then. My handler learned I would be at the party and stopped by to make sure I behaved. I think he worries I'll break down at any moment and start throwing glasses and cutlery, but I'm very stress-resilient."

No doubt true. Colin got to his feet. He could feel his fatigue, and he thought of Fin Bracken's cottage in the Kerry hills. He should be there now, enjoying a quiet glass of whiskey by the fire, or asleep in the loft. But he was here, trying to get information out of a solitary man who wasn't accustomed to telling anyone anything about himself, his plans, his whereabouts or anything else. Oliver York liked to be in control. Colin pictured him as a young boy, in this very room, hiding while his parents were murdered in front of him. A desire to be in control wasn't that hard to figure out or understand.

"Where does Claudia live in London?" Colin asked.

"She has an apartment in Kensington."

"Why was she at Bracken Distillers last week?" Colin asked.

Oliver gave a tight shake of his head. "Other than

stumbling on the Bracken-Sharpe connection, I have no idea." He stifled an obviously fake yawn. "I look forward to seeing the rocky Maine coast again. How is Rock Point these days?"

"Warming up," Colin said, aware of Oliver studying him keenly.

The Englishman drew the heavy drapes, his back to Colin as he continued. "You haven't been home in a while, have you?"

"It's May. It's warming up in Maine. Way it works. Don't read anything else into it."

Oliver turned as he finished closing the drapes. "Mr. Friendly," he said with the smallest of smiles. "Did your personal business in Ireland include arranging your honeymoon with our fair Emma?"

"I'm not talking to you about my travels, Oliver. Or my honeymoon."

"Definitely testy." He eased back to his chair, his expertise in martial arts showing in his fluid, controlled movements. "I am a patriotic Englishman. I don't need to tell you the perils of the antiquities trade. Even the legitimate trade can serve as the gateway to serious crimes. It's easy to be fooled, or to fool others. Someone shows up in London with artifacts he says were discovered in his grandmother's closet after her death, but it turns out they were pillaged from an archaeological site in North Africa. There are international protocols, but not everyone adheres to them. Ancient works end up in the wrong hands. Money ends up in the wrong hands, funding thieves, scoundrels and murderers. Throw in regional and international conflicts, and we can end up with a profoundly dangerous mess on our hands."

"Do you believe Claudia Deverell is involved in the illegal antiquities trade?"

"I can't say for certain. Of course, some believe any trade in antiquities is unethical. But that's a different fight, isn't it? Talk to Emma," Oliver added, picking up his Scotch glass. "When do you go home?"

No reason not to tell him, Colin decided. "Tomorrow. We're not on the same flight."

"Thank goodness. Do you need a place to stay tonight? Martin can prepare the guest room."

Colin had no idea where he was staying, but it wouldn't be under the same roof as Oliver York. "I'm good but thanks."

"Take the book," Oliver said, handing Colin the volume by Alessandro Pearson. "You can read about ancient mosaics on your flight. There are some spectacular photos, too. I'm not implying you aren't up to reading books without pictures."

"Of course not." Colin noticed Martin Hambly in the doorway and took the cue. "Good night, Oliver. Thanks for talking with me."

"Anytime. As you can see, Martin has recovered from his ordeal this winter."

"Bashed on the head and left for dead, you mean?" Hambly asked, giving Colin a faint smile. "I do try to be precise in the description of my various ordeals."

Oliver rolled his eyes. "The drama. Martin's been spending more time at the farm. He's training a puppy. Martin insists Alfred is my puppy, but he isn't. He's an ill-tempered wire fox terrier, but he's helped Martin enormously in his recovery."

"Maybe a dog would help you, too," Colin said.

"I could get you and Emma a puppy for your wedding."

"Stick to sheepskins."

London was cool, damp and dark, but it wasn't raining. Colin walked to Claridge's, an upscale art deco hotel in the heart of Mayfair London. He was convinced that Oliver hadn't told him everything, perhaps at MI5's insistence. If so, Colin didn't blame MI5. If he had a guy like Oliver by the short hairs, he wouldn't want him conferring with anyone else, either.

When he arrived at Claridge's, he settled into a comfortable booth in the main-floor bar. Timothy Sharpe, waiting on a stool at the bar, brought his drink over to the table. Colin noticed Tim's stiff gait, the slight wince as he settled into the booth. He was only in his fifties, but the chronic pain he'd suffered for a decade had taken its toll. "Hello, Colin," he said. "Good to see you."

"Same here. Thanks for meeting me."

"Faye sends her regards. She was relieved when you called, I think. I'd been pacing—just my usual aches and pains, nothing to do with my father's return to Heron's Cove." Tim smiled, although the hint of pain in his green eyes didn't ease. "I suppose there's time yet for that. I doubt I've considered all the possible ramifications of Wendell Sharpe being back on Maine soil for the first time in a decade."

"Emma's there now, too," Colin said.

"Yes. I hope her grandfather's presence doesn't get her into trouble with her FBI superiors. Faye and I saw him last week—he attended a friend's funeral."

"Alessandro Pearson."

"Of course. I shouldn't be surprised you already know."

Colin ordered a beer. For half a nickel, he'd stretch out on the cushioned bench and take a nap. He hadn't slept on his flight, the express train to Paddington Station or the cab to Mayfair, and the walk from Oliver's apartment, while not physically taxing, had relaxed him enough that it was all he could do not to drop his head onto the table and nod off.

He and Tim Sharpe exchanged a few pleasantries before getting down to business. "The tea here on Sunday was a relatively small gathering," Tim said. "We received our invitation on Wednesday, so there wasn't much notice, but everything went off beautifully, as perfect and elegant as one would expect."

"Was it a fund-raiser?" Colin asked.

"Definitely not, at least not overtly so. It was sponsored by a small charity—I didn't pay much attention, frankly."

"I don't want you ruffling feathers, but I'd like to know more details. Would you mind taking a closer look?"

"Happy to."

Colin took another sip of his beer, a high-end brand that his future father-in-law had recommended. "See what you can find out about who was behind the party, why now, the guest list—again, without drawing attention to yourself. I don't want you in hot water with MI5 or anyone else. It's not worth it."

"I don't know how a tea-and-champagne celebration of a show at the Victoria and Albert could get me in hot water, but I'll be careful. I always am. It was an unusual event but in no way alarmingly so. Faye and I had a good time."

Tim went on to describe their short stay at the party, including brief encounters with Oliver York, Gordon Wheelock and Claudia Deverell. He'd heard the rumors about stolen mosaics. "I told Emma when I spoke to her earlier—I don't have anything on them. I can't rule out or verify a theft, I have no idea what the identity of the collector might be or even if there is a collector."

Colin placed the book Oliver had loaned him cover-down on the table and noted the color photograph of the elderly author, dressed in desert khakis, standing at some dusty ancient ruin. "What's your take on Pearson's death occurring around the same time these rumors of stolen mosaics started?"

Tim shrugged. "I suppose there could be a connection if the unnamed collector had consulted him. Perhaps something about Alessandro's death—his will, perhaps—triggered the rumors. There are always rumors in this town, and one would expect to hear a few about antiquities at a party celebrating a late antiquity show at a prominent museum. I didn't hear anything that would be of specific value to the FBI—no American connection. Even if Alessandro's death was suspicious—and I haven't heard a hint that it was—he was British, not American."

"I understand," Colin said. "Your old neighbors in Maine are into mosaics."

"The Norwoods, you mean. I had a crush on Victoria Norwood when I was a boy. She married Henry Deverell, a Philadelphia real estate developer. I don't know him well. He's never been interested in Maine and I doubt he's ever been interested in mosaics. The

same with Adrian Deverell, Henry's son by his first
marriage, a real estate developer in Atlanta. Henry and
Adrian were here early last week on business and took
the opportunity to visit Claudia."

Colin drank some of his beer. "A lot of comings and
goings. Did you see them?"

Tim shook his head. "Claudia mentioned their
visit when Faye and I saw her on Sunday. She and
her mother were close. Six months between diagnosis
and death—it's been rough for Claudia. I think she's
starting to get her feet under her again. In any event,
Colin, I haven't heard even a whisper of the Deverells'
involvement in anything illegal." Tim polished off the
last of his drink and set the glass on the table. "But I do
research and analysis these days. I'm not out and about
the way I was in the past. Still, if I hear anything, I'll
let you and Emma know."

"Thanks, Tim."

"Are you all set for your wedding?" he asked. "Faye
and I will be there, I promise. She has her dress picked
out, finally."

They chatted for a few more minutes. By the time
they wrapped up, Tim looked as if he was about to pass
out from pain, but he didn't mention any discomfort.
He insisted on paying for their drinks. Colin thanked
him, and they walked together to the main entrance
of the elegant hotel. Tim had already offered the sofa
in the small apartment he shared with his wife, but
on his walk to Claridge's, Colin had booked a room
at a budget hotel a few blocks away. He'd stayed there
on other trips to London on behalf of the FBI, but he
didn't tell that to his future father-in-law.

Once Tim was in a cab and on his way back to

his apartment, Colin started walking to his hotel. He pictured Emma in London on her grandfather's behalf, after the sisterhood, before the FBI. What if she'd stayed with Sharpe Fine Art Recovery? Colin shook his head. It wouldn't have mattered. He knew, in his gut, he still would have found his way to her. As it was, they'd met over a dead nun at her former convent. If she'd stayed with the family business instead of joining the Bureau, maybe they'd have met over chowder and pie at Hurley's. Simpler.

He got settled into his room. He'd get a few hours' sleep, then it was back to the airport in the morning. But first he called Sean Murphy, who answered on the first ring. "You're up late," Colin said.

"I just arrived back in Declan's Cross."

With Kitty O'Byrne, Colin thought. He had a decent professional relationship with Sean and would be friends if the opportunity arose. He saw no reason not to tell the Irish detective about his visit with their serial art thief. Oliver York was a criminal. Colin couldn't get past that, even if the Sharpes—including Emma, but especially Wendell and Lucas—could. Ten years Oliver had taunted them, and it was let bygones be bygones.

Then again, MI5 had the same attitude.

"I went back to the distillery after I dropped you off," Sean said. "I spoke to Declan and some of the other staff who were still about. An American—a man—did a tour on Monday and asked about Claudia Deverell. I think you know him."

"Let me guess. Gordon Wheelock."

"Exactly so," Sean said. "He's one of yours, Colin. He filled out a form to get on the distillery's mailing

list or no one might have remembered him. He and Declan had a casual conversation. Wheelock mentioned
a woman he knew—this Claudia—had toured the distillery last week. Declan didn't think a thing of it until
we showed up at the distillery."

Gordy Wheelock had taken the time to stop in Ireland on his way from London to Boston. Colin chewed
on that one for half a beat. "Did Wheelock speak with
Mary?"

"Yes. Declan didn't see them but a worker did. I
don't like this, Colin. A retired agent and then Oliver
York. Is this Deverell woman trouble?"

"I don't know her, Sean."

"I can't bar Mary Bracken from leaving Ireland,"
Sean said, his voice tight. "I swear I would if I could.
I phoned Finian, but he says he has even less influence
than I do. He'll keep an eye on her. And you, Colin?"

"As it happens, Mary and I are on the same flight
to Boston in the morning."

"Best news I've had today."

After Colin hung up with the Irish detective, he
glanced at his watch. Late in London, not late in Maine.

Time for a chat with his fiancée.

He texted her. Our English friend was reading up
on ancient mosaics. We need to talk.

10

Rock Point, Maine

"Where are you?" Colin asked. "Having chowder at Hurley's?"

Emma smiled into her phone, as if he could see her. She'd called him the moment she'd received his text. "You know me well. I'm on my way. I thought I'd be there by now but I took a long walk first." She paused, feeling the chill of the evening air. "It's turned foggy."

"It's like I'm there with you," he said, a raggedness to his voice. "I've missed being home. I've missed you."

"I've missed you, too. I can't wait for you to be here. Are you still in London?"

"Yes."

She started into the small parking lot on the harbor that Hurley's, a Rock Point fixture, shared with the working docks. It was early evening, boats reflected in the still, darkening water. She walked toward the docks while she listened to Colin's report on his late-night visits in London with Oliver and her father. As he finished, she noticed a car turn into the parking lot behind her. Its Massachusetts plates weren't unusual but it was no tourist behind the wheel.

Gordy Wheelock climbed out and waved at her. "Hey, Emma."

"Damn," she said under her breath. "Colin... I have to go. I hate this. I could talk to you all night, but Gordy's here."

"He needs to level with you."

"Yes. I'll see you soon."

"Yeah, babe. Soon."

She could hear the longing in his voice, the loneliness and isolation of his undercover life taking a toll now that he was safe in London. Visiting Oliver York and her father wasn't the same as an evening with his family and friends on Rock Point harbor. Colin was valued for his independence, but he could also get into trouble for it—not just with his superiors at the FBI but also with himself. Sometimes he'd push himself past his limits and refuse to acknowledge he needed to take time to decompress. Matt Yankowski had mandated rest after Colin had finished his last mission in October. He took off for Ireland for a few days at Finian Bracken's cottage in the Kerry hills. Emma, uncertain then of their future together, had joined him. Had he gone to the cottage again this time, only to have his break interrupted because of Oliver's visit to Declan's Cross? But why not tell her?

Maybe he hadn't had a chance.

Emma hated to think that Colin had arrived in Ireland exhausted, hoping for a few days of quiet, and then had gotten a call from Sean Murphy—and not about having a friendly pint together, either.

She walked over to Gordy. "Evening," she said.

He grinned at her. "I figured I'd better call or come find you before you put out a BOLO on me. Your voice mail had an I'm-FBI-and-you're-not tone to it. That means you think you learned something about what I'm up to that I haven't told you and you don't like it. I might be rusty but I still have good instincts."

"How's your head?"

"Hurts like hell." Not a hint of surprise or guilt in his voice. "Stomach's a mess now, too, because I've been popping ibuprofen like mints."

"What happened to you last night, Gordy?"

He shrugged. "Not much. What, housekeeping got nervous about my bloody towel? Bellman talked? Doesn't matter. Like I told the bellman, I tripped on the steps while I was out for a smoke and hit my head. Banged up my knee and twisted my hip, too. I chalk it up to jet lag."

"Were you attacked?"

"By steps?"

"Don't lie to me."

"Relax. I was tired. I didn't really start hurting until I walked to your office."

"Housekeeping says you didn't sleep in your bed."

"I didn't. I laid on the floor when I got back to my room to do some yoga pose Joan taught me and fell asleep. Woke up, washed off the blood and went to see you. I don't blame you for looking up my hotel and seeing what's what—I'd have done the same thing—but it was no big deal. Nothing sinister happened."

She pinned her gaze on him, the light from Hurley's bringing out the puffiness in his face, the dark shadows under his eyes—indications of jet lag, bad sleeping, injury and a not-so-great first year of retirement. "You should have told me you fell instead of making up that bit about your sciatica."

"My sciatica *was* acting up. I should have figured you'd check up on me. I was embarrassed, okay? I didn't want to mention my clumsiness." He nodded to the rustic restaurant. The building was up on pilings, allowing the tide to flow underneath it. "Treat you to chowder?"

"And pie."

He grinned. "Of course." He motioned with one arm. "After you."

"When did you arrive in Maine?"

"About an hour ago. Getting my lay of the land. Figured I'd go for a whale watch tomorrow, unless I decide to skip the open house and go home to North Carolina."

"Maybe that would be a good idea."

"Maybe it would. You've looked into the rumors about the stolen mosaics and didn't find anything, right?"

"I'm not discussing this with you."

"Doesn't matter. There are always rumors and some evaporate, and I'm just the kind of retired agent I used to hate. You can relax, Agent Sharpe. You're chasing nothing. Sorry I got you stirred up. I've done stupider things jet-lagged than trip on my own two feet."

They went to Finian Bracken's preferred table in back along the bank of windows overlooking the harbor and sat across from each other. "No armed Donovans?" Gordy asked as he unrolled his flatware, tucked inside a white paper napkin.

"Most of them are out of town."

"Good. Fish or clam chowder?"

"Fish. Thanks."

Their server arrived, a teenage boy Emma didn't recognize but the Donovans undoubtedly would. Emma could use a few of Colin's brothers around now. Having chowder with Gordy wasn't her idea of a relaxing evening. He decided on the clam chowder and asked for extra rolls.

"You're looking for trouble, Gordy," she said as their server retreated.

"When I first knew you, you wouldn't come out and say it like that. You'd think it—*don't mess with me*—but you wouldn't say it."

"Is there anything else you need to tell me?"

"I don't need to tell you anything."

"Technically that's true." She paused, considering her next words. "What about the envelope the cab driver found addressed to you?"

"From my wife. A delivery she arranged. Personal." He grabbed his water glass. "You'll be married soon. You'll see the kinds of things you do when your guy's out of town. I can't decide if I'm offended or impressed you checked up on me."

"Are you the one doing the sniffing around?"

"MI5 was at that party, and maybe I inferred the rest. It doesn't matter. I'm going to enjoy my stay in Maine and go home to my wife, kids, grandkids, golf clubs and fishing rod. I don't have anything you can use, Emma. I'd give it to you if I did."

"Tell you what. You tell me what's going on and I'll decide what I can and can't use."

He drank some water, set his glass firmly on the table and grinned. "Spoken like a proper FBI agent."

"I am a proper FBI agent, Gordy. And you're not

telling me everything. It's not smart. You're out of the loop on investigations. You don't know who the players are anymore. You need to be straight with me about what's going on with the Deverells, antiquities and these stolen mosaics."

"The Sharpes? Want me to be straight with you about them, too? Your grandfather, your parents, your brother?"

"Whatever you have, whatever you suspect—I want it."

His expression softened. "I wish I had anything relevant to give you."

"Let me decide what's relevant. You just talk. You can start with the truth about this so-called trip on the steps while you were out for a cigarette."

"I told you what happened. Call the Boston cops if you want. See if someone reported witnessing an attack last night."

Emma decided not to tell him that Sam Padgett was doing that now.

"Relax, Emma," Gordy added. "The open house is Saturday. I'll be out of your hair by Sunday."

"I hope I don't need to remind you that you aren't here in any official capacity."

"You don't." He sighed heavily, a touch of self-pity in the shake of his head. "I'm here because I decided to accept an invitation to an open house held by your family. I took a side trip to London and heard some gossip. I'm not interfering in an ongoing investigation or anything else. I know the rules. I'm straight as an arrow and square as a box."

Their server returned with their bowls of chowder

and a basket of warm rolls, asked if they needed anything else, then took off.

"Look, you're right," Gordy said, reaching for a roll. "I haven't told you everything, but what I'm keeping to myself has nothing to do with an investigation, old, new or ongoing. It's personal. A lesser agent than you wouldn't even be able to tell I was holding back. Maybe you'll understand when you have to leave the job. If you don't separate your identity from the work…" He growled, disgusted, impatient, and set his roll on his bread plate. "Never mind."

Emma picked up her spoon. She didn't know if Gordy was flattering and manipulating her, or leveling with her, but suspected it was a combination. "Now that you're here, do you believe you overreacted or misinterpreted what you heard in London?"

"Polite way to ask if I'm getting old, rusty and crusty."

"Stop, Gordy. Please. You're the one who came to my office this morning. You'd be doing exactly what I'm doing if you were in my place."

He stared out the window at the fog. "Do you think MI5 was playing me?"

"I have no reason to believe anyone's playing you." Emma dipped her spoon into her chowder, avoiding the chunks of fish and potatoes and going for just the milky broth. She couldn't let Gordy get the better of her. "What about Claudia Deverell? The Norwoods had a special passion for ancient mosaics."

"Is MI5 after her, you mean? Planted the rumors about stolen mosaics to see what they'd smoke out?" Gordy buttered half his roll and took a bite, chewed, swallowed. "That's a damn good roll. Anyway, I'm not in a position to know what the Brits are up to. That's why I came to you." He finished the rest of his half roll and picked up his spoon, tried the chowder. "Damn. That's good stuff. Let's eat, Emma. Tell me about your wedding."

She hesitated but decided to answer. "We're having the ceremony in one of the gardens at the Sisters of the Joyful Heart convent."

"That's great. I'm happy for you." He sounded sincere. "Don't worry. I don't expect to be invited. Did you wear a habit when you were with the good sisters with the joyful hearts?"

"Gordy."

"Well, did you?"

"A modified habit. Gray or brown."

He made a face. "Brown's not your color."

"My time with the sisters is in the past. Where were you at nineteen?"

"University of North Carolina. I wanted to be an FBI agent even then." He scooped up a clam with his spoon. "I had a hell of a career."

"You should be proud," Emma said.

"I wouldn't want to tarnish my legacy now, would I? Is that what you're trying to say?"

"Let me be as clear as I can be. If you have evidence or suspicion of a crime having been committed, or a crime that is about to be committed, tell me. If the FBI can't investigate, I'll get the information to the proper authorities who can." She took in a breath. "Gordy, I'm on your side."

"Thanks, kid. I appreciate that. I'm sorry I got you worked up. I'll say hi to any old friends at the open house and go home quietly to my wife and grandkids."

"You went to a lot of trouble to fly to London."

"It was something to do."

"Alessandro Pearson also fell."

"After he had a heart attack. I fell trying to light a cigarette. Give me a break, Emma. Two out-of-shape old farts taking headers doesn't mean anything. There's nothing suspicious about Pearson's death."

"Did you know him?"

"I talked to him once or twice in the last few months before I retired. I was working on a case involving fraudulent antiquities. I thought it might lead somewhere interesting, but it led to…" Gordy shrugged. "Fraudulent antiquities. Well, not even there. We never made an arrest. You know how it is."

"True."

"Claudia helped with background. I got good stuff out of her. She knows antiquities and that world—the collectors, the dealers, the archaeologists, the middlemen, the controversies, the snobs and the frauds. It's in the file. You can look it up." He tore open a small bag of oyster crackers and dumped them into his steaming clam chowder, then pointed to her crackers. "You're not eating those?"

"Chowder with one of Hurley's warm rolls is enough for me."

"That's why you're still trim and fit. I should have had a salad instead of crackers and rolls."

"Just enjoy yourself, Gordy." Emma slid her package of crackers across the table to him. "Claudia was in Ireland last week visiting a distillery owned by friends of mine."

"The Brackens," Gordy said. "Touring a whiskey distillery isn't a crime."

"Then you knew she was in Ireland?"

"Yeah. She told me." He tore open her crackers, too. "How did you find out?"

Emma dipped her spoon into her chowder, capturing a thick chunk of haddock. She decided on a partial answer to Gordy's question. "I heard through a garda detective I know there."

"You know a lot of interesting people." He held up a hand. "Not criticizing."

"I do know a lot of people."

"As a Sharpe and a federal agent. The Sharpe friends and acquaintances maybe are the most interesting. You're friends with the Brackens. Claudia was on her way here. She has a history with your family. I imagine she was just curious."

"My grandfather's in Dublin, not Killarney."

"Maybe she stopped in Dublin, too," Gordy said.

"How would she know about the Brackens? For that matter, how do you know?"

"No idea about Claudia, but I've kept track of some of your recent goings-on. It's not that hard to find out about them."

"Which recent goings-on are we talking about, Gordy?"

"Last fall you and your now-fiancé got mixed up in the investigation into a missing American in Declan's Cross. That caught my eye, since it's where our serial art thief pulled off his first heist—at least the first one we know about. Not a US federal crime, obviously, but his hits in Dallas and San Francisco were."

"Did Claudia visit Declan's Cross while she was in Ireland?"

"Don't know." Gordy dumped the second bag of

crackers in his chowder. "I suspect her trip had more to do with memories about her mother and your family than with the Brackens or our serial art thief. Probably got stirred up because of the open house and coming back here, putting her place on the market."

"Have you spoken with Claudia since you've been in Boston?" Emma asked.

He glanced at her, a grudging note of respect in his look. "This afternoon, as a matter of fact. I ran into her at a gallery in Boston that sells antiquities and contemporary mosaic art, which I'm guessing you already know since you've got the bit in your teeth. Yank tell you to find out what I'm up to?"

Emma ignored his question. "Where's Claudia now?"

"In Heron's Cove, I imagine. Talk to her if you want, Emma. Talk to your grandfather and brother. If anything's going on, I'm not going to be much help." He settled back and ate some of his chowder. "You found a murdered nun at your old convent. That's how you met Colin."

Emma nodded. "Sister Joan."

"I'm sorry."

His comment—the note of empathy—took her by surprise. She and Sister Joan hadn't had the easiest of relationships, but her murder had been shocking and unexpected, a mad, violent act by a merciless killer.

"I should have gotten to her in time to stop—"

"Don't do that to yourself," Gordy said, interrupting. "You know better."

Emma smiled. "That's the Special Agent Wheelock I know."

He put down his spoon and reached for another roll.

"The truth is, Emma," he said deliberately, thoughtfully, as he broke open the roll, "I've been in limbo. My head knows I'm retired. My heart doesn't. The invitation to the open house on Saturday reminded me that I had some unfinished business of my own. Emotional business. Nothing involving cases." He set his roll on his plate, staring at it as if it could help him somehow. Finally he looked up. "I let myself get worked up over nothing. I don't want to waste limited time and resources. Don't you follow my lead and get worked up over nothing, too."

"You've reconsidered since you came to see me this morning?"

"It was stupid. I was trying to feel important again. I see that now. I never thought I'd fall into that trap, but I did." He grabbed his knife and smeared butter on the roll. "Will you be at the open house as an FBI agent or a Sharpe?"

"I'm always an FBI agent, Gordy."

"You're always a Sharpe, too." He winked at her. "Sorry. I'm glad to know I can still get under someone's skin."

Emma helped herself to a roll, too. She didn't believe everything he was telling her, but she changed the subject and asked to see pictures of his grandchildren. He got out his phone and went through his family photo gallery with her, telling her about each shot. His face lit up as he named each child and described their lives in North Carolina, but there was something else, too. At first Emma thought he was just a little homesick. Then she realized what she saw in him was a mix of longing, regret and a kind of fatalism she sometimes witnessed in cornered perpetrators.

Whether it was fatigue, physical pain or guilt, the photos left no question in her mind that Gordy Wheelock was in emotional turmoil.

He put away his phone and they finished their chowder. Finally, Emma pushed back her empty bowl and looked up at Gordy. "All right. Now that you have a full tummy, you can tell me why you flew to Ireland on Monday."

"Ha. Good one. You get me all teary-eyed over the grandkids and then pounce." His obvious irritation was laced with grudging appreciation. "Who told you about Ireland? This Irish detective? Never mind. I have nothing to hide. I wanted to see Declan's Cross. I only saw photos when I was working the serial art-thief case. You weren't kidding when you said it's a tiny village. I drove through, saw the O'Byrne house—now quite the boutique hotel—and drove into Ardmore. I had lunch, oohed and aahed over the round tower and Saint Declan ruins, then drove to Killarney and did a short tour of Bracken Distillers."

"Why that particular distillery, Gordy?"

"Come on, Emma. Why do you think? I know you and your fiancé are friends with the co-founder, your Irish priest, Father Bracken."

"That's it?"

"And I knew Claudia Deverell had been there last week, but I wasn't checking up on her."

Emma was silent. Gordy stared out at the dark harbor, but she doubted he was taking in the shadows, the silhouettes of boats at their moorings, the dots of lights on the shore or even his own reflection in the window.

"I don't believe you, Gordy. It's time you leveled with me."

"Yeah, yeah. You're right. I've danced around this enough." He exhaled, settling back in his chair. "I feel responsible for Claudia's falling-out with your brother—they had a good thing going, or starting, when I barged into her life. I scared the hell out of her. I was convinced I was about to break open a network that sold illicit antiquities to unsuspecting or indifferent buyers and then used the profits to fund terrorists. It's the terrorists I wanted, not the buyers. Claudia had knowledge I needed."

"You keep saying *I*, not *we*."

"I was at the end of my career. I pushed hard."

"You threatened Claudia?"

"Not overtly. She's protective of her family's reputation. Any hint of wrongdoing would hurt. Sharing her expertise with the FBI was tricky enough, but being under investigation herself, even for an innocent screwup…well, she knew the damage that could cause. Lucas sniffed out trouble and didn't want anything to do with Claudia after that. He has his own reputation to protect."

Emma scooped crumbs off the table with her hand and dumped them into her empty bowl. "None of this is in your files," she said.

"I know. The investigation didn't pan out. I retired. Claudia moved on with her life. Then I got this invitation to the open house…" He sighed deeply, clearly exhausted. "That's all more than you need to know or I need to tell you. I haven't done a damn thing wrong, Emma, except waste your time and not admit that I tripped while out for a smoke. Speaking of which, I still have a hell of a headache. I'm skipping pie and calling it a night."

Emma watched as he pushed back his chair. "Where are you staying?"

"Fleabag self-catering cottages in Heron's Cove. I bet they'll get torn down soon. They're very un–Heron's Cove. Thought about staying someplace in Rock Point but there are too many armed Donovans here." He grinned, his lame humor back. "I did my research."

"You should have told me you were coming and needed a place to stay."

"I'd be welcome at your place with a couple of honeymooners? Or do you have separate bedrooms, being an ex-nun with a priest as a friend? Here I go, out of line again." He chuckled to himself. "This place is great. Looks like a dump but it has decent food. I hate to skip pie but I'll be in Maine a couple of days. I'll have another chance."

Emma kept her gaze on him. "Gordy, you're one of the finest agents I've ever known. If you're hiding something, protecting someone, tell me now and let's figure it out."

"I don't need to wear a tie to the open house, do I?"

"I don't care what you wear," she said.

"I've pissed you off. I think that's a first for me." He got to his feet, giving a small groan as he stretched his lower back. "I'm turning in early. I'm stiff, sore and beat. I'll see you, kid."

He reached for his wallet but Emma shook her head. "I'll buy you dinner."

"I'll let you," he said, then walked around the table and touched her shoulder. "Don't worry, okay? If I had anything, I'd give it to you. See you Saturday."

"Stay in touch, Gordy."

She wasn't sure he'd heard her as he left the restaurant. She debated pie—not whether to indulge but which kind to order. It was early in the season when it came to fresh fruit pies. That, she decided, justified a slice of Hurley's famous—or infamous—chocolate fudge pie.

Once she put in her order, she called Sam Padgett and reported what she'd learned from Colin and then Gordy. "Do you have anything new?" she asked when she finished.

"Filling in some blanks. Agent Wheelock arrived in Boston from London at six thirty last night and stayed at the hotel near the New England Aquarium, ahead of his meeting with you this morning. Backtrack to last week. He flew to London on Thursday night, arriving early Friday morning, and left on Monday morning, flying to Cork and then back from Cork to London on Wednesday and on to Boston. The Ireland flights weren't part of his original bookings."

"This confirms what the Brackens and Sean Murphy told Colin."

"You believe Wheelock's story about why he made the side trip to Ireland?"

"I don't know, Sam. He's mixing truth, half truths and probably a few outright lies. I'm concerned he's working a personal agenda and it's at least close to infringing on something to do with us and he knows it."

"Freelancing. Great. He can muck things up without crossing the line."

"He can also get himself hurt," Emma added.

"Or arrested. I checked with BPD. They don't have reports of other muggings near Gordy's hotel Wednesday night. I'll take a look around tomorrow morning,

see if I can find any steps or if he made them up."
Sam was silent a moment. "This is Gordon Wheelock,
Emma. I didn't have any contact with him before he
retired, but I knew of him."

"I know, Sam. This stinks. Thanks."

"Are you at that place that looks like it's about to
fall in the water?"

"I am. My pie has just arrived."

"Can't go wrong with pie."

One of her rules in life was to avoid eating pie alone,
but, fortunately, thirty seconds after she hung up with
Sam, Finian Bracken entered the restaurant and joined
her at her table—which, of course, everyone in Rock
Point now thought of as his table. He wore a clerical
collar and black suit, looking as if he'd come straight
from hospital visitations or one of his other priestly duties. Colin insisted their Irish friend looked like Bono,
but Emma didn't see the resemblance. Half his parish
was in love with their handsome Irish priest, with his
angular features and midnight-blue eyes. Didn't matter that most of them were white-haired.

"Good to see you, Emma," he said, kissing her on
the cheek.

"You, too. Have you had dinner? I've had chowder
but, as you can see, I'm now about to indulge in pie."

"I've not had dinner. Chowder sounds grand." He
settled into his chair. "We also have a new Bracken
Distillers expression to try."

Emma smiled. "Chowder, pie and Bracken whiskey it is."

11

After Finian finished his bowl of clam chowder and Emma her half slice of chocolate fudge pie, he poured one finger each of the Bracken Distillers twelve-year-old into two glasses and slid one across the table to Emma. "A *taoscán* for you and a *taoscán* for me," he said, using the Irish word his grandfather had taught him. "Declan and I put this expression into the casks ourselves. It seems so long ago. He says it's as smooth and beautiful as we dreamed it would be."

"You haven't tried it yet?"

He shook his head and peered at his dinner companion. "I can see you have a lot on your mind, Emma." He eyed the whiskey without yet tasting it. "The copper gold color bodes well. I wish I'd been there when Declan bottled the first cask. That's always an exciting time for a distillery. We've been waiting all this time for the casking to mature. It seems like an eternity but twelve years in the whiskey world isn't a long time." He smiled at Emma. "Casking to make a new spirit is my favorite part of the whiskey business."

"What kind of casks did you use?"

Finian didn't answer at once. She was obviously trying to keep the strain she was under from affecting their conversation. Perhaps, he thought, talking about whiskey would help her unwind more than any probing questions from him. "Bourbon casks sourced through the Speyside cooperage," he said. "The whiskey business is even more competitive now than it was when we chose the casks. We knew the whiskey would be good. A good few *taoscáns* were sampled along the way to the bottling." He raised his glass. *"Sláinte."*

Emma gave him a half-hearted smile and raised her glass. *"Sláinte."*

Finian knew her as a careful, limited drinker, not simply because she was an FBI agent but because of her personal taste. He took a sip, savored the roundness on the palate, the gentle sweetness, and waited for the finish, long and maity, with a tease of early summer honey. The twelve-year-old was everything Declan had promised, and everything he and Finian had dreamed of in a different day.

"It's good," he pronounced, setting his glass on the table. "The fifteen-year-old is special, indeed, both the peated and unpeated expressions, but this is as special in its own way."

Emma tasted hers, with the slight look of surprise and uncertainty she had when tasting whiskey. "I see what you mean. It was worth the wait. I can't explain why but it makes me think of Ireland."

Finian suspected that wasn't the idle remark she wanted him to believe it was. He envisioned the old distillery in the Kerry hills that he and Declan had bought in ruins and transformed into a thriving business. In the years since Finian had entered seminary and the priesthood, Declan had expanded Bracken Distillers, establishing it as a quality independent brand—ever with the unwavering conviction that his twin brother would return. *You'll be back here making whiskey one day, Fin. I know you will. That's your true calling.*

Whatever the case, Finian was following this path he was on, wherever it took him. Right now it had taken him across the Atlantic to a small fishing village, where he was presently enjoying whiskey with a troubled FBI agent.

"Sean Murphy phoned earlier," Finian said. "He told me about Mary's encounter with Oliver York in Declan's Cross. I can understand why you look preoccupied."

"Have you spoken with Mary?"

"I rang her but didn't reach her. She's in Dublin— she's staying at Aoife's studio. And no," he added, "I haven't spoken with Aoife, either." A tender subject she was, too, Finian thought. He and beautiful, intense, artistic Aoife had shared a mad weekend together in Declan's Cross in the blur between the deaths of his wife and daughters and his call to the priesthood.

"Did Sean mention his visit with Colin at the distillery?"

Finian nodded without comment. Colin's trip to Ireland was to have been a secret between the two of them.

"Have you spoken to Colin?" Emma asked, her deep green eyes on Finian.

"Not in weeks," he said.

She reached for her water glass. "Declan's Cross was a bit of a detour for Mary if she was on her way from Killarney to Dublin. Was she on distillery business?"

"She wasn't there to see Oliver. She didn't know he was at the O'Byrne House, at least according to Sean and Kitty both. You've heard Mary's arriving tomorrow for a visit? I haven't had a chance to tell you. I haven't seen you since we made plans."

"You're welcome to make plans to see your sister without telling me."

Finian found Emma's obvious tension disconcerting, in part because she was typically steady and analytical, but mostly because they were discussing his family and friends. But there was something else, too. He observed the tightness about her and wondered about Sean's call—what his garda friend had left out more than what he'd said. There'd been more to the call than a friend checking in with him ahead of his sister's visit.

"I hope you know you can talk to me anytime, Emma," he said quietly.

"Thank you."

For now, perhaps it was enough for her to know he was there, as a priest and as a friend. "It looks as if we'll have proper spring weather while Mary is here." Finian glanced out the windows at the darkened landscape. "Spring comes later to the Maine coast than I expected. She says she's looking forward to staying with me at the rectory. She hasn't stepped foot in a church since her confirmation, one with a roof, at least. She loves exploring church ruins."

"Was that why she was out at the ruins in Declan's Cross today?"

"I imagine so," Finian said, studying the young

woman across from him. "Emma, I realize Oliver York doesn't live his life on the straight-and-narrow, but he isn't dangerous, is he? You'd tell me if you were concerned he would harm Mary or anyone else."

"I'm sorry," Emma said, sitting straight. "I didn't mean to alarm you."

Finian felt some of his own tension ease. Her vigilance and suspicion were contagious, but she had a more benevolent attitude toward the English mythologist and art thief than either her fiancé or their garda detective friend—not that any of them had overtly confirmed to Finian that Oliver was a thief.

"When did you last hear from Oliver?" Emma asked.

"Last week."

She was clearly surprised. "When last week?"

"Tuesday or Wednesday. He phoned to tell me he'd scored one of the last bottles of the peated Bracken fifteen-year-old. He was proud of himself, but I don't think that's why he called. He wasn't his usual cheeky self. I chalked it up to fatigue and a touch of melancholy brought on by memories and whiskey."

"Did he mention where he was?"

"No, and I didn't ask. He and I aren't good friends, Emma." Finian knew he didn't have to explain the endless complexities and peculiar charms of the wealthy, isolated, solitary Englishman. "I asked him if he'd been in touch with you. He said the last thing he needed was the bloody FBI breathing down his neck. His words. He said he had his hands full with MI6, or maybe it was MI5. I thought he was joking, but he wasn't, was he?"

"It's hard to say with Oliver."

One of her studied nonanswers. "Have you spoken with Oliver yourself?"

"Earlier today."

"Sean said Oliver returned to London."

"Yes."

A relief, Finian thought—even if a temporary one, since Oliver did have a way of getting about if he so desired. He'd been using an assumed name, Oliver Fairbairn, when they'd all first met him last autumn.

Emma tried more of her whiskey, grimacing in that way she had when sipping spirit. "Definitely smooth, but you're the expert." She set down her glass, her whiskey drinking clearly at an end for the evening. "What do you and Mary have planned to do while she's here?"

Finian launched into the sketchy plans for his sister's visit, but he was keenly aware that Emma was in no way off duty. It was as if she were waiting for him to drop some tidbit, or accidentally answer a question she didn't want to ask outright. But he couldn't for the life of him imagine what Mary Bracken, who'd never been to the US and worked in an independent family Irish whiskey distillery, could know or have done to interest the FBI.

When they finished their chat—and Finian his *taoscán* of the twelve-year-old—he walked with Emma up from the harbor to Colin's house. She remained tight, restless and tense, unusual for a woman who was typically analytical and in control.

The evening was cool and quiet, the air clearing with nightfall. Perhaps it was opening the twelve-year-old or his sister's imminent visit, but Finian felt out of place and far, far from home—and yet, inexplicably, he didn't question he was where he was called to be. His twin brother and his youngest sister, he knew, would never understand.

"The fog's lifted sooner than I expected," Emma said as they navigated the narrow residential streets of the small fishing village. "It's a beautiful night, isn't it, Fin?"

"It is." He smiled, welcoming her use of his first name. His friendship with Colin was more natural, had come easily to them both. It was different with Emma, in part because of her past as a religious sister. But it *was* the past, and he considered her a friend.

But her lighter mood didn't last, and she was again preoccupied when they reached the house she and Colin shared. "Good night, Fin," she said. "Thank you for the company—and the new Bracken whiskey."

"Anytime. You know where to find me if you need anything."

She smiled. "I do. Thank you."

Finian entered the rectory through the front door and noticed at once how chilly it was. He'd left early that morning and had been lulled into the fine spring weather and hadn't shut the windows. With the fog and now nightfall, the temperature had dropped. But he didn't mind. After almost a year in Rock Point, he was comfortable with the changeable weather and his tidy, comfortable home next to St. Patrick's Holy Roman Catholic Church. Built in the 1890s, the house needed work, but he appreciated its nods to decades past—original moldings, old-fashioned light switches, 1960s wood paneling in the den.

The dining room beckoned with its stillness and shadows. To welcome him to Rock Point, the church ladies had covered the table with an Irish lace cloth. He had yet to use the table. He always ate in the kitchen, even when he had company, which he seldom did.

Mary would be fine eating in the kitchen.

Finian shuddered at the thought of his youngest sister encountering Oliver York up by the ruins in Declan's Cross.

Had she *followed* the Englishman?

Leaving the question hanging, Finian went into the kitchen and put on a kettle to boil. The small electric kettle had been his purchase. He made Irish Breakfast tea and took it with him into the den. With the five-hour time difference, it was too late in Ireland to ring his sister again. Phoning her at this hour would only stir up trouble. It would be impossible to convince her a middle-of-the-night call was casual, no worries.

Oliver could have concealed his presence in Declan's Cross if he'd wanted to. He had the skills and brazenness to slip into secured museums, businesses and homes and steal art. Slipping into a small Irish village without being seen would pose no problems.

Finian poured his tea and sat at the kitchen table. He could phone Aoife O'Byrne, who often worked late into the night, but that was the long hand of temptation touching him.

Best not to think about Aoife, much less contact her.

He could get up early and check in with Mary before her flight.

He was halfway through his tea when his phone vibrated next to him on the table, signaling an incoming text message.

It's true, then. Mary is visiting you in Maine?

Finian grimaced when he saw the message was from Oliver York. He typed his response. Yes. Where are you?

London. I walked with Mary in Declan's Cross this morning.

I heard. Pure coincidence?

No. Speak with her.

Finian didn't have a chance to send a message before another came from the Englishman.

Be well, my friend. Yours ever, Oliver.

Finian almost rang him anyway, but he knew Oliver would communicate only on his terms. If he'd wanted to talk, he'd have called. Finian felt like throwing his phone but settled for placing it firmly back on the table.

Should he ring Emma about Oliver's texts?

No, not tonight. There was nothing in them that she didn't already know. Mary had little if any interest in art or even the theft at the O'Byrne house a decade ago that had launched Oliver's career as an accomplished art thief. She was curious by nature, and she longed for adventure—and she worried about him, the brother she didn't understand.

Finian got up and brought his tea dishes to the kitchen.

He reminded himself that Mary was a capable, professional woman who managed her life perfectly well without his interference. She'd been in college, studying business, when his wife and two small daughters had died. He'd disappeared after the unfathomable tragedy, first into grief and whiskey, then into seminary and now the priesthood—a small parish on the southern Maine coast.

I feel abandoned, Fin. We all do.

Mary had never been one to hide her true feelings, or to keep them to herself.

Finian's gaze fell to a shelf by the table, at the framed photograph of the five Bracken siblings and their parents on their south Kerry farm. He and Declan had been seventeen, filled with their dreams, their lives before them. Their parents had gone to God too soon: their mother struck by cancer, their father by a heart attack and a stubborn refusal to see a doctor, particularly after the tragic deaths of his two small granddaughters. Caught up in his own grief and self-destruction, Finian had failed to see that his father wasn't taking care of himself. But truth be told, his father had hidden from all five of his children that he was hurrying himself into the grave.

Finian had been a time bomb himself in those dark days after his wife—his dear Sally—and their little Mary and Kathleen had started their sailing holiday without him. Busy with work, he'd intended to join them, but their reunion was never to be, at least not in this life.

He believed his mother, also named Mary, for her mother, had greeted her daughter-in-law and granddaughters in heaven.

His youngest sister had told him she believed no such thing.

He returned to the dining room and the cabinet

where he kept the Bracken 15, the last of the peated expression he'd casked all those years ago, before tragedy, before the thefts in Declan's Cross, before he'd heard of the Sharpes and the Donovans or had ever met an FBI agent, an English thief or the O'Byrnes on the south Irish coast.

12

Gordy dropped his things at his cottage after driving around Heron's Cove and trying to talk some sense into himself. He hadn't been straight with Emma and she knew it, but what could he do? He was caught between the proverbial rock and hard place.

It was early in the season and no one was at the two other cottages on the property, located in the marshes and woods a half mile from the more picturesque and desirable Heron's Cove waterfront on Ocean Avenue. His cottage had one bedroom, a bathroom and a combination kitchen and living room, with lobster buoys and cheesy paintings of lighthouses on the white-painted walls. But the place was clean, convenient and quiet, and that worked for him.

He didn't stay. Joan would tell him he was a worm in hot ashes.

His throat tightened with emotion. He should never have taken Claudia's call last week. Should have hung up on her when he did pick up. Should never have gone to London. Should have bowed out of attending the Sharpe open house.

So many should-haves the past year and a half. Before that—before attractive, alluring Claudia Norwood Deverell—he'd lived and worked by the book. Right and wrong. Do or don't.

But his behavior wasn't Claudia's fault. It was his own.

"Love you, Joanie," he whispered as he went back outside, shivering since it was spring in Maine and not spring in North Carolina.

He left his car in the pitted dirt driveway of his cabin and walked toward Ocean Avenue, expecting he'd turn around before he reached the water. As he'd thought, Claudia hadn't shown up after her conference call—if there'd even been a conference call. He'd finally gone down the hall in her friends' apartment and checked the bedroom. He hadn't found a suitcase, cosmetics, shoes—she'd been packed and ready to go when he'd walked into the gallery.

He had her cell phone number and had debated texting her she needn't have bothered giving him the slip. What could he do to her? *He* was the one who'd done wrong, whose reputation was on the line. She was his victim.

Unless he could prove she was involved in the world of so-called blood antiquities.

But it wouldn't matter. He'd still be the FBI agent who'd stepped over the line.

He'd left the apartment keys on a kitchen counter and rented a car for the drive to Maine. At one point in the past week of emotional lurches and delusions, he'd envisioned driving up here with Claudia.

"Idiot," he muttered.

The action wasn't in Boston, anyway. Claudia might

be persona non grata with Lucas Sharpe, but she was in Heron's Cove and her father and brother would be at the Sharpe Fine Art Recovery open house on Saturday.

Gordy had tucked the incriminating photos in an inner jacket pocket. He hadn't figured out what to do with them. He'd let himself get caught up in too many fantasies—things he didn't even want if push came to shove but that nonetheless had him in their grip. He told himself he was trying to make things right, but was he? Then why had he thought about Claudia's smile on the flight to London, imagined her welcoming him with a hug and a kiss, the promise of more sweet nights together?

And how could he make anything right? What was done was done.

Maybe he'd heed the warning and go home. It wasn't his fight anymore. It was up to young agents like Emma Sharpe to prevent ancient art and cultural artifacts ending up funding murderous scumbags and their plots, their bombs and their missiles, guns and ammunition.

He could feel the freshness of the breeze off the water and see a few lights in the summer homes up ahead. He liked it here. Heron's Cove reminded him of Cabot Cove on *Murder, She Wrote*. His mother had loved Jessica Fletcher. He could imagine himself retiring here. He wasn't crazy about the condo complex in North Carolina where he and Joan lived now, but it was close to the kids and she liked being back "home." It had amenities—beach, pool, tennis, health club, access to a golf course. He needed to get off his butt and enjoy himself.

He walked down a single-lane road between two

large summer homes. He could see stars glittering on
the horizon, their light glistening on the dark ocean
waters. On a knoll to his left, the Norwood-Deverell
summer home was lit up inside and outside, as if its
occupants were afraid of the dark out here on the southern Maine coast, far from their lives in London, New
York, Atlanta and Philadelphia. Later in the season,
there'd be more people around, but as Gordy crossed
Ocean Avenue to the water, he saw only a few houses
with any lights on.

A movement caught his eye, and he paused, shoving his hands in his pockets as he recognized Claudia
in a window, laughing with her brother, Adrian, who
was as successful in Atlanta real estate as his father
was in Philadelphia real estate.

Isabel Greene was standing on the porch smoking
a cigarette. She was facing northeast, as if something
had caught her eye farther up the street. Gordy doubted
she saw him. He fought an urge to join her and bum a
cigarette. He'd tossed the pack he'd bought last night.

He glanced up at the window to the sunroom where
he and Claudia had made love.

Figured it was one of the few that remained dark.

He followed Ocean Avenue down to Wendell
Sharpe's old house, now the state-of-the-art offices
of Sharpe Fine Art Recovery. When he'd been here
last year, Gordy hadn't stopped to say hi to Lucas or
whoever else was around. He'd rationalized his trip to
Heron's Cove as work-related, but there was no way he
could rationalize screwing Claudia Deverell.

He cut through a parking lot by the inn next door
and walked down to the docks on the tidal river. A
breeze had kicked up, and he could hear waves beat-

ing against boats and wooden posts and washing onto the riverbank with its polished stones.

"Special Agent Wheelock." Wendell Sharpe emerged from the shadows up by the marina next door to the Sharpe house. "As I live and breathe."

Gordy grinned. "For however long you live and breathe. You're scrawnier than ever, Wendell. All those years worrying about messing up and ruining your reputation keeping you spry?"

"I don't know about spry but I don't feel a day over eighty."

"You've developed a sense of humor now that you've retired. I've often imagined what I'd find if I turned over all the rocks in your past and saw what squirmed out from under them."

"A few things I don't know are there, no doubt. The odd corrupt FBI agent, perhaps?"

Gordy let that one go. Wendell looked younger than his years. He wore a lightweight jacket unzipped over a dark turtleneck, khakis and boat shoes, looking maybe less at home here on the coast than when Gordy had seen him last in Dublin. That could be the circumstances, running into an FBI agent who reminded him of days gone by.

"We worked okay together for a long time," Gordy said. "Well, not 'together.' You had your interests and I had mine."

"Still do," Wendell said. "Lucas is here. Care to join us for a nightcap?"

"No, thanks. I'm just out for an evening stroll."

"I understand you were in London last week. I was there early in the week for Alessandro Pearson's funeral. I believe you knew Alessandro."

"Not well enough to attend his funeral," Gordy said, keeping any sarcasm out of his tone.

"He was a scholar and that I'm not. I'd already planned to stop in London to see Tim and Faye before I came here. You saw them, didn't you?"

"You know I did, Wendell." Gordy inhaled deeply, noting the faint scent of salt in the air. Stronger was the smell of dead fish. Maybe it was seaweed. He'd grown up on the North Carolina coast but had never learned much about the ocean—sand, rocks, tides, clams, crabs and all the rest of it. "I don't know what I'm doing here," he added, half under his breath.

"Oh, I think you do," Wendell said, turning to face the river. "It's a pleasant evening for this time of year. I thought the fog might settle in for the night, but it didn't. The air's different here than in Dublin."

"Have you missed Maine?"

"I miss the people here. The people who were once here."

Gordy felt the older man's nostalgia but tried not to let it worm its way into him. "If I were you, I'd give up Ireland," he said cheerfully. "It's a smaller world these days, but Dublin is still across an ocean and in a different country. This place is great. It's easy to forget what a beautiful part of the world Maine is. You have family here. Lucas has a house in the village, Emma and her fiancé have a house up the road in Rock Point and work in Boston. Your son and his wife won't stay in London forever. Don't they have a house here?"

Wendell nodded without glancing at Gordy. "I like how you have my life all sorted."

"I should work on my own instead?"

"Not for me to say. I was born in Ireland. My folks

immigrated to Boston when I was a tot and we ended up here." Wendell's voice was quiet, steady, as if he'd been out here contemplating the past. "They loved Heron's Cove. They worked hard. I was damn lucky, Gordy. Damn lucky."

"They'd be proud of you," he said, meaning it.

"Maybe. I don't know. They believed in an honest day's work, I'll say that." He pulled his gaze from the river and glanced back at the Sharpe house, up above the docks, a light on over the back porch. "My wife and I used to have a glass of wine out on the back porch, rain or shine, cold or warm. Her insights were always spot-on. Even with the renovations, every inch of this place still reminds me of her."

"Is that good or bad?"

"It just is."

Gordy thought of his own wife back in North Carolina. He wanted to call her. He wanted to hear her voice. He felt the weight of the photos in his jacket pocket. He needed to burn those bastards first.

He watched a dinghy bob in the waves. "I'll bet your wife kept you from walking into walls and blind alleys," he said to the old man next to him.

"Constantly." Wendell's voice lightened, and he seemed to pull himself out of his reflective mood. "I learned so much from her and always benefited from her insights. Tim has her analytical abilities. So does Emma, but she employs them with the Feds rather than the family business."

"She's good, Wendell."

"Yeah. I know. Lucas is more like me, except he doesn't have my rougher edges. Grew up in a different Heron's Cove than I did."

"You're all closemouthed," Gordy said.

"Part of the job."

"I just had chowder with Emma. It turned my stomach. Should have ordered the fish chowder like she did. I think I'm developing a thing with shellfish."

Wendell scrutinized him. "Sure it was the chowder?"

Gordy ignored him. "She's coming into her own as an agent. It's great she's getting married in a couple of weeks. Did you know the Donovans when you lived here?"

"I bought a lobster or two from them. Otherwise, no, not really."

"Emma's fiancé is probably putting his career on the line marrying a Sharpe. You Sharpes must give Matt Yankowski headaches. Not my problem. Are you staying in town through the wedding?"

"That's my plan."

"That's known as a noncommittal answer," Gordy said.

Wendell gestured toward the marina. "Let's walk. I stiffen up faster than I used to."

The dock was wide enough for them to walk side by side. Up ahead, a decent-size yacht was in the water, ready for the summer. Gordy had kept thinking he would get into boats but he never had. No time. He'd been all about the job.

"Most of the people attending the open house are rolling it into a long weekend or vacation," Wendell said. "You're on your own. Things okay with you and your wife?"

"Yeah. We're getting used to having each other around all the time. Some days I swear I get on her nerves just because she can hear me breathing. To be expected, I guess. I wasn't around a lot the year before I retired. I guess part of me wanted to tie things up in a nice, neat bow, but it's not the nature of the work."

"Treasure this time together with your wife, Gordy."

He tugged on a thick rope tied to a metal hook on a post. "We've been thinking about traveling. It's not too late to do a round-the-world cruise, is it?"

"Hell, no. You're still a young man."

"I like how you think." He let go of the rope and continued walking next to the older man. "Talk to me about Oliver York, Wendell."

"I was waiting for this. Once Tim told me Oliver had been at the party in London…" Wendell sighed. "I'm not sure what I can tell you. I don't know Oliver well."

"Well enough."

"I doubt anyone knows Oliver York well, Gordy."

"Is he our serial international art thief?"

If he'd meant to catch Wendell off guard—and he wasn't sure he had been—he'd failed. Wendell glanced sideways at him. "Why are you asking me? Ask your friends at the FBI."

"They aren't going to tell me if he's under active investigation. Come on, Wendell. Is this guy the one thief the great Wendell Sharpe couldn't catch? He taunted us for a decade. You in particular."

"The thief did, yes. After every theft, I'd receive a tiny, hand-carved stone Saint Declan's cross. Cheeky bastard, whoever he was—and I'm not saying it was Oliver York."

"You're not saying it isn't, either."

"Talk to the FBI, Gordy."

"Right. I'll do that." He eyed Wendell, and for the first time since he'd heard Claudia's voice on the other end of the phone, he felt his old instincts as an agent kick in. He laughed. "I'll be damned, Wendell. This crazy Brit *is* our thief."

"I didn't say that."

Gordy paid no attention to the half-hearted protest. "He wasn't on my radar. Was he on yours? Never mind. I know. Talk to your FBI-agent granddaughter. Obviously we can't make an arrest. What do you know about York's relationship with the British intelligence services?"

"He isn't my problem—or yours, since you're not on the job any longer."

"You're dodging the question. MI5 must be protecting him. He must know things that can help them given his escapades the past decade. He never stole antiquities, though."

Wendell slowed his pace, the breeze catching the ends of his thin gray hair as he turned to Gordy. "I'm retired, too. It does take some getting used to, and I retired in my eighties instead of…what are you, sixty? Sixty-five? You're young, Gordy. Enjoy your life. Find something to do with your interests and skills. Leave the likes of Oliver York to active agents like Emma and whoever took your place in Washington." The old man gave a quick smile. "Not that anyone could replace you."

"Flattering me or mocking me?" Gordy forced a grin. "Don't answer. From what I hear, you're not retired. At best you're semiretired. I'm a simple man, Wendell. If Oliver York's a thief, he should be prosecuted."

"By whom? Who has jurisdiction? Who has the evidence in hand for a successful prosecution? Anyone? Whatever you or I think should or shouldn't happen, there does need to be sufficient evidence to bring him—or anyone—to trial."

"I'd get the evidence if I were still in the saddle."

"Easy to say when you're not in the saddle. The FBI won't waste agents' valuable time on a losing venture. All the stolen art has been safely returned to its owners."

"Everyone's happy and this Oliver York character gets to use his unique skills and insights to play James Bond instead of stealing paintings. Is the FBI using him, too?"

Wendell stood still and fastened his gaze on Gordy. "Whatever you're up to, Agent Wheelock, don't go it alone. Talk to Emma, or to her boss if you don't trust her. I don't need to tell you that ex-agents meddling in current matters often don't have the whole picture."

"They also aren't welcome."

Wendell blinked as if he didn't understand what Gordy was saying. Then he blew out a breath and shook his head. "Blast, Gordy, don't be a fool. You'll get yourself or someone else killed."

"Don't send flowers to my funeral. I'll haunt you."

"Duly noted." Wendell was silent a moment. "Go home, Gordy. Live your life."

"The world has moved on, has it?"

But Wendell was obviously done. He pointed toward the ocean in the distance. "As a boy, I used to think the stars and water met on the horizon. I remember my father explaining why that wasn't the case. This is quite a spot—impressive natural beauty in a quaint village."

He turned abruptly to Gordy, his eyes narrowed to slits. "Are you going to tell me who gave you the beating?"

Gordy realized he'd let his confident facade slip as he and Wendell had walked on the docks. Also, the old guy had gone a round or two with tough guys in his day. "I've been burning the candle at both ends. I'm not as young as I used to be, and I've put on weight in the past year. I'm tired is all."

Wendell shook his head. "You look stiff and sore. It's not age, Gordy. You're not that old, for one thing, but I know the aches and pains of old age. This is different. Someone clock you?"

"I fell down a flight of stairs while I was out for a smoke last night. I hurt myself worse than I thought."

"I've seen a few beatings in my day. Experienced a few, too. I tried to hide a few, too."

"The way it goes sometimes. You wouldn't hire someone to have a go at me, would you, Wendell—or have a go yourself?"

"I'm flattered you consider me up to giving a man twenty years younger a beating. The rest I'll ignore. I don't assault people. Neither does Lucas, if that's your next stupid idea. You should tell Emma you were attacked, or have you already?"

"I shouldn't have said anything. I was speaking hypothetically. I wasn't attacked. I told Emma about the fall. Even if I was attacked—and I wasn't—it's not an FBI matter. Nothing they could do, anyway. Nothing locals could do, either, if I was just in the wrong place at the wrong time and had no description."

"Were you robbed?"

"I tripped, Wendell. I didn't knock myself out but I did go flying."

"That isn't the whole story. What are you leaving out?"

"I almost had a damn heart attack."

"That's what happened to Alessandro," Wendell said quietly.

"Oh, geez, don't go off half-cocked. It was just an expression." Gordy's head was pounding, as if talking about the incident was making it hurt more. "I can take care of myself. Boston isn't my favorite city and tripping last night didn't improve my opinion. You like it?"

"Boston is a great city."

"Ha. Another reason we'll never be good buddies. Good night, Wendell. You still have my cell phone number? Call me if you have any thoughts you'd like to share. I'll see you on Saturday if not before. I wish I'd stayed at an inn with a decent breakfast but I'll make do. My mother never cooked breakfast. We always had cereal out of the box."

"Is she still alive?"

"Lost her two years ago. She had a good, long life, but I guess it's never easy to say goodbye."

"That it isn't."

Nothing in Wendell's expression conveyed whether he was remembering his own mother, a hard-working woman who'd cleaned toilets at the big houses up the street.

"Will Oliver York be here on Saturday?"

"I'm not in charge of the guest list."

Gordy grinned. "Not what I asked, but whatever. You two aren't colluding, are you?"

Wendell zipped up his jacket. "Now look who's going off half-cocked," he said lightly.

"York doesn't need money. He must like the thrill

of stealing. Maybe he gets his jollies out of taunting people like us. Think he's taking advantage of whatever he's doing to stay out of prison to have some fun with his old nemesis Wendell Sharpe?"

"I'm going to watch the stars for a little while. Enjoy your stay in Heron's Cove, Gordy. The place across the street has good lobster rolls if you've a hankering for fresh Maine lobster."

"Yeah. Thanks." Gordy started down the dock, then paused and turned back to Wendell. "By the way, why didn't you tell me Emma had been a nun?"

"It wasn't relevant to our work together," he said. "And we're not buddies."

The old man said nothing, and Gordy went on his way. He was used to working with a team and having clear protocols, but he didn't have to worry about them now, either. He felt like he was flailing, and maybe he was, but he had freedom to maneuver. He could give second chances, and he didn't have to worry about the dangers of personal involvement.

When he arrived back at his cottage, Gordy turned on the overhead light. The place was clean and had a homey, old-fashioned feel to it that appealed to his fatigue and his nostalgic mood. The website said all three cottages had been renovated. He'd take their word for it, but they didn't look that renovated to him. But he didn't care either way. He'd be here for a couple of nights, and the location suited him with its proximity to the Sharpes and the Deverells. He didn't care about being near the picturesque village's inns, shops and restaurants.

He unpacked, took a shower and ate some more

ibuprofen. He'd picked up a fresh bottle before he'd left Boston. His head continued to ache from its close encounter with the stone steps last night. His attacker had done a number on him, more so than Gordy had realized, but he hadn't received further threats since he'd received the photos. He would find a place to burn them and toss the ashes in the ocean. Didn't matter if there were copies or they were on the internet. He didn't want them on *him*.

He was still a ballsy FBI agent. He would fix this.

He called his wife. It was her dinner night with friends but he left a message. "I love you, Joan. I always have, from the seventh grade on. I'm sorry for any of the dumb-ass things I've done over the years. I miss you. I'll be home soon."

He grabbed the envelope with the photographs and went back outside. His scrapes and bruises felt better. Best he could do right now. He went behind the cottage. There was a small brick terrace with a picnic table and an old charcoal grill. Owners might want to add that to the renovations, he thought, as he lifted off the rack. He placed the photos in the grill bed, the image of his bare ass faceup as if to remind him what an absolute toad he'd been. How would he feel if some FBI agent had pulled on his daughter what he'd pulled on Claudia?

He'd been FBI to the core except for that one transgression. But it was enough. Even now, a year later, its discovery would destroy his reputation, endanger his marriage and cause a major scandal for the best law enforcement agency in the world. He'd dedicated his *life* to the FBI.

He managed to set the photos on fire with his

lighter, although it took a few tries because the grill was wet. The flames were easily visible in the dark, but he was well out of range of any passing cars—and there was no foot traffic out here. It was too early in the spring, there was no beach or picturesque rockbound coastline. This wasn't the place for an evening walk.

He was so keyed up, his entire body ached. Who could have taken the photos? Why? Why wait until now to threaten him with them? He didn't want to get sucked into the black hole of speculation but the questions came at him fast and furiously.

Whoever had sent him the incriminating photos likely had copies on a thumb drive or in the cloud somewhere, easily reproduced, but at least this set was no longer in his possession. He had plausible deniability that he'd ever seen them. What more could he do? If someone wanted to put his bare ass on the internet, go for it. It hadn't been a good time in his life, in his marriage. It was easy to forget that.

While the fire died down, he went inside and collected a spatula and a metal saucepan. When he came back out, the ashes were still smoking but he didn't see any flames or red. He scooped up as much of the ashes as he could, dumped them in the pan and got in his car.

He drove to a remote stretch of coast between Heron's Cove and Rock Point, parked and got out. The wind was blowing hard now. Instead of flinging the ashes into the water as he'd planned, he walked down to the rocks and squatted, wincing in pain as he dumped the ashes into the incoming tide. Even so, a few ashes managed to blow up into his face, as if to remind him what he was doing was illegal and wrong—or maybe just to curse him.

When he got back to his cottage, he could barely keep his eyes open.

Time to get some sleep.

He'd start again tomorrow.

13

Emma awoke thinking Colin was next to her. She swore she could feel his weight on the bed, but that wasn't possible. For one thing, she was in the guest room, not the master bedroom down the hall. Her idea, given their upcoming wedding.

She turned over onto her back and meditated—or tried to. Life with a certain undercover agent hadn't had a positive effect on her meditating abilities.

As if to prove her point, her phone buzzed with a text from him. Awake?

She smiled. Yes. Where are you?

Dublin Airport.

She glanced at the time. Five in the morning. It would be 10:00 a.m. in Dublin. With Mary Bracken?

Yes. Home soon.

Be safe.

Emma set her phone on the bedside table. She could get up and go for a run, or she could head to Hurley's for breakfast. It opened early for the lobstermen.

"Or I could do both," she said, throwing back the covers.

She opened the bedroom's small closet to its meager contents. She hadn't moved many of her clothes to Rock Point and had opted against storing anything of hers in the master bedroom. Not yet, at least. That still felt like Colin's space, and, as a practical matter, it would take some serious work to sort through what stayed or went to make room for anything of hers.

And it would take both of them.

She decided against a run and chose a skirt that would see her through the day, including lunch with Colin's mother. Ten minutes later, she was dressed and in the kitchen, sighing at the contents of his refrigerator. Since she hadn't gone shopping, the shelves were as barren as they'd been last night. Hurley's definitely was the best option.

She needed coffee and a game plan. She'd stayed up late after walking back to the house with Fin Bracken and did some research into Gordy's last months on the job. He'd looked into fraudulent antiquities—outright fakes—that had landed up with a New York dealer and used it as an excuse to dig deeper, obviously with the hope he'd unravel a larger network involving terrorists and terrorist funding. Officially, the investigation had withered and died. But Gordy's notes were vague and, she now knew, incomplete.

Whatever he was up to now, there was no suggestion he'd left behind anything that would have haunted him into retirement—or anything involving antiquities of any description and none involving the Deverells or Sharpe Fine Art Recovery.

He hadn't been forthcoming then and he wasn't being forthcoming now.

Emma felt her frustration mount, as it had last night, in part, she knew, because of Gordy's relationship with her and her family, her grandfather in particular. She'd also checked in with Yank last night. He'd sounded as frustrated as she was.

She went into the front room. The fireplace was cold, unlit since late winter. Evenings were still often cool enough for a fire, but she hadn't bothered on her occasional visits during Colin's frequent absences. He'd only been here a few times since February to light one himself.

Emma fingered a book he'd been reading and had left on a table by the fireplace. A history of Irish whiskey. She smiled. Finian must have loaned it to him.

She returned to the kitchen and headed out through the back door and around to the driveway and her car. It was a beautiful morning, but she decided to drive down to the harbor instead of walking as she had last night. She could pick up a dozen of Hurley's doughnuts after breakfast and take them to Heron's Cove for her brother and grandfather and whoever else was around.

As she pulled into the small lot, her contact at Scotland Yard returned her call. She parked and turned off the engine. The harbor sparkled under the bright morning sun; there wasn't a trace of fog in the air.

After apologizing for not getting back to her sooner, the British detective informed her that he had no report of mosaics of any description having been stolen from a London collector, identified or unidentified.

Any talk to the contrary was just that—talk. He wasn't surprised that guests at a party celebrating a museum show of Mediterranean art and objects from late antiquity would be jabbering about looted, pillaged, stolen, fraudulent and otherwise questionable antiquities.

Emma didn't disagree, although *jabbering* was the Scotland Yard detective's word.

"What about the Deverells?" she asked, deliberately vague.

"Nothing lately. Last year there were a few rumors that Claudia Deverell got mixed up with fraudulent antiquities, but we have no reason to believe she herself committed a crime."

"Alessandro Pearson and Claudia's mother worked together to create training programs for mosaic conservation and preservation," Emma said. "If I may be so bold, I suggest you take another look at his death."

"You may be so bold, but why?"

"Nothing specific."

"Anything to do with one of your own turning up at the London party? I assume you're aware Gordon Wheelock was in town. Interesting that he's surfaced and now you're calling."

"Yes," Emma said, not going further. "What else can you tell me?"

"Your grandfather was at Alessandro Pearson's funeral. Did you know?"

"I did, yes. He's in Maine now. I'm bringing him doughnuts."

"Wish you could bring me doughnuts." The British detective paused. "I'd keep an eye on your grandfather if I were you, Emma. He could be getting dotty. He met with Oliver York while he was in London, and I don't need to tell you about our eccentric mythologist, do I?"

"Are we dancing around something here?"

"Not at all."

"Can you tell me about MI5's presence at Claridge's on Sunday?"

"I've a call I need to take. Please stop by when you're in London next. I'll buy you a pint."

Emma stared at her phone after the detective disconnected. "Well, well."

Decidedly one of those conversations that was more interesting for what hadn't been said than for what had been said. She needed more information. It was possible, however, that Gordy had let his imagination run wild given the combination of Alessandro Pearson's death, the vague rumors about stolen mosaics and recognizing an MI5 contact from his FBI days. Throw in an enigmatic English mythologist/suspected art thief, her grandfather, attractive Claudia Deverell and the Norwood-Deverell family's relationship with the Sharpes, and Gordy had the ingredients for a full-blown conspiracy theory. He could simply have taken the ball and run with it—exaggerated the importance of coincidences and vague rumors, and allowed speculation and drama to propel him to her office.

But that wasn't like the senior agent she'd known and respected, and it didn't explain the bloody towel in his hotel room, the mysterious envelope, his side trip to Ireland or his apparent interest in the Deverells.

Whatever the truth about the various events and rumors of the past couple of weeks, Emma hoped Gordy had gone home. If there was anything to uncover, she'd be the one to do it, and through official channels.

She got out of her car and walked down to the pier. The tide was up and most of the lobster boats typically crowding the harbor were out checking traps. As a teenager, Colin had worked as a lobsterman with his brothers. He'd joined the Maine marine patrol after college and then found his way to the FBI. He'd never expected to do deep-cover work, but Matt Yankowski had seen his potential given Colin's high degree of independence, his quick thinking, his strong, reliable gut instincts. Yank had come to Maine to talk to Colin about that first mission. They'd met here, at Rock Point harbor.

On that same visit, Yank had driven out to the convent where Emma, a young novice, had been on the verge of professing her final vows. He'd made it clear he didn't think she was destined to spend the rest of her life as a religious sister and wanted her in the FBI, but he'd never expected her to fall in love with his deep-cover agent a few short years later.

Emma turned away from the water and headed into Hurley's. Could MI5 have floated the rumors about stolen mosaics? But why would they? Could Oliver York have done it on his own, without their prior approval? Anything was possible with him. Claudia Deverell? Gordy?

Then there was one Wendell Sharpe...

Emma groaned and put her questions aside as she ordered the dozen doughnuts and, on the spur of the moment, coffee to go. Once back in her car, she helped herself to one of the doughnuts—Hurley's doughnuts were a legend on the south coast—and called it breakfast.

She drove to Heron's Cove but discovered her

brother and grandfather were in a meeting. She wanted to talk to them but she wasn't prepared to barge in on clients—and she wasn't, she reminded herself, part of her family's business.

She helped herself to a second doughnut and left the rest with the receptionist.

By midday, Emma didn't have any solid reason to postpone her lunch with Colin's mother. Between one thing and another, they'd canceled and rescheduled several times, but with just a few weeks until the wedding, today was the day.

"Just so happens Colin's thirty thousand feet above the Atlantic," Emma said under her breath as she climbed out of her car. She'd found a spot almost in front of the restaurant, located in a narrow, weather-shingle building in the village of Heron's Cove. Her slim skirt, print top, sweater and simple flats weren't girlie-girl but were dressy enough for a prewedding lunch at one of the area's better restaurants, and respectful of the occasion.

A call from Sam Padgett delayed her entrance into the restaurant. "Oliver York is due to arrive in Boston any minute," Sam said.

"Alone?"

"As far as we know. I just told Yank. Not a happy camper. I suggested he put cold compresses on his forehead to prevent a migraine."

Emma had no reason to doubt Padgett had done exactly that, given his sense of humor. "I have a hunch where Oliver's headed," she said.

"So do I. I'd almost drive up to Maine for that show."

"Are you going to meet him at the airport?"

"On my way there now. You and Yank had the same thought. Scary, isn't it?" Sam didn't wait for an answer. "We'll stay in touch."

They disconnected as Emma entered the restaurant, her mind less on lunch with her future mother-in-law than it had been. Rosemary had arrived first, and Emma joined her at a small window table. A fit and vibrant woman in her sixties, Rosemary kept her dark, graying hair short and undyed, and she had blue eyes, a lighter shade than those of her husband, and a heart-shaped face that tended to soften her features. She was the wife of a retired police officer and the mother of four hardheaded sons who, as she'd told Emma early on, still managed to keep her on her toes. She loved being an innkeeper. It would be a mistake, Emma knew, to underestimate her in any way.

"I bought a pottery vase at the sisters' shop," Rosemary said after she and Emma exchanged a greeting. "Did you ever teach at the studio?"

The restaurant, coincidentally, was across the street from the art shop and studio run by the Sisters of the Joyful Heart. "I never did, no," Emma said. "The sisters didn't have the shop and studio when I was with them, so I was never a teacher."

"Well, it's a lovely vase. It's a simple blue—no wild blueberries or lupine. It's just what we need to perk up the kitchen. I think your friend Sister Cecilia made it."

"I wouldn't be surprised."

Emma noticed Rosemary had also worn a skirt to lunch. She favored classic, functional styles she could keep in her closet for years. She'd once told Emma that fashion trends didn't interest her. She set the bag with her vase on the floor next to her chair. "Sister Cecilia is going to be your only bridesmaid, is that right?"

"That's right," Emma said. "We've become good friends."

"You two met last September after Sister Joan was killed. Awful business that was. Do you have many female friends who aren't nuns, Emma?"

She'd become accustomed to Rosemary's bluntness and took no offense. "I do, and some but not all will be at the wedding. Between the FBI and my family background, my friends are spread all over the world."

"A friend in every port but none to go to a movie with on the odd weeknight. Entering the convent in your late teens must have affected your formation of friendships." Rosemary peered at Emma with an intensity that reminded her of Colin. "And you have no sisters. What about female cousins?"

Emma shook her head. "I have a small family."

"It's hard for me to relate," Rosemary said. "Well, if there's anything I can do to help with the wedding, don't hesitate to ask. I know your mom's in London. I'm right here. By the way, tell her I've decided on blue for my dress at the wedding, unless she's changed her mind about wearing rose."

Emma promised she would relay the message. They ordered lobster bisque, salads and iced tea. Rosemary caught up Emma on Donovan and Rock Point goings-on, including the latest on Mike's security work in Africa, Andy's upcoming trip to Ireland and Kevin's training in Washington. "I assume you've told me what you can about what Colin's been up to," Rosemary said. "He asked us all not to talk about his work."

Given that three of Rosemary's four sons were or

had been involved in the military or law enforcement, Emma expected she had come to accept, if not like, that she wasn't privy to all they did. Until last fall, Colin's family had believed—or pretended to believe—he worked at a desk at FBI headquarters in Washington.

"I had a text from Colin when I got up this morning," Rosemary added, glancing out the window. "He says he'll be back today. You knew?"

"I had a text this morning, too," Emma said without further comment. She didn't want to get into a competition with Rosemary about what Colin told his mother versus his fiancée—and she doubted Rosemary did, either. She was experienced and pragmatic, but, at the same time, she was aware her FBI-agent son operated in a secretive and dangerous world. Emma suspected the question about the text arose more from concern and curiosity than envy she might know more about Colin's work.

Which, Emma thought, she really didn't.

"Having three sons out of town at the same time is strange," Rosemary said. "Mike's in his element protecting those volunteer doctors, but he'll be happy to be back in Maine."

"How's Naomi?"

"Intrepid as ever. She's back in Nashville. She's crazy about Mike but careful not to get too far ahead of herself."

From what Emma had seen of Naomi MacBride, *careful* wasn't really in her vocabulary. Now an independent intelligence analyst based in her hometown of Nashville, she'd worked with Mike in his army days, when she was at the State Department. She was back in Tennessee, having recovered from a knife wound she'd incurred on a wintry Maine day while uncovering a bad operator among her friends in private security. Emma had gotten caught up in that search, too.

"Emma?"

"Sorry. I was thinking about Naomi. I'm glad she's doing well."

"So am I," Rosemary said. "Kevin's due back this weekend. Andy might as well be out of town—he's preoccupied with finishing work on that antique lobster boat that's been such a bone of contention between him and Julianne."

Andy Donovan's on-again, off-again relationship with Julianne Maroney, a Rock Point native, was very much on again. Andy was due to take off any day for Cork, Ireland, where Julianne was completing a graduate-level internship in marine biology. The antique lobster boat in question had once belonged to her grandfather.

"I think Andy's bought Julianne a ring," Rosemary said. "He won't tell me."

The conversation moved to the upcoming wedding of her second-born son. Emma joined her future mother-in-law in indulging in wild blueberry pie, heated, with a scoop of vanilla ice cream. "I had doughnuts for breakfast, too," Emma said. "I should run to Acadia and back this afternoon."

"I've taken up running," Rosemary said cheerfully. "I'm up to thirty minutes without stopping."

"That's great."

"Thank you. I've no interest in running races. Where are you off to after lunch?"

"I'm going to stop at the convent to check out a few things for the wedding."

Rosemary pushed her empty pie plate aside. "The convent gardens will be gorgeous for the wedding. I've been wondering, Emma—did the thought of children enter into your decision to go into the convent?"

"I didn't reject anything. I embraced something, or at least that's what I thought I was doing." Emma paused, debating how to explain—what to say to satisfy Rosemary's curiosity without going too deep. "The process I went through prior to making final vows helped me clarify that I belonged elsewhere."

"The convent wasn't a true calling, you mean? You won't get cold feet about marriage, will you?" Rosemary gasped. "I'm sorry. Forget I asked that. I haven't even had wine. I'll blame the rich food."

Emma smiled. "It's okay. I don't mind saying that I won't get cold feet."

"I believe you and it's wonderful, but it's not okay that I asked. I can hear Colin telling me to mind my own business. He hasn't had much chance for real romance in his life with all the secret stuff he does. I've been patient, but I admit I'm ready for a wedding. Mike and Naomi seem serious about each other. I doubt Andy and Julianne will wait much longer—although it's possible she'll be so mad at him when he pops the question that she'll say no. Kevin's had a revolving door lately." Rosemary sighed, shaking her head. "I don't ask."

Emma gave up on the last of her pie. She'd had enough sweets for the week, never mind the day. "Colin and I are both the first in our families to get married," she said. "It's new territory for all of us."

Rosemary watched a couple with two young children walk past the restaurant window. "Raising four boys didn't exactly put me in a hurry for grandchildren, although they were cute little devils. Mike and Colin took off to the harbor on their own when they were tots. They wanted to get themselves blueberry muffins at Hurley's. The police brought the two miscreants home. I thought Frank would die when he found out, but I thought they'd gone into the water. Muffins didn't seem so bad." She chuckled at the memory and turned back to Emma. "What was your life like growing up?"

"I read a lot. No muffin adventures."

"We're all different," Rosemary said warmly. "I'm delighted you and Colin found each other. Frank and I are here for you, Emma. I want you to know that."

"Thanks, Rosemary. That means a lot to me."

They left the restaurant together. Rosemary paused at her car, the spring sun highlighting the soft lines in her face. "I almost forgot—we're looking forward to having your English friend stay at the inn this weekend. He's arriving later today."

Emma frowned. "My English friend? You don't mean—"

"The strange one. Oliver York. I think that's his name."

Oliver? Emma contained her reaction. The man had nerve. She nodded stiffly. "Yes, that's his name, but I wouldn't call him a friend. When did he make his reservation?"

"Yesterday. He reserved over the internet with a note saying he'd be at your open house tomorrow and was eager to be back in Rock Point. He's not a problem, is he? All you need is a gate-crasher."

Emma didn't correct Rosemary on her use of *your* for the open house. An innocent mistake that would have no effect. Oliver's presence, on the other hand, was another story altogether. "Oliver isn't a gate-crasher but I'll check in with him when he arrives."

"Of course. I'll shoot you a text. I had a feeling…" The older woman sighed. "Never mind. I enjoyed lunch, Emma. Thanks for taking the time."

"My pleasure. It's always great to see you."

"You, too."

She thought Rosemary meant it, even if they both understood she'd never imagined Colin marrying a woman who was not only an ex-nun, but also a Sharpe, an art historian and an FBI agent who specialized in art crimes. And Rosemary was getting used to Mike's new love interest, too, although she was ignorant of her firstborn's history with feisty Naomi MacBride. Naomi's rekindled relationship with Mike Donovan and their time together at his cabin on Maine's remote Bold Coast seemed to have helped her recover from her knife wound.

Complicated, the Donovan men and their women.

Emma smiled as she climbed into her car. She was happy to be in that mix.

But before she started the car, she called Sam Padgett.

He answered on the second ring. "How was lunch with your future mother-in-law? Did you have that lobster and blueberry pie?"

"As a matter of fact, we did. Lobster bisque, though, not lobster rolls. I've had enough calories already today to keep me going for a week. I'm heading up to my old convent. I'll take a long walk while I'm there."

"Not much makes me shudder, but the mention of nuns will do it."

Emma smiled. "Good to know."

"I was about to call you myself. I don't know if Colin's been in touch but you could say that your mutual friend Oliver York landed in his custody. Oliver, Colin and charming Mary Bracken are currently on their way up there in Oliver's rented car. I gather Colin has access to various Donovan vehicles, and Mary's meeting her brother and therefore doesn't need a vehicle."

"I see."

"Oliver's get-out-of-jail-free card will only get him so far. That's my news. What's up with you?"

"I called to tell you that Oliver's booked a room at the inn Colin's parents run," Emma said, keeping her tone neutral.

Sam let out an audible breath. "Oh, boy."

"Yeah. Thanks for the info, Sam."

"Sure thing."

"We'll stay in touch."

She disconnected and checked her messages. There was nothing from Gordy Wheelock, her family, Scotland Yard, MI5, Oliver York or a certain Special Agent Colin Donovan, on his way home to Maine.

Would Oliver volunteer where he was staying?

Possibly, possibly not.

To be on the safe side, Emma texted Colin the information. Even if he was driving, he'd see the text before he arrived in Rock Point.

14

Emma parked at the end of the curving, tree-lined drive that led to the main gate to the convent of the Sisters of the Joyful Heart. She got out by a tall wrought-iron fence, the air fresh and cool out on the small peninsula where the sisters lived and worked. She noticed the pungent scent of the white pines and spruces that grew along the driveway and the other side of the fence.

A small stone statue of Saint Francis of Assisi greeted her by the gate. It was a creation of Mother Sarah Jane Linden, the convent's foundress and a talented artist who had encouraged young Wendell Sharpe in his early days in art recovery. Guided by her vision and commitment, the fledgling order had purchased a run-down nineteenth-century estate just outside Heron's Cove and then had begun a long process of building and renovation. They'd installed multiple gardens and trails to aid in their mission of art education, preservation and conservation. Mother Linden had died years ago, but the two dozen or so religious sisters continued her vision of an order that was at once modern and traditional, hardworking and playful, isolated and connected to the wider community.

Although Rosemary Donovan had been astute in her observations about the unintended and long-lasting effects of Emma's brief time as a novice, Emma had never regretted it. Her months living there were in the past, but still a part of who she was.

Sister Cecilia Catherine Rousseau opened the main gate and greeted Emma warmly. She wore a dove-gray tunic and skirt with a simple silver profession cross hanging from her neck and a gold band on her left ring finger. A wide black headband held back her chin-length light brown hair. With the warm weather, she wasn't wearing a sweater or jacket, just her sturdy walking shoes. She'd professed her final vows last fall, shortly after she and Emma met, and was a dedicated art educator. She'd been giving Emma painting lessons, but they'd been infrequent lately due to work schedules and Emma's less frequent trips to Maine.

"Thanks for seeing me," Emma said.

"I've been doing some research for you. Come."

They went through the main gate and followed a paved walk to the motherhouse, part of the original estate. Built in 1898, the stone mansion had leaded-glass windows, several covered porches, multiple dormers and, as Emma recalled, some serious drafts. But Sister Cecilia didn't linger, instead leading Emma through an expansive, colorful flower garden with late-season tulips, bleeding hearts and other spring flowers, to a wide lawn above a tumble of boulders that led to the sea.

"Mother Aquinas knows you're here," Sister Cecilia said. "I'm not sneaking around."

Not that she was above it, Emma thought. "I wouldn't want you to get yourself into trouble."

"Am I officially an FBI informant?"

"No, Sister—"

"Kidding," she added quickly, her eyes bright with excitement. "I was having a Julie Andrews moment. You know, when she played Maria von Trapp in *The Sound of Music* and the nuns at her former convent helped her and her new family escape the Nazis. But Colin isn't exactly a Captain von Trapp, is he?"

Emma smiled. "He hates *The Sound of Music*."

"Why am I not surprised?" Sister Cecilia kept walking, now toward the estate's former tower, an unusual structure that had been converted into the studio where most of the convent's conservation work was done. "As you know, we focus primarily but not exclusively on religious art. We don't take on antiquity conservation, restoration and preservation. We're familiar with ancient works, particularly very early Christian art and artifacts, but we have limited capability in that field."

"Then that hasn't changed since I was here."

"We can recommend specialists who handle works directly or on-site. Education in handling antiquities is a huge priority. You mentioned ancient mosaics when you called. They're a good example of where one wrong move can lead to disaster—you can literally end up with a pile of dust and bits and pieces. It's like Humpty Dumpty, who couldn't be put back together again. It's not always the case, of course, but best to know what you're doing."

A gust of wind blew off the water, and Emma noticed a lobster boat heading northeast, no doubt on its way back to Rock Point after checking its traps. She turned back to Sister Cecilia. "Did the Norwoods or Deverells ever ask for help with their antiquity collection?"

"Not that I could find in the records. I haven't had time to do a thorough search, but I'd be surprised if there's anything there to find. But the man who built this estate—Edward Hart, a railroad magnate—was great friends with Horace Norwood, the man who built the Norwood summer house in Heron's Cove and started the Norwood family's antiquities collection. Edward and Horace traveled to the Mediterranean together at least a half-dozen times."

"I don't recall that Hart had much of an antiquities collection."

"Not here, that's for certain. I asked one of the retired sisters, and she says there are a couple of trunks and chests that were left here and she believes they could be from Hart's travels. I think one of the trunks is now a coffee table in the rec room." Sister Cecilia sighed, tucking a few stray hairs back under her headband. "Not quite as exciting as discovering a rare mosaic."

Emma had no memory of the trunks and chests and wondered if they'd been unearthed after her departure from the convent. A social connection between two wealthy men with homes in southern Maine at the turn of the last century wasn't unusual or provocative, but she was appreciative of Sister Cecilia's efforts and thanked her.

"I'll see if I can learn anything more. If nothing else, it's fodder for the biography of Mother Linden I'm writing." She paused as they came to the stone tower.

"I hope whatever you're into with all this turns out to be a tempest in a teapot."

"I hope so, too," Emma said.

With her regular duties to tend to, Sister Cecilia left Emma by the converted tower and headed onto a path, a shortcut through a small orchard to the sisters' large vegetable garden. A few of the many gardens on the convent property were off-limits to guests, which, of course, Emma realized she was now. She rarely pictured herself out here in her late teens, absorbed in her studies and a life that seemed distant and yet still so real to her now.

She shoved her hands in her pockets and squinted out at the ocean. The lobster boat had disappeared. In a few short weeks, she and Colin would be married on the lawn above the sea, next to a garden bursting with late spring flowers. She'd never imagined such a moment as a postulant and novice. She smiled, thinking of how surprised her nineteen-year-old self would have been.

She watched a trio of seagulls perched on a giant boulder past the tideline. A cormorant popped out of the water, then dived again. It was out here last September, after the terrible murder of Sister Joan Fabriani, that Emma had spotted a lobster boat hung up on the rocks, its rugged operator making his way up to the convent.

Colin Donovan, dispatched by Matt Yankowski to keep an eye on her.

Colin had never run a boat aground in his life. It had been a ploy to get up here and catch her off guard without having to explain he was an FBI agent. He'd just returned home to Maine after a long, difficult, dan-

gerous undercover mission. She remembered the toll
the months of constant stress had taken on him. She'd
seen it in his eyes that first day. What would he be
like this time, coming home from this latest mission?

She fingered her engagement ring. She and Colin
had fallen in love fast and hard, and he'd proposed to
her in a Dublin pub on a rainy November night. She
hadn't needed time to think. She'd said yes without
hesitation, and she'd never once, even for a heartbeat,
questioned or second-guessed herself since.

The cormorant surfaced again, riding a swell as
the seagulls swooped off the boulder, crying loudly
and quickly disappearing around the tip of the peninsula. Emma imagined her life here, before her months
working with her grandfather in Dublin, before the
FBI Academy and now these first years as a special
agent—before Colin Donovan of Rock Point, Maine.
Could that Emma Sharpe have guessed she would be
having her wedding here on the first Saturday in June?

She took the main walk back through the convent
grounds, refocusing on Gordy Wheelock and his real
reasons for showing up in her office yesterday. As she
reached a pine grove by the convent gate, her mother
called. Faye Sharpe had never pretended to understand
Emma's decision to enter the convent, and she hadn't
hidden her relief when Emma left—not that her mother
had had the FBI in mind as her next career choice. But
her main focus, then and now, was her pain-stricken
husband, not her two adult children.

"Where are you now, Emma?" her mother asked.

"The convent. The gardens are going to be beautiful for the wedding."

"I can imagine. You must be getting excited."

Emma smiled. "I am."

"Well, I won't keep you. We did some research on the party at Claridge's this past Sunday. You'll never guess who was behind it."

"Not…" Emma gritted her teeth. "Oliver York?"

"I know. Of all people, Emma. It took a bit of work to find out. He sponsored the party through a small charitable foundation his grandparents set up in honor of his parents, after their deaths. It's based in Stow-on-the-Wold, not far from the York farm, and it has one part-time employee."

"Did you suspect Oliver was behind the party before you started digging?"

"Not a clue," her mother said frankly. "We learned about the foundation first, then about his involvement with it. It does just enough to keep it legal and in existence. I doubt anyone else realized the party had anything to do with Oliver."

"What about Granddad?" Emma asked. "Was he involved with this party?"

A long pause. "Nothing would surprise me, but we haven't discovered anything that points to Wendell. Colin and your father had a chat last night at Claridge's. I think he's getting used to what it means to be marrying a Sharpe. It took me some getting used to, and things were much less complicated then. One of us wasn't a federal law enforcement agent, for one thing."

Emma didn't detect a hint of criticism in her mother's voice. "That is a fact," she said.

"I won't keep you. Enjoy your time at the convent. I have to say, you never got into these tangles when you were a nun."

"That's true."

"Then again, it could have been you last fall instead of Sister Joan…" Her mother cleared her throat, as if she didn't want to imagine such a scenario. "Your father and I like Colin. We're still figuring out when we can get there for your wedding."

"It'll be great to see you, but everyone will understand if Dad has a flare-up."

"We need to give ourselves enough margin that it won't matter if he does. We will be there, Emma."

She told her mother about Rosemary Donovan's choice of blue for her mother-of-the-groom dress, and they chatted a few more minutes. When they hung up, Emma looked back toward the water, part of the converted tower visible through the trees. Her parents had seldom visited her at the convent, or since she'd joined the Bureau, for that matter. They'd become more and more insular since her father's fall. Emma had found herself increasingly reluctant to ask anything of them—to be a burden to them in any way. But she had to admit she very much wanted them at her wedding.

She continued on the walk, enjoying the dappled shade and the smells of pine needles, sea and freshly mown grass. "I'll see you at my wedding," she said to Saint Francis as she returned to the parking lot.

A man was leaning against her car. Dark hair, a sport coat, a collared shirt with a loosened tie…

Colin.

Emma's knees almost buckled. That would have been very un-FBI of her, but she rallied and crossed the parking lot to him. "I was just talking to Saint Francis," she said.

"He's a tough act to follow."

Colin stood straight, looking tired but alert—and

like himself, the man who'd jumped out of the lobster boat that day last September, who'd dropped onto one knee in the Dublin pub and proposed to her, who'd searched for her when she'd gone missing in February. The man who'd carried her upstairs to his bedroom, who'd made love to her in front of more than one Irish fire.

"It's good to see you," she said, a catch in her voice.

"You, too, babe. Damn…"

He held out his arms, and she fell into them, felt them tighten around her. She breathed in the smell of him, relished having his muscular, hard body envelop her. Only now, with him here, close, did she acknowledge that a part of her had been afraid that this time he wouldn't make it home.

"I just got here. I figured I'd wait for you. I didn't want to interrupt you in case you were meditating with your nun friends."

"I was planning our wedding and decompressing after lunch with your mother."

"Even more reason not to interrupt you. Did you warn my mother you're armed and dangerous?" But he didn't smile as his gray-blue eyes settled on her. "It's been a while but it seems longer. It's good to see you. It's good to be home."

"You wouldn't want to miss spring in Maine."

"If you say so. It's chilly right now."

A hint he'd been in a warmer climate during his weeks of silence? Emma brushed her fingertips across his cheek. "Good flight?"

"Long. I read about ancient mosaics. Oliver loaned me Alessandro Pearson's book."

"It's fascinating, isn't it?"

"It has its moments." He curved his hand around hers. "You have that look, Emma."

"Today was supposed to be a vacation day, but I've been working on figuring out what Gordy, Oliver and my grandfather are up to between a few personal things. I've already had doughnuts and pie."

"Not the break you imagined, except maybe for the doughnuts and pie."

"Colin…" She smiled at him. "I'm just glad you're back. The rest doesn't matter."

"Are there security cameras out here? Would the nuns go nuts if I kiss you?"

"No security cameras, no sisters hiding in the trees."

"Not that it matters because I'm going to kiss you anyway, unless you tell me no."

"I'm not going to tell you no."

His mouth was close to hers before she finished. She put one hand on his upper arm and the other on his face as he drew her closer, kissing her softly, tentatively, as if he were taking into account their surroundings, or perhaps his own rawness after his long weeks away, his long day at airports and on planes.

He stood straight and winked at her, some of his natural Donovan cockiness back. "More to come."

"You're on. Who gave you a ride out here?"

"You don't want to know."

"Oliver."

"Himself. We dropped off Mary Bracken at the rectory and drove up here. I figured I could get a ride back with you."

"You got my text? Oliver's staying at your parents' inn."

"Yeah. Thanks for the heads-up. He told me as we

crossed into Rock Point. He said the idea of staying
with us lost its charm when he realized he'd have to
share a bathroom—never mind that we'd have said no.
Then he said he'd debated asking Fin Bracken but figured that would be rude with Mary in town."

"Oliver York worrying about being rude," Emma
said. "Imagine that."

Colin sighed. "Yeah, imagine. My dad loves him.
Offered to try his hand at proper English scones if Oliver wants them while he's here."

"A shame we can't tell the truth about him."

"It wouldn't matter. Pop's done chasing criminals.
Mom loves having him done. If their guests are good
talkers, pay their bill and don't steal anything of value,
they're fine."

"It wouldn't matter to them Oliver's an unrepentant art thief?"

"Not if he's entertaining, which he can be." Colin
touched the knuckles of one hand to her cheek. "Damn,
Emma. I've missed you. What do you say we have
chowder and whiskey with the gang and I carry you
upstairs for the night? Or are you still into this separate-
beds thing until the wedding?"

"Colin…"

He grinned. "That's what I thought." He headed toward the passenger side of her car. "You good to drive?
I'm a little ragged."

"I'm good," Emma said, pulling open the driver's
side. She eased behind the wheel as he climbed in next
to her. "Where to first?"

"Let's pay Oliver a visit and see how he's getting
settled in at the inn. My father makes great afternoon
tea these days."

"Sounds good."

"You can fill me in on what's going on with Gordy Wheelock on the way. I talked to Sam Padgett for two seconds at the airport. I bet he knows more about Gordy than Gordy does about himself at this point. I never want to have to hide anything from that guy. But first," Colin added, reaching over to her and tucking a strand of hair behind her ear, "tell me the latest on our wedding and what I can do to help."

15

Claudia had walked almost to the Sharpes before she stopped in the middle of the sidewalk, telling herself she needed to change her mind and give it up, not try to see Lucas while she was here. If they ran into each other, okay. But why try to make it happen?

She'd done the same thing last night, aware of how much darker it was here than in London. The endless black of the Atlantic had freaked her out. It was as if the ocean wanted to grab her and suck her into its depths to teach her a lesson, punish her for her transgressions. Every wave crashing on the rocks made her jump, but she'd refused to look down at the tide. Panicky and shaky, afraid she'd let the sea take her, she'd forced herself to focus on the lights in the inn, the Sharpe house and the little restaurant across the street.

If it was her weird reaction to the dark ocean that had prompted her to turn around, then she supposed she ought to be grateful, because as she'd started back up to her family's longtime summer home, she'd spotted Gordy Wheelock crossing Ocean Avenue from the Sharpe house. She'd waited, unmoving in the shadows, trying to control her rapid, shallow breathing, trying to ignore wave after wave surging below her, until Gordy finally disappeared up a side street next to the restaurant.

Back home, she'd sat on the porch and thought of her mother's love for Heron's Cove until she calmed down enough not to attract the attention of her father, her brother and Isabel. Finally under control, she'd congratulated herself. She'd avoided Gordy *and* she'd avoided embarrassing herself with whichever Sharpes were at the Sharpe house—now just the Sharpe offices.

Today was another day, with fresh urges and temptations, a fact of life for her whenever she was in Heron's Cove. She hadn't realized it until she'd met Gordy here, but it had happened before, from the time she was a small child. She remembered wandering down to the rocks on her own, without telling anyone, terrifying her parents. Usually good, always responsible, she'd broken free here in ways she hadn't anywhere else.

Her mother hadn't seen it. *You were only four, Claudia. That's what four-year-olds do.*

It was always like that, the understanding, the minimizing, but her mother hadn't been around for her only daughter's encounter with Gordy Wheelock in the sunroom.

Claudia shoved her hands in her pockets, imagining Heron's Cove when Horace Norwood, her great-grandfather, had built his summer house more than a century ago. She didn't remember Wendell's parents when they worked at keeping the place up in every way—maintenance, housekeeping, mowing, pruning, planting. They'd overseen household projects and looked after the property during the off-season. She remembered her mother talking about them. She'd loved them like family, she'd said. No one had ever had a qualm about leaving valuables at the house or letting the Sharpes have a key.

A different time, Claudia thought as she glanced out at the water, not at all frightening now under the late afternoon sun. She could hear her mother's laughter as the two of them had searched for tide pools among the rocks. *I love a sand beach, Claudia, but there's truly nothing like the rugged, rocky coast.*

It wasn't a specific memory of a specific time but one of many memories of many times. Before her father won the battle and they'd stopped coming to Maine on a regular basis, Claudia had gone on countless excursions searching for tide pools with her mother, and her mother would always say the same thing about rocks versus sand.

But the memory of her mother's laughter faded, and Claudia realized Lucas Sharpe was down on the rocks. "Lucas!" she called brightly, waving to him as she left the sidewalk.

He looked up, and if he grimaced or cursed under his breath, she couldn't tell.

She took a dirt path toward the water, until it disappeared among the boulders that formed this stretch of coastline. She stopped on a flat-topped hunk of granite just above Lucas. "Are you relaxing or catching dinner?" she asked.

"Getting air." He was standing on a barnacle-covered boulder, the low tide inches from his feet. It wouldn't be long before the boulder again would be submerged in salt water. "Hello, Claudia."

Hearing his voice, seeing those green eyes and that

fit, lanky body, reminded her why she'd become so obsessed with seeing him again here in Heron's Cove. She'd had a chance with Lucas Sharpe, and she'd blown it. She could blame Gordy for using her the way he had, but it was her own actions that had driven this good-looking, intelligent, decent man from her.

"It's great to see you, Lucas," she said, managing to keep her voice from sounding too strangled, too desperate. "I just got in from London via Boston. Heron's Cove never really changes, does it? Not on the surface, anyway. Are you traveling as much as ever?"

"A fair amount. It comes with the job."

He didn't sound desperate at all, only cool, in control. Claudia crossed her arms on her chest. "It's colder down here close to the water. Funny how I forget. I heard you've been in London a few times this past year on business and to see your parents. Next time you're in town give me a ring. I'd love to take you for a drink. Just two old friends from Heron's Cove."

"You're from Philadelphia and you live in London. You didn't grow up here."

If he regretted his barbed comment, or even realized it stung, she saw no sign of it. She jumped onto another boulder, avoiding ones with barnacles. She was dressed for boulder-hopping in her slim pants and hoodie, but she was sure the barnacles would shred the bottoms of her walking flats. She'd packed light for the trip and they needed to do double duty. Any clothes she might have left at the house were at least a decade old. There were stores in Heron's Cove, but she didn't want to go shopping. It would be another unbearable reminder of happy days with her mother.

"You must be looking forward to the open house

tomorrow," she said. "It was decent of you to invite us. I'm afraid I won't be able to make it. I'm not going to be here long, and I have a lot I need to do to get the house ready."

"Whatever works for you, Claudia."

She didn't know what to say. Lucas seemed unwilling to acknowledge there'd been anything between them—as she had been yesterday with Gordy, despite their having slept together. Of course, she and Lucas *hadn't* slept together. But there'd been something there. Common interests, common history and a deep physical attraction. She felt it now. She knew he'd felt it last year.

He took a long step off the barnacle-covered rock to one to her right. "Agent Wheelock will be there tomorrow," he added.

"I saw him in London."

"So I heard."

Claudia would have preferred Lucas deny ever having entertained the thought of a romantic relationship with her than remind of her brief affair with an FBI legend. She'd never been sure how much Lucas knew, but it didn't matter. He suspected. He had a business to protect. Any hint she'd had an inappropriate relationship with a federal agent would send him running.

She decided not to mention she'd been the one to call Gordy last week.

"He seems to be enjoying retirement," she said. "He's expecting another grandchild soon. I let him tag along to a party on Sunday. Your parents were there. I'm sure they told you. I also saw your grandfather last week at Alessandro Pearson's funeral."

"I know you and Alessandro were friends. I'm sorry."

"Yes, his death was a shock. He was elderly, but it's still hard to believe…" She stopped herself, narrowing her gaze on Lucas. "Am I missing something, Lucas?"

"I doubt it."

Just the barest undertone of contempt. She swallowed. "You and your grandfather don't believe there's any issue with Alessandro's death, do you?"

"We don't do death investigations," he said.

His coldness took her aback, but she kept her footing on the boulder. "I know you aren't happy to see me here, but please don't worry. My focus is on getting the house ready to sell. My father and brother and Isabel don't know anything about our past. I intend to keep it that way."

"We had dinner together a couple of times when I was in London and we went to a show. Your attentions were elsewhere at the time. There's no going back, Claudia. I'm not here to judge you or mess up your life."

"But you don't trust me." When he didn't respond, she glanced up at the steep bank to the Norwood house. *Her* house. "My mother gave up coming here because my father prefers the Outer Banks. He never developed a fondness for cool, foggy Maine evenings. I love them—snuggling up under a cozy wrap while everyone else is sweating to death or condemned to air-conditioning on a hot summer night. My father, on the other hand, would prefer to sit on a sandy beach in a pair of shorts, with a cold beer. Adrian's like that, too. What do you like, Lucas?"

"I haven't had much time for relaxing lately."

Obviously she hadn't caught him in the greatest mood. She attempted a smile. "I'm not complaining about the Outer Banks, mind you. It's gorgeous there. I suppose I'm nostalgic because of my mother."

"I'm sorry, Claudia," Lucas said. "I know you must miss her."

"Thank you."

"Stop by tomorrow if you'd like," he added. "It's fine with me either way."

"Because I don't matter to you."

But as she spoke, a swell broke over the boulder he'd vacated and almost reached the one where he was now standing. Claudia wasn't sure if he'd heard her. He hopped onto another boulder, gave her a quick wave and started back up to the sidewalk.

She stayed and watched more swells rise and roll in over the rocks, giving Lucas a chance to get back to the Sharpe Fine Art Recovery offices. She'd driven past his antique house in the village that morning and noticed a black cat in the window. The cat seemed to be staring at her, as if it knew all her secrets. She'd wondered if Lucas had a romantic life, or if he were consumed by work—if he might decide he wanted to rekindle a relationship with her, after all.

Lucas...why don't you move your offices to New York or Boston?

Heron's Cove is where Sharpe Fine Art Recovery started. It's like its soul is there. It also works well. We're removed but not too removed.

You can be objective.

Exactly. With technology, it's even easier to manage a more out-of-the-way location than it was when my grandfather started the company sixty years ago.

He's been in Dublin for the past fifteen years. That's helped, too.

My mother always has had such respect for you and your family and the work you do.

Lucas had spoken to her with such ease and friendliness over that first dinner in London, before her mother's cancer diagnosis. Claudia wanted it to be like that between them again, but now she despaired of that ever happening. It wasn't that he hadn't put the past behind him, she realized. He'd put *her* behind him.

A slip into an ankle-deep tide pool finally drove Claudia inside. She went upstairs to her bedroom, its turquoise-and-white décor unchanged from when she was ten, and changed her pants, shoes and socks. The sun had leaked out of the sky, and the afternoon, what was left of it, had turned cool. She gazed out at the sea and fought tears. A week ago, she'd been in Ireland, touring Bracken Distillers, feeling like a stalker as she'd traced some of Lucas's steps there and tried to understand what he and his family had been doing this past year, since she'd laid her mother to rest.

Mary Bracken had been charming and knowledgeable—and open. Claudia remembered being open with people, before Gordy Wheelock had inserted himself into her life, before her mother's death, but she'd never possessed Mary's natural innocence. Her openness had been more a conscious way of acting and being. She was a Norwood, after all. She'd taken her cue from her mother's ease and graciousness with people. Mary Bracken was more vivacious, a bundle of energy and amusing one-liners as she'd led the tour.

She must be in Maine by now for her visit with her

brother. She'd said she didn't know the Sharpes as well as he did as the parish priest in a small fishing village near Heron's Cove.

Claudia opened a window. She could hear the ocean crashing on the rocks, sounding so close it was almost as if the waves and water could overtake her. She found herself wondering what it would be like to let herself go out to sea with the tide. Would anyone miss her?

Frightened by her train of thought, she pulled herself away from the window. As she turned, three framed black-and-white photographs of various Norwoods greeted her on the wall by the door. In the center was her mother at seven or eight, standing on the front lawn with the ocean in the background. Could she ever have imagined the twists and turns her life would take—that it would end too soon, at the age of sixty-six?

Of course not, Claudia thought, annoyed with herself. Little girls didn't think of such things.

She went downstairs and found her father and brother in the kitchen, arguing about afternoon drinks. "Claudia," Adrian said cheerfully, "you decide. Martinis or gin and tonic, inside or outside?"

She relaxed at the mundane conversation. Nothing about FBI agents, failed romance, the Sharpes or the Norwood antiquities. "It's not hot enough for gin and tonic," she said. "But it's not too cold for drinks outside. How's that?"

"Martinis it is," Adrian said then winked at their father. "I won't gloat."

Claudia watched as her father got out three martini glasses. "I'll take the high road and not sulk," he said. "Can't go wrong with either. You'll join us, Claudia?"

"I'd love to."

"It's your house," Adrian said. "Lucky you. I found a mouse hole in the laundry room today. It's perfectly formed. I half expected a cartoon mouse and cat to burst out. Isabel says she's worried about bats."

"Bats in the attic and mice everywhere," Claudia said with a laugh. "Definitely time to sell the place. In the meantime, make my martini dry and strong, Dad."

Her father and his son by his first marriage were both impressive men, she thought, fair and handsome, successful in business, decent at golf and tennis and with no axes to grind against her or her mother's family. Born to a Main Line Philadelphia family, Henry Deverell had married his college sweetheart—Adrian's mother—but they divorced when Adrian, their only child together, was four. Eighteen months later, Henry was married to Victoria Norwood, a young antiquities enthusiast from an even wealthier family. Claudia was born the next year. Although Adrian was raised by his mother, he and Claudia had spent alternate holidays and such together growing up, and he seemed to bear no ill will toward their father. After a short-lived marriage in his twenties, Adrian had told Claudia last night he was seeing someone and expected to ask her to marry him when he returned to Atlanta. He'd asked about her love life but she'd dodged the question.

They made martinis, added the appropriate olives and headed out to the front porch. "You were obsessing on your walk, weren't you, Claudia?" Adrian asked knowingly. "Go to the open house. I don't know what went on between you and the Sharpes but they're too civilized to kick you out. No one else knows you had a falling-out or will care if they do know."

"We didn't have a falling-out," Claudia mumbled, sitting on a wicker rocker. Its cushion needed replacing and its frame needed painting, but it was sturdy and comfortable.

Her father frowned. He sat on her mother's favorite settee across from Claudia. "Who don't you want to see at the open house?"

"No one," she said, clearing her throat and forcing herself to stop mumbling. She didn't want her father and brother to suspect she had anything to hide. "Adrian's talking through his hat. I have no problem with the Sharpes, and as far as I know, they have no problem with me. I just have a lot to do here and a short time in which to do it."

"So it's a time-management issue," Adrian said, clearly skeptical. He sat on a chair that wasn't in great shape; it creaked under him. "Whoa. Almost spilled my martini. That would have been a catastrophe."

Claudia sighed at him. "It's good you worry about the important things, Adrian."

He grinned. "Isn't it?" He sipped his martini. "Excellent as always, Dad."

Their father had his gaze narrowed on Claudia. "You didn't cross Wendell Sharpe, did you, Claudia?"

She shook her head. "Of course not."

"Did your mother, before she died?"

"No, Dad."

"There's history between the Norwoods and the Sharpes."

Adrian set his martini on a small table. "Maybe that means you'll find a few interesting skeletons in the closet when you go through this place. That could be fun."

"You visited me in London before you came here," Claudia said. "You've seen for yourself how dull my day-to-day life is."

Her brother gave a mock shudder. "Incredibly dull."

Her father crossed one leg over the other. "What a night," he said. "It's colder than I'd like but it's beautiful here. That never was my problem with this place."

"What was your problem?" Claudia asked, keeping her tone mild.

He shrugged. "It's in Maine."

She took another couple of sips of her martini and then got up, glancing out at the ocean at dusk before she went inside, leaving the two men to their drinks.

Isabel was curled up in a cozy chair by the unlit fireplace in the front room. She put aside a book she was reading and smiled. "Did you see any creepy-crawly things in a tide pool while you were out on your walk?"

Claudia felt her mood lightening. "I didn't see a tide pool, but I wasn't thinking about creepy-crawly things."

"I always think about them when I'm near the sea. I'm not your ocean type, I'm afraid, but what a beautiful day it's been. I don't blame you for wanting a good walk. Of course, you're used to this place. Starfish, periwinkles, seaweed and whatnot wouldn't faze you."

"This is true." Claudia pointed toward the entry and its main stairs. "Would you like to join me? I'm going upstairs to the room where my mother stored bits and pieces of the family collection. A bit of an eccentric move on her part, but I'm finally going to start sorting through them."

"If you find any loose stones and glass that I can use in my mosaic art, I'll take them."

"Consider it done."

Isabel threw off the blanket on her lap and eased to her feet, stretching and yawning, then giving a little shiver. "I'm ready for a fire and you're probably planning to leave your bedroom windows open tonight."

"It could happen," Claudia said, grinning.

They went upstairs to the large back bedroom that Claudia's mother had converted into a storage room for sturdy art and artifacts that she deemed able to withstand the conditions, and God knew what else. Claudia unlocked the door and pushed it open. "After you," she said, her throat tight with unexpected emotion.

Isabel crossed the threshold and then stopped. "Oh, my." Her light mood vanished. "Claudia. It's like you can feel her presence, isn't it?"

"Yes, it is."

"There's more here than I ever imagined."

"During the last months of her life, Mother gathered pieces from various locations—friends, her home in Philadelphia, other rooms of this house—and stored them in here. She did it on her own. She didn't want Dad or me to help. She'd planned to have me here last summer and we'd go through them together."

"But she didn't make it," Isabel said in a whisper.

Claudia tried to ignore her own emotion. To get through what she had to do here, she needed to stay objective, professional. "I wonder now if it wasn't a kind of hoarding on her part—part of her way of saying goodbye to this world."

"That would be so like Victoria." Isabel's eyes brimmed with tears. "It's just so sad."

"I think my mother would want to see it as..." Claudia sought the right words. "Hopeful and loving."

"Do you think there's anything of real value in here?"

"If there is, it's not likely to be from the ancient past. Maybe I'll find an old ring someone dropped in 1937 or something."

"That would be fun." But Isabel sniffled, blinking back tears. "You've rented out the house for years. Do you think it's possible a renter or two could have made off with anything?"

Claudia shook her head. "We haven't had anyone in here since Mother was diagnosed, but we never left anything of value out for renters." She scanned the clutter of boxes, chests and trunks, then sighed. "*Now* do you see why I can't waste time on parties?"

"But you're in your element here," Isabel said, smiling. "Just like your mother."

"Thank you for saying that."

"It's true. I'm sorry that Agent Wheelock used your relationship with your poor dying mother to throw you off balance. You know I suspect he used you. I don't know how far things went between you two and I don't need to know." Isabel made a face. "Bastard. Then to have to see him in London and now here."

Claudia didn't explain *she* was the one who'd called Gordy last week, after Alessandro's death, the Claridge's party invitation on her desk, the open house coming up—and her father and brother in town, invited to the Sharpe open house by Wendell Sharpe himself. She'd felt like calling him was a way to take control of the situation. That seemed silly and delusional now.

"I don't want to think about Gordy Wheelock," she said quietly. "Not in here, of all places."

"Of course not. Sorry. Just one thing, Claudia…for

my own peace of mind." Isabel paused, clearly debating whether to continue. "Did he coerce you? Did he plant something on you—an illicit antiquity of some sort can't be that hard for an FBI art crimes agent to find—or did you make an innocent mistake and he used it as leverage?"

"What if the answer is neither?"

"Your mother asked me to look after you, not because I'm any steadier than you are, but because you inherited so much from her—and not just this house and the Norwood collection. Her faith in people."

Claudia attempted a smile. "Calling us naive, Isabel?"

"Kind," she said without hesitation. "You always assume the best in people."

"And you don't?"

Her friend grinned. "Oh, good heavens, no. Claudia, Claudia. You have a wonderful family and your mother was taken from you too soon. You weren't ready, but how could you have been? The cancer was found so late…too late."

"We're all coming out of the shock bit by bit. Father and Adrian are there, I think, and I'm almost there."

Isabel looked skeptical but didn't respond right away. She stepped past a wooden crate. "Well, let's have a quick look around. If we find any old, loose tesserae with no home, I'd love to have them for my work, but even better would be to find a decent intact mosaic in here. That would be terribly exciting. But either way, you and I aren't going to spend the evening digging through boxes and crates. I'm taking you down the street to that lobster place. I checked out the wine list online. It's downright decent, and we won't have to worry about driving back here. We can stagger."

"Sounds like a perfect evening."

"I promise I won't let you throw rocks at the Sharpe windows if you overimbibe."

Claudia laughed, relaxing, but she knew she and Isabel wouldn't find any surprises stored in the bedroom—and they wouldn't get drunk tonight. But maybe the greatest fun was in imagining it could be so.

16

Colin breathed in the smells of Rock Point harbor and relished the sight of the quiet water, the docks, the working boats and Hurley's, unchanged in decades never mind the past month. Emma came around the front of her car and eased in next to him. "It must be strange not to have at least one of your brothers here to greet you."

"A record," he said. "They've all promised to be here for the wedding."

My wedding, he thought. He'd never expected to be the first brother down the aisle. Kevin or Andy, the two youngest, had seemed more likely, although for no other reason than they'd stayed in Rock Point. Kevin and Mike weren't here now, and maybe that was just as well with Oliver York in town. A text from Fin Bracken had changed his and Emma's plans about catching up with the art thief at the inn. Oliver was joining Fin and Mary at Hurley's.

Colin had let his folks know he was back in town. He'd see them later. He hated the idea of Oliver staying at their inn, but he had a feeling his father, former cop that he was, had a good idea that their English guest bore watching.

He slipped his hand into Emma's and they went into the restaurant together. Colin knew most of the people at the tables, but it wasn't crowded. By his past standards, he hadn't been gone long—nor did anyone have a clue where he'd been or what he'd been doing. But that was good, he thought. He preferred keeping his undercover work and his life here separate.

A few hellos and he and Emma made it back to Fin Bracken's favorite table along the windows overlooking the darkening harbor. Mary had the seat with the best view. "Emma, Colin," she said in her distinctive Irish accent. "Welcome! What a place this is."

She started to her feet, but Emma shook her head. "No, no, please don't get up. You must be tired."

"Dead tired," Mary said cheerfully, keeping her seat. "It's the middle of the night in Ireland, but I'm so excited to be here, finally. I didn't sleep a wink on the flight, but that's good. I'll go to bed at a normal hour for the East Coast."

Colin had sat a half-dozen rows behind her but could verify she hadn't slept. He hadn't, either. Deep into his book on ancient mosaics. Reviewing his conversations with Yank, Emma and Oliver. Pushing back his frustration with losing his time in Ireland to plan his honeymoon. Plenty to keep him awake for seven hours.

He pulled out a chair for Emma and then sat next to her.

"It's wonderful to be here," Mary said. "I've been wanting a chance to see where Fin's been living all these months."

"Good that you waited until spring," her brother said. "I don't see you navigating icy roads and frigid temperatures." He eyed Colin across the table. "Good to see you, Colin."

Colin grinned. "You, too, Father Fin."

Finian leaned toward his sister. "Colin knows I loathe being called Father Fin."

Mary laughed. "I don't know, I think it suits you."

"That's the jet lag talking," Fin said.

"How do you like Maine so far?" Emma asked, addressing Mary. "Is it at all what you imagined?"

"It's *exactly* what I imagined."

But Mary wasn't hungry, obviously, and her eyelids were visibly heavy as she agreed to her brother's suggestion of clam chowder. Colin indulged in fish and chips, as if to confirm to himself that he was finally and truly home.

Emma was ordering grilled scallops when Colin noticed Oliver enter the rustic restaurant. He felt himself stiffen, but Oliver had a happy spring in his step as he joined them at their table. He wore a battered Barbour jacket that belied its expense and his wealth, a dark sweater, cords and sturdy, expensive walking shoes.

"I got lost walking from the inn," he said, pulling out a chair, clearly not expecting anyone at the table to believe him. "What a splendid evening. I find the sea air therapeutic after a long flight."

"It's therapeutic anytime," Colin said.

"Perhaps not in winter when the temperatures dip to below zero Fahrenheit. I used to be able to convert Fahrenheit to Celsius in my head, but now I don't bother. It's like becoming fluent in a foreign language. After a certain point, you just know." He plopped onto his chair and grabbed a stray bag of oyster crackers. "I miss these when I'm home in England."

Mary giggled. "You have such a sense of humor, Oliver."

"That he does," Finian said half under his breath.

Emma leaned back in her chair. "Oliver, what are you doing here?"

"You remember. Your grandfather personally invited me to the open house tomorrow. You can ask him. He'll remember. His memory hasn't deteriorated with age. Certain lives might be easier if it did."

"I won't argue with that," Emma said. "But he wasn't serious. Lucas hadn't set a date."

"He has now, and here I am. I was worried Wendell had changed his mind about the invitation but he reiterated it when I saw him in London last week. When I discovered his son and daughter-in-law weren't going to be at the open house, I was concerned about him flying alone. I flew to Dublin to convince him to join me on my flight, but he'd already left. I decided to pop down to Declan's Cross for a quick visit." He tore open the oyster crackers. "Aren't you relieved I spared you from asking?"

"We're tough FBI agents," Colin said. "We don't mind asking you questions about your Irish travels."

Oliver dumped out the crackers on a paper place mat. He looked completely relaxed, but Colin suspected he looked relaxed even when he was slipping into locked museums. "Did you tell Emma that Martin got a puppy?" he asked.

Colin took in a calming breath. He didn't care about Oliver's puppy.

"Colin and I haven't had a chance to discuss puppies," Emma said, perhaps marginally more interested.

"Yes, one can imagine," Oliver said dryly. "He's a wire fox terrier. He's energetic. He needs room to roam. He stays at the farm. He hasn't been to London yet. I wouldn't mind if he had accidents on the library rug, but Martin and the house staff would have fits."

"I can manage without a house staff," Colin said, picking up his glass of water, "but I've decided I need a manservant."

Oliver sniffed. "Martin would scowl at you for being condescending. He's my trusted personal assistant and friend. He worked for my grandparents before he inherited me."

Colin sipped his water. "I rest my case. You're Batman."

Oliver turned to Mary. "I don't know how I'd have managed if you hadn't been with Agent Donovan and me for those two hours in the car this afternoon." He peered at Emma. "And you, Agent Sharpe. Are you sure you want to marry this man?"

"Oliver," Colin said.

"No worries. I can see from our Emma's expression that she has no plans to cancel the wedding."

Finian pushed back his chair. "Mary, would you care to help choose a whiskey for the table? We must celebrate your safe arrival."

She took the hint and got to her feet. "Ah, yes. Whiskey. My world."

"This place must have a passable Scotch," Oliver muttered.

The two Brackens either ignored him or hadn't heard. They retreated to the bar and its display of whiskeys. Of course, Finian was already familiar with every bottle on the shelf. Colin knew he was giving his FBI friends a chance to speak to Oliver alone.

"Let the interrogating and throttling begin." Oliver yawned. "It's late in London. A good throttling might wake me up."

"We're not interrogating or throttling you," Emma said.

"Are you speaking for Agent Donovan as well as yourself?" He nodded toward Mary up at the bar. "She's prettier than one would expect of Finian's sister, isn't she? He's a good-looking bloke, but I'm surprised the look of the Bracken men translates to the Bracken women. I met Mary this winter but didn't pay much attention until yesterday in Declan's Cross."

"You can't think you're falling for Mary Bracken," Colin said. "Fin will kill you."

"He's a priest."

"He wasn't always a priest."

"Well, he needn't worry," Oliver said. "I have an entirely brotherly attitude toward her. I didn't see Aoife when I was in Declan's Cross. I wish she'd paint porpoises again. Any hope for her and our Father Fin?"

Colin set his water glass on the table. He glanced out at the harbor, saw a couple of guys he knew down on the docks. He hadn't imagined having dinner with Oliver York on his first night back home. He shifted back to Oliver. "We'll walk you back to my folks' inn after dinner. We can talk there."

"Fewer witnesses," Oliver said.

Emma rolled her eyes. "You can quit with the drama, Oliver."

"Is it a busy time these days with your work, Agent Sharpe?"

"Always."

"But it doesn't keep you from fretting about me, does it?"

"No."

Colin grinned, appreciating Emma's directness.

The Brackens returned to the table with a recommendation of a Scotch that passed Oliver's inspection. Colin half expected Gordy Wheelock to wander in next, but he didn't. Emma had called his home number in North Carolina earlier but didn't get an answer. With any luck, he'd taken her advice and flown home and his wife was at the airport to pick him up. If Gordy believed he'd overreacted and overstepped, that was the best outcome, whatever was really going on with Oliver, this London party and his arrival in Maine.

The bartender brought over the glasses of Scotch. Their server brought the chowders and plates of scallops and fish and chips. Oliver said he was sticking to oyster crackers. Colin took in a breath. He felt a surge of emotion. He was home.

Finian held up his glass. *"Sláinte."*

His sister, Emma, Oliver and Colin did the same. Colin limited himself to a couple of sips of the smoky Scotch, as he knew Emma would, too.

A few minutes into their meals, Oliver, nursing his Scotch, turned to Finian. "Has Father Callaghan been in touch with you about his plans for his return to Rock Point?"

Colin noticed a change in Finian's expression and realized Oliver's question wasn't entirely speculative.

He knew something. "We can talk about this later," his priest friend said. "Mary's tired."

His sister shook her head. "Not that tired. What about Father Callaghan?" she asked, addressing Oliver. "Did you see him when you were in Ireland?"

"I stopped in Ardmore before heading to Declan's Cross and ran into the good father on the cliff walk. We finished the walk together. Did you know Father Callaghan during your nun days, Emma?"

She bristled in that subtle way Colin recognized. It meant she wasn't talking about her "nun days" with Oliver. "Not well," she said evenly.

"He's trim and fit these days and quite taken with the land of his ancestors," Oliver said. "His Irish sabbatical has agreed with him."

Mary frowned. "But he's coming back here to Rock Point, isn't he?"

"I wouldn't know," Oliver said vaguely.

"Fin," Mary said, swinging around to her brother. "He *is* coming back, yes?"

Finian sighed, looking uncomfortable, and finally shook his head. "No, he's not. I've only just found out myself. He's retiring from parish work. He's taking a part-time post in Cork."

"Oh." Mary paused, abandoning her chowder as she stared at her brother. "Then the church here will have to find another priest. You're coming home in June."

"That's only a couple of weeks from now," Finian said. "Father Callaghan delayed his final decision until the last possible moment. I can't leave the parish in the lurch. I'll stay on at least for a while."

"How long is *a while*, Fin?"

"I don't know yet is the honest answer. We've plenty

of time to discuss my plans. How do you like the chowder?"

Mary eyed him suspiciously. "Finian Bracken..." But she didn't finish, clearly tired. "The chowder's brilliant." She struggled to smile. "I'll want pie."

"Pie's always a good choice at Hurley's," Colin said. He glanced at Oliver but couldn't tell if he'd known his comment about Father Callaghan would stir up trouble between the Brackens. Probably. "You should give up on the oyster crackers and have pie, Oliver."

"Perhaps another dram of our passable Scotch," he said, then shifted to Mary. "What do you plan to see while you're in Maine?"

She hesitated, then smiled, looking less strained. "Everything," she said, her smile broadening. "I've a list."

The Rock Point Harbor Inn, locally known as the Donovans' inn, was located on a cove up past the village, in what was reputedly an old sea captain's house complete with a widow's walk. Oliver didn't protest when Emma and Colin both insisted on walking back with him. It was a beautiful spring night, and Colin would have held Emma's hand if not for their company. He at least appreciated being in familiar surroundings. His parents had their own quarters separate from the inn, but were considering converting a small cottage at the back of the property for themselves and using their current space for more guests.

Oliver led the way into the front sitting room as if he owned the place. "Look, our lovely innkeepers left fresh fruit, milk and cookies. Care for anything?"

"We're not staying," Colin said.

"Thank heavens for that." He grabbed a small plate and loaded it with fruit and cookies. "The Scotch and the walk to the harbor front and back woke up my appetite. You two can relax. I'm fairly certain none of my MI5 colleagues followed me here, but they know where I am."

"They're not your colleagues," Colin said. "They're your watchdogs."

"Well, there's that," Oliver said good-naturedly.

"If you put one toe out of line, they'll open the files on you," Emma added.

"Imagine how dull that would be for them." Oliver pointed to a grouping of a couch and two chairs. "Please, have a seat. Colin, you can stretch out on the couch if you'd like. I'm tired but you must be thoroughly exhausted."

"I'm fine, Oliver."

"As you wish." He sat on the couch himself, placing his plate on the coffee table. "MI5 hasn't demonstrated a keen interest in mythology, particularly my specialty of Celtic mythology, folklore and legends. But I know what you mean about stepping a toe out of line. I can't walk Alfred at the farm without worrying an agent will pop out from behind a tree." He turned to Emma as she sat in one of the chairs. "Alfred's the puppy."

"Have you ever walked him?" she asked.

"Not exactly but I was speaking hypothetically."

She leaned back, watching him eat a few strawberries and grapes. "Do your handlers know you threw the party at Claridge's on Sunday?"

Oliver's gaze settled on her. He ate more fruit. Colin sat on the chair opposite Emma. Finally, Oliver wiped his fingers on a cloth napkin, got up, poured tea into a mug and returned to the couch. "I prefer a cup and saucer but one manages. Tell me, Emma, did your father ferret out this tidbit? Your mother? Not that Texan agent. Padgett."

"It doesn't matter," she said.

"To you, maybe. To answer your question, yes, my MI5 colleagues are aware the philanthropic foundation set up in memory of my parents sponsored the party."

"Was this rumor about stolen mosaics your idea, too?" Emma asked.

"Mosaics happen to be a Norwood favorite and were Alessandro Pearson's specialty," Oliver said.

Colin could see Emma's impatience but doubted Oliver would care. "Trying to smoke out a few bad guys, Oliver?" Colin asked, hearing the sarcastic edge to his voice.

Oliver didn't react. "I aim to please, but I'm not an intelligence agent or a law enforcement officer. I'm a mythologist. Rumors and concerns are quite different from solid leads on wealthy collectors and dealers recklessly buying and selling ancient works of dubious origin. If I were a collector, I would want to be sure I wasn't buying something from people bent on murder, wouldn't you?" He didn't wait for a response. "If I could smoke out a few unscrupulous dealers and collectors, I'd be happy to do so."

"Is that why you're here?" Emma asked.

"I'm here for the Sharpe open house."

"Right," she said, plainly skeptical. "How did you put together your guest list for Sunday?"

"The foundation took care of it, with my guidance. MI5 wasn't involved. It was a spur-of-the-moment event. I don't have my eye on anyone in particular if that's what you're wondering. The show at the Victoria and Albert was convenient. It provided a natural reason for us to focus on people interested in antiquities."

"You invited my parents," Emma said.

"Of course. That was a courtesy. How could I throw a party and not invite them?"

"Even if it wasn't obvious it was your party?"

"I keep a low profile. Nothing unusual."

"How many parties have you thrown, Oliver?" Colin asked.

"A first time for everything."

"Oliver," Emma said, "was my grandfather involved with this party?"

"He was here in Maine, Agent Sharpe."

"He wasn't here when the invitations went out. Did you two cook up this party because of Alessandro's death?"

"No."

Emma smiled faintly. "I think that's the first time you answered the question I asked. I hope it's a true answer."

"I don't lie. It's too hard to keep track." He sank back against the soft couch cushions. "I could fall asleep right here. I'm staying in the room where fair Naomi MacBride stayed this winter. Don't worry, Colin, no one volunteered the information—I asked. How is Naomi? Well, I trust?"

Naomi had been out to the York farm in the Cotswolds that winter, prior to her arrival in Rock Point. Plucky and nosy, Mike called her, but he knew, as Colin did, that she was also a good intelligence analyst. "She's fine," he said.

"Excellent to hear." Oliver stifled a yawn. "I'm

going to take my tea up to my room and call it a night. You must be tired, too, Colin—Agent Donovan. Or don't FBI agents need sleep the same as we mere mortals do?"

"We need sleep," Colin said. He glanced at Emma. "Any more questions?"

"Not tonight," she said, getting to her feet.

Colin rose, too. "Be good, Oliver. Don't make me come back here in the middle of the night."

"I won't. I wouldn't want to get thrown out before sampling a Maine inn breakfast."

"We'll see ourselves out," Emma said.

The night was still and clear, cooler than Colin had expected. He took Emma's hand as they walked back up to his house. "I used up a lot of patience not strangling Oliver on the drive here. He's eccentric and unorthodox, but MI5 won't let him drift too far off the beam."

"If he and my grandfather are colluding…"

"Wendell knows where the edges of the beam are, Emma. He might stick a toe off the edge but he won't go over."

"He's in his eighties. He's been preoccupied with this trip home to Heron's Cove, and I'm sure Alessandro's death hit him hard and reminded him of his own mortality. Maybe he doesn't care."

"Not Wendell. Meanwhile, where's our meddling retired agent?"

"I hope he's in North Carolina but I doubt it."

"We could be chasing the nonexistent shadows of Gordy Wheelock's last case."

"That wouldn't be a bad outcome—a retired agent who got carried away with a few innocent coincidences that also got my grandfather and Oliver stewing and brewing."

"Better than we're missing something important."

"Yes."

"Alessandro Pearson worked in some dangerous areas during his career. He spent his last years focused on the preservation of mosaics in particular in their original context. He must have known all sorts in that world. Dealers, collectors, experts, ordinary workers."

"Possibly a terrorist or two," Emma said. "At least sympathizers."

"Scotland Yard's taking another look at his death?"

"Yes."

They'd done what they could for tonight. Colin suspected Emma knew it as well as he did. "We don't have a lot, Emma. A British archaeologist is dead. A known art thief threw a party in London. A former agent came to you to check out rumors and possibly lied about tripping on stairs, and your family's having an open house at their new Maine offices."

"Yank wants me to find out what Gordy's up to."

"And now me, too." They went into his house through the front door and paused in the small entry by the stairs. Colin eased his hand from Emma's and took her in his arms. "Meanwhile, how's the separate bedroom working out?"

"It was easier when you weren't here."

"I am here."

She smiled. "Yes, you are."

She laughed then. It was a good sound. The best. "Emma…"

"You don't have to carry me up the stairs, Colin."

"If I wanted to?"

"I wouldn't stop you," she said.

"Good, because imagining this moment got me through some rough nights."

He heard her intake of breath as he tightened his hold on her and lifted her, relishing the feel of her taut muscles, her soft breasts and the scent of her... her clothes, her hair, her skin. He hardly noticed her weight as he bounded up the stairs.

They both were laughing when they fell on his bed together.

"Emma," he whispered. "Emma, Emma."

"I can't believe you're back. At dinner and then with Oliver at the inn, I kept wanting to stare at you, just to be sure..."

"I'm here."

He kissed her, felt her hands on his waist, tearing at his clothes. It didn't take long before his pants, jacket and the rest were in a heap on the floor, with her skirt and top and tights—hell, the tights—scattered somewhere in the small, dark room. He managed to get her under the covers before he took her, knowing she was as ready as he was. His fatigue, the long hours crossing the Atlantic, the drive up here, the questions and frustrations all fell away as he made love to this woman who had transformed his life and would soon be his wife.

"I love you, Colin," she said, clutching him, crying out with her release.

All he could manage was to say her name again, but he knew it was enough.

Colin had drifted off when Emma's phone vibrated on the bedside table, waking him. She reached for it, glanced at the screen, then showed it to him. A text from Gordy Wheelock: Went for a whale watch and got my head screwed on straight. Going home. See you, kid.

Colin returned the phone to her. "Feel better?" he asked.

She shook her head. "No."

"Me, either."

17

Mary entered her brother's office at St. Patrick's Holy Roman Catholic Church of Rock Point, Maine. She was here at last, in this place he lived and worked. It was at once simpler and humbler than she'd expected, having relied on his vague descriptions, hunts on the internet and her own presuppositions for images. She fingered the cover of a thick book on Finian's desk on the history and geology of the Iveragh, one of the peninsulas jutting into the Atlantic on the southwest Irish coast. The book was one of the few familiar objects in the prosaic office. He'd stopped at the church to check on donations parishioners had dropped off for a rummage sale.

Her brother the whiskey man, sorting through old clothes and dishes.

Nothing about his life here made sense to her, except perhaps whiskey and chowder with his friends—but they were FBI agents, not fishermen. At least Emma and Colin were. Mary couldn't figure out Oliver York.

"You're still here," Finian said, obviously surprised

when he returned to his office. "I thought you'd be off to bed by now."

"It's not even ten o'clock."

"Here in Maine," he said.

"Which is where I am."

"Yes." He went around his desk chair and grabbed a sweater off a peg. "Oliver York, Sean Murphy, this retired FBI agent." He paused, coming back to her. "Is there anything else I should know about your recent adventures?"

"They're hardly adventures. I ran into Oliver by accident in Declan's Cross, and I meet all sorts on distillery tours."

"Are you certain you ran into Oliver by chance?"

"By fate instead, you mean? There's nothing romantic between us. He's sexy in his own English aristocratic way, I suppose—"

"Mary."

She grinned. "I can still be the pesky little sister. Do you know the Deverells? They have a summer house in Heron's Cove. Claudia Deverell did a distillery tour last week. Her name seems to strike a nerve with everyone."

"Not with me, nor should it with you, if I might be so blunt."

"As if I could stop you. Don't worry, I've no intention of sticking my nose into affairs that are clearly none of my business. But you have interesting friends, Fin. Oliver seems to be a bit of both friend and…" She sighed. "I'm not sure what. Too tired to think of the right word. Sean made it perfectly clear he doesn't consider Oliver a friend at all. What are your objections to him?"

"Sean can speak for himself, but I will put it this way—Oliver York lives in a different world from yours or mine."

"I can see that he lives in a different world from me," Mary said. "I don't know about you. Oliver's world is yours now, too, isn't it? Your friendship with these two FBI agents has sucked you into a few adventures of your own."

"You're here for a visit, Mary. It was just chance you were on the same flight as Colin and drove up here with him and Oliver."

"But Emma and Colin are your friends, aren't they?"

"Yes."

"You just don't want me to flirt with a wealthy Brit."

"He has a difficult past. It undoubtedly influences who he is now."

Mary could read layers and layers into that statement, but she was too tired. Every nerve in her body seemed to cry out for a soft, comfy bed. "Well, I'm here to have fun. Remember what fun is, Fin?" She gasped immediately, horrified by her remark. "I'm so sorry."

He shook his head. "It's okay."

She followed him out of the office and across a paved drive to the rectory. He'd sent photos when he'd first arrived in Rock Point, giving her an idea of where he lived, but it was different seeing the simple house and church on the southern Maine coast. She loved the traditional cottage he and Sally had rebuilt outside Killarney. It was so *them*. But there was no Fin and Sally anymore, there was just Fin, and if this place felt foreign and different, Mary supposed it was because she no longer knew her brother and the man he'd become. It was as if he'd exorcised anything that could remind him of his past, whether in his heart or his surroundings.

And she used the word *exorcised* deliberately, because it truly was as if he regarded any thought of his wife and daughters as the devil in possession of him.

Perhaps that wasn't fair, but Mary couldn't deny that was what she at least wondered.

They entered the kitchen and he went straight to the sink and grabbed the kettle. "A cup of tea will settle you down and help you sleep."

She sank into a chair and looked up at a cross above the table. "Do you believe you're here in Rock Point because of your sins, Fin?"

He turned on the tap and filled the kettle. "I'm here because I'm replacing Father Callaghan while he's on a one-year sabbatical in Ireland."

"You're also here because you answered a call to the priesthood," she said, hearing the combativeness in her voice.

"That was a while ago, Mary. It's old ground for us to traverse again."

She didn't back down. "Were you called because of your sins?"

"Let's have tea."

"You don't have to heed a calling," she said, pulling out a chair at the table. "I know that much. You can ignore it. You have a choice, even if it's a call you believe is from God."

"That's true. I also went through an exacting process of discernment that tested that call before I was accepted into the priesthood, perhaps more exacting because of my background."

"As a previously married man and father," she said.

"Yes." He set the kettle onto its stand and flipped the switch. "What's your calling, Mary?"

"To teach people about whiskey." She liked that as tired as she was, she'd been able to answer without hesitation. "You're running from yourself, Fin. I don't care what discernment process you went through. You fooled everyone including yourself. Including God, for all I know."

"Mary…" He sighed, looking as tired as she felt. "What do you want from me?"

"I want you to return home and marry Aoife."

He didn't seem surprised or offended by her answer. "Aoife has her own life."

"You were protective of her when she was here last fall."

"Because there was a killer on the loose."

"More than that. But never mind. You don't have to marry Aoife. You can marry anyone. Marry the barmaid at your favorite Killarney pub. Or don't marry anyone, just come home and be with your family."

He leaned against the counter, studying her a moment. "How's your romantic life these days?"

"Well, now that Oliver York is off my list of possible suitors, who knows?" Mary grinned at Finian. "It scares you that I'm all grown up now, doesn't it?"

He laughed. "It terrifies me."

He made tea, a lovely peppermint suitable for her delayed bedtime and her jet lag, and with a bit of luck it would also soothe her mad curiosity about the obvious tensions between the FBI agents and Oliver York, Gordon Wheelock and Claudia Deverell—just for starters. She recognized so much had been left unsaid since her encounter with Oliver and then Sean Murphy yesterday. Bumping into Colin Donovan at the airport that morning with a ticket on the same flight as hers couldn't have been merely a happy coincidence.

Then there was the dark, handsome FBI agent who'd met them at the airport in Boston. "Special Agent Sam Padgett," he'd said in a deep, drawling accent when he'd introduced himself.

Be still my heart.

Mary decided not to share that particular reaction with her priest brother, but as they had their evening tea together, she couldn't hide her excitement about the open house tomorrow. "I can't help it, Fin, I'm fascinated by the Sharpes and their work, and by Oliver. Kitty thinks he's half in love with Aoife, but he's so solitary. He has some soul connection at crosses. Either that, or he had something to do with the theft. Confessional. You'd never tell, would you?"

"You're exhausted, Mary."

"I am." She staggered to her feet. "I'll see you in the morning."

"If you're up early, help yourself to anything you need. Hurley's opens at four for the lobstermen."

"*Four?* Remind me not to fall for a lobsterman."

Finian smiled. "Sleep well. I'm glad you're here."

"I am, too." She hesitated. "I won't harass you about being a priest anymore. I promise."

"You can ask me anything and say anything to me."

"Thank you," she said, almost running into a wall as she exited the kitchen.

* * *

After Mary went up to bed, Finian sat outside on the front steps, enjoying the stillness and relative warmth of the clear, starlit spring night. At least it wasn't winter. Whatever Father Callaghan's plans, Finian dreaded staying in Rock Point for another Maine winter. The Donovan brothers told him he needed to take up snow-shoeing, cross-country skiing or ice fishing—or all three. Downhill skiing was another possibility, with a number of alpine resorts in northern New England, but it wasn't a favorite of the Donovans.

A movement by the church caught his eye, and he spotted Oliver York walking down the quiet residential street. Finian wasn't surprised, although he couldn't explain why.

Oliver waved and came up the walkway. "Mind if I join you?"

"Not at all."

"You'd think I'd have no trouble dropping off to sleep, but it's not the case. I went up to my room and looked out at the night sky and realized how far away London is, and I kept thinking I might not get back this time." He shrugged. "But that's what I always think when I travel."

Whether because of MI5 or his heists—or both? Finian decided not to ask. Oliver would be just as jet-lagged as Mary but he was a more experienced traveler, well aware of the disorienting effects a dramatic time change could have at first.

He looked up at the sky as if it held answers, then sighed and scraped a hunk of mud off his shoe, using the bottom step. "I don't want to take one crumb of Maine mud back to England with me. I'd probably be stopped at the airport, anyway. US customs would be looking for an excuse to lock me up."

"Not UK customs?"

He grinned. "Them, too." The idea didn't seem to bother him. "Frank Donovan says he makes the best blueberry muffins on the Maine coast. I believe him. I'm learning not to argue with a Donovan or engage in nuance. He also not too subtly let me know he still keeps a loaded firearm at the ready. A fun bunch, these Donovans."

"No truer friends."

"Or more undying enemies. I'm walking off tonight's cookies, and my own malaise. I'm the snake here. How are you, Father Bracken?"

"We're putting together the annual spring rummage sale."

"Will there be a bake sale, too?"

Finian had no idea if Oliver was genuinely interested or being sarcastic. "Of course," he said. "There are quite a number of excellent bakers in the congregation."

"You'll have to leave the open house early for Saturday services. I'll keep an eye on Mary if she wants to stay on. I can give her a ride back here."

"Emma or Colin can run her back here, or she can get a taxi. No need to trouble yourself."

"It's no trouble." Oliver put a hand on his lower back and stretched. "I didn't fly first class. I wish now I had. No worries about tomorrow, Finian. I wouldn't trust me, either, given what you know and think you know about me, but I promise you that I'm entirely trustworthy when it comes to the youngest Bracken.

She's prettier than you are, my friend, but this you already know."

"Mary's the only one unaware of how pretty she is."

"She's also smart, lively and perhaps not as innocent as she seems."

"Oliver."

"Easy. Our FBI friends will be keeping an eye on me, no doubt. It will be interesting to see who will be there tomorrow. Do you know much about the use of mosaic art in the domes and wall panels of early Byzantine churches?"

"Very little. I'm too busy sorting rummage goods these days."

"The building of churches exploded in the eastern Roman empire after the fall of Rome in 476 CE finally killed off the western empire. That the spectacular Byzantine mosaics in places such as Ravenna, Italy, and Madaba, Jordan, have survived the centuries is nothing short of miraculous. I'm interested in the incorporation of classical mythological motifs in images depicting Christian narratives, but that's for another day."

Finian smiled. "I'm afraid I know more about whiskey than I do ancient mosaics."

"But you'd recognize an image showing Christ's triumph over death, wouldn't you?"

"I would think so."

Oliver's gaze was steady, nothing about this conversation spontaneous or innocent. "No desire to decorate your office or St. Patrick's sanctuary with a couple of fifteen-hundred-year-old mosaics?"

"I can't fathom such a thing."

"Rock Point's a salt-of-the-earth place. I remember last fall you were planning a bean-hole supper. Or maybe you'd just had one. Either way, not sorry I missed it."

"Your loss," Finian said, amused. "Why are you interested in ancient mosaics, may I ask?"

"You may ask but I don't have a good answer. Rumors. Speculation."

"Rumors and speculation about what, Oliver?"

"Missing mosaics that no one knows who owned or anyone can describe. It's easier to move stolen art and antiquities that aren't well-known. The *Mona Lisa* would be recognized by even the most indifferent border agent. Some works of art present specific transport challenges. Mosaics, for instance, can turn to rubble if not properly and carefully handled."

Finian nodded, more interested now. "I knew quite a few avid art collectors in my days as a distillery executive. What about you, Oliver?"

"The Yorks were never into art collecting. Most of what I own in London and at the farm is rubbish. Pretty paintings of dogs and foxes and such that are primarily of sentimental value with little if any monetary value. The frames are generally worth more than the art itself. You'll have to come back to the farm, Fin. Bring Mary. We have plenty of room."

"Thank you for the invitation. It's good of you to think of us."

He grinned. "But you're never bringing your sister for a visit, right? It's okay. I've no one to blame but myself for the reluctance of friends to visit. I've made my own bed, as they say."

Finian felt a cool breeze and got to his feet. "It's been a long day for you."

"Yes, it has," Oliver said quietly. "Good night, Father Bracken."

No cheeky *Father Fin* this time. "Was this visit soul work or were you hoping I'd give you information?"

"It was an impromptu visit with a friend. The visits to Bracken Distillers by the retired FBI agent and Claudia Deverell likely have no direct connection with your family in Ireland, or with Mary's visit here. At least as far as I can see." He paused. "Thought you'd want to know."

"Are they of interest to the FBI or UK authorities— or to Irish authorities for that matter?"

"You're the one with friends in those places," Oliver said.

"Good night, Oliver. Welcome back to Maine."

18

Still with no food in the house, Emma and Colin decided on a late breakfast at Hurley's. They'd discussed going to his parents' inn for breakfast but opted to let them do their thing. Oliver would be jet-lagged and hungry, and he'd been looking forward to a real Maine inn breakfast. Emma left it to Colin whether to walk or drive to the harbor, since it was his first day home, but she wasn't surprised when he chose to walk on the bright, clear, crisp May morning.

When they arrived on the harbor, Frank Donovan texted his second-born son that his English guest was showing off photos of his puppy over wild blueberry muffins. "He's ingratiating himself," Colin muttered. He looked as if he wanted to about-face and go on to the inn after all, but he shook his head. "Let's stick to our plan. I like dogs, but I'm good with not being subjected to Oliver's puppy photos."

"Where do you suppose he got the name Alfred for the pup?"

"Batman," Colin said without hesitation. "Oliver went on one day about superheroes and mythology."

Emma glanced at him. "Sorry I missed that one."

He grinned. "I'm sure you are."

Andy Donovan, dark-haired, blue-eyed and rugged like his three brothers, was on his way out of the restaurant as they started to a table in the back. He and Colin greeted each other, Andy quickly filling in his older brother on his upcoming departure for Ireland. He'd spend a week with Julianne, then fly home with her in plenty of time for Colin's June wedding. "Franny's in Ireland now," Andy added with a grimace, referring to Julianne's grandmother. "She'll be heading home as I arrive."

"I thought she wanted you to escort her to Ireland since it's her first overseas trip," Colin said.

"Julianne talked her out of it." Andy shuddered. "I still get hives thinking about being on a plane with Franny Maroney for six or seven hours. When she landed, she handed Julianne a list of all the sights she wanted to see. I think they've done them all. Julianne says she'll be ready to hang out in a quiet cottage for a week before she comes home. Works for me."

"I'll bet it does," Colin said with a grin.

Andy went on his way, and Emma sat across from Colin at a small table by the windows overlooking the harbor. "Is your life starting to feel more normal?" she asked him.

"Starting. Normal is having Oliver in England."

And Gordy Wheelock back in North Carolina, Emma added silently.

"But let's enjoy our breakfast," Colin said. "I don't know if I trust your brother to serve real food at the open house. I'm going for a full all-American breakfast and throwing in one of Hurley's doughnuts for good measure."

Emma had a simple cheese omelet. Halfway through breakfast, the Scotland Yard detective called. He'd checked the autopsy report on Alessandro Pearson. "There was a substantial bruise in the middle of his back. It was attributed to the fall, but we're taking a closer look at the forty-eight hours before his death. His death didn't raise a single alarm here."

"Understood. Thanks for letting me know."

"You'll do the same with your findings," he said, not making it a question.

After breakfast, on their walk back up to Colin's house, Emma got another call, this one from Sam Padgett. "Good day for an open house," Sam said. "Weather-wise, anyway. I don't know about anything else. You aren't in Heron's Cove yet, are you?"

"Not yet."

"Then I'm not interrupting. I'm on my way to Gordy's hotel again. BPD doesn't have anything on assaults within a couple of blocks before midnight on Wednesday. I went out there last night to have a look for myself, maybe find a potential witness—someone who routinely hangs out around there or walks that way. No luck. I located a couple of possible spots for the steps where he could have tripped. I don't know what good that'll do, but I'll take a look again now that it's daylight."

"Maybe Gordy did trip on his shoelaces," Emma said.

"You don't believe that."

"No, I don't." She told him about Gordy's text. "I texted him back. So far no response."

"He didn't say whether he's leaving before or after the open house. Let me know if you need me to check into whale watches. When I considered joining HIT, first thing I thought of was, hey, I'll be in New England, I can go whale watching."

"You'd love it," Emma said, biting back a smile.

"No doubt." He was clearly not at all serious. "By the way, Yank told me to tell you he's not coming up there today for the party. I think it's something to do with his wife's knitting shop, but I'm not asking. Could be he doesn't want to run into Wheelock or get in the middle of this thing—whatever it is. All I got. Later, Emma."

She disconnected and slid her phone into her jacket pocket. Back at the house, she showered and changed into a dark navy jacket and pants, a crisp white shirt and her pistol, in a hip holster, concealed. Colin, too, dressed professionally in a charcoal-gray suit and tie. They weren't attending the Sharpe Fine Art Recovery open house as regular guests or, certainly, as hosts. Emma was convinced her brother and grandfather would not only understand her and Colin's approach to the day, but also expect it.

They drove to Heron's Cove in Colin's beat-up Maine truck, a small but important step, Emma knew, in his return to normalcy. Sam Padgett hadn't been kidding about the weather. The open house couldn't have landed on a better Saturday in May given the warm, sunny conditions. Emma was pleased especially for her brother, who was greeting guests at the front door when she and Colin arrived.

Lucas grinned as they headed up the front walk.

"Well, don't you two look like a pair of FBI agents," he said.

Emma laughed. "Imagine that."

"Welcome home, Colin. Help yourselves to food. We've hired a great local caterer. A few guests are here but it's still early."

"What about Gordy Wheelock?" Colin asked.

Lucas shook his head. "He's not here yet."

"But you still expect him?" Emma asked. "He didn't bow out at the last minute?"

"As far as I know he'll be here today. I haven't seen him but Granddad ran into him out on the docks the other night. He said Agent Wheelock looked like hell but blamed jet lag and overindulging during his first year in retirement. Listen, thanks for coming, both of you. We don't expect a big crowd but we'll have a good time. We won't run out of food, that's for sure."

No question about the food, Emma saw right away when she and Colin entered the house. Servers were carrying trays from the kitchen loaded with a variety of temptations, including mini lobster tacos, crab cakes, lettuce wraps, cheese, fruit and a variety of cookies.

Emma took the opportunity to text Gordy: We're at the open house. See you soon?

No immediate response. She also called but got his voice mail and left a brief message.

Colin glanced around the refurbished front room. "Last time I was in here, it was unfurnished. Looks good. Lucas is a forward thinker. He won't want Gordy dragging him into the past. Yank said Gordy looked off when he saw him on Thursday."

Emma nodded. "He wasn't himself but not alarmingly so."

"Do you think he could have gotten a bad health diagnosis?"

"A bad diagnosis and then he flies to London, Ireland and Boston and then drives up here?"

A server approached them with a tray of mini crab cakes. Colin helped himself to one but Emma was still full from their late breakfast. "Maybe it was a psychiatric diagnosis," he said as the server retreated. "Would the Gordy Wheelock you knew come all the way up here for a party and then not at least stop in for a few hors d'oeuvres? Even if he realized he'd been a fool over these rumors about stolen mosaics, would he just go home?"

"Not the Gordy Wheelock I know."

Lucas took a break from his post by the front door and joined them, snatching a couple of crab cakes. "Mingle, you two. Mingle. You're scaring people from coming in here."

"I doubt that," Emma said. "Colin and I haven't seen each other in a while. Has Oliver York arrived?"

"He's upstairs. Granddad's giving him the grand tour."

Lucas excused himself to greet more guests. Emma started toward the stairs in the entry, but Henry and Adrian Deverell and Isabel Greene entered the front room, drinks in hand as they greeted Emma. She introduced Colin. "The Rock Point Donovans," Henry said. "Yes, we used to buy lobsters from your family."

"I think your dad ticketed me once for speeding," Adrian added cheerfully. "But I don't go way back in this area the way my stepmother's family does."

"Claudia sends her regards," Isabel said. "She's swamped with a mile-long to-do list up at the house."

"It's cathartic for her to go through her mother's things," Henry said. "There's a timing to it, I think. One day you just know you're ready to tackle the job and you have to dive in before the moment passes. I know it was that way for me when my mother passed away. That was over a decade ago, and not a day goes by that I don't think of her. Now it's that way with Victoria. We all miss her terribly."

"Victoria left Claudia the house and the Norwood antiquities collection," Isabel said. "They're an enormous responsibility as well as a constant reminder of the mother she lost too soon, but it was the right thing for Victoria to do. Still, it's been difficult and isolating for Claudia emotionally. I don't think she'd mind my saying so."

"It's no secret she and her mother were close," Henry said.

Isabel nodded in sympathy. "I still can't believe she's gone. Sorry if we're being morose. It's our first trip back here since Victoria's death." She turned to Colin. "I hope you're not lost, Special Agent Donovan. I was Victoria's friend and became Claudia's friend."

Adrian polished off his drink. "It'll be interesting to see if Claudia discovers anything new and interesting in the house. Victoria loved to squirrel things away but she generally kept careful records. I'm the worst at record-keeping. But just what Claudia needs, one more old urn or coin." He leaned toward Emma with a grin. "Don't tell anyone I said that."

"Anyone who gives a damn is right here and heard you," Isabel said.

He winked. "Subtlety isn't my long suit. As far as

I'm concerned, an ancient mosaic might as well be Home Depot bathroom tile."

Isabel swatted him on the arm. "You're the worst, Adrian. I suppose you say the same about my mosaics?"

"We could call your work bespoke bathroom tile. How's that?"

His father looked amused. "As you can see, Emma, my son doesn't have the same appreciation for ancient art and artifacts that Claudia does. The two couldn't be more different."

"Claudia also appreciates my mosaic art," Isabel said, clearly not offended by Adrian's remarks. "This rat Adrian does, too, but he loves to tease. Have you ever seen an ancient mosaic floor in its archaeological context, Emma?"

"I have," she said, aware of Colin's stillness next to her. "I had the good fortune to visit a dig in Tunisia that uncovered the intricate mosaic floor of a classical Roman villa. It was fantastic. The design depicted the flora and fauna of the region."

"Mosaics really do provide us with a visual story of life in the ancient world," Isabel said. She gestured with her glass as Oliver came down the stairs. "Mr. York here could tell us about the myths and legends depicted on mosaics, couldn't you?"

"Some, no doubt," he said.

A server arrived with a tray of drinks, and Adrian exchanged his empty glass for a glass of champagne. "One of my interior designers in Atlanta insists that staging a condo with a few well-chosen antiquities helps it sell faster and at a higher price. It's best to use real antiquities but she says good fakes will do the trick."

"Are you serious?" Isabel asked.

"Totally serious. Most people have no idea about any of the controversies and protocols involved with the antiquity trade. There are bragging rights to having a bust of Apollo or a Spartan coin on your living room shelf."

"There's endless fascination with the ancient world," Henry said, his tone neutral. "You must deal with illegal antiquities in your work, Emma. It's far too easy for unscrupulous dealers to fake provenance. Victoria was as careful as possible, and her father and grandfather before her. But I wouldn't be surprised if we discover a fake or two in such a vast collection."

Oliver pointed down the hall toward the kitchen. "I thought I saw a bald eagle from an upstairs window. It was flying above the river. I was excited. Then Wendell Sharpe spoiled the fun and told me it was an ordinary seagull."

Isabel burst into laughter. "That must have entertained Wendell no end."

"I think he's still chuckling," Oliver said. "I do want to see a bald eagle while I'm here."

Emma had no doubt Oliver hadn't thought he'd spotted a bald eagle. He'd simply wanted to change the subject. But Henry and Adrian spotted someone else they knew and moved on, and Isabel chased a tray of hors d'oeuvres.

Oliver made a face. "Here I am alone with you two. Have you seen the Bracken siblings? They were on the back porch when I went upstairs. Mary's having the time of her life. Fin is keeping a close eye on her. You people do have a knack for trouble."

"I'm not convinced you aren't stirring up a little trouble of your own," Colin said. "You have a knack for it, too, along with drama and manipulation."

"I'm a—"

"You're a simple mythologist, yes, I know." Colin pointed at the ceiling. "Want to show me the upstairs? We can collect Wendell."

"After you," Oliver said.

Emma didn't follow them upstairs. Instead she rejoined Isabel and grabbed a glass of sparkling cider from a tray. "Not me," Isabel said. "I want alcohol in my drinks since I don't have to worry about driving. If I stumble into the river or the ocean, someone will pluck me out before I drown. The great weather is drawing people out. Cabin fever must be brutal here in the winter. But it's a great party, Emma. Thanks for having me."

"You'll have to thank Lucas."

"Lucas. I felt the cold wind blowing from him when we arrived. He'd never be openly rude, but it's obvious he'd rather we weren't in Heron's Cove. Well, you can tell him for me that Claudia is my friend and he's wrong not to trust her, or forgive her or—I don't know, give up on whatever grudge he has against her."

"That's between the two of them," Emma said, sipping her cider.

Isabel sighed, rolling her eyes. "Sometimes I wonder what it takes to get a pulse out of you Sharpes. Honestly, you're a cool, calm, collected bunch. Wendell has more heat than you and Lucas, but I bet he doesn't lose control, either. I suppose you can't get riled up easily in your line of work." She waved her hand, almost splashing champagne out of her glass. "I have the feeling I'm misbehaving. Thank you for letting me get that off my chest. Now we can smile and enjoy ourselves. Henry and Adrian don't plan to stay long. I'll leave when they do." She raised her glass. "I'm afraid I inhaled this—the one before it, too."

"Time for food, maybe."

"I had champagne at Claridge's on Sunday. It was more expensive than this one but I liked it less. Your former agent had a glass, too. Where is he? I thought he was coming today."

Emma helped herself to a tiny lobster taco, although she wasn't hungry. "How well do you know Agent Wheelock?"

"Not at all."

"I haven't seen him since Thursday. Have you?"

Isabel shook her head. "I haven't seen him since London. Claudia has. I hope she changes her mind and stops in today. She loves champagne." She waved to someone behind Emma. "Excuse me, won't you? I see someone who bought one of my first mosaics. I must say hello."

She scooted off, and Emma went through the kitchen, which was bustling with caterers, and out to the porch. It was crowded with guests. Some she recognized, some she didn't, but she was deliberately keeping a low profile. This wasn't her event.

She set her glass on a table and stood at the top of the steps. More guests wandered through the yard, bordered by hedges on one side and hydrangeas on the other. So much had changed but it was still very much the house where her grandparents had lived and worked for decades. Emma walked down the steps and across the yard to the retaining wall above the docks. The sun sparkled on the river. The waterfront was stunning on a beautiful late spring day, but she found herself feeling more distant from Sharpe Fine Art Recovery than ever.

And still no Gordy.

"The Deverells asked me to say goodbye," Lucas said, joining her. "Isabel Greene went with them. She shot me daggers on her way out. Colin is upstairs with Oliver and Granddad. I think they're trying to pin him down about his plans for your honeymoon."

"Uh-oh. Does he need me to rescue him?"

"Nothing fazes Colin. Well, you walking down the aisle in a wedding dress might." Her brother tilted his head back, his green eyes warm in the bright sun. "You don't have any doubts about getting married, do you, Emma?"

"None. But let's not talk about me right now. Today's your day, Lucas. You're in your element. I can see you're proud of the new offices. You should be."

"I am, and thanks. We all knew we needed to renovate, but I didn't expect new offices to be such a boost, not just for me but for the entire staff. The work took longer than I expected but everyone says it always does. We're reenergized. Granddad seems happy with how everything turned out. He's enjoying his suite."

"Mom and Dad will be thrilled, too."

"I did a virtual tour with them. They'll be here for your wedding, Emma. I know they will." Lucas glanced back at the house. "Today's turnout is better than I expected. I never thought I'd like this work, but I do. It suits me. I had something to prove, but I had room to maneuver and make a few mistakes. There's a certain freedom in modest expectations." He paused. "Anyway, Henry Deverell invited us up for drinks and a bite later on. You, Colin, Granddad, me, the Brackens. Oliver York. I'm not sure I like the idea of him getting lumped in with us."

"Will you go?"

"I haven't decided."

"I've never been clear on what you have against Claudia," Emma said.

He shrugged. "We got together a few times when I was in London. It didn't go further than that. It was a difficult time for her. She'd just quit the auction house to spend more time with her mother. Victoria never had a chance with the cancer. Claudia flew back and forth between London and Philadelphia, with side trips to New York. She was exhausted, physically and emotionally. She needed a friend."

"And you couldn't be that friend or she wanted more than a friend?"

"Maybe a little of both. It doesn't matter."

"She helped Gordy Wheelock around that same time," Emma said.

"I think he was a welcome distraction for her," Lucas said evenly. "Always good to help the FBI. She loves talking about antiquities, mosaics in particular. She and I didn't click. That's the long and the short of it. We had an awkward parting of ways. We're seeing each other for the first time since then, and it's a bit strained. That's all. If you have any other questions, Emma, can they wait?"

She nodded. "Of course."

"You must be pleased Colin is back. All good there?"

"All good. He's decided to buy a tux. Figures he'll need one being married to a Sharpe."

Lucas laughed. "Just because Granddad, Dad and I own tuxes doesn't mean we enjoy wearing them." He pointed with his champagne glass toward the marina. "Isn't that Mary Bracken?"

It was, indeed. Mary spotted them and waved, making her way down the docks. She hoisted up the hem of her long, casual skirt and climbed up around the edge of the retaining wall. "What a fun day," she said, smiling at Emma and Lucas. "I love Dublin, but I can't believe your grandfather ever left this place. I didn't realize it's right on the water. I could watch the boats and the birds and the people all day."

"It'll get a lot busier after Memorial Day," Lucas said.

"That's the unofficial start to the marina's summer season," Emma added. "Has Finian gone back to Rock Point?"

Mary nodded. "He had to prepare for Saturday services. He told me he hated to leave, but I didn't believe him. He never liked parties even before he was a priest. It's so good to see him. He's a good priest, isn't he?"

"I think so," Emma said.

Mary looked past her at the riverbank below the inn and parking lot. "That's Claudia Deverell, isn't it?"

Emma turned to Lucas. "I'll go down and say hi."

He took the hint. "Come, Mary," he said. "Have you ever tried Maine lobster?"

"Please tell Claudia hello from me," Mary said.

She and Lucas started across the lawn together to the house. Emma squeezed between the hedges and went down to the riverbank. The tide was going out, leaving behind strands of seaweed among the wet sand and polished stones.

"That was Mary Bracken I saw on the docks, wasn't it?" Claudia pointed vaguely toward the marina, past the Sharpe house. "It's hard to believe we just saw each other in Ireland. Today's a change from the dreary weather we had the day I did my Bracken distillery tour. Anyway, hello, Emma. What an absolutely gorgeous day."

"It is," Emma said. "I can imagine Mary does a great distillery tour."

"Informative and entertaining. It was my first. I enjoyed it. I love the history of the place. I hadn't realized Declan and Finian are fraternal twins. They were quite the visionaries. I saw the brother who's a priest now. If my brother ever announced he was entering seminary, I'd know he'd lost his mind. Finian Bracken seems suited to it from what I hear. It must be strange for Mary, getting used to him as a priest."

"I'm sure it has its moments," Emma said.

"You must know, since your family had to get used to you as a nun—or an almost-nun, at least. At least your convent and Father Bracken's parish are in a beautiful place. Rock Point has its charms, but I guess I'm spoiled by Heron's Cove." Claudia bit her lower lip. "Can I blame that remark on fatigue and a lapse in good manners?"

"No problem."

"Mary Bracken's part of the world on the southwest Irish coast is beautiful, too," Claudia said, sounding less awkward. "I know you must be curious, Emma—I chose Bracken Distillers because of today's open house and my return here. It wasn't one of those small-world moments. I'd heard about the Brackens' friendship with your family." She shrugged. "It just seemed like the thing to do."

"Sounds as if you had a busy week before you headed here."

"Very. Intense, too, with Alessandro Pearson's death and funeral." Claudia toed at a stone embedded in the sand. "You've caught me in a gregarious mood. I put off coming back here. It's been easier than I thought it would be, maybe because I did wait. Every nook and crevice of the house reminds me of my mother. Walking along Ocean Avenue and listening to the waves..." She breathed in again. "It's as if she's with me."

"I'm sorry for your loss," Emma said simply.

Claudia nodded without comment, her eyes welling with tears. Finally she got the stone loose, swooped down, scooped it up with one hand and pitched it into the river. It disappeared with a plop, barely causing any ripples. "I thought I'd see Agent Wheelock here," she said.

"I did, too." Emma stayed above the tide line, where the stones were dry, not stuck in the sand. "When did you see and speak with him last?"

"Early afternoon on Thursday. He stopped to see me at a small gallery on Newbury Street owned by friends of mine. Isabel shows her work there—Isabel Greene. She was here."

"We chatted briefly."

"She's very opinionated," Claudia said. "She can be protective of me because of my mother and their friendship. It's a little odd because Isabel and I are close to the same age. Obviously you know I helped Agent Wheelock with an antiquities investigation. I don't know any details because he didn't tell me, but the case must be in his files. My part wasn't a big deal."

"What exactly did you do?" Emma asked.

"I gave him a tutorial on the antiquities trade and assorted controversies through the centuries and took him through the work my mother and Alessandro started on mosaic preservation training. Antiquities 101, basically. Gordy said he'd be here today, but he didn't sound enthusiastic. He didn't look well when I saw him on Thursday. I assumed he was just tired, but maybe he was coming down with something, too."

Emma picked up a small stone and rubbed the smooth, pale blue-gray surface with her thumb. "Did you ask him to come to London last week?"

"No, but I called him and that's why he came." Claudia squatted down and picked through wet stones, choosing one about the size of an egg. "I was upset about Alessandro's death—Alessandro Pearson. You knew him. He died suddenly, and I was coming back here…" She stood with her stone. "I called Gordy on impulse. I wanted to talk to him. We'd become friends and stayed in touch on and off after his retirement, at least for the first few months." She captured a few windblown strands of her fine blond hair and tucked them behind her ear. "Look, Emma, I have nothing to hide. I did my best to help Gordy last year, as I would have you or any other FBI agent, or your grandfather or parents or brother, for that matter. I put him in touch with Alessandro if he needed more information. I'm not a scholar like he was. Then he retired. Gordy, I mean, not Alessandro."

"It must be tough, losing Alessandro so soon after your mother," Emma said.

Claudia flung her stone, watching it plop into the water. "At least he was almost ninety and died of a heart attack. My imagination and emotions got the better of me last week. I just wanted to hear Gordy tell me everything was okay, from the point of view of a friend and an experienced investigator." She stooped, grabbed another stone and stood straight again. "I know many people in my work. Every single one of them has been honest and reputable—dealers, scholars, collectors, educators, conservationists. They might not agree on every topic involving antiquities, but they aren't mixed up in looting, pillaging, fraud and funding terrorists."

A lobster boat puttered through the narrow channel from the ocean into the river, creating gentle waves as it made its way to its mooring. "Did you and Agent Wheelock discuss Alessandro's death or stolen mosaics when he was in London last weekend?" Emma asked.

"Not specifically, no. He's become cynical, Emma. He didn't believe me when I told him I had no reason to think any foul play was involved in Alessandro's death. I was just worked up about coming back here."

"When did you decide to go to Ireland?"

"About ten minutes after I called Gordy. It's a short flight. I really was worked up. The only connection between calling Gordy and Ireland is being here. The open house today. Going through a house that's been in my family for generations, with all its memories. Seeing people I've known since childhood." She tossed her stone into the dissipating waves created by the lobster boat. "I think Gordy understood. He had an amazing career. It had to be hard to let go."

Emma watched Claudia as she stared out at the

water. "And you haven't spoken to Gordy since Thursday at the Newbury Street gallery?" Emma asked.

Claudia shook her head, grabbing more stray strands. "I stood him up. I told him I'd meet him at my friends' apartment and I never did. I could see he was in a mood and I was already in enough of one myself. I picked up Isabel at the train station and we came straight here. I didn't call, text or email him. I'm not proud of it. I thought he'd stay the night in Boston, but he didn't." She turned and motioned vaguely with one hand toward the street. "I saw him out here Thursday night. We didn't talk, if that's your next question. I don't know that he saw me."

Emma was silent a moment. "How close were you two?" she asked finally.

"I know what you're asking and I'm not going to comment." Claudia brushed bits of mud off her hands from her stones. "I knew Gordy would be in touch with you and you'd have questions. I know my father invited you all up to the house. I hope you'll join us." She shifted her gaze to Emma. "I should go."

"Why don't you come in and see the new offices?"

"Another time, maybe. Is it weird for you, Emma, seeing the changes in the house your grandparents called home for so long?"

"I saw the plans and the work being done over the fall and winter."

"It wasn't a shock, then. That must help. And, of course, your grandfather is still with us."

"Very much so," Emma said.

Claudia smiled, looking slightly more relaxed as she headed up the riverbank and out to the parking lot and past the inn. Emma waited a few moments, then flung her stone into the river. She waved to the lobsterman, a guy she knew from Rock Point, and started back to the house.

"Gordy, Gordy," she said softly. "It's time we had a real talk, my friend."

The upstairs offices bore no resemblance to the bedrooms they'd once been. Colin had only been up there once before the carpenters had started ripping the place apart. The transformation from old house to modern offices was a testament to Lucas Sharpe's vision and tenacity. Wendell Sharpe obviously approved. He insisted on giving Colin and Oliver a grand tour. Other guests came upstairs for a look and greeted the renowned art detective with a kind of reverence that obviously made him uncomfortable.

"You look as if you could throw things, Agent Donovan," Oliver said as he, Colin and Wendell entered Lucas's office, which overlooked the tidal river.

Wendell grunted. "Don't give him any ideas."

"Excellent point. Combine boredom, jet lag and frustration, and out the window we go. Hell of an end to a good party." Oliver pointed to a tray a server had left behind on a desk, with an array of bite-size cookies. "These will improve your mood."

"My mood's fine," Colin said.

Wendell's eyebrows went up slightly but he said nothing.

Colin glanced out a window in Lucas's office. He could see Emma down on the lawn. He turned back to her grandfather and the thief. "You two can tell me about London last week."

"Oops, Wendell," Oliver said, "looks as if the FBI knows about our devious plotting."

"I wish you were as funny as you think you are," Colin said.

Oliver sniffed. "Who's trying to be funny?"

"Don't let him get under your skin, Colin," Wendell said. "Oliver knows you'll put him on a plane back to London before you'll arrest him. We weren't talking about anything interesting. I wish we had been. All anyone wants from me is my take on the changes I've seen in the world of art and antiquities since I started this business sixty years ago. I feel like a damn dinosaur."

"Henry Deverell and his son were here with Isabel Greene," Colin said. "Did you see them when you were in London last week for Alessandro Pearson's funeral?"

Wendell Sharpe didn't skip a beat. "They didn't attend Alessandro's funeral if that's what you're asking. Claudia did. I was aware they were in town. Isabel Greene lives in London part of the year. They both were at the party at Claridge's but Henry and Adrian had gone home by then. Me, too, as it turns out."

Oliver peered at the cookies. "I want more of those lobster tacos but they're not making their way up here. Shall we go downstairs?"

"Hold on," Colin said. "Wendell, what did you and Gordy Wheelock discuss the other night?"

"The past, parties, Oliver and the British intelligence services."

"There," Oliver said, nodding out the window. "It *is* an eagle. I'm off before I miss it."

Colin didn't stop him. Neither did Wendell. "Come

on," Colin said. "You can tell me about your conversation with Gordy on the way downstairs."

But Wendell's recap didn't explain what Gordy Wheelock was up to, where he was or why he hadn't responded to Emma's messages. Colin walked back to the kitchen with the old man, passing several newly arrived guests. "Wendell, if you have anything that can help us understand what's going on, you need to tell me."

"I'm not the one you need to talk to."

"You know who and what Oliver is. You'd be wise to steer clear of him, but you know that. You don't need me to tell you. What have you two cooked up?"

"I'll admit I helped Oliver with his tea at Claridge's. Hardly a capital offense. He thought the tea would be a good way to gather information and get an idea of what people were talking about after Alessandro's death."

"Do you believe his death was due to natural causes?"

"*He* might not have thought so as he plunged down those steps, but the medical examiner said it was a heart attack. He didn't die instantly and he got banged up in the fall, yet it wasn't what killed him."

"I hear a *but* in your voice."

"But the rumors of stolen mosaics and his death are quite the coincidence, aren't they?"

Colin couldn't deny it. "Go on."

"I'm sorry he died before we could have a pint together last week. Perhaps he was agitated about these stolen mosaics and that prompted his heart attack. I don't know. I'm speculating. Oliver wasn't in contact with him if that's your next question, and as far as I'm aware Gordy Wheelock didn't arrive in London until after Alessandro's death."

"What about the Deverells?"

"You'll have to ask them. I was in London a short time. I'd lost a friend, if not a close friend at least one I will miss. I visited my son and my daughter-in-law and I came on here, back to Maine."

Not *home to Maine*, Colin noted. An elderly couple greeted Wendell, and Colin left them and went out to the back porch. Emma smiled as she came up the steps. "I just felt a surge of pure, simple happiness seeing you here," she said. "Home safe and sound again."

He pointed to a corner of the porch. "Did your easel get tossed during renovations?"

"It's tucked in a closet. Lucas says I can paint here anytime, but I'm ready to move on. My last lobster boat almost looked like a lobster boat, and painting here won't be the same with all this new stuff in the house."

"Proper electrical sockets, efficient heat, toilets that flush the first time..."

She grinned. "I was thinking in terms of new kitchen cabinets."

"The fun stuff."

She eased in close to him. "Maybe I'll set up an easel on the porch at Rock Point Harbor Inn and get into painting shore birds. Sister Cecilia is convinced I can do it."

"My folks like Sister Cecilia. Lots of things to paint at the inn. You could try your hand at a still life and paint my father's wild blueberry muffins."

"That would be something."

He gazed down at the docks. "What's on your mind, Emma?" he asked.

"I don't like it that Gordy hasn't shown up today."

"I don't, either."

"I don't see him turning around and going home without stopping here first. It's possible, but I don't see it. If nothing else, he knows I'm asking questions. He'd at least text me that he's back in North Carolina."

Colin nodded. "If Gordy's hiding something, he'd do a better job of reassuring you and getting you off his back. If he's not hiding anything, he wouldn't waste your time."

Emma was silent a moment. She ran her fingertips across the freshly painted porch rail. Colin noticed the ring he'd placed on her finger in November. Some days, he still couldn't believe she'd said yes to marrying him. But it felt right. No question.

"I'd like to take a look at the cottage where Gordy's staying," she said. "I think I know where it is. It's one of three or four cottages about three quarters of a mile from here."

"I know them. Walk or drive?"

"Drive. It's quicker."

19

Emma rolled down the passenger window when Colin turned onto a shaded dirt road lined with white pines and spruce trees. She breathed in the evergreen-scented spring air. She wasn't surprised Colin knew the way to the cottages where Gordy had said he was staying. This was his turf as much as hers, and probably more so given his and his family's Maine law enforcement experience.

She'd tried Gordy again. Cell phone, home phone, email, text.

Nothing.

She stared out her window at the woods. "A friend of mine's parents owned these cottages when I was a kid. They sold them and moved to Jacksonville when we graduated high school."

"Where's your friend now?"

"In Florida, too, at least last I heard. She's a physical therapist. We didn't stay in touch, but I heard from her last year after Sister Joan died. She'd seen the news in the papers and got in touch with Lucas, and he let me know. We emailed back and forth a few times. It was good but we don't have much in common." Emma paused, noticing a gray squirrel zipping out to the end of a pine branch. The truck rattled on, bouncing over ruts and rocks, and she didn't see where the squirrel went. She turned to Colin. "I don't have a lot of close friends from my childhood."

"Neither do I. I arrested half of them when I was with the marine patrol."

She had no idea if he was serious. "I won't have a big bridal party."

He frowned at her. "Emma, did my mother get you thinking about this?"

"I was thinking about it before we had our lunch yesterday. Being a Sharpe, being with the sisters—it affected my formation of friendships, especially in my teens and early twenties."

"It was my mother," he said, downshifting. "Want me to tell her to back off?"

That was Colin, she thought. Cutting to the chase. "She doesn't need to back off. We had a lovely lunch."

"You told her you have friends, they just don't all live within ten miles of you like hers?"

"I phrased it differently."

"Have to be direct with her. No pussyfooting. If you give her an opening, she'll ram right through it. She's tough but fair. I wasn't kidding. I learned some great interrogation techniques from her." He grinned. "She told me you wore a skirt to lunch."

"I'll be her first daughter-in-law."

"But not the last at the rate things are going with Mike and Naomi and Andy and Julianne." Colin slowed the truck, his expression turning serious as he nodded up ahead. "Is that Gordy's car?"

Emma nodded. "The one he rented."

The black sedan, the sole vehicle in the cul-de-sac, was parked in front of the middle cottage. Colin pulled in behind it, threw the truck into Reverse, shut off the engine and reached for his weapon in quick, smooth motions. "Emma," he said.

"I see."

A body lay across the threshold of the front door of the cottage. A man, unmoving. Emma could make out an outstretched arm, a hand, a shoulder. Thinning gray hair.

"It's Gordy," she said, drawing her own pistol.

She and Colin got out of the truck simultaneously, met at the hood and approached the cottage. He went to the left of the door and she to the right. Any hope Gordy was unconscious was eliminated when they got close to him. His face was tucked in the crook of his outstretched arm, as if he might have lain down on the threshold for a nap—except nothing about his features said he was sleeping. He was dead, and he'd been dead awhile.

Emma ignored the twist of pain in her gut and focused on Colin. They needed to clear the cottage for assailants, anyone else injured, dead or hiding. They went in, moving quickly through the small structure, checking the living area, bedroom, bathroom and closet. There was no one. The bed was still made but a small suitcase had been unpacked, clothes neatly stacked on top of the dresser. The shower had been used, a towel hanging to dry on a rack.

The back door was locked, no windows were open or broken.

Colin holstered his pistol and returned to the body.

Emma did the same, standing back from him. He had more experience with death investigations than she did. "Can you tell what killed him?"

"Not yet."

There was no immediate, obvious indication of how he'd died—no visible blood, trauma, bullet or knife wound or other injuries. Emma didn't see any signs of a struggle. "Do you think he could have been hurt worse when he fell at his hotel on Wednesday?" she asked. "Some kind of slow bleed and he just collapsed?"

"Maybe but I doubt it."

"If he was attacked and had a chance to fight back, he would have. He said he was rusty, but he had decades of training and experience. He'd have put up a fight."

Colin stood next to her and touched her shoulder. "Let's go outside. I'll call it in."

She nodded. She glanced at the kitchen area but didn't see groceries. A metal spatula and saucepan were in the drainer next to the sink, as if they'd been recently washed and set to dry—by Gordy? The cottage's housekeeper?

Emma followed Colin out of the cottage, skirting Gordy's body. The afternoon sun beating on Gordy's rented car and the driveway struck her as incongruous, wrong, even, with a fellow agent—a friend—lying dead. She barely heard Colin as he stood by his truck and reported the death to the local police. Heron's Cove didn't have a big police department. The Maine state police would lead the investigation.

Colin disconnected and turned to Emma. "They told us to sit tight," he said. "I would have, too."

Emma squinted at him against the bright sun.

"Claudia Deverell said she saw Gordy crossing Ocean Avenue Thursday night after he talked to my grandfather. Unless she's lying or was mistaken, Gordy was alive then."

"The text last night," Colin said. "It sounded like him?"

"Yes."

"We'll look for a phone when the locals get here." He glanced back at the body. "It's off season. I'm not surprised he wasn't found sooner. Unoccupied cottages in a relatively isolated location can attract people looking for trouble."

"Gordy could have surprised someone going through the place. He was out of shape. He'd put up a fight but a close call wouldn't necessarily go well for him." Emma held up a hand, as if stopping herself. "I know we can't jump to conclusions."

"I'll let Yank know what's going on."

As much as he and Gordy hadn't got along, Emma had no doubts that Matt Yankowski would be saddened to learn about Gordy's death. And frustrated. "He should have trusted us," she said.

"I'm sorry, Emma. I know you worked with the guy."

While he called Yank, she walked down the dirt driveway a few yards, taking a moment to stand in the sun and breathe. She glanced up at the sky, noticed the green of a tall spruce tree against the blue sky. Another deep breath, and she got out her phone. She needed to give Sam Padgett the news.

"Damn, Emma," he said after she'd updated him. "That's not what I was expecting to hear. I was actually about to call you. If you want me to wait—"

"No, go ahead, Sam."

"I just finished meeting with the bellman I mentioned. Turns out he took a picture of a golden retriever puppy in front of the hotel and also caught in the background someone putting an envelope through the open window of a cab. He says it's the envelope that the cab driver found and gave to him. You can't see much in the photo, but I had him text it to me and I'm texting it to you."

"You mean you can't see the person with the envelope?"

"That's right. The main event is the puppy. I assume you'll look for it in Wheelock's things."

"Thanks, Sam."

"No problem." He paused. "No way any of us could have predicted this, Emma."

He disconnected without waiting for her to respond. A few seconds later, the photo arrived, and she checked it on her screen. An adorable puppy, a cab and part of a figure, mostly hidden by the cab. If not for the bellman's description, there'd have been no way to guess what was happening from the photo.

The local police arrived first, followed quickly by the state detectives. Colin knew a few of them. "We're on this, too," he told the lead detective, who didn't argue.

20

From the moment she crossed the threshold into the foyer of the Deverell house, Mary fell in love with the sturdy, faded grande dame of a place with its magnificent views of the Atlantic and the stunning Maine coast. She'd have loved a tour of the entire house but settled for the first floor. Every room had a unique charm. She smiled to herself as she went out to the large, curved front porch. She inhaled the sea air. This place, the open house and handsome Lucas Sharpe and Adrian Deverell and mysterious, sexy Oliver York— how could she go wrong?

Ah, yes, Mary Bracken, you are going to have a grand time in Maine.

"I can't imagine tearing down this place," Mary said to Isabel Greene, who'd explained that was a real possibility. "Would a new owner be able to put up some new monstrosity?"

Isabel shook her head. "Not on this section of Ocean Avenue. There are strict regulations governing what people can build between the inn next to the Sharpe offices and the nature preserve about a mile up the road. The idea is to preserve the historic and natural beauty of the area."

"That's a relief, then."

"Where do you live, Mary?"

"I have a flat in Killarney. Have you ever been to Killarney?"

"I've never been to Ireland. I keep saying I will, but I just haven't done it, even though I spend about half the year in London." Isabel sat on the wide porch rail, a breeze catching the ends of her hair. "I suppose you haven't had a chance to be homesick yet."

Mary tightened her denim jacket around her in the stiffening breeze. "I won't be here long enough to get homesick. Where's your family?"

"I don't have much of one. I have a brother in New York. Our parents are gone."

"Mine are, too, but I have two older sisters and two older brothers."

"I saw Father Bracken leaving today," Claudia said, coming through the front door out to the porch. "I know he and your brother Declan aren't identical twins, but they do look a lot alike. Quite a good-looking guy to lose to the priesthood."

Mary made no comment. She noticed whitecaps on the horizon and a small yacht making its way toward the river and, presumably, the marina next to the Sharpe offices. She'd enjoyed checking out the boats and docks during the open house. Once Finian had returned to Rock Point, she hadn't known anyone there except Emma, Colin and Oliver. She hadn't wanted to monopolize their time and wasn't up to a great deal of socializing with strangers after her long trip yesterday. Anyway, she socialized all the time in her work. It had felt good to go off on her own to look at boats.

She sat with Isabel and Claudia on wicker chairs and had iced tea as they engaged in an amiable, free-flowing conversation. They were discussing whiskey when the police and Colin and Emma arrived. From their grim expressions, Mary knew instantly they'd come with terrible news.

Claudia gasped, clutching her shirt just above her heart. "Something's happened. Isabel…"

"Steady," her friend whispered. "Steady, Claudia."

A middle-aged man introduced himself as a state police detective. Colin and Emma stayed to one side, silent as the detective explained his reasons for being there.

A dead FBI agent…

Mary had to fight her way through the fog of jet lag and shock to comprehend what they were saying. The FBI agent who'd died was the American who'd toured the distillery that past Monday. Gordon Wheelock. And he hadn't just died. He'd been killed. But Mary wasn't even sure if that was what the detective had said or if it was what she'd inferred, or if someone else had said it.

The men came out to the porch. Henry Deverell and his son as well as Oliver York and Wendell Sharpe.

Mary remained on her chair, but Claudia and Isabel both had jumped to their feet and Isabel had an arm around Claudia as they both absorbed the news.

The detectives said they had a few questions they wanted to ask. Mary didn't think they could possibly mean to include her in that statement, but it wasn't true. "Mary," Emma Sharpe said, "would you mind going through Gordon Wheelock's visit to Bracken Distillers on Monday? It could help us understand what's happened."

"I don't mind. I'll do it, of course."

"I don't understand what this man's death has to do with us," Henry Deverell said.

No one answered him. Mary went with Emma and a female detective to a far corner of the porch, where they could chat. She heard someone crying and glanced back, just as Claudia Deverell collapsed onto a chair, her face in her hands as she sobbed. Mary glanced at Emma, who was taking in Claudia's reaction to the retired agent's death. Everyone else was visibly upset and shaken, but Claudia was completely broken up.

As she related the details of Special Agent Wheelock's visit to the distillery, Mary thought of Sean Murphy two days ago in Declan's Cross, trying to talk her out of this trip. That his instincts had proved right and she would encounter danger and violence, if not a direct threat to her, was no comfort at all.

Would the police want to question Finian, too?

When the detective finished, she thanked Mary and withdrew. Emma didn't go with her. "I'm sorry, Mary," she said.

"Did you know Agent Wheelock?"

"I worked with him in art crimes."

"He said he knew your grandfather..." Mary didn't finish. She'd already told the detective, and Emma had been there, quietly observing. "Otherwise we only talked about whiskey and the distillery. He said he's a bourbon man." But she realized she was talking more to herself than to Emma. She gave herself an inward shake. "I can go back to Rock Point now?"

Emma nodded. "Do you have a ride?"

"I'm leaving now," Oliver said, joining them. "I can return Mary to her brother."

Emma didn't look enthusiastic, but Mary jumped at the chance. "Thank you," she said, rising.

"You'll be at the inn?" Emma asked him.

"There, the rectory or Hurley's. Promise."

"Be where I can find you, Oliver."

"As you wish, Agent Sharpe."

Oliver had driven to the Deverell house from the Sharpe offices and parked in front. Mary shivered in a breeze off the water that an hour ago she'd have found refreshing.

"I'm glad our boys and girls in blue didn't block me in," Oliver said, touching Mary's wrist. "Other side, Mary. We're driving on the right."

"Of course. Sorry."

She went around the front of the car and got in, suddenly fighting tears. "Did you know Agent Wheelock?" she asked Oliver as he climbed in next to her.

"Of him."

"I can't imagine his death had anything to do with his visit to Ireland."

But Oliver pretended not to hear her. As he pulled onto the street, Mary noticed the strain at the corners of his eyes and mouth, unsettling, she thought, in such an irreverent, unflappable sort. She debated texting Declan or Sean, but what could they do from Ireland?

Services were wrapping up when Oliver pulled in front of St. Patrick's rectory. Mary unfastened her seat belt but couldn't seem to make herself move. "Thank you," she said, her voice hoarse with emotion.

"I can wait with you until your brother is finished."

She shook her head, rallying. "No. You go on. I'll see you later, I'm sure. Thank you."

"Except for that last bit, it was a fine day, wouldn't you say?"

But his cheeky remark didn't quite take, and he seemed to know it. Mary thanked him again and got out of the car. By the time she walked down to the side entrance, Finian was crossing the driveway between the rectory and the church to her. From his expression, she knew he'd already learned about Gordy Wheelock's death, whether from Emma, Colin, a parishioner or even Oliver, she couldn't guess. She supposed it didn't matter.

"Mary," Finian said, opening his arms.

They embraced and, enveloped in her brother's priestly garb, reassured by his presence, Mary could only think that she wanted him to say a prayer. But she didn't ask him to. Instead they went inside, and he put on a kettle for tea.

"What happened, Mary?" he asked her.

"The FBI agent who visited the distillery this past Monday is dead, and from the way the police are acting, I think he was murdered." She took in a shallow breath. "And I think they suspect the killer was at the open house today, or at least had something to do with it. I don't know it for a fact, but—" This time she gulped in air. "I've never been involved in a homicide investigation."

"Ah, Mary."

She sniffled, glaring at him. "A year ago you'd have been shocked at such an event, but you're not now, are you? It's these friends of yours. These FBI agents. Oliver. Wendell and Lucas Sharpe. Even Sean Murphy. I wonder if it started last year, before you came here—when you helped Sean with the smugglers."

"When what started?"

"This affinity you have for danger and dangerous people. *That's* your calling, Fin. It's got nothing to do with God. It's about you."

He didn't look upset, offended, chagrined. He was listening to her, she realized, but that only agitated her more.

"I'm not one of your bloody parishioners," she said.

"No, you're not. You're my sister. I'll make tea, and you tell me what's happened. Then we'll talk."

"You'll talk, too?"

"Yes, I'll talk, too."

Finian's first impulse when Mary finished was to drive her to Boston and put her on a flight to Ireland. Instead, they walked to the Donovans' inn, not because it was what he wanted to do but because it was what she needed. As he'd suspected, she hadn't had the patience to delve into a deep conversation about his vocation and his friendships since arriving in Maine almost a year ago.

A death investigation. A likely murder.

Mary...

Finian shuddered next to her, but if she noticed, she said nothing. He doubted she had noticed. She seemed to welcome getting out in the fresh air, moving—seeing Oliver again. Finian reminded himself she didn't know Oliver was a serial art thief. From Mary Bracken's point of view, Oliver York was kind, intelligent, mysterious and quite good-looking. He was also as much an outsider in the current drama as she was.

Of course, Finian knew that wasn't the case. The dead FBI agent would have investigated the American thefts Oliver had committed. Oliver had visited Declan's Cross, arriving just in time to bump into Mary, who'd escorted both Claudia Deverell and then Gordon Wheelock on distillery tours.

In Finian's experience, Oliver would skirt the truth to the point it was effectively a lie, and he used his adventures—and not just burglarizing—to keep his personal demons at bay, to alleviate the pain and distress of the helpless little boy inside him who'd endured a terrible ordeal.

But would he kill anyone?

No.

Finian shook his head, confident that the man who'd driven his sister back to Rock Point today wasn't a killer. Even so, Finian felt tight-lipped and tense. It was his fault Mary was here, in the middle of another violent mess involving his friends. He would trust Emma, Colin and Colin's brothers with his life, but that didn't mean he'd trust them with his sister's tender sensibilities…her innocence.

Colin greeted them on the main walk to his parents' inn. He kissed Mary on the cheek. "I'm sorry about today," he said simply.

"It's the way of things sometimes." Her ashen face and slight, anxious smile belied her words. "Is Emma with you?"

He shook his head. "I stopped to see my folks. Oliver isn't here. I want to talk to him."

Finian got the message. "We'll see him another time, then."

"Thanks, Fin."

"The man today—he was murdered, wasn't he?"

Colin's eyes told the story. Yes. Murder. But Finian knew his friend wouldn't—perhaps couldn't—say the words out loud. "I'll see you later," he said instead.

As Finian turned with Mary, she stopped abruptly, spinning back around to Colin. "I think there was something between Claudia Deverell and Agent Wheelock," Mary blurted. "I felt it when he was at the distillery, and I felt it again today when you all arrived with the terrible news."

"Do you have any reason to believe she already knew he was dead?" Colin asked.

Mary blanched, looking unsteady on her feet. "No, no, that's not what I mean at all. I have no evidence for you, I'm afraid. I told the detective everything I know, and that's all I can do."

"If you think of anything else, get in touch with the detective, or with Emma or me. Don't hesitate, Mary. We'd rather have you err on the side of telling us too much than too little."

"I understand," she said, her voice strong and clear. She stood straighter, squaring her shoulders. "I hope you find whoever is responsible for Agent Wheelock's death."

Colin gave a curt nod. "We will."

This time, Mary didn't turn back. As she and Finian walked up to the rectory, he realized this wasn't the bubbly Mary Bracken he knew—the little sister he'd wanted to show a little of Maine and Boston. She'd been so young when his wife and daughters had died. For months, he'd disappeared into grief and drink, and then into seminary and the priesthood. He'd envisioned himself serving an Irish parish but Father Callaghan of Rock Point, Maine, had decided to spend a couple of nights at the newly opened O'Byrne House Hotel in Declan's Cross. Finian, fresh out of seminary, had been there to visit Sean Murphy, the garda detective who'd investigated the untimely deaths of Sally and little Kathleen and Mary Bracken.

"I can see why you're needed here," Mary said as they crossed a narrow residential street. "I can see why God called you to this place, if that's how you describe it and what you believe happened. When I looked into Colin Donovan's eyes just now, I could feel the dangers and risks and hardships he's faced—the great responsibility he and Emma and those like them have taken on. It's not a Hollywood movie. They're real people."

"That's true, but if I'd found only fishermen here, it's still where I'm meant to be."

"But you didn't find just fishermen, did you?" She kept her eyes focused on the road in front of them, her pace picking up along with the wind. "Emma and Colin have fallen in love with each other in spite of the complications of their families and work, or perhaps because of them. Do you think Emma's time as a religious sister prepared her for the life she has now?"

"Perhaps so," Finian said.

"And Oliver. I think he's lonely."

"Don't let him fool you."

"Why do you suppose he's never married?" Mary asked, matter-of-fact.

Finian wasn't sure he liked this turn in the conversation, but he wanted Mary to feel free to say whatever was on her mind. "There's yet time for Oliver to find someone."

"For you, too, Finian."

He made no comment. Her voice was so quiet, he wasn't positive she'd meant for him to hear her, although he suspected that was a rationalization for his silence.

They came to a corner and stood in the shade of a maple tree as a car passed in front of them. But as Finian started to cross the street, Mary didn't budge. He waited, noting that the wind had reddened her cheeks but otherwise they were still pale. She cleared her throat. "You don't— Fin, you don't believe God deliberately took your family from you, do you?"

"I believe a terrible sailing accident took them."

"Yes. There's that." Mary walked briskly across the street and up a slight hill past three small houses. She eased off on her pace. "Have you thought more about how long you'll stay on now that Father Callaghan has decided not to return?"

"I haven't, Mary."

"But your time here is winding down. You'll come home soon, won't you? Home to Ireland, I mean."

"I no longer think of home the way I used to."

"No, I suppose you don't." She hooked her arm into his, as if she were determined to be cheerful. "Well, you're still my big brother and I'm still your nosy little sister."

He smiled. "All true, all good."

She released his arm, her mood turning palpably serious again. "Does Sean Murphy know what happened today—about the death of this retired FBI agent?"

"I haven't spoken to him."

"He'll want to know given this man's time in Ireland, and because Claudia Deverell and Oliver York were in Ireland, too. In case they were up to anything there."

"I expect so."

Finian took Mary's questions as his cue and checked his phone. He saw a text waiting for him from his garda detective friend. A dead FBI agent, Fin? Call me.

It was late in Ireland, but when Finian arrived back at the rectory with Mary, he left her to sort out what she wanted to do for dinner and stepped out onto the back steps to phone Sean.

"Tell me what you know, Fin," Sean said.

"It's not everything."

But his friend listened to what Fin could tell him, and grunted as if in pain when he finished. "How's Mary?"

"Today's been a shock for her."

"I'll ring her next."

Finian nodded as if Sean could see him. "Are you still in Declan's Cross?" he asked.

"For now."

After they hung up, Finian returned to the kitchen. Mary was rummaging in the cupboards. She was properly chagrined at a man's untimely death, but at the same time Finian also recognized that his youngest sister had never experienced anything like the Sharpes, the Donovans, Oliver York and their dangerous, intriguing world.

21

Oliver's room wasn't the one where Naomi MacBride had stayed in February. It was down the hall, a sunny corner room with views of the front and side yards. Colin used the master key to get in. He'd sent his folks to Hurley's for dinner. His mother had wanted to talk—make sure everything was okay with him after today, smack on arriving home—but his father had taken the hint. They'd cleared out, and Colin had headed upstairs.

On his own, Oliver wasn't that neat. His things seemed to have exploded out of his battered soft-sided leather suitcase. The room had been cleaned that morning, which no doubt helped. Colin noted the expensive shaving gear, Floris aftershave and a bristle hairbrush, none of it brand-new. Oliver struck him as the sort who bought classic quality and replaced it only when he had to.

Colin returned to the bedroom. He'd left the room door open, which allowed Oliver to walk right in. "And here I thought I hadn't latched the door properly and the wind blew it open." Oliver tossed his waxed-cotton jacket on a chair. "Hello, Colin. I suppose you're going to tell me you're doing the turndown service?"

"Why not? I like to help my folks. Do you want me to put on soothing music for you?"

"I enjoy the sounds of the wind and waves. Were you looking for anything specific?"

"Besides towels that need to be replaced? Let's say Gordy Wheelock's phone is missing. I'd like to find that. Then let's say there's an envelope about the size of a book that was given to him at his hotel in Boston, and it's also disappeared, its contents unknown."

"You'd like to find that, too," Oliver said.

Colin shrugged. "I'd settle for the contents. Money, notes, blackmail material, recipes. Whatever it is."

"What about a murder weapon? A gun, a knife—a crowbar, perhaps?"

A rock, Colin thought. The state guys had found a baseball-size rock in the grass by the cottage's front door that was the likely murder weapon. It looked as if someone had been inside the cottage, surprised Gordy and nailed him on the head with the rock, about where he'd hurt himself on Wednesday night. It was unlikely whoever it was had grabbed the rock on impulse but instead had had it in hand, for use as a weapon.

But Colin wasn't giving any of that information to Oliver.

He noticed Oliver was still waiting for a response. "I'd take a murder weapon, too," he said. "Agent Wheelock was injured Wednesday night when he fell down stairs in Boston. You were at the O'Byrne House Hotel in Declan's Cross then, but an associate of yours could have pushed him."

"Or it could have been an accident. He could have

been killed in a robbery gone bad, or he surprised a deranged person who decided the cottage belonged to him, or something along those lines. We can all speculate, Agent Donovan."

"If you're connected to Gordy Wheelock's death, Oliver, your friends in MI5 can't protect you."

"They wouldn't want to and I wouldn't blame them. What are your plans now that you've seen to the turndown in my room?"

Colin nodded toward the door, still open to the hall. "Fin Bracken gave my folks a bottle of Bracken fifteen-year-old to celebrate the opening of the inn. I know where they keep it. Can I offer you a glass?"

"If I say no?"

"It's the peated expression. Only a few bottles left. You'll like it."

"Then I accept," Oliver said. "Will Emma be joining us?"

"No."

"And my hosts?"

"Out."

Oliver's eyes narrowed, but he stood back and motioned with one arm. "After you, Agent Donovan."

Colin let Oliver get settled in the front room and grabbed the Bracken 15 and two glasses out of a locked cabinet in the dining room. When he returned, his guest was examining a watercolor painting of the Cape Elizabeth lighthouse hanging above the sofa. "My mother got it at a yard sale. It's not worth anything."

"It's rather charming, though, isn't it? People who stay here must love lighthouses."

"Lighthouses are all automated these days."

"Ever the wet blanket, aren't you, Agent Donovan?"

"Just stating a fact." Colin poured the whiskey and handed Oliver a glass. "Fin and Mary Bracken stopped here a little while ago. You drove Mary back?"

"I did. The fear and fatigue in those midnight-blue eyes reminded me why I live a quiet, solitary life. Don't fret, Colin. Lucas Sharpe is more Mary Bracken's type, but he'd have to move to Killarney and take up whiskey-making. It's in that Bracken blood of hers. She's not going anywhere. If you'd like, I can psychoanalyze her."

"Thought you were a mythologist."

"I believe Mary was deeply affected by the deaths of her sister-in-law and nieces, and it's had a delete-rious influence on her romantic relationships. She's afraid. She doesn't want to suffer her brother's fate—to lose the people she loves. That's why she's having such a hard time with Finian's vocation and his move to Maine. She feels she's losing him, too."

Colin sat down with his whiskey. "She tell you that?"

"I'm psychoanalyzing," Oliver said. "I could be an FBI profiler, don't you think? A keen observer of human nature."

"A profiler who can also break into museums. That'd be something."

Oliver raised his glass. "Cheers."

"Yeah. Cheers." Colin sipped the whiskey, watching Oliver do the same.

"Long day, Agent Donovan."

"Yes."

"Agent Wheelock wasn't killed in a break-in and robbery, was he?"

"How well did you know him?"

Oliver cupped his drink. "I didn't know him at all."

"But you kept an eye on him," Colin said. "Part of your fun as a thief was taunting the people trying to catch you. Gordy Wheelock was one of them."

"I live in the Cotswolds and London. Agent Wheelock was based in Washington during his years with the FBI. This past year, he's been retired in North Carolina. I've never been to North Carolina. Look it up if you don't believe me."

"He spent time in London."

"I didn't offer him the guest suite at the flat," Oliver said lightly, raising his glass to his mouth. He hesitated, then took another sip. "It is a fine whiskey."

Colin could feel fatigue and impatience burning up his nerve endings. It was late, and if all had gone according to plan, he'd either be at a pub or looking up at the stars above Kenmare Bay from Finian Bracken's cottage. But here he was, talking to Oliver York about a murdered retired FBI agent. "When did you learn Agent Wheelock was in London this past week?"

"Soon after he arrived. Friday, I believe it was."

"How?"

Oliver set his drink on a coaster on the coffee table in front of him. "Wendell Sharpe told me."

"He was here in Maine by then."

"He phoned me. He believed one way or another Gordy—that's what Wendell called him—was in London because of Alessandro Pearson's death. Wendell had the open house coming up. Gordy would be there. He wanted me in the loop. The invitations for the tea party at Claridge's had already gone out. I wasn't surprised when Gordy showed up with Claudia Deverell."

"You threw the party in order to…what? Smoke out a few bad guys funding terrorists with stolen antiquities? No wonder MI5 was there. They had no idea what you were up to until the day of the party, did they?"

"The day before. They agreed to let it go forward. Whatever their agenda, mine was to continue my rather ambiguous efforts to gather information on the illegal antiquities trade. I'd helped British intelligence uncover a smuggling scheme over the winter. I'd heard vague rumors about stolen mosaics and thought I might hear more at the party."

"You invited Claudia Deverell because of her family's collection?"

"I'd invited Adrian and Henry, too, but they left London before the party. Isabel Greene came. And Gordy Wheelock, of course," Oliver added.

Colin studied the Englishman, noted that he looked rumpled and tired. As determinedly cheeky and energetic as he was, he wasn't impervious to the trials of the day. Finally Colin put his whiskey glass on a side table. "Are you the unnamed collector, Oliver?"

"What would I do with Byzantine mosaics? Now, Aoife O'Byrne's watercolor of porpoises in Ardmore Bay is altogether different."

Colin wasn't going to be distracted. "If you're not the collector, who is?"

"I don't know."

"But you have an idea."

Oliver gave a tight shake of the head. "I don't speculate."

"Let me speculate, then. It was Alessandro Pearson. He wasn't a collector, but he floated the rumors." Colin settled back in his chair. "What do you think?"

"Now I understand why Emma isn't here. She'd have stopped you by now."

"She's with her grandfather and brother, asking the same questions." He got to his feet, looked down at Oliver. "Make sure we have the times and places you met Agent Wheelock and everything you talked about."

"You have them already," Oliver said simply.

"Did you tell the state detectives you were here last under an assumed name?"

"Consulting with Hollywood under a pseudonym is perfectly legitimate." Oliver rose, following Colin out to the front porch. It was dusk now, the harbor quiet and still in the fading light. "I'm sorry about Agent Wheelock. I truly am. If his death is related to any unfinished business he had concerning illegal antiquities, he should have trusted us."

Colin bristled at *us* but said nothing as he walked down the steps. He glanced back, saw that Oliver was watching him. But there was no smart-aleck remark from the English thief. He gave a quick wave, then went back inside, presumably to the rest of his rare peated Irish whiskey.

Fog rolled in, cool and damp, and Colin lit a fire in the fireplace. Emma had been in the living room, staring at the unlit fireplace, when he'd arrived. Now they were sitting side by side on the floor, leaning against the front of the couch with their legs out straight. He'd pushed the coffee table aside and kicked off his shoes. He could sense Emma's pensiveness as she grappled with the events of the past few days, particularly finding Gordy Wheelock—a man she'd known, worked with, admired.

"The detectives are convinced Gordy burned something in the grill behind the cottage," she said. "He cleaned up but not enough. He left a few ashes behind. It could have been someone else—the person who killed him, for example—but he had a lighter on him, and it explains the saucepan and spatula."

"He got rid of the ashes," Colin said.

"Evidence. Whatever was in the envelope."

"Was he being blackmailed?"

A chunk of dried oak bark caught fire, creating a burst of orange flames. "Blackmail, or information he wanted to keep secret for other reasons—to protect someone else, maybe."

"Directions to buried treasure."

She leaned against his upper arm. "For all we know that's true. It could have been a robber who decided to burn a few things he didn't want, just for the hell of it, then ran into Gordy and killed him in a panic."

"Or the ashes are unrelated to Gordy's death."

"This is why we're trained to gather evidence and see where it takes us. We can't allow ourselves to get tunnel vision or locked on one theory."

Colin slipped his arm over her shoulders. "But?"

He felt her intake of breath more than heard it. "But Gordy burned evidence, and he didn't fall the other night, and it all goes back to his work last year and his abrupt retirement. I checked his files. He didn't keep extensive records his last two months on the job. In fact, I'd say they weren't adequate, especially compared to his earlier notes."

"Skimping was out of character for him?"

"Yes. There had to be something between Claudia and Gordy."

"And whatever it was broke the rules," Colin said.

"Granddad knew, or at least guessed." But her certainty evaporated. "He was tired when I saw him."

"An improper relationship between a legendary FBI agent and a contact could be one of those things your old granddad didn't put in the Sharpe files. Would he have told Lucas?"

"I suspect Granddad has a few things he'll never speak of to anyone and take to the grave with him. An affair between a married FBI legend and a source, the daughter and granddaughter of old friends from Maine, might be one of them."

"Could Claudia have been his CI, not just a resource?"

"If she was, it was unofficial. I keep going back to Alessandro Pearson and his friendship with Claudia and her mother. They worked together on antiquity preservation in some hot spots on the Mediterranean. Since we're speculating by the fire, I'll go out on a limb and say he could have been onto a pipeline of illicit antiquities, particularly mosaics, and was concerned profits from their sale were going to some very bad guys. And I'll say he had help dying."

"The bruise on his back?"

"Surprised and shoved from behind, just like Gordy. Only Gordy survived and lied about it, where Alessandro had a heart attack and died." Emma gazed at the fire, the flames settling down after the oak-bark surge. "Gordy was a good agent with top-notch instincts. He didn't lose that in a year. He'd figured out something. He wasn't sure what to do. He had conflicting loyalties, and probably a few things about himself he wanted to hide. He came to me for information, a sense of what

I knew and didn't know about Alessandro's death, Oliver, this tea party in London."

"He should have been straight with you."

Colin got up and took another oak log from a stack of wood on the hearth. He set it on the fire and then grabbed the black-iron poker and adjusted the burning logs. He didn't know if he was doing that much good, but he'd imagined himself doing just this, keeping a fire going, sitting in his living room on a foggy, chilly Maine evening with his fiancée.

He sat down again, one knee up as he stretched out his right leg along Emma's left leg. "If Gordy suspected Oliver and Wendell were colluding and whatever they were up to could expose his shortcomings, missteps or actual wrongdoing, and MI5 was involved, he'd play it close to the vest with you."

"Who killed him, Colin?" Emma didn't wait for his response. "I hope your friends in major crimes don't suspect Granddad or Lucas was involved. Granddad doesn't drive in the States—he shouldn't in Ireland—and Lucas was busy with the open house. That doesn't rule them out, I know, but they didn't kill Gordy."

"He wanted to keep you on his team in Washington, didn't he?"

"Yank already had HIT in mind and wanted me for it once he got the green light. Gordy didn't like that. I think it had more to do with his dislike of Yank than with wanting to keep me. Yank didn't care. He's pragmatic. He wanted me to have broad experience and get what I could from my time with Gordy."

"Yank never imagined the two of us together. Talk about bucking the bureaucracy. You were complicated the day we met. Rather I'd been a lobsterman for real?"

"You are. You're just also an FBI agent."

"I have options, within FBI, outside of it. Whatever it takes, Emma. You know that."

She smiled. "You could always help your parents with the inn and guests like Oliver."

"Not one of my options, but I like your sense of humor."

"Wendell and Lucas won't stonewall the investigation."

"I know. I'm sorry this happened. We'll do what we can to help with the investigation but we're too close to all the players. I know the state guy in charge. He'll chop us to the ground if we overstep." He lifted her onto his lap and slipped his arms around her, drawing her close. "Think we'll have rain on our wedding day?"

22

Gordy's dead...dead...dead...

Claudia hadn't budged from the porch since the police had left. Isabel had brought her dinner, but she had managed only a few bites. Now it was dark, foggy, cold, the sort of Maine night her mother had loved.

It was real, Claudia thought, nursing a glass of white wine.

This force in her life for more than a year was gone. It was as if the last of the terrible, intrusive pressures she'd faced during her mother's final months had released her from its grip. She hated herself for feeling this way, but it was undeniable: this utter, blissful relief that Gordy Wheelock was actually, absolutely, without any doubt gone.

Dead.

"I'm glad," she said aloud, as if to convince herself it was okay to feel that way.

She'd done the right thing, and now she had only to sort through the Maine house and get it on the market. Her mother's sometimes indiscriminate storing and collecting would make the process more time-consuming and complicated, but it was nothing compared to having a renowned FBI investigator on her case.

She heard the front door creak open. In another moment, her father joined her in the grouping of old wicker chairs. "How are you, Claudia?" he asked.

"It's been a day," she said.

"It's emotional enough being back here without anyone turning up dead. The detectives won't say he was murdered, but it's clear from their questions he was. I'm sorry about what happened. He must have just been in the wrong place at the wrong time. Ah, Claudia. My dear Claudia." Her father sat on a chair facing the dense fog over the Atlantic and the immediate coastline. "Your mother loved this place. I know it's hard for you to give it up."

"It's time, though."

"Yes. I'm trying not to have an opinion."

"Oh, you have one, you're just not offering it."

Adrian mounted the steps from the front walk. Claudia smiled at him. "I didn't know you were out there."

"I was taking a walk. I scooted out back, got as far as crossing Ocean Avenue and decided this is how idiots like me get killed on foggy Maine nights. It's amazing to me how such a beautiful day turned into this—pea-soup fog and a dead FBI agent. I'm sorry, Claudia, I know you two were friends, but damn, my stomach still hurts from when the cops swarmed."

"It was because of me," Claudia said. "I'm the one who brought Agent Wheelock into our lives."

"He asked for your help, and you gave it to him." Her brother sat next to her, opposite their father. "That's not a bad thing, Claudia. I hope he arrested some bad guys as a result of your expertise."

"I do, too, but he never said."

"Who do you think killed him?" Adrian asked.

Claudia heard her father's quick breath at the frank, direct question, typical of her brother. "Let's not do this, Adrian. Leave the investigation to the police. We don't have answers and we're not responsible for getting them. Claudia, what's that you're drinking?" When she told him, he made a face. "I'll want something stronger."

"While you two both are here..." She hesitated but decided just to say it. "I'm putting the house on the market as soon as I can. Mother loved it here, but it's not for me, not any longer. But I'm also finished with London, too. I have enough money for a fresh start. I'm thinking about California. Carmel, maybe. I have a few friends there."

"*Your* friends, Claudia?"

She knew what her brother was asking. Her friends, not just her mother's friends. "That's right," she said, without any defensiveness.

"I hope you know I'm here for you," her father said.

"I do, Dad, thanks. It's been a tough year for you, too."

He didn't respond. What was there to say? He and Adrian went inside, but Claudia stayed out on the porch. She was shivering, but she shut her eyes, listening to the sounds of the waves through the fog. She remembered sitting out here with Gordy on a foggy night after they'd made love. He'd been something in bed. But what a mistake, for both of them.

23

Mary had trouble sleeping. Ireland seemed so very far away. She lay in the unfamiliar bed in St. Patrick's rectory and shut her eyes, remembering walks in Killarney National Park with Sally and little Kathleen and Mary, both named for Mary Kathleen Bracken, their great-grandmother. For months after they'd drowned, Mary had worried Finian would follow them into the grave. He'd jump into the bay or drink himself to death. His love of the distillery—his and Declan's plans, the dozens of barrels of whiskey maturing for brighter days, the beautiful smells and the hard work—hadn't sustained him.

Off to seminary he'd gone.

Mary had expected he'd tire of the restrictive life, or come to realize the call he'd heard had arisen more from sobering up and deciding not to kill himself with drink after all. What an awe-inspiring experience it must have been to hike the Iveragh Peninsula and see it without the haze created by his alcohol abuse.

At the very least, Mary had expected he'd flunk his classes.

But he hadn't, and now here she was in Maine, visiting her priest brother, his return home in jeopardy.

Ireland *was* home for him. She didn't believe a word of his nonsense about having a different idea of home now that he was a priest.

Yet after dinner—he'd ordered pizza from a local shop—Mary had wandered through the rectory. Other than a bottle from Bracken Distillers on his shelf, she'd discovered little sign Finian had a foot in his homeland. Even after one day visiting him, she better understood the appeal of this place. She'd offered to go find his friends with him—knew that was what he would do if not for her presence—but he'd insisted on a quiet evening. He'd coped with the tricky aftermath of adrenaline dumps of his own during his months on the Maine coast. He'd warned her she might have trouble sleeping. *You don't have to witness or experience violence to experience its effects.*

She rolled onto her stomach and rearranged her pillow, then gave up and jumped out of bed and raised a window. The rush of cool night air and its faint hint of salt brought her out of her uncontrolled thoughts. Both her feet were firmly in Bracken Distillers and she would go home to Ireland in a few days.

If only Finian would go with her.

Mary finally slept but awoke too early. It wasn't just the five-hour time difference between Maine and Ireland, although that was a big part of it. It was also the return of her obsessing. She kept picturing Gordon Wheelock on his distillery tour not a week ago. He hadn't been in the best shape, but she'd never have believed he'd be dead by Saturday.

She didn't want to wake Finian, so tiptoed down the stairs to the kitchen. She left him a note on the counter. He'd be awake soon for Sunday church services. She was ambivalent about attending. Right now she didn't trust herself not to leap up during the offering and tell his flock to send him home to his family.

A walk would help her decide whether she should find something else to do for her Sunday morning.

She slipped into her jacket and headed outside. The fog wasn't as dense as last night, but it was holding on. She shoved her hands into her jacket pockets and was startled to feel something hard and foreign in the left pocket. She yanked out her hand, but she immediately realized whatever was in there wasn't alive and going to bite her. She dipped her hand back in and withdrew what she immediately saw was an old-fashioned key.

Slowing her pace, she placed the key in her palm and had a look. She didn't recognize it and couldn't imagine how it had landed in her jacket. She'd have remembered putting it there. It was too small to be the key to the rectory's front or back door, or to a church door. A cabinet, perhaps, or a drawer or even a trunk.

Had Finian tucked the key into her pocket by mistake, thinking it was his jacket? Or just for a moment's safekeeping, and then he'd forgotten about it? He might have done it when she'd gone to his church office, but she couldn't think of when he'd have had the opportunity.

She'd worn the jacket almost nonstop since leaving Ireland, only taking it off at night and for a few minutes yesterday at the Sharpe open house, before she'd gone down to the docks, and again at the Deverell house, before the police had arrived.

Surely she'd have noticed the key by now if someone had slipped it into her jacket in Dublin, but she couldn't say for certain she'd put her hands in her pockets since then. She must have done so.

She returned the key to her pocket and continued her walk. A bit of a mystery, but more than likely it had simply ended up in the wrong jacket yesterday. Perhaps its owner had already missed it and launched a query with the Sharpes.

Without giving it much thought, she went toward the Rock Point Harbor Inn. She debated a moment before mounting the porch steps and ringing the doorbell. Rosemary Donovan came to the door and immediately invited Mary to join them for breakfast.

"Are you sure?" Mary asked, suddenly hungry.

"Absolutely," Rosemary said, already leading Mary back to the kitchen. "Frank's made enough for a platoon and we've only Oliver staying here."

Which meant he was the only one in the kitchen, at the table with tea and a plate full of food.

Rosemary took her coffee with her into another room, leaving Mary to help herself to a sideboard spread with bowls of cut fruit and natural yogurt, a variety of cereals, granola, cheese and cold meats, boiled eggs, a loaf of freshly baked bread and a plate of blueberry muffins.

"They're Maine wild blueberries," Oliver said as Mary put a muffin on a plate.

"They look delicious."

Everything looked delicious. She added fruit and cheese to her plate and set it across from Oliver while she made tea, pouring hot water from an urn and choosing a green tea.

"I loathe green tea," Oliver said. "It tastes like grass to me."

"Now you sound like my brother Declan. He drinks black tea and that's it."

"Good man. I occasionally get daring and drink mint tea."

She smiled at him. "I'll bet you do more daring things than drink mint tea."

She sat at her plate, feeling less rattled than she had since the fog had descended on Rock Point late yesterday, leading to her restless night. Of course, it wasn't just the fog that had unnerved her.

"I want to go to Heron's Cove," she said, making the decision and speaking it out loud at about the same time. "Finian's working and I don't have a car. Are you doing anything this morning? Can you take me?"

"I'd be happy to, but what about Emma and Colin?"

"They're FBI agents," Mary said, as if that explained everything.

But Oliver seemed to understand. "And they don't forget it, trust me."

She showed him the key and explained how she'd found it. "Someone must have dropped it yesterday at the open house or later at the Deverell house. The open house is most likely. Then someone else put it in my pocket thinking it was mine. Or thinking my coat was theirs."

"You don't recognize it?"

"Not at all. Do you?"

"I've never seen it before."

"It can't have been in my pocket for long. I'd have noticed its weight even without putting my hand in my pocket." She sighed. "I'm sure it's nothing."

"Given the circumstances, I can see why it got your attention." Oliver ate the last bit of his muffin. "That's my third. I didn't have dinner last night and woke up starving. Frank Donovan offered to whip up an omelet for me, but there's plenty here, even for a starving Englishman." He peered at her. "I see dark circles under your eyes, Mary."

"No wonder, is it?"

He shook his head. "No. No wonder."

"Do you suppose we'll hear from the detectives again today?"

"Only if they have follow-up questions I would think." He patted his stomach. "As much as I'm not one for rambles, I could use a good one now after this breakfast. When do you want to leave for Heron's Cove?"

"As soon as possible."

"All right, then. Give me ten minutes to get cleaned up and I'll meet you in the front room—unless you're still in here indulging in muffins."

"A second cup of tea, perhaps."

"That's how it starts. A second cup of tea, and then suddenly the muffin plate is empty. But they say blueberries are packed with healthy antioxidants. Healthy something, anyway. Enjoy. I'll be down in ten." He rose, glancing down at her. "If you change your mind and decide to take your mysterious key to our FBI friends, we can do that first."

Mary finished her plate of food and got up for more. As Oliver had warned, one really couldn't resist. The time change was also wreaking havoc on her internal clock, making her hungry and suppressing her appetite at inconvenient times. In Ireland, she'd be having lunch by now—as good a justification as any for eating enough at breakfast for two meals.

Feeling better with a full stomach, she arrived in the front room just as Oliver was coming down the stairs. He moved with such grace and control. She had so many questions about him, in part because of the way Sean Murphy and Finian bristled whenever they said his name.

They took the coastal route to Heron's Cove, stunning with the last of the fog burning off, sunlight breaking through departing clouds and shining on the water, waves sweeping in over rocks and boulders.

No one was at the Sharpe house.

Mary hadn't expected that. She sat next to Oliver, frowning, trying not to let him see her frustration—her sudden, irrational fear.

"Mary," Oliver said, "I suggest you give the key to Colin and Emma and let them figure it out. If it's nothing, it's nothing."

"You're right, of course."

"No *of course*, but I am right this time."

When Oliver pulled up at Colin's house in Rock Point, Colin was at his truck out front, about to leave. Mary jumped out. Colin sized up the situation immediately, but she explained about the key and showed it to him. "Do you recognize it?"

"No. You're sure it appeared in the past two days?"

"I'm positive. It's old, don't you think?"

"Looks it." He turned to Oliver. "Did you put the key in Mary's jacket?"

"No, and I didn't see who did."

Colin shifted back to her. "I'd like to show it to Emma. If you think of anything else or discover it belongs to the church or rectory after all, give me a call or text me."

"I will," Mary promised.

"Finian will be furious with Oliver for taking you to Heron's Cove."

"Try arguing with a Bracken," Oliver muttered. "Better I go with her than she go alone, wouldn't you say?"

"I'll drop her off at the rectory and see you later. I don't have a sister, but if I did—"

"She'd be a Donovan," Oliver offered, finishing for him. "Mary here is a strong woman, but she doesn't live in your world. Best get her home. I'm guessing the good father still has a temper."

"Thank you, gentlemen," she said, "but I can find my way back to the rectory on foot. It's only a short distance, and it's turned into a beautiful day. Oliver, thank you for driving me to Heron's Cove. Colin, will you let me know if you solve the mystery of the key? I promise I won't feel like a fool if it turns out to be the key to Lucas Sharpe's wine cabinet."

"Stay in touch, love," Oliver said, kissing Mary on the cheek.

As Oliver got back in his car, Colin held the driver door open. "Pop's making lobster salad. He's about to invite you to lunch. You wouldn't want to be rude."

"You want me where you can find me."

"My brother Andy caught the lobsters himself."

"An offer I can't refuse," Oliver said, noncommittal, and got behind the wheel.

Colin stood back, letting Oliver go on his way. But as Mary started toward the rectory, Colin eased in next to her. "We can walk or we can drive," he said amiably. "Your choice."

"I'd like to walk. I indulged at breakfast at your parents' inn."

"Mary…" Colin walked with her a few steps in the shade. "We have no reason to believe you or anyone else is in danger—but you might want to stick close to your brother for now."

"Fin knows something I don't about Oliver, doesn't he?"

"Oliver's a character." Colin's voice softened, but there was nothing soft about his eyes. "I'll call my folks and have them or Andy drop off lobster salad and rolls for you and Fin. How's that?"

Mary smiled. "Brilliant, thanks. It's a fine day for a picnic."

Finian didn't care about muffins, lobster salad, rolls, the old key, who'd been home and who hadn't been home. He cared only, Mary thought, that she'd gone off to Heron's Cove without telling him—without thinking. He didn't say *without thinking* but she knew he wanted to. Despite the nine years difference between them in age, his years as a seminarian and now as a priest, she knew her brother.

"I'm sorry," she said. "I was thoughtless."

"You were *reckless*."

"I wouldn't go that far. I left you a note. I meant it to cover whatever I got up to this morning. I'd have told you I was going to Heron's Cove, but I didn't want to interrupt your preparation for mass—and as it turns out, I arrived back here before mass ended."

"Seconds before."

And not enough time for him to miss seeing Colin Donovan amble off. Mary sank onto a chair at the kitchen table. "I haven't seen you this livid since I wandered off after the lambs when I was six."

"You were five." But there was a spark in his eyes—amusement, affection. Something. He sighed, putting an arm around her. "All's well that ends well, then and now."

"Were you upset I didn't attend mass with you?"

"Not at all."

"I haven't been to mass in years. I miss some of the rituals. I love old church ruins. Oliver has an affinity for the ruin in Declan's Cross, perhaps because he was left in one as a boy. He was found by a Catholic priest. Do you suppose that's why he's drawn to you? You both also have tragic pasts."

"Oliver's an interesting man."

"That's almost word for word what Colin Donovan just told me."

Finian hugged her close. "It's good to have you here, Mary. I'm sorry the circumstances aren't better."

"I don't mind for myself. I mind for this man who died and his family and friends. Ah, Fin…" She realized she was trembling with emotion. "I can see why your friends need you and appreciate you."

"Thanks for that, Mary."

She sniffled. "But I still want you to come home."

24

The fog was finally lifting on the small peninsula where railroad magnate Edward Hart had built his Maine paradise and the Sisters of the Joyful Heart now lived and worked. Emma hadn't thought about these sorts of mornings in a long time, when she'd be toiling in a garden or meditating by a fountain in the fog, knowing it was sunny in Heron's Cove. When she'd arrived at the convent thirty minutes ago, she couldn't see the water even from the main garden. Now, in a meditative garden open to visitors as well as the sisters, she could see gray swells rolling onto the rocks and boulders below her.

"You're pacing, Emma," her grandfather said. "It's wearing me out. Sit down, will you?"

She spun around at him. He was seated on a wooden bench facing a golden sundial situated amid clusters of yellow tulips, junipers and pots of multicolored pansies. Later in the season, the tulips and pansies would give way to summer flowers, always with an eye toward creating a soothing, restful spot for contemplation. Emma had been contemplating, but she hadn't been restful.

Her grandfather studied her, nothing about him frail, tentative, or that would suggest he was off his game. He wore a windbreaker and chinos that looked as if he'd pulled them out of a box in the attic, but Lucas had cleared out everything. No way would he have kept a pair of their grandfather's old, frayed pants.

"You had evidence of a corrupt FBI agent and you didn't tell me."

"Not corrupt. Human."

"Granddad."

He sighed, no hint of impatience. "I didn't have evidence. I had an inkling. What was I going to do, knock on the FBI director's door with an inkling an agent was having a fling with a source?"

"You could have knocked on my door."

"And put you in the position of dethroning the great Gordy Wheelock? You weren't working with him then. He wasn't your problem."

"Another agent having an affair with a source, potentially coercing her, opening himself up to blackmail—Granddad, that *is* my problem."

"You keep using these declarative statements. I don't know for a fact even now, sitting here with you pacing, that Gordon Wheelock and Claudia Deverell had an affair. Do you?"

Emma lowered her arms to her sides. She'd had them crossed on her chest as she'd paced. "We've talked with Gordy's widow. She knew. She didn't tell him, but she knew. They'd been having troubles with their marriage. His career had been all-consuming for him and the future scared him."

"Her words?"

"Yes. His reputation meant a lot to him. To both of them. She talked to him on Thursday evening. She wasn't alarmed when she didn't hear from him on Friday."

"Are you sure she didn't send someone after him?"

"Right now, Granddad, I'm not sure of much. Joan Wheelock didn't believe her husband was rekindling his relationship with Claudia or trying to make things right somehow."

"He was on a case. The last case that he left unfinished."

Emma noticed more of the ocean was visible, bluer with the lifting fog. "There's what we know and there's what we think we know. It's best not to confuse the two."

Her grandfather rose, only his use of the bench arm suggesting any infirmity. "Maybe Joan Wheelock did some stepping out of her own. The world isn't as black-and-white for me these days, Emma. My eyesight isn't as good as it used to be—I see a lot of shades of gray."

"Any 'inkling' Gordy coerced Claudia?"

"I always suspected he had something on her, or enough. She was in a state because of her mother. She'd do anything to protect the Norwood reputation. If Gordy found out something shady about their family, Claudia would have been devastated."

"Did Lucas know about her and Gordy? Is that what affected their relationship?"

"Probably. We've never talked about it. Lucas is a better catch than old married Gordy was, even in his heyday. He and Claudia are closer in age, they have similar interests and backgrounds, they're both single and world travelers. It could have worked."

Emma noticed dew or mist dripping on the sundial. Her grandfather and her brother had suspected—*strongly* suspected—Claudia Deverell had had an affair with an active FBI agent, and they hadn't said a word to her.

"You're a Fed, Emma," her grandfather said quietly.

In other words, she'd excluded herself from Sharpe confidences. "Did Mum and Dad know about Gordy and Claudia?"

He shook his head. "They're both in London. With Claudia there, too—let sleeping dogs lie, you know?"

"Sure, Granddad."

"Mad?"

She let out a breath. "No. No, I'm not mad. I excluded myself from the family business when I came here to the convent. Then I went back for a while. Working with you in Dublin was special. I learned so much."

"You were a good student," he said. "I'd have loved for you to stay with the business and take over the Dublin office, but that was about me. You had to decide what was right for you." He nodded to the sundial. "I remember when Sarah Jane—Mother Linden—made the sundial. I told her it could get her into trouble and she should stick to good religious symbols. She scoffed. She was a smart, kind woman, Emma. You learned a lot from being here, too."

They took a path past the tower and on to the walkway, through the pine grove. Emma matched her grandfather's slower pace. Being here, in this place imprinted with his friend and mentor's vision and spirit, had obviously affected him. Emma had counted on that when she'd collected him and brought him out here.

"Granddad, is someone using the Norwood collection to help sanitize the provenance of illicit antiquities?"

"I don't know for certain."

"Is that what Alessandro believed?"

"Yes."

And Gordy, Emma thought. At least he'd suspected. And what part did Oliver York and MI5 play? But she didn't go there.

"That world's a morass," her grandfather said. "I stay out of it as much as possible."

"A wise choice."

"That's part of the attraction of the FBI for you. I choose my morasses. You wade into all of them."

She made no comment. Wendell Sharpe was welcome to his theories about his sole granddaughter's choices in life.

As they reached the front gate, she spotted Colin's truck parked next to her car.

"The law is here," her grandfather said, pointing.

Emma smiled. "I am the law, too, Granddad."

"As if I could forget, even if I wanted to."

They went through the gate, sunlight streaming through the pine branches and shining on the small parking area. Colin got out of his truck. "Hey, Wendell. Maybe you can help with this one." He turned to Emma. "For what it's worth, Mary Bracken found a key."

He didn't seem that excited, but Emma and her grandfather both recognized it immediately. "It's similar to the key to an old Victorian chest here at the convent," she said.

"I remember moving the thing after Sarah Jane bought this place," her grandfather added. "I was all for junking it but she liked it."

Emma noticed Colin's frown and explained further. "Horace Norwood and Edward Hart often traveled together. There's probably a similar chest at the Norwood-Deverell house in Heron's Cove. Claudia's been going through it. She could have dropped the key and someone found it and put it in Mary's pocket by mistake."

"Or deliberately," Colin said.

"If we're right and it's Claudia's key. Let's find out."

They quickly formed a plan. Emma would return Wendell to his guest suite at the Sharpe offices and meet Colin at the Norwood-Deverell house.

She took the key, handing it to her grandfather to examine on the ride back to Heron's Cove.

25

Claudia pushed open the door to the bedroom her mother had used for storage and let Oliver York go in ahead of her. She'd been surprised when he'd arrived at the house, asking to have a look at some of the Norwood antiquities—out of curiosity, as a mythologist. She wasn't sure she entirely believed him but had no objection to bringing him upstairs. Her father and brother were out sailing with friends, and Isabel was in her bedroom, packing for her flight home.

Oliver glanced around at the jam-packed room. "One can imagine the reaction of an artisan of two thousand years ago discovering one of his creations stuffed in a container here, in a place he couldn't have known existed." He glanced back at Claudia. "Do you know which pieces your mother collected as opposed to her father and grandfather?"

"For the most part, yes. I won't know for certain until I go through everything. My mother was more the stickler for documentation than my grandfather and great-grandfather."

"But she added to the collection herself?"

Claudia nodded. "Oliver…what's this all about?"

"You saw Alessandro Pearson the day before he died."

"Yes." She hadn't hesitated but did now. "Why? How did you know?"

"Did you ask to see him or did he ask to see you?"

"He wanted to see me. We had tea. Look, I have nothing to hide. Why are you questioning me? Who *are* you?"

He stood in front of a stack of wooden crates, filled, she knew, with Grecian pots and urns. "An English mythologist. I'm not with law enforcement, Claudia."

"It wouldn't matter if you were. I have nothing to hide. Alessandro called me. He was worried my mother or I had been duped, used by terrorists and fraudulent scumbags to help them sanitize antiquities coming out of hot spots on the Mediterranean—to give them a provenance. It wouldn't matter if the pieces in question were legitimately obtained but had just got caught up in the conflicts and chaos in their origin countries."

"The poor fellow who discovers a few ancient pieces in the back shed?"

"All right, more likely Alessandro was worried about looted works." She shrugged. "It was all so vague. Then he died, and I was coming back here."

"And you called Gordy Wheelock," Oliver said.

"That's right. I never expected him to come to London. I couldn't stop him from going to the open house—I was glad he didn't. I thought he'd gone home. I was as shocked as anyone to learn he'd been killed."

Oliver took a few steps toward her. "Claudia, I believe your life could be in danger."

"What? Are you trying to scare me? Why? What do you think I've done?"

"You looked after your beloved mother and left yourself open to being used. You'd do almost anything to protect your mother's legacy, but not quite as much as Gordy believed."

She drew herself up straight and squared her shoulders. "You need to leave."

But in the next split second, Claudia realized she was too late.

Colin parked across from the Norwood-Deverell house and jumped out of his truck as he saw Lucas Sharpe starting across Ocean Avenue. "Hold on, Lucas. What's up?"

"Granddad was telling me about the key Mary Bracken found in her jacket. It reminded me of a chest I helped Victoria Deverell move upstairs on her last visit out here. It was old—mid-nineteenth-century I think she said. Her grandfather and Edward Hart came back from one of their trips with twin chests, and each kept one. She wanted it for storage."

"Was Claudia with her?"

Lucas nodded. "Henry stayed in Philadelphia. Isabel Greene came up for a day. I don't know that it helps figure out how the key ended up in Mary's jacket—assuming it's the same key. Just wanted to let Emma know. She walked up here after dropping off Granddad."

"Thanks, Lucas. Go back and stay with your grandfather, okay? We'll be in touch."

"Colin? Is everything okay?"

"Sam Padgett texted Emma and me on my way here.

Isabel Greene didn't take a train to Boston from New York or anywhere else on Thursday."

"But Claudia picked her up. They drove up here together. Why lie?"

"That's what I want to know. She needs to explain."

"She must know you'd check, after yesterday. Maybe she and Claudia aren't such great friends after all."

Colin gave a curt nod and started across the street.

A single shot came from the house.

Emma.

He turned to a shocked Lucas. "Take cover and call 911. Do it now, Lucas."

Colin drew his weapon and broke into a run.

Emma intercepted Claudia pushing open the door to a bathroom at the top of the stairs. She was shaking, in a full panic with the gunfire. "Oliver pushed me out of harm's way. She's mad…" Claudia gulped in more air, her skin splotchy from hyperventilating. "She's looking for me. She'll kill Oliver."

"Where is she now?"

"She was hiding behind a chest…in the bedroom. We didn't see her."

"She's still there?"

A nod, tears spilling down her cheeks.

"Where's Oliver?" Emma asked.

"Hiding. He dove after he pushed me. She… Isabel shot him."

"Is anyone else in the room?"

Claudia shook her head. "I don't think so. Dad and Adrian have gone sailing."

"You saw them leave yourself?"

"Yes."

Emma held her by the shoulders. "I'm going to keep you safe, but I need you to listen to me. Stay in the bathroom. Lock the door. Wait for an all-clear."

Claudia did as Emma asked.

Gun drawn, Emma edged to the open bedroom door. Colin materialized beside her.

"Isabel—it's Emma. Emma Sharpe. We'll figure this out. Let's keep everyone safe."

"A little late for that, Emma," Isabel, her voice clear and steady, said from inside the room.

"She's to your left of the door," Oliver called out. "Two meters in, with a nine-millimeter pistol pointed in my general direction."

He was finishing his statement even as Colin and Emma moved in unison, entering the room. Isabel had one chance to lower her weapon, and she took it, placing it on the floor. Emma kicked it aside as Colin tackled her, got her in cuffs and arrested her.

"It was self-defense," Isabel said, cool. "I know you can't take my word for it now, but you'll see. Claudia will do everything to protect her mother and the damn Norwood reputation."

Oliver stood up from behind a chest. "Bloody hell," he said.

"Did she shoot you?" Emma asked him.

"Not really."

"Yes or no, Oliver," Colin said.

"A little. I'm not a fan of guns." He dusted himself off, wincing in pain. Emma noticed blood dripping down his left arm onto his hand. "I think you'd call this a graze. I'm in a bit of pain but nothing a good Scotch won't cure."

Colin shook his head at him. "All that tai chi isn't very helpful with bullets."

"I ducked in time to avoid a bullet to the heart because of it. I could have dispatched this—this woman, but imagine the paperwork."

"What the hell were you doing here, Oliver?"

"Looking for mosaics looted from one of Alessandro Pearson's former archaeological sites." He steadied his gaze on Isabel. "You killed Alessandro and you killed Gordy Wheelock."

"I haven't killed anyone."

"You put a key in Mary Bracken's pocket," Emma said. "Why?"

"Claudia did it. I saw her. You'll soon learn the truth."

"You wanted her to take the fall," Oliver said. "Bloody coward."

Isabel's lips thinned as she smirked at him. "Claudia used her dying mother's odd behavior to cover up laundering antiquities. She continued after Victoria's death. Alessandro found out." She glanced at Colin. "It's all right, Agent Donovan. You've read me my rights. I'm fine."

He said nothing. Emma walked over to the chest where Oliver had hidden. "It's much easier to sell antiquities from the Norwood-Deverell collection than a looted archaeological site," she said. "Hide them in an old chest, 'discover' them and claim they were here for years. This particular chest isn't valuable. You could always just take an ax to it. You don't need the key. You only need what's inside."

"Alessandro's mosaics," Oliver said. "You create a

history and a provenance and sell them to some hedge-fund manager who thinks he's doing good and getting something valuable in return."

A flash of disdain from Isabel. "Not quite the lonely, eccentric mythologist, are you?"

"No, I am. I'm also observant, and I liked Alessandro and don't appreciate you shoving him down a flight of stairs. Thought you'd get lucky with Gordy in the same way?"

"It was Claudia," Isabel said. "All Claudia."

26

"One mistake or foible is the death penalty with you lot, isn't it?"

Colin gaped at Oliver. Only word for it. Oliver's comment got to him. They were at Fin Bracken's back table at Hurley's. Oliver, Emma, Wendell and Colin, something of the odd man out since he wasn't into art thefts. He liked it that way. He could offer Emma a different perspective.

"Note, Oliver," Colin said, "that we didn't kill anyone today."

"I'd have been fine if you'd killed that woman. She shot me, you know. I refused opioids at the emergency room and now I wish I hadn't. Every throb of pain reminds me of those cold eyes when she trained her weapon on me."

Colin gritted his teeth. "You didn't see her eyes, Oliver. You were ducking."

"I was speaking metaphorically. Of course, I wouldn't have wanted you to execute her, but I was rather hoping she wouldn't lower her weapon and you would be justified in using deadly force."

Wendell, sitting across from Colin, shook his head. "It's the adrenaline talking."

"I've no adrenaline left," Oliver said. "Every ounce in me got dumped when Isabel jumped out from behind a cupboard with that bloody gun. It belonged to Henry Deverell, by the way. She told me. She sneaked it out of its locked case. Of course, she blamed Claudia."

"Kept that key, I bet." Wendell muttered.

As cheeky as he could be, Oliver had done well today. Colin couldn't deny it. He and Emma couldn't talk about the investigation but Oliver and Wendell could provide their insights. Sam Padgett had talked to the cab driver who'd found the envelope. He'd insisted he hadn't looked inside, but dogged Padgett got it out of him. He'd looked. There'd been photos of a man who fit Gordy's description and an unidentified woman having sex.

That explained the ashes, Colin thought.

Gordy's phone had turned up in Claudia's bedroom in Heron's Cove. Isabel must have sent the text message on it before she'd planted it there, already assuming the police would eventually have cause to search the place.

Claudia had finally admitted to her affair with Gordy. He'd crossed several lines with her. His marriage on the rocks, his preliminary investigation into so-called blood antiquities fizzling, retirement looming, he'd succumbed to temptation. A mistake or a foible—he shouldn't have done it, and he'd paid a heavy price for trying to keep it quiet, whether for Claudia's sake or just for his own.

"Isabel's a risk-taker," Wendell said. "She chose mosaic art in part to give herself an excuse to go into dangerous areas. The FBI, MI5 and MI6 will want her to name her associates. I bet there's a terrorist or two among them. Alessandro was convinced that was the case."

Colin couldn't say so, but he knew Isabel was talking to investigators. She'd killed Gordy, lying in wait for him while he'd disposed of the ashes from the burned photos, and she'd hastened Alessandro Pearson's death, both in an effort to cover her own tracks. She'd done her best to frame Claudia, right down to wearing one of Claudia's scarves and sweaters when she'd delivered the envelope—Sam Padgett had found a witness who'd provided a description to go with the partial of her in the photo he'd gotten from the bellman. Colin was convinced Isabel had hoped out-of-shape Gordy would die of a heart attack when she'd pushed him, just as Alessandro Pearson had.

"Alessandro didn't know who was responsible for laundering illicit antiquities through the Norwood-Deverell collection," Oliver added.

Wendell nodded thoughtfully. "I hope he didn't die believing Victoria or Claudia was responsible. Claudia made a mistake with Gordy at a tough time in her life."

Oliver waved a hand. "Don't try to plead her case with these two," he said.

Emma rolled her eyes. "We just can't discuss details of the investigation with you. Don't read anything into our silence."

"Isabel expected to get away with everything," Wendell said. "Claudia made it easier because of her grief over her mother and her guilt over Gordy. I wish I'd known sooner what he was up to. I'd have throttled the guy. By the time I'd figured out he and Claudia were having an affair, it was already over."

"When did you and Oliver start colluding?" Emma asked, her green-eyed gaze on her elderly grandfather.

Wendell raised his eyebrows. "That's like asking when did you stop beating your wife? There's no good answer."

"Sure there is," Colin said. "You say the date. Last week, last month, last year."

"Not last year," Wendell said "A year ago I didn't know Oliver was…well. You know what I'm saying."

Oliver picked up his water glass. "A year ago I was in Hollywood consulting on a ghastly horror film. The director wanted to use obscure Nordic myths. It was a challenging time."

For two cents, Colin would have thrown the guy into the harbor. On the other hand, he was happy Oliver hadn't been killed or seriously injured today. A couple of days' rest and he might be able to reconcile those two conflicting emotions.

"MI5 gives you room to maneuver," Emma said.

"A long rope. Like your new FBI director with Matt Yankowski and his secret unit."

"It's not secret," Colin said. "If it was secret, you wouldn't know about it. You're clever, Oliver, but not that clever."

"My handlers are happy with my help when they get it. They don't ask questions. Some rocks needed to be turned over to see what squirmed out. Gordy Wheelock had a chance to live a good life in retirement. He wanted to make things right, but he went about it in the wrong way. He should have plopped everything on your desk."

"You should have done the same," Wendell said,

"but returning the art you stole and helping MI5 are a start."

Colin noticed Mary and Finian enter the restaurant. They managed to look both shaken and relieved as they approached the table.

"Time to switch to whiskey," Finian said, to which no one argued.

Claudia stood on the porch and looked out at the starlit view her mother had so loved. The police and FBI had finished their work at the house, but the storage room was still taped off. They'd found beautiful mosaics depicting an ancient vineyard in the old chest that she, Isabel and Lucas had carted upstairs. Claudia knew right away they didn't belong to the Norwood-Deverell collection. But that was the beauty of Isabel's scheme, wasn't it? She'd planned to sell them without Claudia ever having seen them. She'd done it before, but this time, with these particular mosaics, Alessandro Pearson had become suspicious.

She'd been willing to sacrifice them in order to frame Claudia. The chest, the missing key. Isabel had slipped it into Mary Bracken's jacket on purpose.

It's Claudia. All Claudia.

Her only consolation was that her mother wasn't here to witness such a betrayal.

"I'm sorry, Claudia," Adrian said, joining her at the porch rail. "What a day."

"Mom and I trusted Isabel. We thought she was our friend, but she played us—she used us."

"Not enough money and excitement being an artist, I guess."

"She knowingly funneled money to terrorists."

"Probably," Adrian said.

"I've been flailing for two years—ever since my mother was diagnosed. I couldn't see straight, make good decisions. I was paralyzed, afraid of hurting myself and you and Dad even more than I already had."

"Your mother loved you," her father said from the shadows. He eased in next to her, opposite Adrian, and put his arm around her. "You and this FBI agent helped and hurt each other at a vulnerable time. Let it go, Claudia. Your mother wouldn't want you to tear yourself up."

"Isabel took pictures of us. Gordy and me. Here. The police asked me, and I know it was Isabel."

"She hurt you more than Gordy Wheelock ever did. Be strong now, Claudia, as you go forward with your life. It's what your mother would want." Her father hugged her close. "She loved antiquities but she loved you more."

When Mary arrived back at the rectory with her brother, they sat in the kitchen with a pot of tea, and she started to talk. Words tumbled out. She couldn't stop them. Finian wasn't returning to Ireland in a few weeks. He hadn't gotten the priesthood out of his system.

"You're where you're meant to be," she said. "Ten years ago, you were meant to be a husband, a father and a whiskey man. But if the church lets priests marry, Aoife O'Byrne will be here in a heartbeat."

"I don't think Rock Point would suit her," Finian said, amused.

"Maybe you aren't meant to be together in this life. I don't know. Maybe her forbidden love for you works for her on a certain level. She can bury herself in work. She's in Declan's Cross for an extended period of painting. Fin…" Mary took a much-needed breath. "Your dangerous men and women hold on to deep secrets and have seen the darkest in life. They need you."

"And you, Mary?"

"You're my brother and I love you, and that's enough, wherever you are and whatever you do with your life."

"That's not what I mean."

And she could tell from his expression that he was seeing into her soul, into places she had locked off from herself. "I still can't bear thinking about them. Mary and Kathleen especially. I hate myself for it. I wish I had your faith. I think of them drowning…"

"You're stuck in that moment." He rose, took her hand. "Come with me."

He led her into the dining room of his simple home and he took a framed photograph from a sideboard and handed it to her. Sally and little Mary and Kathleen were laughing, pointing to a rainbow arcing high over Kenmare Bay.

"That's how I think of them," Finian said. "Now and forever, with all my love."

Mary touched the glass, as if she were touching the happy faces of her sister-in-law and nieces, soaking in their laughter. She placed the photograph back in its spot.

"A walk on a fine Maine evening?" her brother asked. "Sean tells me there's a lad at the distillery who has his eye on you."

"Is he mad about the events of today?"

"Boiling. What's this lad's name?"

"You think I know who it is?"

"I know you do."

She laughed and grabbed her coat.

In the morning, Emma brought Hurley's doughnuts to Heron's Cove and sat out on the back porch with her grandfather. "Isabel Greene was into money, risk, excitement and dangerous men, and she's not as clever as she thought she was. She didn't care if she was funneling money to terrorists. You'll follow her trail and break up some nasty plots and arrest some nasty people."

"No doubt in my mind," Emma said. "Lucas told me he's never hosting another party here. Maybe ever."

"The open house was my idea. I can't say it was one of my best ideas but it did get word out that Sharpe Fine Art Recovery is entering a new era. It's no longer just old Wendell Sharpe in an Irish cap with a ledger and pencils."

"Have you ever in your life owned a ledger?"

"You were right. I belong there. Born in Dublin, and I will die there. My life here in Maine is in the past. The memories…" His lively, aged eyes filled with tears. "I feel alive in Dublin. Here I just want to crawl into the grave with the woman I loved with all my heart and soul."

"Granddad…"

"Don't cry. Be glad your grandparents had that kind of love for each other." He cleared his throat and smiled through his tears. "Reminds me of you and Colin."

"I couldn't ask for more. Granddad, please don't stay for the wedding. You need to be home, and it's no longer here in Maine. Mary Bracken will be flying to Dublin in a few days. Why don't you go with her?" Emma took his hand. "And don't fly back for the wedding, either. Take a walk in St. Stephen's Green and think of us. Colin and I will see you soon enough."

"Emma, are you sure?"

"Yes. No question. Here." She handed him a chocolate-covered doughnut. "Indulge."

He smiled, and they sat back, enjoying doughnuts and coffee and the quiet morning.

27

When Emma took her father's arm on the clear, warm June morning of her wedding, it was as if every moment of her life flashed before her, bringing her here, to this time and place—and to the handsome, rugged man waiting for her in his tux, his three brothers beside him.

Her father walked down the lush green grass aisle with her, showing no sign of the pain that haunted his life. Ahead of her, Sister Cecilia, her friend, carried flowers from the convent gardens. On each side were gathered friends and colleagues. Matt and Lucy Yankowski, Sam Padgett, other members of HIT, Julianne Maroney and her grandmother, Naomi MacBride, Lucas, Mother Superior Natalie Aquinas.

Emma smiled at her mother, lovely in her rose-colored dress. Rosemary Donovan looked beautiful in blue and had tears in her eyes as her second-born watched his bride-to-be approach him.

Colin winked at her, and she knew he was telling her not to overthink.

Emma laughed, happy and in love as she eased in next to the man she was marrying.

Their Irish honeymoon was Colin's doing. Five blissful days together, with no work interruptions.

He'd meant it to be a secret from everyone—family, colleagues, friends, perpetrators—but they were busted. He could tell the moment he and Emma walked into upscale Ashford Castle. He'd dug deep into his bank account for two nights in the cheapest room, which wasn't cheap, but they were greeted with a room upgrade, champagne, a spa appointment for Emma and a kayak tour of the historic Lake Corrib.

A note with the champagne explained:

Although I wasn't invited to your wedding, I wanted to celebrate with you.

Oliver, in conjunction with assorted Donovans, Sharpes and a certain Irish priest.

PS: Don't worry, we'll stay out of your way.

"If the Sharpes don't get me kicked out of the FBI," Colin said, "Oliver will."

"He did help us catch some serious bad guys."

"We're two very lucky people, Emma," he said, taking her into his arms. "I love you."

"I love you, too, with all my heart and soul."

Colin poured the champagne. This time was for the two of them, on their own, but they weren't alone.

* * * * *

AUTHOR'S NOTE

Liar's Key took shape and came to life for me on one of my visits to Ireland. We were touring Dingle Distillery, an independent venture on the southwest Irish coast, where a cask named for Finian Bracken, Emma and Colin's Irish priest, has been maturing for several years under the careful watch of our great friend John Moriarty. And I knew Mary Bracken would visit her brother in Rock Point, the small Maine fishing village where he's serving a struggling parish. Of course there would be trouble and she'd be in the thick of it. My whiskey education continues. It's an endlessly fascinating subject! Many, many thanks to everyone at Dingle Distillery for the private tour, and especially to John.

I also want to thank my daughter, Katherine Jewell, a historian who generously pointed me in the right direction on a number of questions involving the ancient world. It's not her field, but, of course, she knows people. One of her expert friends managed to spark another story that's now percolating…

And I must take a moment to thank my wonderful editor, Nicole Brebner, and editorial assistant Margot

Mallinson for their patience, insights and support as I dove into this story. A big thank-you, too, to everyone at MIRA Books and to my agent, Jodi Reamer. As I write this note, I'm diving into the next Sharpe & Donovan novel, inspired by a walk in the English Cotswolds countryside.

If you're new to the Sharpe & Donovan series, the first book is *Saint's Gate*, when Emma and Colin meet over the murder of a nun at Emma's former convent. A lot's happened in their lives since then!

To learn more about my books, please visit my website, CarlaNeggers.com, and sign up for my newsletter, and join me on Facebook (Facebook.com/carlaneggers), Twitter (Twitter.com/carlaneggers) and, now, Instagram.

Thanks and happy reading,
Carla

*Keep reading for an exclusive sneak peek at
the next thrilling story in
the* SHARPE & DONOVAN *series
from* New York Times *bestselling author
Carla Neggers.*
THIEF'S MARK
Available soon from MIRA Books.

1

South Irish Coast

Colin Donovan read the text he'd just received. He was on his way into the second-floor drawing room at the O'Byrne House Hotel in tiny Declan's Cross, not far from historic Ardmore on the south Irish coast.

Have you run into our English mythologist by chance?

Colin read it again before he showed his phone to Emma Sharpe, his bride of ten days, who was studying a Jack Butler Yeats Irish landscape once stolen by the English mythologist mentioned in the text. "It's from Finian Bracken," he said.

She glanced at the screen. "Have you answered?"

"No."

"Does Finian know we're in Declan's Cross?"

"I wouldn't be surprised."

"He's in Maine, isn't he?"

"As far as I know. I'll ask him."

Emma moved to another painting, a vibrant Irish sunrise by Aoife O'Byrne, a prominent contemporary Irish artist who'd slept with Finian before he'd become a priest and probably still loved him. It was all Colin knew, and he'd have been fine not knowing that much. The affair had occurred before Finian had become a priest and long before he had arrived in struggling Rock Point, Colin's hometown on the southern Maine coast, to serve the local parish. He'd meant to stay a year and then return home to Ireland, but he was still in Rock Point. Colin didn't know if Aoife, now an internationally acclaimed artist, had something to do with that. She was holed up in a cottage outside the village, alone, painting. He and Emma hadn't visited her. Loving a man who couldn't love her was perhaps one of the ways Aoife rationalized her solitary life, or so Emma had speculated. Colin was better at figuring out the minds of illegal arms traffickers than he was at figuring out the minds of artists.

Several of Aoife's paintings were on display in the drawing room. Her older sister, Kitty, had converted their uncle's rambling seaside house into the boutique hotel after his death, but the drawing room had always been the drawing room. Emma had wanted one last look before she and Colin headed to Dublin, then on to London in the morning for meetings with colleagues.

Back to work, he thought.

He looked out at the tranquil sea, a light turquoise under the bright midday June sun. For the past ten days, he and Emma had been a pair of honeymooners, enjoying Irish hotels, food, scenery and hospitality. They hadn't discussed their work with HIT, their

Boston-based FBI unit, but that didn't mean it was far from their minds. Emma specialized in art crimes. The O'Byrne House Hotel, where they'd stayed last night, had been the first known target of Oliver York, a wealthy Englishman, mythologist, gentleman farmer and serial art thief. Emma and her grandfather, a private art detective, had chased him for a decade before finally uncovering his identity last fall. Oliver had since returned the art he'd stolen in at least eight cities across the world—including two in the U.S.—and in Declan's Cross. Only an unsigned landscape believed to be an early work by Aoife O'Byrne remained missing. Aoife didn't speak of it. Oliver didn't speak of any of his thefts. He was working with MI5, with the understanding he would never be prosecuted in England or anywhere else for his crimes.

And now Finian Bracken was asking about him.

It couldn't be a coincidence.

Colin pulled his gaze from the view and texted his priest friend: Where are you?

Rock Point. You?

Declan's Cross.

Love to Kitty and all.

No Oliver. Why did you ask?

It was a few beats before Finian responded. Priestly curiosity.

Colin frowned at his phone. What did that mean?

Before he could type another question, another text came from his friend and confidante in Maine.

Must go. Love to Emma.

Colin gritted his teeth and slid his phone in his jacket pocket. No point texting or trying to call Finian.

Emma came and stood next to him. He noticed the sunlight on her fair hair, lightening her green eyes. "Anything else from Finian?" she asked.

"He's in Rock Point. That's all I got out of him."

"He and Oliver have struck up an odd friendship."

"All of Oliver's friendships are odd," Colin said.

She smiled. "You two will never be friends, will you?"

"No. Neither will you and Oliver. You just have more patience with him. He did send us a nice bottle of champagne for our wedding."

"And the sheepskins," she added.

He felt some of his tensions ease. "He does have good taste."

Colin hadn't known either Emma or Oliver a year ago when he'd met Finian Bracken on the pier in Rock Point. He'd been home for a brief stay, feeling the effects of a long, dangerous deep-cover mission that would linger on for a few more months. Emma had grown up in Heron's Cove, a classic, picturesque coastal village a few miles south of Rock Point, but they hadn't run into each other until September. Now here they were, married.

He smiled at her. "Ready to head to Dublin?"

"The last night of our honeymoon. It's been good, hasn't it?"

He slipped an arm around her and kissed the top of her head, smelled the freshness of her hair. She'd pulled it back for their drive north. "Definitely good."

Ten days without hearing from or about Oliver York had been some kind of record of late, but Colin kept that observation to himself as they headed down the sweeping stairs to the main floor. They said their good-byes to some of the staff—Kitty was out—and went to their car, a small Audi that could handle even the narrowest, most twisting Irish road with ease. Their luggage was already in back. They had packed light. Hikes, reading, a few nice dinners, long, lazy nights and long, lazy mornings hadn't required a steamer trunk.

Colin did the driving. Emma was thinking. He could tell Finian's text had stirred up that analytical mind of hers. When they reached the motorway, she received a text. "It's from Granddad. He wants to meet us at the Shelbourne instead of his place."

"Why?"

"He wants to buy us a drink." She was silent a moment. "Finian and now Granddad. The texts could be unrelated, and Granddad didn't mention Oliver. Let's hope if they're up to anything it's just honeymoon mischief."

"I could have booked our honeymoon in Australia."

"That would have been fun, too, but we'd have missed our Irish rainbows."

"Even if it's in your grandfather's guest room, we'll make the most of the last night of our honeymoon."

"Twin beds," she said.

Colin grinned at her. "We'll persevere."

It wasn't Colin's first time in Dublin, but it was his first time at the Shelbourne Hotel, a landmark nineteenth-century brick building on the north side of St. Stephen's Green in the heart of the city. He and Emma sat in armchairs across from each other in the bar, its tall windows looking out on the busy street and across to the green on the warm, sunny late afternoon. Two women at the next table had a half-dozen Brown Thomas bags at their feet and pink-colored drinks in front of them. The crowd appeared to be a mix of shoppers, tourists and office workers—and now a pair of honeymooners.

Emma stared at the long, polished wood bar as if she were contemplating what order to drink, but Colin knew better. She was preoccupied, thinking. He'd learned to give her space to work. She'd said little on the drive up from the south coast. They'd agreed to wait and speak to Wendell before getting in touch with Finian again.

Their waiter appeared and they ordered drinks, a pint of Smithwick's for Colin and a glass of champagne for Emma. "Oliver, Finian and Wendell all know today's the last day of our honeymoon," she said after the waiter withdrew. "Did you mention to anyone in your family that we're heading to London?"

"I haven't been in touch with my family since the wedding."

"Your folks, your brothers—"

"None of them."

"I haven't, either. I haven't talked to anyone in your

family or mine, just a few texts with Granddad to arrange today."

"Speak of the devil," Colin said, nodding to the entrance.

Emma's octogenarian grandfather paused, scanning the bar crowd. Colin got to his feet, and Wendell waved and made his way to their table. Wiry and in good shape, he wore his usual rumpled khakis, sport coat and bowtie. He'd been in a months-long process of retiring from the day-to-day running of Sharpe Fine Art Recovery, the company he'd founded sixty years ago in the front room of his Heron's Cove home. He'd relocated to Dublin, the city of his birth, fifteen years ago after the death of his wife, but the main offices were still in Maine, run by his grandson, Emma's older brother. No one believed Wendell Sharpe would ever fully give up his work as a private art detective.

He shook his head as he reached their table. "Could you two try to look less like FBI agents?"

"We *are* FBI agents, Granddad," Emma said, rising, smiling. "It's great to see you."

They embraced, and when she stepped back, Wendell shook Colin's hand. "Welcome to Dublin. Good honeymoon?" He grinned. "Don't answer." He pulled out a chair and sat with a heavy sigh. "Beautiful day. I walked from my place."

Colin's pint and Emma's champagne arrived. "What're you drinking, Wendell?" Colin asked.

"Sparkling water. I like to keep my head about me when I'm with the feds."

A typical Wendell Sharpe exaggeration, but Colin made no comment and ordered the water.

"You two go ahead," Wendell said. "Tell me about Declan's Cross."

Emma picked up her champagne. "We were there last night. Kitty's hung the two recovered Jack Butler Yeats paintings in the drawing room. They're amazing. I don't know where our English friend kept them for the past ten years, but there's no sign of wear or damage."

"The cross?"

"At home back above the lounge mantel."

Colin didn't have all the details of the art Oliver York had stolen on that first heist on a bleak November night. He did know that John O'Byrne, Aoife and Kitty's uncle, had discovered the sixteenth-century wall cross buried in his back garden when he'd had landscaping work done fifty years ago. It was silver, inscribed with symbols honoring Saint Declan, an early-medieval Irish patron saint who'd founded a monastery in nearby Ardmore.

"Nothing's changed since that first heist, and everything's changed," Wendell said quietly. His water arrived, and he drained about a third of it. He set the glass on the table. "Your secret Irish honeymoon didn't stay secret for long, did it?"

"It didn't stay secret at all," Colin said. "Everyone knows we're here."

"You chose Ireland for Emma. Tough to think of you as a romantic."

Colin drank some of his beer. "Not going there, Wendell."

The old man grinned. Emma sipped her champagne. "It's been a perfect honeymoon, Granddad. It's nice of you to invite us here. Any particular reason for the change in plan?"

He glanced around the elegant bar. "We're getting looks. I've lived in Dublin for fifteen years but I don't recognize a soul here. It's got to be you two."

Colin made no comment. They weren't getting looks. It was a diversion tactic. No one near their table seemed to be paying any attention to them much less was sneaking looks at them. He and Emma were dressed casually but suitably for their surroundings, not in the hiking clothes they'd worn much of the past ten days in the Irish countryside.

"Granddad," Emma said.

"I thought we should celebrate your marriage at a special place instead of my neighborhood pub. I didn't make it to your wedding. Least I could do is buy you a drink." He nodded to their drinks. "Glad you two didn't go for an expensive whiskey. I'm retired."

Emma gave him a skeptical look. "Semiretired at best."

In the months since Colin had come to know her— to fall in love with her—he had learned to steer clear of meddling with or even trying to understand her deep-seated, often impenetrable relationship with her eccentric family. She hadn't known he was planning to take her to Ireland for their honeymoon until he'd told her after their wedding, but he thought she might have guessed. Staying with him in Dublin had seemed like a good way to start the re-entry process back to their normal lives. Family, friends, their work with the FBI.

"When do you two go back to work?" Wendell

asked. "You'll get home in time to do a load of laundry, buy some milk and coffee?"

"We fly back to Boston this weekend," Emma said. "We'll be at our desks on Monday."

"I thought Colin didn't have a desk."

"I don't," Colin interjected. "I get to nap on Emma's couch once in a while."

"Ha. Don't worry. I'm not going to ask what you really do for the FBI. I have a surprise for you." Wendell held his glass in one hand. "I've booked a room for you here at the Shelbourne. Figured it's a better choice for the last night of the honeymoon for a pair of newlyweds than my guest room."

Emma folded her hands on her lap, eyeing her grandfather with a cool steadiness Colin had come to know and appreciate. "Thank you, Granddad, that's generous of you, but we'd have been happy in your guest room."

"You'll be happier here."

Emma unfolded her hands and touched a fingertip to the rim of her champagne glass, nothing casual about her move. "The Shelbourne is gorgeous, but having a drink with you is a great wedding gift. We don't want you to overspend."

"Don't worry, I won't end up on your front stoop with my bag."

She sighed, a tightness in her eyes that indicated both love and suspicion. "Are you having your place painted or something? If it's inconvenient for you to put us up, you could have just said so."

"It's not inconvenient." Her grandfather settled into his comfortable chair. "This place was built in 1824. I saw that when I booked your room. These walls ooze Irish history. Princess Grace stayed here back in the day. She had Irish roots. What a beauty she was. Tragic end to her life."

Colin snatched up his pint glass. Wendell was engaging in pure, in-your-face evasiveness. No wonder he'd stuck to sparkling water. Colin took a drink, reining in his impatience, and turned to Emma. "Do you want to get the truth out of him or do you want me to? Or do you want to pretend drinks and a night at the Shelbourne are a last-minute wedding gift?"

"They're a surprise wedding gift," Wendell said, unruffled. "They're not last-minute."

Emma sipped her champagne, returned the glass to the table and glanced first at Colin and then at her grandfather. "But Colin's right, isn't he, Granddad? You *are* hiding something."

He plucked the slice of lemon out of his glass, squeezed it, tossed it back in and then took a drink. "You two missed your jobs while you were on your honeymoon, didn't you? You're rested and ready to pounce on an old man. I shouldn't have mentioned expensive whiskey and being retired. Put you on alert."

"When someone does something out of the blue, out of character, most people will notice," Emma said. "It doesn't take being an FBI agent."

"Helps, though."

Colin gritted his teeth. "Spit it out, Wendell. Why don't you want us at your place?"

The old man locked eyes with his grandson-in-law. "All right. I tried to keep you two out of it. I give up." He paused. "My place is a crime scene."

Emma stiffened visibly. "What kind of crime scene?"

"Looks as if someone slipped inside while I was out running errands this morning after breakfast. Gutsy to break in when it was broad daylight. I didn't have much time to think with you two on the way. Path of least resistance was to put you up here." He shrugged his bony shoulders. "One of the hazards of having FBI agents in the family."

"You didn't call the police," Colin said, making it a statement.

"No point. Nothing they can do." Wendell rolled his shoulders as if he were in physical pain. "Damn, I'm getting old. Fifty years ago I wouldn't have spilled the beans this fast. *Ten* years ago. I should have just had you over to the house and handed you a broom to clean up the glass."

Emma went still. "Glass?"

"Guest room window. That's how the intruder got in. Do you have a car? Where are your bags? You can check in after your drinks. I booked your room under Donovan. I assume you're using Sharpe professionally?"

"Unless you land in prison," his only granddaughter said. "Then I might reconsider."

"Ha, I wouldn't blame you."

"We turned in our car when we arrived in Dublin and took a cab here. We left our bags with the bellman." Emma reached out a hand and placed it on Wendell's thin wrist. "Why don't we get settled and then walk over to your place and have a look?"

"You can call the gardai in the meantime," Colin added.

Wendell scowled at him but turned to Emma with a smile. "Good plan. Take your time. I won't touch anything, but you two have no jurisdiction here. I'm not calling the gardai before you get there. Just so we're clear."

"Have you told anyone else about the break-in?" she asked.

"No, and I don't plan to. I didn't plan to tell you but Colin here had his thumbscrew-look on and I caved." Wendell raised his glass, almost empty of sparkling water now. "Bottoms up, kids."

Colin called his oldest brother, Mike, while Emma freshened up in the bathroom of their elegant third-floor room. He stood at the window and looked down at St. Stephen's Green across the street, imagined himself walking on its meandering paths with Emma, holding her hand, laughing as they had so much over the past ten days.

Back to reality, he thought as Mike answered on the second ring. "What's up?" Mike asked without preamble.

"Not sure. Where are you?"

"Rock Point. Mulching. Naomi's on a job."

Naomi MacBride was Mike's fiancée, a private intelligence analyst recently recovered from a knife wound. They planned to spend the summer at Mike's place out on Maine's Bold Coast, where he was a wilderness guide. Lately, though, he'd dipped back into his old world as a Special Forces operator, doing contract security work with other former soldiers. Then there was mulching. It would be at their folks' inn on

Rock Point harbor. All four brothers helped out when they could.

"Have you seen Finian Bracken lately?" Colin asked.

"This morning. Breakfast at Hurley's."

"What about Oliver York? Is he in town by any chance?"

"Not that I know of." A wariness had crept into Mike's tone. "Another Brit was here, though."

"Who?"

"Don't know. White male, late fifties, maybe early sixties. Stocky. English accent. I didn't see him myself. Franny did. Says she ran into a Brit at the church on Monday."

Franny Maroney was the widowed grandmother of their younger brother Andy's fiancée, a marine biologist. "Franny should have been CIA," Colin said. "Did she see this man with Fin?"

"No. He said he was meeting him and waited in the sanctuary. Bad news?"

Colin told Mike about Finian's texts. "Could be nothing," he added when he finished.

"Not likely if you and Fin Bracken are involved. Anything else I need to know?"

"Wendell Sharpe's invited Emma and me for a drink at a five-star Irish hotel."

"Instead of his local pub? I'd be suspicious."

"I am," Colin said, his tone not as light as he'd intended.

"Have fun. Hi to Emma. I'll report back if I find out anything. See you two lovebirds when you're back home."

Mike was gone before Colin could say thanks.

Home. He could almost feel a sea breeze, taste the

salt in the air, as if he were standing on the pier in Rock Point, looking out at the harbor with Emma at his side. They'd go into Hurley's, a local favorite, for whiskey with his brothers and Fin Bracken, or walk up to the house he'd bought when he was single, wondering if his undercover work with the FBI had obliterated any chance he had at a normal life—a wife, a family. Now it was his and Emma's house, with her pies in the freezer and his beer in the fridge.

She came out of the bathroom. She'd freshened up her makeup. Colin could tell these things now. Noticed them. Noticed everything about her, including the continued strain in her Sharpe-green eyes.

He put out his hand. "Let's go see your grandfather."

THIEF'S MARK by Carla Neggers.
Available August 29, 2017, from MIRA Books.

New York Times bestselling author

CARLA NEGGERS

returns to charming Swift River Valley, where spring is the time for fresh starts and new beginnings.

Kylie Shaw has found a home and a quiet place to work as an illustrator of children's books in little Knights Bridge, Massachusetts. No one seems to know her here—and she likes it that way. She carefully guards her privacy in the refurbished nineteenth-century hat factory where she has a loft. And then California private investigator Russ Colton moves in.

Kylie and Russ have more in common than they or anyone else would ever expect. They're both looking for a place to belong, and if they're able to let go of past mistakes and learn to trust again, they just might find what they need in Knights Bridge…and each other.

Available now, wherever books are sold!

Be sure to connect with us at:

Harlequin.com/Newsletters

Facebook.com/HarlequinBooks

Twitter.com/HarlequinBooks

MIRA®

www.MIRABooks.com

MCN1867

Turn your love of reading into rewards you'll love with

Harlequin My Rewards

**Join for FREE today at
www.HarlequinMyRewards.com**

Earn **FREE BOOKS** of your choice.

Experience **EXCLUSIVE OFFERS** and contests.

Enjoy **BOOK RECOMMENDATIONS**
selected just for you.

PLUS! Sign up now
and get **500** points
right away!

Earn **FREE REWARDS**
HarlequinMyRewards.com
Join Today!

MYR16R

Get 2 Free Books,
Plus 2 Free Gifts –
just for trying the Reader Service!

CARLA NEGGERS

(limited quantities available)

TOTAL AMOUNT	$ _____
POSTAGE & HANDLING	$ _____
($1.00 for 1 book, 50¢ for each additional)	
APPLICABLE TAXES*	$ _____
TOTAL PAYABLE	$ _____

(check or money order—please do not send cash)

To order, complete this form and send it, along with a check or money order for the total above, payable to MIRA Books, to: **In the U.S.:** 3010 Walden Avenue, P.O. Box 9077, Buffalo, NY 14269-9077; **In Canada:** P.O. Box 636, Fort Erie, Ontario, L2A 5X3.

Name: _____

Address: _____ City: _____

State/Prov.: _____ Zip/Postal Code: _____

Account Number (if applicable): _____
075 CSAS

mira

Harlequin.com

MCN0817BL